PELICAN COVE COZY MYSTERY SERIES OMNIBUS COLLECTION 2

BOOKS 5-8

By

LEENA CLOVER

Parfaits and Paramours – Pelican Cove Cozy Mystery Series Book 7

By Leena Clover

Truffles and Troubadours – Pelican Cove Cozy Mystery Series Book 8

By Leena Clover

Join my Newsletter

Get access to free books, exclusive bonus content, sneak peeks, giveaways and much more. Also get a chance to join my exclusive ARC group, the people who get first dibs on all my new books.

Sign up at the following link and join the fun.

Click here → http://www.subscribepage.com/leenaclovernl

I love to hear from my readers, so please feel free to connect with me at any of the following places.

Website – http://leenaclover.com

Twitter – https://twitter.com/leenaclover

Facebook – http://facebook.com/leenaclovercozymysterybooks

Email – leenaclover@gmail.com

Waffles and Weekends – Pelican Cove Cozy Mystery Series Book 5

Chapter 1

Jenny King's cheeks flamed with embarrassment as she observed her friend Heather over the rim of her wine glass.

It was Valentine's weekend and the four couples had met for dinner at The Steakhouse, Pelican Cove's only fancy restaurant. Jenny, Heather and Molly were close friends. Jenny considered Jason Stone a friend too. He was the only lawyer in Pelican Cove and was currently dating another lawyer from the city. He had pursued Jenny for a while after she came to live in Pelican Cove. But Jenny had made her choice. She looked up into the blue eyes of her date. Adam Hopkins, the sheriff of Pelican Cove smiled back at her.

Heather Morse cuddled with a man much older than herself. She had been dating Gianni Costa, Dr. Gianni Costa, for the past few months. The flamboyant fiftyish man had set up shop as soon as he moved to the small seaside town. He flirted outrageously with his patients, most of whom were older ladies who liked being flattered by the silver-tongued Casanova.

Jenny watched as Heather engaged in behavior her grandmother would not approve of. Adam nudged her and cleared his throat.

"What did you do last night?" Jenny asked her friend Molly.

"Chris and I had a romantic dinner at home. We didn't want to spend our first Valentine's Day at a restaurant."

"We went for a canoe ride after that," Chris beamed, looking lovingly at Molly. "Molly loves those."

Jason's date spoke up.

"We went to a hot new restaurant in town. I know the chef personally. He's about to get his first Michelin star."

"The weekend's going great, then," Jenny said happily. "Don't forget you are all coming to Seaview tomorrow."

"Isn't it a bit cold for a barbecue?" Kandy, the city lawyer, asked.

"We'll have a fire going in the pit," Jason assured her. "Seaview is a great place to be, any time of the year."

Jenny still couldn't believe she was the proud owner of a sea facing mansion. Dumped by her husband of twenty years, she had grabbed her aunt's invitation like a lifeline and come to visit her in the small seaside town of Pelican Cove. A barrier island off the coast of Virginia, Pelican Cove was the perfect place to lick her wounds. Jenny's aunt Star had let her wallow for a few weeks and urged her to start working at the local café. Neither of them knew she was going to be a big success. Jenny had started baking and cooking with the local produce and turned the Boardwalk Café around. Tourists flocked to the café to taste the delectable treats Jenny created on a regular basis.

"Your parties are legendary, Jenny," Heather nodded. "Gianni and I can't wait for tomorrow."

"Have you settled in at Seaview?" Molly asked Jenny.

Jenny had been charmed by the big three story house adjoining her aunt's cottage. She had bought the house with her divorce settlement and spent a big sum of money renovating it. The discovery of a skeleton in her garden had been unexpected. But Jenny had soldiered on and moved into the house with her aunt.

"It's a great house," Jenny told her friend. "I'm loving it more each day."

"And having Adam there helps," Heather remarked with a wink.

When Jenny first came to Pelican Cove, Adam and Jason had both fallen for her. Jenny found herself pursued by two handsome, eligible men. They were as different as chalk and cheese. Jenny had chosen to date Adam, the more unpredictable of the two.

"Adam's living on the third floor," Jenny said curtly. "It's not what you think."

"Why do you protest so much?" Heather pouted. "I don't care where he lives. By the way, as far as appearances go, you two live in the same house."

Adam grew uncomfortable. He tucked a finger in his collar and tried to loosen it. His roof had fallen in a few weeks ago and he had been forced to move out. Jenny had insisted he stay at Seaview until his house was fixed. Their living arrangement had set tongues wagging.

Jenny told him she didn't care what people said.

"Let's not talk about 'appearances', Heather," Jenny fumed.

"Simmer down, you two," Jason Stone said lightly. He gave Jenny a knowing look. "Are you denying you and Adam are a couple?"

"Jenny's just being a good friend," Adam protested. "I would have come and lived with you, Jason. But you didn't offer."

Dr. Gianni Costa looked bored with the conversation.

"Basta!" he exclaimed. "How about another round of drinks? They are on me."

He ordered an expensive bottle of wine for the table. Dr. Costa had plenty of money and he believed in spending it.

"I am looking forward to this party at your home," he told Jenny. "I want to see this spot where they found that skeleton."

"There's nothing to look at there," Jenny said bluntly. "We put a water fountain on the spot."

The bottle of wine arrived and Dr. Costa and Heather drank most of it. He insisted on getting the check.

"My treat," he told the others. "You can pay next time."

Heather stumbled out of the restaurant with the good doctor, both of them swaying a bit.

"I hope you're not driving," Adam said anxiously. "Can I give you a ride somewhere?"

He had opted to be the designated driver for the group.

"We want to walk home," Heather slurred. "It's such a beautiful night."

"Not more beautiful than you, my pet," Gianni Costa murmured.

He clutched Heather's hand in his and waved goodbye to the group.

"Ciao friends," he cried with a big smile on his face. "Heather and I have our own little party planned."

He took a couple of steps and stumbled. He let out a burp and Heather giggled.

"You're totally wasted, Heather," Jenny clucked, shaking her head. "Maybe we should see you home safely."

"I'm going to Gianni's," Heather whispered in her ear. "You go have fun with Adam."

There was another round of goodbyes and the group finally dispersed. Adam drove Chris and Molly home.

"You think she'll be alright?" Molly asked Jenny.

"She's thirty five, Molls, not thirteen," Jenny said with a sigh. "I think she can take care of herself."

"Heather's changed a lot, hasn't she?" Chris muttered.

Chris Williams had been in love with Heather Morse since third grade. Everyone knew they had an understanding. Heather had shocked everyone the previous summer by deciding to date other people. Chris had found himself falling for Molly, the shy, soft spoken librarian. Chris and Molly found they had a deep connection. They were very much in love.

"What does Heather see in Gianni?" Jenny wondered, her frustration evident in her voice.

Jenny and Adam watched a movie after getting home. Adam had let her pick Casablanca in honor of the special weekend.

Jenny hummed a tune as she mixed some batter for her special waffles the next morning. The café opened a bit later than usual on Sunday. Most of her regular customers turned up for breakfast, eager to indulge in whatever sinful treat Jenny dished up.

Jenny greeted Captain Charlie as she threw open the doors of the café. He was her favorite customer, always first in line when the café opened.

"Got those waffles?" he asked her. "I've been dreaming about having them for breakfast."

Jenny brought out a platter with hot waffles drizzled with a fresh berry sauce. Captain Charlie smacked his lips as he cut into his food.

"Delicious!" he pronounced after the first bite.

"Do you want chocolate sauce too?" Jenny asked him. "Or some chocolate covered strawberries? I saved some for you."

Jenny chatted with people as she offered them a choice of fresh berry sauce or melted chocolate to top their waffles. Some opted for both.

Jenny's friends began walking in around eleven. They were an odd group of women, young and old. Betty Sue Morse, Heather's grandmother, was the unopposed leader of the pack. She was a force to reckon with even in her eighties. Jenny's aunt Star and café owner Petunia Clark formed the rest of the old guard. Jenny, Molly and Heather provided the young blood, although at 45, Jenny was much older than Heather and Molly. The ladies called themselves the Magnolias and met at the café every morning.

Betty Sue was busy with her knitting as usual. All the Magnolias were dressed warmly because they wanted to sit out on the deck. The café's deck sat right on the sand, facing the Atlantic Ocean.

"How was Valentine's Day?" Betty Sue's voice boomed. "I hope you girls are behaving yourself?"

Molly blushed prettily, making Petunia and Star laugh.

"Chris and I can't wait for the barbecue at Jenny's," Molly said. "You are coming, aren't you, Betty Sue?"

"Of course I am," Betty Sue nodded. "I am looking forward to it."

"Why don't you invite John?" Star asked.

John Newbury was Betty Sue's estranged husband. Betty Sue turned red at the mention of his name.

"Why would I do that?" she sputtered.

"It is Valentine's weekend," Star teased. "Don't you want to spend some time with your honey?"

The older ladies proceeded to tease Betty Sue mercilessly. Jenny thought it was cute how Betty Sue broke out in a sweat every time her husband was mentioned.

"Where's Heather?" Molly asked innocently.

Jenny shook her head meaningfully and tried to warn Molly. But Betty Sue had already heard her.

"She's fast asleep in her bed," Betty Sue complained. "Wouldn't budge.

I had to take Tootsie for her walk myself." She looked at Jenny and Molly inquiringly. "How come you two look so fresh? Didn't Heather get any sleep at all last night?"

Jenny hastily changed the subject.

"Did Chris give you a gift, Molly?"

Molly leaned forward and showed them a new pair of earrings she was wearing. The ladies exclaimed over the heart shaped jewelry.

"Did Adam get you anything?" Molly asked.

Jenny smiled and shook her head. She hadn't expected fancy jewelry but she had hoped Adam would get her a memento of some kind. He had brought her breakfast in bed, along with a posy of her favorite roses from the garden at Seaview. Jenny told herself she didn't need fancy gifts. She had received enough of those from her ex-husband. They had meant nothing in the end.

She felt her heart skip a beat and looked around. Adam strode along the beach and ran up the café steps.

"Hello ladies," he greeted them.

His eyes softened as they met Jenny's. Adam looked apologetic. Jenny knew that look. She braced herself for what Adam would say next.

"Where is Heather?" Adam asked Betty Sue.

"Don't ask!" Betty Sue said with a roll of her eyes. "She's sleeping like the dead."

"Funny you should say that," Adam said tersely.

The Magnolias were staring at him now.

"Spit it out," Star said. "You have some bad news."

"Gianni died in his sleep last night."

A collective gasp went through the group.

"Are you sure?" Molly burst out. "Maybe he's just passed out."

"I am sure, Molly," Adam said with a sigh. "I need to talk to Heather."

Jenny sat down with a thump. They had all seen Heather go home with Gianni Costa. She had probably been the last person to see him alive.

One of the last people, Jenny corrected herself.

"How did he die?" she asked Adam fearfully.

Adam's brow furrowed as he answered her.

"It's too early to say, but looks like he was drugged."

Betty Sue had put her knitting down for a change. She had been trying to get a word in.

"What does Heather have to do with that flashy doctor? She barely knew him."

Chapter 2

Jenny walked to the police station with a wicker basket on her arm. The lunch rush at the café had died down and she was off to have lunch with Adam. She had packed chicken rolls and slices of carrot cake.

Adam Hopkins sat with one leg propped up on a chair. He was a veteran who had been deployed in war zones. He had been shot in the leg and still struggled with the old injury. He had a mercurial temper which flared every time his leg bothered him.

"How are you, Jenny?" He had a special smile for her.

Although Adam and Jenny lived in the same house, their work schedules were such that they barely saw each other.

"Hungry?" Jenny asked, unpacking the basket.

Adam took a big bite of the roll and gave her a thumbs up.

"Yum! What is it?"

"It's a new Asian style chicken recipe I am trying out," Jenny explained, taking a dainty bite of her own sandwich.

They made some small talk while they ate. Adam finally polished off the last bite of cake and wiped his mouth with a tissue. He gave Jenny a grave look.

"I got some news about Mrs. Bones."

'Mrs. Bones' was the nickname Jenny and the girls had assigned the skeleton that had been discovered in Jenny's backyard. For a long time, Jenny and her friends had believed that the skeleton belonged to a missing girl from the area. That theory had been shot down. Now Jenny suspected something else.

"Tell me, quick."

"It's a woman, as you already know," Adam began. "A woman about fifty years old. She's been buried for thirty some years."

"Anything else?" Jenny asked with bated breath.

"They found a broken collar bone, probably a childhood injury."

Jenny's eyes shone with excitement.

"Finally, something we can verify. Betty Sue might know about this."

"Do you really believe that's Lily?" Adam asked.

Jenny nodded sadly. The tragic history of Seaview flashed before her eyes. Seaview had been home to the Davis family, one of the pioneer families of Pelican Cove. Old man Davis had lived there with his entire family. A big storm had wiped out most of them, leaving only his daughter Lily, his son's wife and his grandson alive. Ann Davis, the son's wife, had taken her baby and Lily and moved away. Lily came back thirty years later with her husband and children. But tragedy struck again. Lily lost her daughter to a freak virus. Then Lily herself disappeared one night. The general impression in town had been that Lily abandoned her family and ran away with another man. As more information surfaced about the skeleton, Jenny was sure Lily had met an untimely end.

"She's the only fiftyish woman who went missing from these parts," Jenny reminded Adam. "And no one heard from her again."

"You know what you are implying?" Adam asked, leaning back in his chair.

He pulled a bottle of pills from a drawer and tried to unscrew the top. Jenny took the bottle and opened it for him.

"Lily was killed," Jenny said flatly. She looked impatient as Adam popped a couple of pills in his mouth and washed them down with a sip of water. "That's obvious, isn't it? She didn't bury herself in my garden."

"You may be right," Adam continued. "Someone bashed her head in."

"Poor Lily," Jenny mumbled.

"One more mystery for you to solve, huh?" Adam teased.

"Aren't you going to tell me to stay out of it?" Jenny asked with surprise.

Adam didn't like anyone meddling into police business. He and Jenny were often at odds with each other because of it.

"It's a cold case," Adam shrugged. "There's not much anyone can do."

"But Lily deserves justice!" Jenny argued.

Lily's son had died the previous year. Her husband was in a senior home in Texas. No one was going to come and ask the police to find Lily's murderer.

"Maybe you can do something about it," Adam said mildly.

"Are you actually giving me your blessing?" Jenny asked incredulously.

"Just be careful," Adam warned, "and keep me updated."

Jenny walked to the seafood market to shop for dinner. Chris Williams filled her order. They chatted for some time and Jenny walked home. Dinner was a lively affair with her aunt's special friend Jimmy Parsons joining them. Jimmy had been better known as the town drunk for several years. He had recently turned his life around and was dating her aunt. He spent a lot of his time at Seaview.

Jenny and Adam went for their usual walk on the beach after dinner. Jenny threw a ball for Tank, Adam's yellow Labrador. Tank had moved into Seaview with Adam. He adored Jenny and could be seen following her through the house, his tail wagging.

The next morning, Jenny couldn't wait to meet the Magnolias. She baked a fresh tray of banana nut muffins and had the coffee ready. Betty Sue arrived, her needles clacking with force as she took in the guests at the café. Heather followed behind, looking morose.

"How are you holding up, Heather?" Jenny asked.

Heather's eyes filled up.

"How would you be doing in my place?"

"I didn't know you were that close," Jenny sympathized. "I mean, sure, we know you had some fun with him. But did you actually care about him?"

"Of course I did," Heather cried. "Gianni made me happy."

Betty Sue refused to acknowledge Heather's connection to the dead doctor.

"Stop mooning around, girl," she ordered. "Pour me a cup of coffee."

Molly stumbled into the café, holding on to her Coke-bottle glasses. Star wasn't far behind.

"I can smell spring in the air," Star said as she doodled a drawing on a paper napkin.

Star was an artist who painted landscapes and seascapes. The tourists loved her work. She had a gallery in town and Jenny had helped her set up a website. Star worked hard in winter and spring to replenish her catalog. The tourist season would ramp up soon.

"Spring Fest is around the corner," Betty Sue reminded them. "We need to work on it."

"Barb's back early this year," Star observed.

Barb Norton was a local woman who took an active part in all the town events. She spent winter in Florida with her daughter but got back in time to organize the spring festival. The Magnolias liked to give her the cold shoulder but they had to admit she was resourceful.

"She'll be around soon enough," Petunia said softly.

"Can we talk about Mrs. Bones?" Jenny butted in. She had been trying to find the right moment to talk about Lily. "Did Lily ever have any accidents as a child, Betty Sue?"

Betty Sue paused from her knitting and narrowed her eyes.

"Lily was a hellion. My Daddy was quite strict with me but old man Davis let Lily roam around the island. She swam with the watermen's kids and could outrow them any day."

"So you two didn't play together?"

"I'm coming to it," Betty Sue said irritably. "Lily came to visit a lot. We could play in our yard but I wasn't allowed to go out with her."

Jenny wished Betty Sue would get on with her reminisces. She tried to curb her impatience.

"One afternoon, we snuck out and walked to one of the bluffs. Someone had tied a rope swing on an oak. I got sick just looking at it. Lily scrambled up and made me push the swing."

"Is this going anywhere?" Heather asked with a yawn.

Betty Sue barely heard her. She was lost in the memories of her childhood.

"Lily begged me to push harder every time. We were both yelling, Lily with abandon, me with fright. Suddenly, she flew in the air and crashed to the ground."

"She broke her collar bone, didn't she?" Jenny asked urgently.

Betty Sue's mouth dropped open.

"Don't interrupt, Jenny," Star quipped. "Let her finish."

"She's right," Betty Sue said, pointing a finger at Jenny. "I'll never forget that day. Lily had a nasty scrape on her chin and a broken bone. She was howling for hours. We were both grounded for weeks after that."

"Mrs. Bones has a fractured collar bone," Jenny said softly.

"So there's no doubt it's Lily?" Betty Sue asked sadly.

"It's beginning to look like that," Jenny said, placing her hand on Betty Sue's. "The police might run some more tests. Then we'll know for sure."

Betty Sue's face hardened as she looked at Jenny.

"I want you to clear Lily's name. They didn't just kill her. They destroyed her reputation."

"I'm going to do my best," Jenny promised her.

"What about Gianni?" Heather wailed. "Aren't you going to find out what happened to him?"

"Gianni Costa died in his sleep," Star snapped. "He had one drink too many."

Petunia seconded Star.

"What kind of doctor was he, anyway? He should have known when to stop."

"He didn't drink that much," Heather argued. "We all drank wine at the restaurant."

"What about after he got home?" Molly asked. "He must have had a few more drinks then."

Heather had no answer for that. She didn't remember much of what had happened after they reached Gianni's home. But she wasn't ready to admit that.

"You're all just bad-mouthing him," Heather insisted. "Jenny needs to find out the truth."

"Hold on, Heather," Jenny protested. "That's not my job. The police will look into it. What do you think I am? Some kind of detective?"

"It won't be the first time you solved a murder," Heather said sullenly.

"That was different," Jenny said.

"She's right," Betty Sue spoke up. "That doctor was a menace. Good riddance, I say."

"Grandma!" Heather cried. "You barely knew him."

"Jenny has her hands full with Mrs. Bones," Molly reiterated.

Heather opened her mouth to argue. A loud voice hailed them from the boardwalk.

"Yooohoooo …"

A short, plump woman scrambled up the café steps.

"Hello Barb," Star drawled. "The Spring Fest committee doesn't meet for three more days."

Barb Norton sat down next to Molly and tried to catch her breath. Jenny offered her a cup of coffee. She took a sip gratefully and looked around at the assembled women.

"Forget the Spring Fest."

"Are you stepping down as Chairperson?" Star asked eagerly. "It's my turn now, anyway."

Barb glared at Star.

"The Spring Fest will go ahead as planned. I am here on important business."

"What's got your panties in a wad?" Betty Sue thundered.

"Dire things are afoot, Betty Sue," Barb Norton said urgently. "We need to gather everyone for an emergency town meeting."

"What's the matter now?" Jenny asked.

Jenny had lived in a city most of her life. Small town politics was new to her. She was still amazed by how the people came together to discuss and dissect every small issue. There was a committee for everything, Jenny had found.

"Our very way of life is being threatened," Barb said dramatically.

She flung a finger at Betty Sue.

"Those Newburys are doing it again. And your husband is responsible."

"What is John doing now?" Betty Sue asked mildly.

"Drugs!" Barb declared, her bosom heaving. "The Newburys are getting into the drug business."

"What nonsense!" Betty Sue dismissed.

Jenny, Heather and Molly shared a swift glance. They were trying hard not to laugh. Barb Norton pounced on them.

"You find this funny?"

"Stop being fanciful, Barb," Star said curtly. "Get to the point."

"The Newburys are planting cannabis in their fields," Barb declared triumphantly. "They are going to sell it too, right here in town. John Newbury signed a lease on that empty store on the corner of Main. Eddie Cotton owns that store. He told me himself."

"Are they opening a medical marijuana dispensary?" Jenny asked.

"I don't care how they sugarcoat it," Barb sniffed. "We cannot have drugs in Pelican Cove."

Chapter 3

Jenny added a generous amount of ground cinnamon to her waffle batter. She added some orange zest to the berries bubbling away on the stove. She was fixing a special batch of her waffles based on Barb Norton's request. The Spring Fest committee had met the previous night but hadn't reached consensus on a single point. Jenny had suggested consulting Mandy. Everyone had agreed to that suggestion.

Mandy James was a consultant the town had hired before. She had helped them win the Prettiest Town in America tag. Jenny was sure she would have plenty of ideas about how to make Spring Fest bigger and better. A conference call had been set up and the ladies were going to gather in the café to talk to Mandy via video conference.

Jenny fussed over arranging the perfect plate of waffles and wished Heather would hurry. Barb wanted a picture of the waffles for the Spring Fest flyers. Jenny also wanted to post the picture on the town's Instagram page.

"Merchandise!" Mandy James said resolutely. "Anything you can think of – t-shirts, tote bags, baseball caps – something for everyone. You make money this year and get free advertising for the next. And swag! You need to give away swag."

Mandy was on a roll. The Magnolias groaned as Mandy rattled off one suggestion after another. They hadn't missed this aspect of her personality.

"Hold on, Mandy," Jenny said. "Heather's taking notes."

"Aren't you recording this?" Mandy asked.

"We prefer to take notes the old fashioned way," Barb Norton bristled. "Now tell us what this swag is."

Mandy spent a few minutes explaining how they could give away small items like pens or key chains with the town's logo on it.

"Get some big items for the raffle," Mandy ordered. "Everything should have the town's web address on it."

Jenny's mind was working furiously, thinking about ways to spread the word about the Boardwalk Café.

"Why don't we get some special tees printed?" she asked Petunia. "We can put a pretty picture on them, like these waffles, along with our name and address."

"Whatever you think is right, dear," she said uncertainly.

Jenny turned toward the screen and spoke to Mandy.

"What about having a concert on the beach? I know you shot my suggestion down last time, but the Spring Fest seems like a good time for some music."

"That's an excellent idea, Jenny," Mandy approved. "Why don't you start contacting a few bands?"

Barb started working on the waffles while the women threw ideas around.

"You don't know what you are missing," she told Mandy. "When are you coming for a visit? Jenny's come up with plenty of yummy recipes since you left."

"Let me check my calendar," Mandy said seriously. "I will try to make it there for the Spring Fest. No promises, though."

Heather sat with a camera in her lap, staring into space. Molly nudged Jenny and tipped her head at Heather.

"We need to do something," she hissed.

"Looks like she's really grieving for Gianni," Jenny shrugged. "We need to get her out of this funk."

"How about a trip to the city?" Molly asked. "Let's catch a movie and get her favorite dinner."

The girls decided to talk to Heather after the conference call ended. Barb Norton made Jenny fix a fresh plate of waffles and ordered Heather to take a few dozen photos from all angles. She went off on another mission after that. The girls finally heaved a sigh of relief.

Heather didn't want to go to the city.

"How can I enjoy a movie when my sweetie just died?" she wailed. "How heartless do you think I am?"

"How about a visit to the spa?" Jenny offered. "My treat."

"Have you been biting these?" Molly asked, picking up Heather's hand and peering at her nails.

Vanity won and Heather agreed to tag along to the spa. Molly chattered continuously as Jenny drove off the bridge that connected the island of Pelican Cove to the mainland. Heather stared out of the window, tears streaming down her cheeks. Jenny gave her a worried glance.

"You need to pull yourself together, Heather."

Heather pulled out a few tissues from a box on the dashboard. She blew her nose and nodded wordlessly.

"I didn't realize you were so attached to him," Jenny continued.

"Gianni cared about me. I might have had a future with him."

Jenny bit her lip and forced herself to stay quiet. Had Heather really been thinking about marrying a man fifteen years her senior? She thought of the flamboyant doctor with his flashy clothes and diamond earring. His shirt had been unbuttoned every time Jenny met him, exposing his hairy chest.

"You'll find someone else," Molly soothed.

Molly's comment didn't go down well. Jenny believed Heather hadn't forgiven Molly for hooking up with Chris.

"You take as much time as you need, Heather," Jenny said diplomatically. "We can put up your profile on that dating site again."

"It's a mobile app," Heather corrected her. "No one uses websites anymore."

"Why don't we take a new photo after our spa visit, hmm?" Jenny soothed.

Heather seemed to rally around a bit after that. They chose a three hour package at the spa. Jenny found herself relaxing after a long time as she let herself be scrubbed and massaged. They went to Heather's favorite restaurant overlooking the Chesapeake Bay for a late lunch.

"I'm starving," Heather said. "I'm getting the blackened sea bass."

The girls ordered different entrees and switched them around after a few bites. Jenny couldn't resist ordering the bourbon pecan pie for dessert.

"Thanks for doing this, girls," Heather said on the way back. "I almost feel human."

Jenny squeezed Heather's hand.

"We're here for you, sweetie. Just let us know what you need."

Jason was sitting out on the patio with Star when Jenny got home. She was happy to see him.

"Jason!" she exclaimed happily. "We hardly see you anymore."

Jason sprang up and hugged Jenny. "You're glowing, Jenny."

"After what I spent at that spa, I better," Jenny joked. "What brings you here?"

"Kandy's busy with a case," he told them. "And I've cleared my desk too for a change. So I thought I would enjoy an evening at Seaview."

"You're always welcome here," Star said warmly.

She had a soft corner for Jason and preferred him over Adam. She made sure she told Jenny about it plenty of times.

"Is Adam home yet?" Jenny asked.

"He just left," Star said gleefully. "He's working till midnight."

"How's Nick?" Jason asked. "Haven't seen him in a while."

Jenny's son Nick was a sophomore in college. Jenny rubbed a small gold charm that hung around her neck. Nick had gifted her a charm for Mother's Day ever since he was a kid. They hung around Jenny's neck on a chain. She had the habit of rubbing the charms whenever she missed her son.

"He should be here for Spring Fest," Jenny said. "Hopefully even before that."

"Did you hear about John Newbury's plans?" Star asked Jason. "What do you think?"

"I think he's got guts," Jason said. "But the Newburys never cared about the town folk."

"Surely they won't do anything illegal?" Jenny asked, wide eyed.

"Having the law on their side won't be enough," Jason explained. "Communities around the country have protested against these dispensaries."

"Aren't they supposed to help sick people?" Jenny asked.

Jason let out a sigh.

"The amount of people they can help is less than the ones they can harm, I guess. People are afraid of the ramifications, and rightly so."

They argued over the pros and cons of growing medical cannabis in a small town like Pelican Cove.

"You can be sure of one thing," Star said. "There will be a protest, and a big one. Those Newburys better be ready for it."

Jenny insisted on cooking Jason's favorite pan seared fish in a wine butter sauce. He had brought a bottle of local wine Jenny loved. They lingered over chocolate brownies and ice cream on the patio. Jason had built a fire in the pit. The scent of roses and gardenias perfumed the air. Water gurgled in the stone fountain.

Jenny sighed with pleasure as she looked around her. This was her home now.

The Magnolias were all fired up about the Spring Fest the next day. Star had produced some designs for the festival T-shirts. The ladies pored over them, arguing over which one best represented Pelican Cove.

"I like this one with just the crab," Molly said. "It's simple but elegant."

"I prefer this one," Heather opposed her. "Crab, oyster, sea bass in a basket and the light house and beach in the background. It's all the best of Pelican Cove."

"Did you post that photo of the waffles on Instagram?" Jenny asked, bringing out a plate of warm muffins.

"Already done, Jenny. It has some five thousand likes. Get ready to make plenty of waffles."

Adam Hopkins came in sight, flanked by two men in uniform. He was leaning on his cane heavily, wincing with every step.

"Is your leg bothering you?" Jenny asked with concern. "Have you taken any pain pills this morning?"

Adam gave her a quelling look. He didn't like being fussed over in public.

The two men accompanying Adam had gone to stand beside Heather.

"What are you doing here, boy?" Betty Sue demanded.

"You need to come with us, Heather," Adam said curtly.

Jenny put her arms on her hips and glared at Adam.

"Not again! You are making a habit of this, Adam. I think you like coming here and harassing us."

"Just doing my job," Adam muttered.

"What has my child done?" Betty Sue asked imperiously.

"Heather was seen going home with Gianni Costa the night he died. We need to question her."

"You don't think I hurt Gianni?" Heather asked fearfully. "I cared for him. Very much."

"We can discuss all that in my office," Adam told her. "Let's go."

"Jenny!" Heather's eyes filled with panic as she looked around at the group. "What am I to do?"

"You'll have to go with him," Jenny said with a sigh.

"We are right behind you," Star said, getting up.

Heather looked bewildered as she stood up and followed Adam down the café steps. She kept glancing back at her friends, looking wild eyed.

"I'm calling Jason," Jenny said, rushing inside the café.

Betty Sue Morse had dumped her knitting on the table. She looked ashen. Molly helped her up and the ladies started walking down to the police station. Jenny ran a few steps and caught up with them.

"He'll meet us there," she said breathlessly.

Jason Stone was pacing up and down the police station lobby when they got there.

"She's inside. Don't worry. They can't hold her for long."

"I thought my Heather was rid of that awful man," Betty Sue sobbed.

"Hush, Betty Sue," Jenny warned. "Be careful what you say."

"I'm not afraid of anyone," Betty Sue puffed up. "Least of all, that beau of yours."

Jenny knew Adam had a job to do. His way of carrying out his duties often rubbed her the wrong way. Jenny realized none of that mattered in the present situation. If Heather was in trouble, she would do anything to help her clear her name.

Heather came out of a tiny room an hour later, looking bewildered. The Magnolias surrounded her immediately, throwing all kinds of questions at her.

Heather gently pushed them away and stared at Jenny.

"I need your help, Jenny. Are you going to find out who killed Gianni?"

Chapter 4

Jenny thought about Heather while frosting chocolate cupcakes. Heather had come to mean a lot to her. She was like her baby sister. Jenny resolved to do whatever needed to help Heather. The first step was going to be getting some background information on Dr. Gianni Costa.

Gianni had been in town only a short time. No one knew much about his past. Jenny had looked for his profile on social media the previous night. He had posted some photos of the beaches at Pelican Cove. There were some photos with Heather plastered to his side. But all the photos only went back a few months. There was nothing about his family or his previous life. Jenny had brought her laptop to work. She was going to dig deeper as soon as she got a chance.

Jenny fired up her laptop after lunch and began looking for Gianni Costa. Jenny was surprised when an address showed up for Gianni in Delaware. It was a small town on the coast, roughly a hundred miles from Pelican Cove.

Jenny felt a surge of energy as she spotted a phone number next to the address. She fed the number in her cell phone and crossed her fingers as she hit the green icon that would dial the number.

The phone barely rang twice before it was answered. The woman sounded brusque, as if she was just stepping out of the door.

"Does this number belong to Dr. Gianni Costa?" Jenny asked.

"Who is this?" the woman shot back.

"My name is Jenny King. I live in Pelican Cove."

"Are you Gianni's harpy?"

"Excuse me?" Jenny sputtered.

"Are you that girl he's been hanging out with lately?" the woman asked patiently.

"I'm not," Jenny said firmly. "I'm her friend."

"What do you want?"

"May I know who I am talking to?"

"Gianni's wife. Mrs. Gianni Costa."

The woman's smug tone carried over the phone line. Jenny found herself speechless.

"I didn't know Gianni was married," she finally managed to blurt out.

"You and everyone else, sister!"

"I would like to talk to you about Gianni," Jenny burst out. "Do you think we can meet?"

"You have my address," the woman said in a bored voice. "Give me a call when you are in town."

Jenny hung up. She was still trying to digest the fact that Gianni was married. Had Heather known about it?

Star came into the café's kitchen and flopped down into a chair. Her face was set in a frown.

"Had a fight with Jimmy?" Jenny teased.

"How old do you think I am, girl? Sixteen?" Star was rarely short with her.

"What's wrong, then?" Jenny asked, offering her aunt a freshly frosted cupcake.

Star considered the platter before her and chose one from the center. She took a big bite and licked the frosting off her lips.

"Are you reading minds now?" she asked Jenny.

Jenny waited patiently. She knew her aunt was just trying to buy time.

"There's a new art gallery in town."

"Where?"

"It's on the other end of town," Star explained. "Near to where all the rich people live. It's the first place they see when they come down the hills."

"Who told you about it?"

"I heard someone talking about it at the market. He has a big collection all ready to go."

"Why are you worried? People love your art."

"They didn't really have a choice all this time," Star grumbled. "My gallery was the only place you could get paintings of the region."

"And now you have competition," Jenny summed up.

"More importantly, the buyers have a choice," Star said.

Her fear and uncertainty were written clearly on her face.

"What if they don't like my stuff anymore?"

"I don't think that's possible," Jenny said loyally. "How long have you been doing this? Thirty years, forty? You are a pro at this. It's evident in your work."

"Art is subjective," Star pointed out. "What if people like his work more than mine?"

"You said it yourself," Jenny smiled. "Some people might like this new guy's paintings and some will like yours. Tourist trade is picking up in Pelican Cove. And most people roam around on Main Street. Anyone walking on the boardwalk or the beach can see your art gallery. They can't help but walk in."

"You think so?" Star asked.

"I know so. And we have your website set up too. You have more orders than you can fill right now. I don't see why you are getting so worked up."

"I have always been the only artist on the island," Star muttered.

"Have you met this guy yet?" Jenny asked. "What's his name, anyway?"

"Frank something," Star said. "He's not from around here. I can't understand why he came to Pelican Cove."

"Go meet him," Jenny suggested. "Introduce yourself."

"He could be a recluse," Star mused.

"So? He'll turn you away. But you will have tried."

"I think that's a good idea. Can I take some of these cupcakes with me?"

"That's a great idea," Jenny said brightly. "He's going to like you, don't worry. Everyone does."

Star could be outspoken but she was always ready to lend a helping hand. Although she wasn't born in Pelican Cove, she had endeared herself to the locals. After forty odd years on the island, she was almost a native.

"I guess I can finally talk shop with someone," Star said eagerly.

"That's the right attitude," Jenny cheered. "You'll be fine."

Jenny pulled out one of the fancy boxes they had recently ordered. With more and more people wanting to carry Jenny's sweet treats away with them, Petunia had suggested they print some fancy boxes with the Boardwalk Café's logo on them. Jenny packed four cupcakes in the box and tied it with a satin ribbon.

"Does he have any family?" she asked. "Will these be enough?"

"I don't know," Star shrugged. "I guess I'll find out."

Star took the box and went out. Jenny hoped she would hit it off with the new artist.

The phone rang. It was Betty Sue. Jenny was almost done with her day's chores. She rushed to the Bayview Inn to see what was wrong with Heather. The next hour was spent consoling Heather and letting her cry on her shoulder. Jenny didn't think it was the right time to tell Heather about Gianni's wife.

"How long is she going to mope around like this?" Betty Sue said worriedly.

She was twisting her lace handkerchief in her hands. Her hands were never still, even when she wasn't knitting.

"We have to give her time, Betty Sue," Jenny sighed. "Grief is personal, I guess. We can't predict how long she will take to get over Gianni."

"I hate that man," Betty Sue spat. "He misled my Heather when he was alive, and now he's messing with her even after he's dead."

Jenny fully agreed with Betty Sue.

"Why don't you find some dirt on him? I'm sure he wasn't a good man."

Jenny debated how much she wanted to reveal to Betty Sue.

"I'm working on it," she nodded. "Although I'm not sure if it will make a difference. Gianni has become some kind of hero in Heather's eyes."

Betty Sue surprised Jenny by what she said next.

"Heather needs to go out on a date. Why don't you fix up something for her on that Internet?"

"She has to be ready to meet other people, Betty Sue. Don't worry, just give it some time."

"You need to get some dirt on that man, and soon," Betty Sue insisted.

"I did find out something," Jenny finally admitted. "I spoke to his wife today."

Betty Sue sucked in a breath.

"Keep digging, Jenny. Make my Heather smile again."

Jenny went to the seafood market to shop for dinner. Chris met her as soon as she entered.

"The catch just came in," he told her. "I put aside all your favorites for you."

Back home, Jenny drew a bath for herself. She lit some scented candles and poured herself some lemonade. The hot water soothed her and she dozed a bit in the big clawfoot tub. The renovators had suggested installing a jetted tub in the lavish bathroom but Jenny had opted against it.

She dressed in her favorite faded jeans and an old sweatshirt and hopped down to the kitchen. There was some warmth in the air but she craved something rich and comforting. She slid a bread pudding in the oven and made her special whiskey and butter sauce to go on top. Then she made a simple sauce with olives and cherry tomatoes to go with the fish.

Star regaled them with an account of her encounter with the new artist.

"He didn't say much, but his eyes gleamed when he saw the cupcakes."

"Nobody can resist those cupcakes," Adam said lovingly, placing his hand over Jenny's.

"You have nothing to worry about, babe," Jimmy told Star loyally.

Jenny yearned to go for a walk. Adam and Jimmy loaded the dishwasher and helped clear up. Tank came over with his leash in his mouth and dropped it at Jenny's feet.

Jenny clipped the leash on and hugged Tank.

"Are you coming?" she asked Adam.

Tank strained on his leash, almost dragging her to the door.

The salty breeze and the flowers from the garden perfumed the air with a peculiar fragrance. Jenny closed her eyes and took a deep breath. A familiar arm came around her shoulders and she snuggled close to Adam.

They walked away from the house, Jenny throwing a ball for Tank.

"The contractor called today," Adam told Jenny. "They are almost done at my house. I should be able to move back soon."

"Do you have to go?"

"I've imposed on you long enough."

"Don't say that," Jenny argued. "I've enjoyed having you here at Seaview. The house is big enough."

"So is your heart," Adam crooned in her ear.

He planted a kiss on her head and stared into her eyes.

"I enjoyed these past few months, Jenny. We have been living in a dream."

"And I don't want to wake up from it," Jenny nodded.

"There are things to consider," Adam said cryptically.

Adam's twin girls were at college. They came home periodically. Jenny had welcomed them at Seaview but she guessed they missed their own home.

"Have the twins said something?"

"The twins have said a lot," Adam smiled. "I think I agree with them."

Jenny blushed at the suggestion. They had never discussed the status of their relationship. Jenny maintained Adam was her friend and a guest in her house. And yes, they were dating. What was the next step in their relationship?

"Tank and I are going to miss you."

"You'll still come here for your walk, won't you?" Jenny asked with a pout.

Months ago, she had run into Adam and Tank while walking on the beach. They had struck up a conversation and continued meeting with tacit agreement.

"We will try, but we may not make it out here every night."

"Then stay," Jenny urged. "Don't go yet."

Adam knew he needed to move out of Seaview before he could take any next steps. He had a solid plan and he couldn't wait to put it into action.

"We've got a couple of weeks," Adam consoled her. "But I will be gone by Spring Fest."

"Is something special happening then?"

"Wait and see," Adam grinned. "Now, did someone mention dessert?"

"Don't change the subject," Jenny said, glaring at him with her hands on her hips.

They had reached the patio at the back of the house. Star and Jimmy sat outside, enjoying their bread pudding. Adam pulled out a chair for Jenny.

"Adam's moving out," Jenny told her aunt. "It's going to be just the two of us again."

Chapter 5

Jenny brewed a fresh pot of coffee and wondered how to tackle Heather. Lately, Heather had the tendency of bursting into tears at the slightest provocation. But Jenny wanted to tell Heather about Gianni's wife before she heard about it from somewhere else.

"Can you come here before the others?" Jenny asked Heather over the phone. "We need to talk."

"Whatever," Heather mumbled without an ounce of interest.

She arrived at the café half an hour later, looking like she just got out of bed. Her eyes were sunken and there were circles under her eyes.

"How are you holding up, Heather?" Jenny asked with concern.

"Never mind that," Heather snapped. "Why did you want me here?"

Jenny led Heather to a small table inside the kitchen and made her sit down. Heather declined the offer of a freshly frosted cupcake but grabbed the cup of coffee Jenny poured for her.

"I found something out yesterday," Jenny began. "It doesn't make any difference now."

"What is it?"

"Promise me you won't flip."

"Spit it out already, Jenny!"

"I was looking Gianni up on the Internet." Jenny didn't know how to break it gently. "He was married, Heather. I am so sorry."

"Not for long," Heather said coolly.

"You knew about it?" Jenny burst out. "You never mentioned it."

"It wasn't a big deal," Heather shrugged. "It was a sham of a marriage. Gianni was going to divorce her pretty soon. His lawyer was drawing up the papers."

Jenny reflected over her conversation with Tiffany, Gianni's wife. Tiffany hadn't been aware of the impending divorce.

"Why was he leaving her?"

"She cheated on him," Heather drawled. "Gianni wasn't too happy with that."

Jenny stifled a laugh. It was the pot calling the kettle black.

"Who would be?" she said lamely. "Does she know about you?"

"I don't know," Heather shrugged. "Like you said, it doesn't matter now. What's with all the questions, Jenny?"

The Magnolias came in one by one and Heather went back to sulking in a corner.

Jenny went to The Steakhouse on her way back home. She had left her scarf in the restaurant the last time she was there. The hostess had told her to come and look in their Lost and Found. It was a pricey scarf with a designer label, a remnant of Jenny's old life. She admitted she still had some pleasant memories attached to it though and she didn't want to lose it.

It was an hour before the restaurant opened for dinner. The staff was setting the tables, filling salt shakers and getting the place ready. An attractive young woman Jenny recognized led her to a small office. Jenny spotted her scarf right away.

"Oh good," she exclaimed. "I didn't want to lose it."

"Did you have a good time here?" the girl asked eagerly. "It wasn't our best night."

"I was here Valentine's weekend," Jenny said. "I loved how you decorated the place. It was romantic."

"We try to do our best," the girl said solicitously. "I was referring to that other girl from your party. The one with the older man."

"Heather?"

The girl nodded. "She got into a big fight. You didn't know?"

Jenny shook her head. She had no idea what the girl was talking about.

"There was this other woman, platinum blonde, very attractive," the girl went on. "She was obviously a tourist. She got a table behind yours."

"Go on," Jenny urged.

"Heather got into an argument with her in the restroom. The woman pushed Heather. Heather pushed her back and slapped her. The woman fell and broke a heel. There was quite a ruckus."

Jenny was staring at the girl with wide eyes.

"We didn't hear any of that!"

"Well, the music was loud, I guess," the girl mused. "And we broke up the fight. A couple of the guys helped."

"Heather was gone from the table for some time," Jenny recollected. "I do remember that now. I thought she was fixing her face."

Jenny blushed as she remembered that night. She had been busy holding hands with Adam, thinking of the surprise she had planned for him when they got home. She had barely spared a glance at Heather.

"Heather's much older than me, of course," the girl prattled on. "But I've seen her around with that cute poodle. I never thought she was capable of using her fists."

"Any idea what they were fighting about?"

The girl looked uncomfortable.

"The blonde called Heather a slut."

Jenny had a good idea who the woman must have been. She thanked the girl for the scarf and walked home, lost in thought.

Why was Heather being so secretive? She had kept things from Jenny and also lied to her blatantly. Jenny didn't recognize the person Heather was turning into.

Star was pacing the floor in the great room at Seaview, rubbing her hands.

"What's the matter?" Jenny asked.

"I did something impulsive. I asked that new artist over for dinner."

"That's wonderful," Jenny assured her. "It will give you a chance to get to know him. We can get him talking and find out what his intentions are."

"Do we have enough food?" Star asked. "We don't have fish today."

"You don't worry about a thing. Let me handle everything."

Jenny called Jason and invited him for dinner.

"I need your discerning eye," she laughed over the phone. "We have a special guest."

Jason had just finished wrapping up a case. He agreed to pick up some shrimp from the seafood market.

Jenny marinated chicken breasts in garlic and balsamic vinegar. She plucked rosemary from the garden and crushed it before adding it to the marinade. She would make her special wine sauce to go with it.

Jason arrived a few minutes before the artist. He put on an apron and started chopping salad.

"Where's that grouchy house guest of yours?" he asked with a wink.

"Adam's working late. He won't be home for dinner."

"So I'm a sit in for him?"

Jenny placed her hands on her hips and glared at Jason.

"No good deed goes unpunished, huh. Here I thought you would enjoy a home cooked meal. But I guess I was wrong."

They bantered for a while, comfortable in each other's company. Jenny asked after Kandy but she was secretly glad the slightly overbearing lawyer wasn't with them.

The doorbell rang and they heard Star welcome someone.

"Frank's here," she said as she led a short, stout man in.

Star towered over him, at least a foot taller. The man had long arms and the slender fingers of an artist. His face was pockmarked and he wore his white hair in a crew cut.

"Frank Lopez," he introduced himself.

Jimmy Parsons hovered close to Star, his eyes keenly observing the newcomer.

Jenny brought out her crab dip and Jason poured wine. Frank declined.

"I don't drink," he said, looking at Jimmy's lemonade. "I'll have the same."

"Where are you from, Frank?" Jenny asked.

"I lived in the southwest most of my life," the artist replied. "I guess I got tired of painting canyons and deserts."

There was some polite laughter at that.

"I sold my house, put all my stuff in an Airstream and set off one day."

"Doesn't get simpler than that," Star agreed.

Jenny sensed a longing in her aunt's voice. Her aunt had been a hippie in her younger days. Jenny wondered if she still dreamt of hitting the road.

"How's that working out for you?" Jason asked.

"Much better than I ever imagined," Frank said enthusiastically. "I stop where I want, set up my easel and start painting. It's been great for my art."

"What brings you to Pelican Cove?" Jimmy asked. "Very few westerners venture into our neck of the woods."

"I was in Vermont last fall," Frank explained. "I ran into a family who hailed from the Eastern Shore. They told me so much about the region. I decided I was going to spend the next summer here."

"Wasn't Maine closer to where you were?" Jimmy asked curiously. "It's not a bad spot to paint."

"I was there last summer," Frank laughed. "Painted the cliffs and the mountains ad nauseum. The beaches here are different."

"No place is quite like Pelican Cove," Star said fondly. "Most of the beauty here is untouched. We have our share of tourists, but we are not very commercialized."

"I confess I'm something of a gourmand," Frank said, piercing his fork into a plump shrimp.

Jenny had served dinner and the lively conversation had moved to the dinner table.

Frank complimented Jenny's cooking.

"I'm making it a point to taste local delicacies. The Chesapeake crabs and oysters are next on my list."

"You came to the right place for that," Jenny told him. "Wait till you taste our soft shell crabs."

"I'm also big on meditation," Frank went on. "It helps my art, you know. Peace of mind is underrated."

"I hear you are setting up a gallery?" Star asked, finally broaching the topic that was bothering her.

Frank nodded. "It's temporary. I have landscapes from all over the country. A lot of water colors."

"I mostly use oil on canvas," Star told him.

Jenny served a cheesecake for dessert. Frank went home with a big smile on his face.

"He seems okay," Jenny said. "He'll be gone before fall sets in, Star. You don't have anything to worry about."

Jimmy wasn't too taken with the newcomer.

"I don't buy it," he said. "Peace of mind, my ass."

"You promised not to swear, Jimmy," Star chided him.

Jenny went out to see Jason off. He thanked her for the lovely dinner.

"Are you Heather's lawyer?" Jenny asked him.

Jason nodded.

"So you don't have to tell me everything she tells you?"

"Anything Heather tells me is confidential, Jenny. You know that."

"She's been lying to me, Jason. She knew Gianni was married but she never told us about it."

"Maybe she didn't want you to judge her."

"I can believe that," Jenny said. "But get this. She picked a fight with Gianni's wife at The Steakhouse. What was Gianni's wife doing there? And why was Heather punching her lights out?"

"I'll talk to her about it," Jason promised.

Jenny kept thinking about Heather as she tossed and turned that night.

"What else are you hiding, Heather?" she demanded the next morning.

Heather's eyes were swollen with too much sleep.

"Get off my back, Jenny," Heather snarled.

"I know you punched Gianni's wife. That's not like you."

Heather shrugged.

"What did you do after you went home with Gianni?" Jenny pressed. "You need to come clean if you want me to help you."

"I don't need your help," Heather wailed. "I'm innocent."

"So tell me what you did."

"I must have gone home," Heather said with a frown. "I woke up in my own bed."

"When did you go home?" Jenny pressed. "And how?"

Heather clutched her forehead in her hands as she sat down.

"Leave me alone, Jenny. I don't owe you any explanations."

"You can blow me off all you want, Heather," Jenny said, shaking her head. "But you can't stop the questions. The police will keep asking them and you better have an answer for them."

"I don't remember, okay?" Heather cried. "I went home with Gianni. I think we had a drink."

"You were already drunk."

"So what?" Heather scowled. "I woke up in my own bed the next day. I don't know how I got there. You can ask me the same question a dozen times but my answer will be the same. I don't know."

Jenny balled her fists as she realized how hopeless the situation was.

"I think you're in trouble, sweetie," Jenny said softly. "God help you get out of this."

Chapter 6

"Are you sure she won't be mad at us?" Molly asked timidly.

Jenny and Molly were driving out of town in Jenny's car, headed to the small town in Delaware where Gianni's wife lived. Jenny had wisely decided against taking Heather with them. Normally, the three friends always went out of town together, but this time they had slipped out without telling Heather about their plans.

"Given the way she's acting lately, I am sure she'll throw a fit," Jenny said with a grimace. "Let her. We are doing this for her own good."

"I don't feel so good about it," Molly whined.

Heather had taken the slightest opportunity to belittle Molly since she got together with Chris. Jenny knew her concerns were justified.

"I'll handle her, don't worry."

They drove for over an hour and Jenny crossed the state border. The town they entered seemed to be smaller than Pelican Cove.

"This place looks deserted," Jenny observed. "Hard to imagine a doctor having a thriving practice here."

"Gianni set up shop in Pelican Cove," Molly reminded her. "Maybe he had a clinic in a whole bunch of small towns up and down the coast."

"Hold that thought," Jenny said as an attractive platinum blonde pulled up in a Mercedes convertible.

Jenny waited as the girl tottered on her heels and went inside the rundown diner. Her chiseled face hinted at Botox and her flawless complexion had probably seen some chemical peels. Jenny switched off her car and stepped out.

The girls followed the other woman into the diner. She had bagged one of the three booths inside. The faux red leather was peeling and there was a smell of burnt cheese in the air.

"You must be Tiffany," Jenny said, taking a seat opposite the woman. "Thanks for coming to meet us."

The girls introduced themselves. Tiffany Costa was friendly enough.

She laughed openly and asked the girls how they knew her husband.

Jenny hesitated before replying.

"Gianni knew a friend of ours. Actually, he was dating her for the past few months."

"You're talking about Heather," Tiffany said, fiddling with the sugar sachets on the table.

A tired, grumpy looking waitress came and poured coffee. Jenny took one look at the murky brown liquid and pushed her mug away.

"Do you prefer tea?" the waitress asked her with a smirk. "I've got tea bags."

"You knew Heather?" Molly asked incredulously.

Jenny hadn't told her about the infamous fight at The Steakhouse.

"I saw their photos," Tiffany said wearily. "The whole world saw them, of course. He brought her home once."

Jenny wondered what kind of a cad Gianni had been.

"That must have been hard."

"Gianni had a thing for younger women," Tiffany said. "Younger, beautiful women. He dated them for a while and promised to marry them."

"And?" Molly asked, holding her breath.

"He dumped them when he found someone new."

Tiffany shrugged and took a sip of the coffee. She seemed pretty cool about the whole thing.

"You were fine with all that?" Jenny pressed.

"He always came back to me," Tiffany told them. "So when he was in the mood for these indiscretions, I just looked the other way."

"I'm guessing the lifestyle didn't hurt."

"I made my choice," Tiffany said coldly. "I'm allowed to do that."

Tiffany seemed to get a bit defensive after that.

"Can you tell us anything else about Gianni?" Molly asked.

"What do you want to know?"

"Why did you live in this town, for instance?" Jenny asked. "There must be hardly any patients here."

"This place was just right for Gianni," Tiffany said cryptically.

"How so?"

"Gianni preyed on older people," Tiffany said with a sigh. "People who were not all there," she said, tapping her forehead with a finger. "He fleeced them as much as he could."

"Are you saying he was dishonest?" Molly asked in shock.

"He was a master at duping people," Tiffany said, her eyes gleaming. "He chose small isolated towns where most of the people were senior citizens. They were alone or their kids lived in some city. Either way, they didn't have anyone looking after them."

"What was he doing in Pelican Cove?" Jenny asked, aghast.

"He was done here. Pelican Cove was next on his list. He already had a nice racket going there."

"Why didn't you live there with him?"

"I did," Tiffany said with a shrug. "Off and on."

"Funny we never ran into you," Jenny said, narrowing her eyes.

Most new people in town came to the Boardwalk Café for a meal. Jenny was sure Tiffany had never visited the café.

"That was all part of Gianni's plan," Tiffany explained. "I was keeping a low profile."

"I don't understand," Jenny said coldly.

"He was wooing Heather, right?" Tiffany said with a yawn. "According to Gianni, it was easy to befriend people as a single man. He always showered attention on one of the local girls. That allowed him to get a foot in, meet the movers and shakers in town."

"How smart of him," Jenny said sarcastically.

"He was sneaky that way," Tiffany agreed.

"I don't understand," Jenny said, sitting up. "If you already knew

Heather, what was the fight about?"

"You heard about that?" Tiffany asked with a laugh. "I was just acting on Gianni's instructions."

"Kindly explain …" Jenny said with a roll of her eyes.

"Heather was getting clingy. She probably expected some kind of grand gesture for Valentine's weekend. That's why Gianni invited me there."

"What were you going to do?"

"I just had to show up at that dingy restaurant and tell Heather I was meeting Gianni later."

"I guess she didn't believe you."

Tiffany shook her head, rubbing a spot on her chin. It seemed like she was remembering the fight.

"That girl's got a mean right hook," she said with a shudder. "She told me she was the one going home with Gianni. She warned me to stay away."

"Did you?" Jenny asked.

"I was just supposed to plant a seed of doubt. I got that done."

Jenny peered at Tiffany's face, trying to gauge if she was telling the truth.

"You are sure you didn't go home and lie in wait for Gianni?"

"Gianni was a mean drunk," Tiffany said. "I didn't want to be anywhere near him that night."

"Would you say Gianni was depressed about something?" Jenny asked as a last resort.

The police hadn't mentioned the possibility of suicide but she wanted to rule it out.

"Honey, Gianni made other people cry. He was happier than a pig in mud!"

Jenny thanked Tiffany for meeting them.

"Sure. Call me anytime."

She breezed out of the diner ahead of them. Jenny belatedly realized

Tiffany looked nothing like a grieving widow.

"Heather had a close call," Molly said on the way back.

"You don't believe she was okay with Gianni being married?" Jenny asked her.

"He must have convinced her he was going to leave his wife," Molly shrugged.

"Heather must have lost it when she saw Tiffany at the restaurant," Jenny observed.

Had Heather been angry enough to take revenge?

Jenny and Molly were both hungry by the time they got back in town.

"Petunia must be closing up, but I can rustle up something for us to eat," Jenny promised.

They were surprised to see a group of women arguing loudly at the café.

"We have to do something about this," Barb Norton said, slapping the table. "It's your duty to support us, Betty Sue."

"What's going on?" Jenny asked her aunt.

Petunia, Star and Betty Sue sat on one side of the table. Barb Norton sat on the other side, glaring at them like a judge. Heather was nowhere to be seen.

"Just wait and watch," Star whispered.

Jenny pulled out a bowl of chicken salad and scooped it generously over two large slices of artisan bread. She added sliced tomatoes and lettuce and squirted her honey mustard dressing on top. She cut the sandwich in two pieces and put them on a plate.

Molly and Jenny munched their sandwich as they listened to Barb and Betty Sue.

Betty Sue's needles clacked as she went on knitting, refusing to look up.

"Are you paying attention, Betty Sue?" Barb roared. "We need to go talk to those Newburys."

Betty Sue finally looked up. She had a weary look in her eyes.

"I don't like talking to John about his business."

"His business is threatening the fabric of our society," Barb said pompously. "It's everyone's business now."

"Why don't you go the usual route? Form a committee?" Betty Sue clucked. "We can then draw up some kind of proposal and take it to the Newburys."

"I am doing all that," Barb said sternly. "But we need to push things forward. I say we take a delegation up there right now."

Star giggled at the mention of a delegation. Barb breathed fire on her.

"Is this about the medical dispensary?" Jenny mumbled, chewing on her delicious sandwich.

"Don't talk with your mouth full, young lady!" Barb snapped. "We are talking about the drug farms."

"Same difference," Jenny muttered.

"Are you saying you support this heinous undertaking?" Barb scowled at her. "I was counting on you, Jenny."

"My mind's not made up either way," Jenny said, wiping her mouth with a paper napkin. "I need more information."

"I agree with Jenny," Molly said softly.

"You too?" Barb pounced on Molly. "Have you forgotten what we did to save your job?"

"I am grateful for what the town did for me, Barb," Molly spoke up. "But this is a different issue."

"Stop blabbering," Betty Sue commanded. "You are giving me a headache."

"Put that knitting down, Betty Sue, and come with me," Barb pressed. "We should all go."

"You know Ada doesn't see people without an appointment," Betty Sue pleaded.

Ada Newbury never let anyone forget that she was the richest woman in town. She looked down her nose at everyone and was a trial to be around.

Barb and Betty Sue argued a bit more and Betty Sue finally gave in. They all set off in two cars, Jenny looking forward to seeing someone take Ada down a peg or two.

The guard at the gate let them in when he spied Betty Sue in Jenny's back seat. Ada kept them waiting for half an hour before she emerged, dressed to the nines.

"Ladies," she said with her nose in the air. "Is it an emergency? I am getting late for a party."

"Sit down, Ada," Barb Norton said brusquely. "We have come to talk about this drug farm of yours."

"My husband handles the business," Ada snipped. "People generally take an appointment and meet him in his office."

"Your husband has gone too far this time," Barb quipped. "We need you to bring him to his senses."

"Be very careful what you say next, Barb," Ada said angrily. "Don't forget you are sitting in my parlor."

"We love our town, Ada," Barb said. "It's rustic but simple and we manage it as well as possible with the limited resources we have."

Ada reminded them she donated liberally to those resources.

"The town has always been grateful for your largesse," Barb said firmly. "But we cannot open our doors to a drug business."

"I think there is some misunderstanding," Ada clucked. "We are planning to open a dispensary that will treat people."

"A marijuana dispensary?" Barb said hoarsely. "Over my dead body!"

"Stop being so dramatic," Ada said in a bored voice.

The conversation derailed after that. Ada clapped her hands and a couple of maids ran into the room. She ordered them to escort the women out.

"Now what?" Jenny asked as they stood outside the Boardwalk Café.

"We march on," Barb said, plunging her fist in the air. "Say no to cannabis!" she yelled. "Say no to drugs!"

Chapter 7

Jenny sat in Jason's office, moodily sipping from a bottle of juice. Jason leaned back in his chair with his hands behind his head, staring at a corner.

"Are you sure about this, Jenny?"

"I only have Tiffany's word for it, but why would she lie?"

"I can think of a number of reasons. She says Gianni told her about the girls he dated. But we only have her word for it."

"Any other wife would have been shocked."

"We don't know if she was really okay with all this," Jason warned. "All I am saying is, take anything she says with a pinch of salt. You just met the woman."

Jenny didn't like to be called gullible. She thought she had a good eye for people.

"What about the other stuff she said?"

"That's also her word against his."

"So you don't think he was shady? Any man who can cheat on his wife and sweet talk a young girl into going around with him …"

"We all know what he did with Heather," Jason said, warding her off. "But medical fraud …"

Jason went back to staring in the distance.

"We can't just sit around talking about this," Jenny said. "Let's go out and do something."

"Like what? Raid Gianni's office?"

Jenny's eyes gleamed and a smile lit up her face.

"Who's going to stop us?"

"I'm a lawyer, Jenny. I can't just go breaking and entering."

"We may not have to," Jenny said, springing to her feet.

She almost dragged Jason along with her.

Gianni Costa lived in a ranch style house a few blocks off Main Street. There was another ranch adjoining his which had served as his clinic. The shingle hanging off a pole announced it as the family practice of Dr. Gianni Costa, MD. Jenny walked up to the door and turned the handle. The door opened easily.

"Viola!" she said to Jason. "We are not breaking any laws going through an open door."

"I guess not," Jason shrugged.

Jenny rushed through the waiting room at the front and entered a door marked 'Staff only'.

"He must have kept some records," she mumbled to herself.

Gianni turned out to be a meticulous record keeper. Jenny spotted files in a drawer and started rifling through them.

"What are you looking for, exactly?" Jason asked.

"Anything out of the ordinary," Jenny quipped. "Heather was a patient?" she murmured as she pulled out a thick file.

Her mouth was hanging open two minutes later.

"Look at what this says," she said, pulling at Jason's sleeve. "According to this, Heather was Gianni's patient and visited him every day of the week."

"She visited him alright," Jason sniggered.

"Can you be serious for a minute?" Jenny taunted. "It's all written here. Heather Morse is a patient. There are prescription records too."

Jenny slumped into a chair, looking worried.

"Is Heather sick?" she exclaimed. "Does she have some terrible illness she's hiding from everyone?"

"You're being dramatic, Jenny," Jason said lightly. "She might have had some minor complaint."

"This says she had an appointment every day. There is some kind of code under diagnosis but I don't know what that means."

"Let's go talk to Heather."

Jason sounded resigned. He knew Jenny wouldn't rest until she got to the bottom of this.

Jenny called Heather from the clinic and asked her to wait at home. She started for the Bayview Inn with Jason.

Betty Sue fussed over them when they got to the inn, plying them with hot tea and cookies.

"Why don't you take a nap, Grandma," Heather suggested. "I've got things under control here."

"You're just trying to get rid of me," Betty Sue glowered.

Jenny sighed with relief when she went up the stairs to her room.

"What have you been hiding, Heather?" she asked, turning to look at her friend. "Please tell me nothing's wrong with you."

"What do you mean, Jenny?"

Heather looked bewildered as Jenny narrated what she had seen.

"I never saw Gianni professionally," Heather said firmly. "There must be some mistake."

"As far as I know, there's only one Heather Morse in Pelican Cove," Jenny said stoutly. "Something is fishy here."

"I still go to old Dr. Smith," Heather said again. "He's treated me since I came to live with Grandma."

"So Tiffany was right," Jenny said to Jason, slapping her leg. "That Gianni was doing something illegal."

"When did you talk to Tiffany?" Heather asked, springing to her feet. "She had it in for Gianni."

"I don't care what her relationship was with Gianni," Jenny dismissed. "She told us Gianni cheated his patients. I am beginning to think she was right."

"Just because Gianni's not here to defend himself …"

Heather curled her fists and looked anguished. Her eyes filled with tears.

"Get hold of yourself, Heather," Jenny said, grabbing her by the shoulders and shaking her. "Gianni's gone, and I say you are well rid of him."

"He was a good man," Heather blubbered through her tears.

"He was a nasty crook who was just taking you for a ride," Jenny said mercilessly. "I'm going to prove it to you."

Jenny stomped out of the Bayview Inn, muttering to herself.

"Can you give me a ride home?" she requested Jason. "I have to get ready for dinner. We are going on a double date with Molly and Chris."

"We could have triple dated," Jason said in a hurt tone.

Jenny didn't think she could tolerate another evening with Kandy the lawyer.

"Some other time," she said glibly.

Jenny took a quick shower and agonized over what to wear. She tried on and discarded four dresses. Finally, she settled on a sunflower yellow dress with a cowl neck. She rubbed the heart shaped charm around her neck as she gazed at herself in the mirror. The phone rang just then and Jenny's face lit up when she saw it was her son. She pressed the video button. She needed to see her beloved Nicky.

"When are you getting home, scamp?" she asked lovingly. "A little bird told me you are spending spring break in Pelican Cove."

"No way, Mom," Nick groaned. "You know I am going to Cancun with my friends."

They chatted for a while and Nick hung up after promising to visit soon. Jenny's face lit up in a thousand watt smile. There was a knock on the door.

Adam stood outside, leaning on his cane. He looked handsome in a black silk shirt. His faded jeans hugged his lean body.

"Ready to roll, Madam?" he grinned.

"Are we picking them up?" Jenny asked Adam as she got into the car.

They were going to an Italian restaurant in a nearby town. The Eastern Shore was home to plenty of small towns like Pelican Cove. The area was paradise for foodies, with eclectic restaurants lining the shore from north to south.

"Chris mentioned some errands," Adam told her. "They will meet us at the restaurant."

"Good," Jenny smiled, placing her hand in Adam's.

Molly and Chris were sipping wine and munching on garlic bread when the hostess ushered Adam and Jenny to their table. Jenny let out a shriek merely seconds after she sat down.

"Is that a ring, Molly?"

Molly's face glowed in the candle light.

Jenny whipped her head toward Chris. He was beaming at Molly. Molly clasped his hand in hers and held it up for Jenny.

"Congratulations, man!" Adam said, slapping Chris on the back.

"It's a promise ring," Chris said, clearing his throat. "Sort of a pre-engagement ring."

"Chris surprised me with the most beautiful engagement ring." Molly sounded hushed. "But I thought we would wear a promise ring first."

"But why?" Jenny wailed. "I can't wait to plan your wedding."

"We are taking it slow," Molly said, looking lovingly at Chris. "There's no rush."

"That's just mumbo jumbo," Adam dismissed. "As far as I am concerned, congratulations are in order. We need some champagne here."

They poured the bubbly and toasted the happy couple. Molly chattered nonstop over the osso buco, a slow cooked dish of wine braised veal. They had tiramisu for dessert and Jenny ordered an espresso to round off the meal.

"Am I allowed to tell people about this?" Jenny asked Molly.

"I'll tell them tomorrow," Molly said shyly. "I'm so happy, Jenny," she said later as they waited outside for the men to bring their cars around. "I feel like I'm in a dream."

"Chris is a good guy," Jenny assured her. "You couldn't have chosen better."

"I want to be sure he loves me," Molly said with a hint of doubt in her voice. "Technically, I'm his rebound relationship."

"Is that why you went for the promise ring?" Jenny asked her.

Molly nodded. "I want him to be sure. Very sure."

"You're one brave girl, Molly. Anyone in your position would have dragged Chris to the altar."

"I've been there," Molly reminded her, referring to her previous marriage. "You understand, don't you, Jenny? When I tie the knot again, it will be for the last time."

Jenny reflected over how different Molly was from Heather. Molly was timid but level headed. Heather was headstrong and impulsive. Chris had fallen for both these women at one time or another.

Adam accompanied Chris to the other end of the parking lot. It was late and the lot had emptied while they lingered over their meal.

"So you are almost leg-shackled," Adam laughed as he patted Chris on the back. "How does it feel?"

Chris wrung a hand through his hair. The smile he had worn all evening was nowhere to be seen.

"You know what's happening with Heather?" he muttered. "I felt pressured."

"You don't love Molly?" Adam scowled. "Are you messing with her, Chris?"

"I do love her," Chris said uncertainly. "But what if Heather needs me? I promised I would always be there for her."

"Are you kidding me?" Adam snapped at Chris. "You should have thought of that before you slipped on that ring."

He put his hand on Chris's shoulder.

"I think you are getting cold feet. Happens to the best of us."

"But what about Heather?" Chris asked with a frown.

"Heather will be fine," Adam said. "She left you, Chris. You accepted that and moved on. You need to look ahead now. Molly's a good soul. She will make you happy for the rest of your days."

"I do love Molly," Chris said earnestly. "But I feel responsible for

Heather."

"Heather will be fine," Adam consoled him. "She's not alone. We will all take care of her."

Adam kept quiet about his conversation with Chris. He knew Jenny would fly off the handle if she learned what was going on in Chris's mind. He said good night to Jenny outside her door and limped to his room in search of pain pills.

Jenny brushed her hair and smiled at herself in the mirror. She was happy for Molly and Chris. Chris had always impressed her as a level headed young guy. He would take care of her friend. Her brows furrowed in concern as her phone trilled suddenly. It was past midnight. Her heart thudded in her chest as she thought of her son. She hoped he was fine.

Jenny checked the caller id and crossed her fingers before answering the phone.

"Jason? Is something wrong? Why are you calling so late?"

Jason's voice was heavy with emotion.

"Kandy dumped me."

"What?" Jenny exclaimed. "When?"

"She just sent me an email," Jason said grimly. "She doesn't want to see me anymore."

Chapter 8

Jason refused to speak about Kandy the next day.

"I bet she's just pulling your leg."

"Let's not talk about this, Jenny."

Jenny didn't know what to say. Kandy hadn't seemed like the kind who would settle down, especially in a small, isolated town like Pelican Cove. She had a high flying career in the city. Jenny had been surprised she stuck to Jason all those months.

"Did she give a reason?" Jenny had asked Jason the previous night.

"None," he had lamented. "It just says our lives don't align any more. What does that even mean?"

Jason was putting on a stoic face that morning. Her anguished and hurt friend from the previous night was nowhere in evidence.

"She'll come around," Jenny said again, giving Jason a hug. "If she doesn't, it's her loss."

"What brings you here, Jenny?" Jason asked with a sigh. "Are you just here to console me or do you have something else on your mind?"

"A bit of both," Jenny said grudgingly.

"Shoot. I'm free for the next few hours."

"Do you know the other doctor in town?"

"Old Dr. Smith?" Jason asked. "Sure. I've been seeing him all my life."

"I have an idea."

Dr. Smith's clinic turned out to be a block away from Jenny's home. Jason had called ahead for an appointment. An elderly nurse hugged and kissed Jason.

"Your half yearly appointment is overdue," she scolded.

Dr. Smith was a slim, energetic man in his seventies. Jenny guessed he was a few years older than her aunt. He welcomed Jason with a hug.

"Who's your friend?" he asked with a twinkle in his eye. "Are you finally taking my advice and starting a family?"

Jenny blushed to the roots of her hair. She hastened to explain.

"Oh, you are the young lady the whole town is talking about," the doctor said. "I've tasted most of your goodies. I just haven't had a chance to come into the Boardwalk Café myself. I'm as good as chained to this place."

The small talk went on for a few minutes until Jenny cleared her throat.

Dr. Smith took the hint.

"Look at me ramble on. So what brings you young people here?"

Dr. Smith's face darkened at the mention of Gianni Costa.

"He was a bad one."

Jenny told him about the records in the doctor's office.

"Heather insists she was never his patient. Do you know why he would have a file with her name on it?"

"I can think of a reason or two," Dr. Smith said grimly.

"Would you please look at some of the papers and give them a once over?"

"I have appointments all day," Dr. Smith apologized. "Can you bring the files here?"

"I can get you a few samples," Jenny nodded.

Jason and Jenny went to Gianni's house again. The door to the clinic portion was locked this time. A fan whirred inside and the radio was playing. Jenny rapped her knuckles on the door.

A tiny, shriveled woman opened the door, her eyes full of fear.

"Do you work here?" Jenny asked.

"I was Dr. Costa's nurse," the woman said.

Jenny realized she should have guessed that from the colorful scrubs the woman was wearing.

"You do know Dr. Costa is gone?" Jason asked.

The nurse shook her head.

"I was out of town on vacation. Did he say when he will be back?"

"We are not sure," Jenny said smoothly. "We are here for some paperwork. He said you would give it to us."

Jason was staring at Jenny with his mouth agape.

The nurse led them into the office they had been in earlier. Jenny got rid of the woman by asking for a glass of water. She pulled out the topmost boxes and began taking pictures of the papers in the files.

"Do you know what you are doing?" Jason hissed.

Jenny held a finger to her lips, asking him to be quiet.

The nurse came back with the water.

"I don't think you are allowed to touch that," she said mildly. "Those records contain confidential information."

"Sorry," Jenny said sweetly. "I thought I would save you some time."

She made up a name and asked for a duplicate report. The nurse spent some time rifling through the files.

"I don't see your name here," she said with a frown.

Jenny sensed the nurse was finally beginning to get irritated.

"Why don't you keep looking for it?" she said. "I'll be back later."

Jason berated her as soon as they got into the car.

"You know what you were doing? Getting information under false pretenses. This will never stand up in a court of law."

"I'm not thinking that far ahead," Jenny dismissed. "I just want to find out what Gianni was up to."

Dr. Smith's office was closed for lunch.

"I've never seen a doctor's office close in the middle of the day," Jenny said.

"This is Pelican Cove," Jason reminded her. "And everyone has to eat."

Jenny's stomach growled just then.

"It's time for lunch," Jason said with a smile. "How about going to

Ethan's Crab Shack?"

Jenny smiled approvingly.

"I'd rather not go back to the café. I know I'll put on an apron and start working as soon as I get in there."

Jenny was feeling guilty about leaving Petunia on her own for so long. But her aunt had promised to help out so she could go play detective.

Ethan Hopkins greeted them with a big smile. He was Adam's twin but he couldn't have been more different.

"I've never been here during the day," Jenny said as they found a table by the water.

"What are you in the mood for?" Jason asked. "I am going for the fish and chips."

Jenny chose the grilled seafood salad. Their food arrived in large platters.

"This salad is huge," Jenny said, picking up a fry from Jason's plate.

Jason pushed his plate away after a few bites and lapsed into silence. Jenny let him be.

They made their way back to Dr. Smith's clinic. The old doctor studied all the photos carefully.

"That man was a crook!" he exclaimed. "I want to look at the rest of his files but I am almost certain what's going on here."

"What?" Jason and Jenny asked.

"Healthcare fraud," the doctor said grimly. "I know some of the names here. As far as I know, these people don't have the conditions Costa treated them for."

"So what was he up to?" Jenny asked, fascinated.

"There are fake visits here," Dr. Smith explained. "And false diagnoses."

"Do you know what these letters mean?" Jenny asked, pointing to some gibberish under 'diagnosis'.

"They are diagnosis codes," the doctor explained. "Each group of letters means something specific. Looks like Costa was getting money from the government based on fake data."

"So Heather was never really his patient?"

"Heather and a few others," the doctor nodded. "He's charging for patient visits that never happened. Also for services or procedures I bet he has not performed."

"Could this have harmed his patients?" Jason asked, aghast.

"Hard to say based on this data," Dr. Smith shrugged. "But I wouldn't put it past him."

Jenny thanked the doctor for his time.

"What now?" Jason asked.

"I'm going to talk to Adam," Jenny said stiffly. "Can you drop me off at the police station?"

Nora, the desk clerk, greeted Jenny as soon as she stepped into the station.

"He's not in a good mood," she warned, jerking her head toward Adam's office.

"So what's new?" Jenny said with a roll of her eyes.

Adam's mood was a popular topic of discussion at his place of work. His coworkers tiptoed around him when his temper flared.

Adam sat with his leg propped up on a chair, struggling to unscrew a bottle of pills.

"What do you want?" he snapped, tossing the bottle to Jenny.

She grabbed it and opened it without much effort. She took out two pills and handed them to Adam. Adam downed them with a glass of water and sighed deeply.

"Sit down," he said in a milder tone. "What brings you here, Jenny? I hear you are painting the town red with Jason Stone."

"Hardly," Jenny said with a grimace. "I didn't know you had Ethan spying on me."

"He brought me lunch," Adam said lightly. "You know I was just kidding. So how many laws have you broken today?"

"None that I know of," Jenny said sullenly. "Wait till you hear what I found."

Jenny spoke for the next few minutes. Adam's face was inscrutable as he listened to her.

"When are you going to learn?" he whined when she stopped to take a breath. "You are meddling in police business."

"You mean I am doing their business. Shouldn't you or your men have found all this out by now?"

Adam had no answer for that.

"Have you even met Tiffany?" Jenny demanded. "I think she's a potential suspect."

"You must be right, of course," Adam said sarcastically.

"You think Heather is guilty, don't you? Why not Tiffany? She was a woman scorned. And she was right here in Pelican Cove on that night. In fact, she was at The Steakhouse."

"Are you sure about that?" Adam asked.

"Yes, I am sure," Jenny bristled. "Just talk to the staff at the restaurant."

"I have to follow certain procedures," Adam droned. "I can't just run around the place talking up anyone I meet."

"What about this healthcare fraud? Don't you think that is important?"

"That's just an allegation," Adam said. "We don't know he was doing anything wrong for sure. We will have to bring in some specialists. And if there is any connection to his old clinic in Delaware, this case is out of my hands."

"What does that mean?" Jenny asked with alarm.

She was worried about Heather.

"Based on what you told me, whatever crimes Gianni committed crossed state lines. That puts the case out of my jurisdiction."

"I have no such restrictions," Jenny said. "I just want to take care of Heather. I'm going to keep digging."

"This healthcare fraud could be dangerous, Jenny," Adam pleaded.

"Who knows how many more people are involved. You need to be careful."

"Jason was with me when we went to Gianni's clinic."

"He should have known better," Adam clucked. "Has he lost his mind?"

"He's just being a good friend," Jenny bristled. "Unlike you."

"My hands are tied," Adam said, literally holding his hands up in the air. "You know I can't be partial to you. The whole town knows I'm your house guest."

Jenny tried to calm herself. Adam always got her riled up with his strait laced ideas.

"Is that all you are?" she asked coquettishly.

"Please be careful, Jenny," Adam begged. "I couldn't bear it if something happened to you."

"I can take care of myself," Jenny said, shaking her head. "Don't you think this whole scam business is important? It might lead you to other suspects."

"I never thought of that!" Adam glared at her. "Why don't you leave me alone and let me think about this?"

"I'm leaving," Jenny said, pushing her chair back.

"Want to go out for dinner?" Adam asked. "You must be tired from running around all day."

Jenny smiled reluctantly.

"I don't mind. I was craving something spicy."

Adam made plans to take her to a Mexican restaurant ten miles up the coast.

"Have a nice day, Sheriff!" Jenny said with a wave as she breezed out of Adam's office.

She had stumbled onto her next course of action while talking to Adam.

Chapter 9

Adam and Jenny sat on the patio, sipping wine. Star and Jimmy were watching a movie. It was one of their favorite things to do after dinner. Jenny had been too tired to go for a walk. They had chosen to relax in the garden instead. Tank sat at Jenny's feet, dozing with one eye closed.

Adam looked at the stone fountain in the garden and let out a sigh.

"I have some news for you, Jenny."

"I know you are eager to move back to your house, Adam, but why don't you wait a few weeks more?"

"It's not about that," Adam hesitated.

Jenny peered into his eyes, trying to guess what he was about to say.

"The DNA results are in. There is no more doubt."

"So it was Lily Davis," Jenny said softly. "Or Lily Bennet if you consider her married name."

Adam nodded in the soft moonlight.

"She was here all along, right in her own backyard."

"Do you think she's still around?" Jenny asked with a shiver.

"What nonsense!" Adam dismissed. "We talked about this, Jenny."

"I know, I know … but all those stories about mysterious lights and the house being haunted … maybe Lily was trying to get someone's attention."

"You amaze me," Adam said with a shake of his head. "You are this smart modern woman one instant and the next instant you start talking like some illiterate person."

"I'm just saying …"

"I guess you feel some kind of compulsion to get to the bottom of this," Adam smirked.

"Believe it or not, I do," Jenny said. "I'm going to do everything I can to find out who killed Lily."

"I wish you luck. We don't have too many resources to assign to a case that old, so you might be the only one fighting for Lily."

"I might need your help, Adam."

"Let me know what you need."

"You're not going to yell at me for meddling with police business?"

"Not this time," Adam promised.

Jenny thought of Lily as she baked a batch of blueberry muffins the next morning. She wasn't looking forward to telling the Magnolias about Lily.

Betty Sue came in, clutching a ball of white wool under her armpit. Her knitting needles poked out of a tote bag. Heather followed her, biting her nails, looking lost in thought.

"Is she still biting her nails?" Betty Sue asked Jenny.

Jenny followed them out to the deck with a tray loaded with coffee and snacks. Star was coming up the steps from the beach.

"Where's Molly?" Petunia wanted to know.

"I'm right here," Molly said cheerily, looking pretty in an apple green dress.

Jenny didn't waste any time bringing the women up to speed. Betty Sue crossed herself and muttered a prayer.

Lily had been her best friend since childhood.

"I never believed she abandoned her family," Betty Sue said.

"You say that now, Grandma!" Heather said with a sneer. "But you were quick to blame her, just like everyone else."

"How was I supposed to know what happened?" Betty Sue cried. "She disappeared overnight."

"You should have known," Heather stressed. "You should have trusted her."

Jenny sensed Heather wasn't just talking about Lily. Heather's recent wild streak had driven a wedge between her and Betty Sue.

Jenny called Adam from the café.

"Did anyone file a missing person report when Lily disappeared?"

"I'll have Nora look into the archives," Adam promised. "Why don't you come here in a few hours?"

"Let's meet for lunch," Jenny suggested.

Adam pointed to a thin file on his desk when Jenny entered his office with a basket on her arm. They made quick work of the crab salad sandwich she had brought. Jenny was eager to see what the file contained. She pushed the box of cupcakes she had brought toward Adam and flipped open the file.

"Three pages?" she exclaimed. "That's all?"

"There was nothing suspicious about her disappearance. I am surprised they even filed a report."

"Lily wasn't a loose character," Jenny mused. "Why did people believe she had a lover?"

"I think the general impression was that she had lost it. She had become so unpredictable that people were ready to believe anything about her."

Jenny read the reports as she discussed different scenarios with Adam.

"This is from Ann Davis," she spoke up suddenly. "Ann says she saw Lily get into a car. What was Ann doing here, Adam?"

Adam shrugged his shoulders as he licked frosting off his lips.

Jenny decided to go to the Bayview Inn to talk to Betty Sue.

"Of course! I forgot Ann was in town at that time," Betty Sue said. "She and Ricky were both here."

"What were they doing here?" Jenny asked.

"Seaview was a house of mourning, remember? When Lily lost her daughter, Ann and her son came to visit."

"Wasn't there a lot of time in between? Like months?"

"It was a different time, dear," Betty Sue said with a faraway look in her eyes. "People came for a visit and stayed on. No one was in a hurry to rush back anywhere. And Ann and her son, they were family. Seaview was as much their home as Lily's."

"Ann was the one who saw Lily get into that car," Jenny told Betty Sue. "So either Lily really got into a car and came back, or Ann is lying."

"Did I tell you Lily wanted to sell the house?" Betty Sue asked.

"What? No, you never mentioned that."

"Lily began to hate the place after her girl died. She wanted to get away from this place. She might have put an ad in the paper."

"How did Ann feel about it?"

"You will have to ask her," Betty Sue said.

"That's right," Jenny said, her eyes growing wide. "I have Ann's number. I can talk to her. Why didn't I think of that!"

Jenny hurried home later, determined to call Ann Davis. Jenny had bought her house from her. The woman was in her eighties and lived in Texas. Jenny had met her when she came to Pelican Cove a few months ago.

Ann was surprised to hear from Jenny.

"I miss the beach and your café," she told Jenny. "Ricky and I are thinking of visiting again this summer."

"This is your home," Jenny told her. "You are always welcome here."

Ann asked after all the Magnolias. Jenny finally got to the point.

"I was looking at an old police report," she began. "You told the police that you saw Lily get into a car with someone."

"That's right," Ann said in a strong voice. "Got into a dark sedan late at night and never came back. It was a new moon, and the garden was pitch dark. But I saw it all from my window."

"Did you see who was driving?" Jenny pressed. "Do you remember anything else about the car?"

"I wish I did," Ann sighed. "It might have helped the police find Lily. But I guess she never wanted to come back."

"Didn't the police call you?" Jenny asked.

She told Ann about the DNA results.

"I can't believe it," Ann said, suddenly sounding old. "Poor Lily."

"Did you hear a car again that night?" Lily asked. "Or did you hear any noise in the garden?"

She didn't want to spell out her theory. If someone had come back and dug a pit in the garden, surely Ann would have heard something?

"I had a migraine," Ann told Jenny, dashing her hopes. "I took a sleeping pill and went to bed."

"Did you notice anything odd in the garden in the next day or two?"

"I sprained my ankle on the stairs the next day," Ann told her. "I had to keep it elevated for a week."

Jenny told Ann to call her back if she remembered anything new. She hung up, feeling dejected.

She tried to clear her mind as she made dinner. She went out in the garden and stood staring at the fountain, the spot where they had dug up the skeleton. Give me a clue, Lily, she urged silently. Give me something. She plucked a bunch of dill and went inside.

Jenny poured her orange dill marinade over a pan of fish and slid it in the oven.

"Any luck?" Star asked her as they ate dinner.

Jenny shook her head.

"Everything hinges on Ann's testimony. And Ann insists she saw Lily get into that car. If she's lying, I need a way to prove it."

"Didn't we have a toll booth at the bridge in those days?" Star asked Jimmy.

"That's right," Jimmy nodded. "Kids from the high school worked there most times."

Adam slammed his fork down in his plate and swore suddenly.

"I worked there for a few weeks. How could I not remember?"

"It's okay," Jenny teased. "Memory's the first to go when you're getting old."

"You don't get it, Jenny," Adam said urgently. "The purpose behind that booth was to find out how many tourists came to Pelican Cove. The kid working the booth had to note down the tags of all the cars that came and left."

"And your point is?"

"We can check how many cars crossed the bridge to go out of town that night."

"They keep records from 1991?" Jenny asked doubtfully.

"I'm going to find out," Adam promised.

Jenny greeted Captain Charlie, her favorite customer, the next morning. He was always first in line when the Boardwalk Café opened at 6 AM.

"Here's your muffin, Captain Charlie," Jenny said, handing him a paper bag and a tall cup of coffee. "What do you think about the new dispensary that's opening up in town?"

"I already signed the paper," he told her. "I know they say those pot brownies help with aches and pains, but I ain't going against the town. No Sir."

"What paper?"

"Heather's going around town with it. She'll get around to you soon enough."

Heather came in earlier than usual, holding a clipboard.

"Barb put me to work," she told Jenny. "This is some kind of appeal. It says you're against the marijuana dispensary. Just print your name here and sign next to it."

"You really think it's that bad?"

"I don't think," Heather said, stressing the word think. "When Barb says you have to do something, people generally fall in line."

"I'm not convinced this dispensary is such a bad idea," Jenny argued. "What about all the people it's going to help?"

"Barb says it will harm more people than it will help. Anyway, you can talk about all that at the town hall meeting. Just sign here for now."

"What is Barb going to do with these signatures?"

Heather shrugged.

"I guess she's going to stop the Newburys from getting the licenses they need."

"That sounds vindictive."

"Suit yourself," Heather said. "But get ready to tackle Barb Norton."

Jenny stirred a pot of soup and motioned Heather to sit down. She slid a freshly baked cupcake with pretty pink frosting in front of Heather.

"Lemon with a raspberry filling. Try it."

"I've gained ten pounds since you came into town, Jenny."

"You look as pretty as ever, sweetie."

Jenny patted Heather on her cheek.

"Are Chris and Molly engaged?" Heather asked with a heavy voice. "Why haven't they told me?"

"They are not officially engaged," Jenny explained. "They are somewhere in between." She hesitated before saying anything more. "You know that day is coming though, Heather."

"I've been doing some thinking, Jenny. I know I acted like a jerk these past few months. No wonder Grandma's so mad at me."

"She's worried about you."

"I don't deserve Chris," Heather said, sounding like her old self. "It's my own fault I lost him, Jenny. He's never coming back to me."

Jenny hugged her friend close, feeling sorry for her. She just hoped there was something better around the corner for Heather.

Chapter 10

"I think you should seize all the records in Gianni's office," Jenny argued with Adam. "Have some other doctor study them."

"And why would I do that?"

"You will get a list of all the people he scammed. Any of those could be a suspect."

"I talked to Dr. Smith about those scams," Adam told Jenny. "Gianni was just billing the government for work he didn't do. Most of the fake records deal with treatment that was not provided to his patients. I know it was illegal but it didn't hurt his patients."

"You can't be sure about that," Jenny persisted. "Some people got a wrong diagnosis. He might have written fake prescriptions that made their way to the patient. What if someone actually took the wrong medicine?"

"I can't go running after every wild scenario."

"This is plausible. Think about it a bit and you will agree with me."

"I'll look into it," Adam said in a resigned tone.

"What about Tiffany? Have you questioned her yet?"

"She's coming to town today for an interview."

"She's a woman scorned, Adam. She had a strong motive."

"Let me do my job, Jenny," Adam pleaded. "Please."

Jenny walked out of his office in a huff. She pulled out her cell phone as soon as she stepped out of the police station and called Tiffany Costa.

"Are you coming to Pelican Cove today? Can we meet?"

Jenny gave her directions for the Boardwalk Café and set up a time to meet.

The Magnolias came in for their mid-morning coffee. Betty Sue was looking better than she had in a long time.

"You look happy," Star observed. "What are you hiding, Betty Sue?"

Betty Sue put down her knitting and leaned toward Star.

"Heather talked to me last night. I think she's going to be okay."

"She's a good kid," Star agreed. "I told you she would come around."

Molly and Heather came in together, arm in arm. Molly looked like she was bursting to tell them something.

"I am meeting the parents," she beamed. "Chris is setting it up."

"You know old Pa Williams," Star said. "You have talked to him hundreds of times."

"Not as my prospective father-in-law," Molly said shyly. "I hope he likes me."

"Ma Williams is a good woman," Betty Sue told Molly. "She's going to love you."

"I've known her since I was a kid," Heather added. "I'll put in a good word for you, Molls."

The lunch crowd kept Jenny busy. Finally, she sat down to grab a bite with Petunia.

"Do you need any help with that cake?" the old woman asked.

"I got it, don't worry."

Jenny had started baking cakes for special occasions like birthdays and anniversaries. There was no super market in Pelican Cove where you could just pick up a cake on the fly. So Jenny's little cake business had taken off.

"What is it this time?" Petunia asked as she took a bite of her fried fish sandwich.

"Lemon cake with raspberry filling," Jenny told her, "like those cupcakes I made the other day. It's for a thirteen year old girl. I hope she likes the pink frosting."

Jenny's phone buzzed just then.

"I'm waiting for you. You can come any time."

Jenny hung up the phone and made a fresh sandwich for Tiffany. She took the plate and a pitcher of sweet tea out to the deck.

Tiffany Costa came in, looking like a young Marilyn Monroe. Petunia led her out to the deck.

"Fabulous view!" Tiffany said as she sat down.

Jenny pointed to the sandwich.

"I thought you might be hungry."

"You're a doll," Tiffany squealed. "I'm starving. That grumpy cop didn't even offer me a glass of water."

Jenny was familiar with the grumpy cop's behavior so she wasn't surprised.

Tiffany drained half the glass of tea in one gulp. She attacked her sandwich as if she hadn't eaten in days. Jenny allowed her to settle down.

"The cops found out I was here at the restaurant," Tiffany said.

She narrowed her eyes and looked at Jenny.

"It's a small town. People can spot a stranger from a mile away."

"They asked me a ton of questions. I answered every one of them. I have nothing to hide."

"That's good for you, Tiffany," Jenny said encouragingly.

"What did you want to talk about?" Tiffany asked, wiping her mouth with a tissue.

"My friend Heather is a suspect in Gianni's murder," Jenny said. "Who am I kidding? The police really think she did it. I'm trying to help her out."

"Are you some kind of detective?"

"Not really," Jenny admitted. "I just talk to people and try to find out stuff."

"How can I help you?" Tiffany asked cagily. "You are not trying to incriminate me, are you?"

"I just want to find out the truth."

"I know most people point at the trophy wife," Tiffany bristled. "I'm not just a blonde bimbo, you know."

"Trust me, Tiffany," Jenny said. "You have nothing to worry about if you are innocent."

"Do you think I would be talking to you if I wasn't?" the girl asked.

Jenny decided not to answer that.

"Tell me about Gianni," Jenny urged. "Were you a patient of his? How did you two meet?"

"We met online," Tiffany said wistfully.

Her eyes had a faraway look as if she was remembering happier times.

"He was so handsome!"

"What were you doing at the time?"

"I worked as a dental hygienist in the city," Tiffany told her. "Gianni swept me off my feet. He took me to fancy restaurants, bought me pretty things. Then on Valentine's Day two years ago, he proposed."

"Were you surprised?"

"Not really," Tiffany said. "I have been chased by many men. They always propose to me. It can get really boring."

"I am guessing it was different with Gianni?" Jenny quizzed.

Tiffany smiled.

"I wanted him to take the next step. We had a court wedding but he took me to Aruba for our honeymoon."

"What about your family?" Jenny asked.

"I come from a small town in the mountains," Tiffany explained. "I was raised by an old aunt. She's in long term care now. I don't have anyone else."

"Was he living in Delaware when you got married?"

"Oh yes. I had known that when we were dating."

"When did you learn about the affairs?"

"Two months after marriage," Tiffany said with a scowl. "Gianni was quite open about it. He said it was a ruse. He snared a local girl to get

75

his foot into a new community."

"What about the shady activities? Did he tell you about them himself?"

"I helped him with some filing a couple of times," Tiffany explained. "I had noticed some odd things. But I was quiet about it. He started bragging about it one night when he was drunk."

"And you were fine with that?"

"I had never done anything illegal," Tiffany admitted. "But he gave me a diamond bracelet two days later. I said nothing."

"So he bought your silence."

Tiffany looked uncomfortable.

"I grew up dirt poor. I never had fancy things."

Jenny didn't torment her any further.

"Can I look at the files at your place?" she asked.

"Sure! You can come and get them any time."

"How long did Gianni plan to go out with Heather?"

"Pelican Cove turned out to be smaller than he had imagined. He said he had pretty much exhausted his options here. He had already hired a moving company. He was getting out of here by the end of February."

"What are your plans now?" Jenny asked her.

"I might get my old job back," Tiffany said. "Just to stay busy."

Jenny told her she would visit soon to look at Gianni's files.

Tiffany didn't seem worried about her future. Gianni must have left her well off, Jenny mused as she walked to the seafood market. Chris greeted her with a brilliant smile.

"Hey, Jenny!"

Jenny called her aunt to ask her what she wanted for dinner.

"We have an extra guest," her aunt told her. "That's five for dinner."

Jenny picked up fresh peppers and mushrooms from the local farm. She doubled her usual order of fish and shrimp and remembered they were out of Old Bay seasoning.

"Molly's excited about meeting your parents," she told Chris.

Chris fingered his shiny new promise ring and blushed.

"She's a bit tense too. My mother scares her."

Jenny beamed as she thought of something.

"Why don't you all come to Seaview for dinner? Star will be there, and Jimmy and Adam. It will be a more casual setting."

"That's a great idea, Jenny," Chris said eagerly. "You sure you won't mind?"

"We haven't had company in a long time. Just tell me what your parents like to eat."

"They'll eat anything," he said. "Mom doesn't like spicy food though."

"I'll keep that in mind," Jenny promised. "Let me talk to my aunt and come up with a date. I'll call you."

Jenny was in for a surprise when she reached home. Star had set up an easel on the beach outside Seaview. There was another easel next to hers. Frank, the artist, was standing beside her aunt, brush in hand, talking about something.

"They are having a plain air session," Jimmy told her with a scowl. "That creep's been here since noon. And your aunt has been standing out there with him."

"You mean 'plein' air," Jenny laughed. "It's a French term for painting outdoors."

Jimmy sat in a chair on the patio, staring out at the beach. Jenny knew he wouldn't be easy to spot from the beach, but he had a clear view of Star and her companion.

"Is that the guest we are having for dinner?" Jenny asked.

"He invited himself," Jimmy grumbled. "Said he fancied a nice home cooked meal. He can cook it in his own kitchen, can't he?"

"I thought he lived in a bus."

"He travels in that bus. He's rented a house in town. The bus is parked in his yard."

"Star's just being nice," Jenny said with a smile.

She wondered what Jimmy was worried about. Although her aunt had never said it out loud, Jenny was sure she really liked Jimmy. She wasn't going to be impressed by some vagabond artist.

Adam came home and offered to help with dinner. Jenny gave him the job of chopping the vegetables. She sprinkled Old Bay on fish and drizzled it with olive oil. She set it aside, ready to go in the oven just before they sat down to eat.

"I met Tiffany today," Jenny told him. "Sounds like you were a bit harsh with her."

"I was just doing my job," Adam told her.

"Tiffany's offered to let me look at Gianni's old records."

"That's great," Adam said eagerly. "Dr. Smith is looking at the stuff we found here in Pelican Cove. But that's all I can do for now. The other stuff is off limits for me."

"Adam Hopkins," Jenny said with her hands on her hips. "Are you actually asking for my help?"

"You might be able to go where I can't," Adam said. "Who knows what those records will yield."

"Does Tiffany come into a lot of money?" Jenny asked.

"She's the spouse," Adam shrugged. "Unless we find a will or someone turns up with one, she is his next of kin."

"So she could have killed him for his money."

"We are trying to establish her alibi. We already know she was in town that night. Unless she can prove what time she left town, she had as much opportunity as Heather."

"She also had access to Gianni's clinic and all the drugs he kept there," Jenny reminded him.

Adam agreed with Jenny for a change. Tank came in and sat down on the floor next to Jenny.

"Who's that dude out there with Star?" Adam asked. "And why is Jimmy hiding behind the rose bushes?"

Chapter 11

Adam Hopkins walked into the Boardwalk Café at noon.

"Hello Sheriff," Jenny smiled. "Taking the day off?"

"I'm here for lunch," Adam said. "Care to join me?"

Jenny ladled pea soup in two bowls and placed strawberry chicken sandwiches on a plate. She took the tray of food out to the deck. It was a sunny spring day and the fresh breeze coming off the ocean perked her up.

Adam slurped the soup and pronounced it delicious.

"I asked around," he told Jenny. "Old Asher Cohen had sponsored the toll both all those years ago. He paid the people who worked there."

Jenny's face fell.

"Asher's gone now."

"Asher may not be around but his company, Cohen Construction is," Adam reminded her. "I spoke to Luke."

Luke Stone was Jason's uncle. He ran Cohen Construction, one of the biggest employers in town.

Jenny took a bite of her sandwich and nodded for Adam to go on.

"Asher was very meticulous about keeping records. Luke is sure they have everything from back when the booth was still running."

"When can I look at them?" Jenny asked eagerly.

"Luke's having someone pull them from their records section. You can go there later this afternoon. They are expecting you."

"Sounds great," Jenny said. "You think I'll find something?"

"Whatever you find will be something we don't know now," Adam told her. "Think of it as another piece of the puzzle."

"Yes Sir!" Jenny gave him a mock salute.

Her enthusiasm waned a bit when she saw the three foot high pile of paper set aside for her at Cohen Construction. She sat down and started looking for the right year.

Apparently, the toll booth had been operational for barely a year. It had never actually collected toll. Its only purpose had been to note down the cars entering and leaving the city. Jenny noted down the relevant information and struggled to her feet. Her legs were stiff after sitting in one spot for hours. She hoped the information she had found would provide some value.

Jenny walked back home, thinking about Lily. Lily had grown up in Pelican Cove. She had left town at nineteen and come back several years later with her husband and children. Her husband worked in the city and was traveling most of the time. Her daughter died from a freak virus. Lily's son was in college at that time. According to Betty Sue, Lily had shut herself in her house after her daughter's death. It didn't seem like she had any enemies. She hardly talked to anyone. Why had someone taken her life?

Jenny walked on for a while before she found herself in front of the library. She remembered something Betty Sue had said. Molly greeted her at the desk, looking radiant.

"Chris told me you are hosting us for dinner, Jenny," she beamed. "Thank you so much. To be honest, I was a bit intimidated at the thought of going to their home for dinner. But I'll feel right at home at Seaview."

Jenny spent some time chatting with Molly about the dinner party. She went in to the reference section and began looking at newspapers from 1991. There was no news item related to Lily's disappearance. Jenny found it odd. Why hadn't the Pelican Cove Chronicle printed anything about Lily? She moved to the classifieds section next. She spotted the ad for the sale of Seaview right away. Her eyes popped open at what she saw on the page. Had grief really addled Lily's brain?"

"Not a single car went out of town that night," she told Adam later that night.

They were taking a long walk on the beach after a rich dinner of Star's special six cheese lasagna. Tank ran in circles around them, begging Jenny to throw a stick he could fetch.

"Did anyone come into town?"

Jenny shook her head. "Not after 3 PM that day."

"Did you note those numbers?"

"I did more than that," Jenny told him. "Those same cars left town around 6:30 in the morning and got back by 4 PM. I am guessing these belonged to people who commuted to the mainland."

"Good guess," Adam complimented her. "What about the days before and after Lily disappeared?"

"I didn't see any car leaving town for a day after that."

"Are you saying Lily never got into a car?"

"I'm saying she didn't go out of town for sure," Jenny said. "At least not that night. So this whole story about her running away with someone seems pretty thin now."

"She could have stayed with someone else in town for a couple of days," Adam mused.

"Betty Sue says Lily hardly spoke to anyone those days. I find it hard to believe she had a secret lover."

"So you believe Ann lied?"

"I don't know what to believe, Adam. But it's beginning to look probable. It's Ann's word against Lily's and Lily is not here to defend herself."

"Hmmm …"

Adam lapsed into silence. Tank nudged Jenny, trying to get her attention. She played with him for a while.

"And wait till you hear this," Jenny spoke up. "Lily wanted to sell Seaview. She listed it in the classifieds for twenty thousand dollars."

"What?" Adam exclaimed. "You sure you didn't miss a zero?"

Jenny shook her head.

"It was printed in words too, Adam. I know things were cheaper back then, but surely not that cheap?"

"Why would Lily do that?"

"Betty Sue said she just wanted to get away from here."

"Do you remember Ann and her son owned half the house? I'm sure they didn't go along with that."

"Lily was acting erratic, that's for sure."

Jenny couldn't wait to tell the Magnolias all she had found out. She waited impatiently for Betty Sue's arrival the next morning. Betty Sue walked in, busy knitting something pink.

"Sit down, Betty Sue. I want to ask you something."

"How about some coffee first, eh?" Betty Sue grumbled. "What's got you so twisted?"

Jenny poured out her story.

"Twenty thousand dollars!" Betty Sue exclaimed. "There was a recession around that time but Seaview was worth several times more than that."

"How come someone didn't snap up the property?" Jenny asked her.

A knowing look flashed across Betty Sue's face.

"It was the curse. People around here believed Seaview was jinxed."

"Did Ann want to sell too?"

"Ann came here and liked what she saw. She wanted to live here with Ricky."

"But they went back!"

"I never understood why," Betty Sue nodded. "You can ask Ann about it. She was as eager to stay on here as Lily was to leave."

"Did they get along?" Jenny asked.

"Lily adored Ann when we were teenagers," Betty Sue said. "She was young, sophisticated and married, everything we aspired to as girls. Ann could do no wrong in Lily's eyes."

"Didn't Lily live with Ann for a while?"

"Those two were pretty close once upon a time," Betty Sue agreed.

"But not in 1991?"

"Lily was really hard to be around that time," Betty Sue said reluctantly. "Her mood swings had become really hard to take. She would throw tantrums at the slightest provocation. She didn't talk to a single person for days together. She sat on the balcony at Seaview, staring at the sea, sobbing her heart out for her girl."

"Ann stayed here through all that?"

"She did," Betty Sue said grimly. "She held the family together."

Jenny wondered if Ann Davis had really loved Lily.

Molly and Heather came in, arm in arm.

"Are you all set for this special dinner?" Heather asked with a smile. "Let me know if you need any help. I can give you the skinny on what Chris's mother likes."

"Thanks Heather," Jenny said. "I'm almost ready, I think. Chris is coming around with the fish around four."

"That takes care of the food," Heather said. "What are you wearing, Molly?"

"That new green dress?" Molly said uncertainly.

"Mrs. Williams likes blue. Don't you have a blue dress you can wear?" Heather was trying really hard to be likable. "What about your hair?"

"It's just a dinner, Heather," Jenny rolled her eyes. "Stop scaring Molly."

"I know, but you know what they say about first impressions."

"You're making me nervous," Molly said, beginning to look green. "I tend to puke when I get nervous."

"We can't have that," Heather frowned. "Just be your usual self, Molls. You got this."

Star had set up her easel on the patio when Jenny got home. She was muttering to herself.

"What are you doing, Star?" Jenny laughed.

"I'm trying my hand at water colors," she said. "Not as easy as it looks."

"I thought you hated them."

"I never really gave them a shot. Frank says watercolor is actually the most difficult medium."

"Frank says, huh?"

"A true artist does not shy away from different techniques. Frank says I should think of adding water colors to my portfolio."

"When did you go shopping for all these new colors?"

"Frank lent them to me. He's quite generous, that one."

"Carry on then," Jenny told her aunt. "I have my work cut out for me."

"Are we having company?" Star asked. "I was thinking of asking Frank over for dinner."

"Have you forgotten Molly's dinner party?" Jenny asked her, rubbing a charm around her neck.

She had been missing Nick all day.

"Oh yeah," Star said. "That's tonight? Why didn't you say so earlier?" Star began putting away her stuff. "I'll help you in the kitchen."

Molly's party started off well. Heather had kept her word and helped Molly get ready. Molly was wearing more makeup than usual and she kept touching her face every few minutes.

"Relax," Jenny whispered in her ear.

Pa Williams, Chris's father, was an easy going man. He put an arm around Molly and welcomed her to the family. His wife didn't seem that forthcoming. Her face had a pinched expression.

"She's not a Pioneer," she said to Star. "You know how we feel about that."

A peculiar hierarchy existed on the island of Pelican Cove. A bunch of families who had been the original settlers called themselves the Pioneers. Only five or six families had this honor. The Morse family, Betty Sue and Heather's ancestors were one of them, being the original owners of the island. So were the Stone and Williams families. They had been on the island since the nineteenth century.

Molly's family came from a group called the refugees. Her family had sought shelter in Pelican Cove after the great storm of 1962, a deadly storm which had wrought massive destruction up and down the coast.

Time didn't move very fast in Pelican Cove. Family background mattered a lot.

"Your son loves this girl," Star hissed. "Can't you be happy about that?"

Star herself was a chicken necker, a term the islanders used for someone who wasn't born there. She had come to Pelican Cove in the 1970s and never gone back.

"You wouldn't understand," Mrs. Williams told Star. "And what is this love you speak of? My son was in love with Heather Morse since third grade. I don't know how this girl managed to snare him."

Molly overheard them and turned red. Her eyes filled up and threatened to spill over. Jenny took her by the arm and led her inside.

"She doesn't like me," Molly stuttered.

A wild look had come into her eyes.

"I can't marry Chris without their blessing. What am I going to do?"

"She's in shock," Jenny soothed. "Your engagement is kind of sudden."

"We are not even engaged," Molly cried. "And now his mother doesn't approve of me."

"Chris loves you," Jenny said firmly. "He's going to stand by you no matter what, Molls."

"Do you really believe that, Jenny?"

Jenny crossed her fingers behind her back and nodded at her friend.

Chapter 12

"Jenny, it's for you," Petunia called out.

Jenny put down the piping bag she was holding and answered the phone.

"This is Dr. Smith. You gave me this number."

"How are you, Doc?" Jenny greeted him. "Any update?"

"Can you come down to my clinic?"

"Give me an hour," Jenny said and hung up.

She immediately dialed Jason's number.

"I don't know what he's come up with. Do you want to go with me?"

Jason pulled up outside the Boardwalk Café half an hour later. Jason seemed to have lost weight since the last time Jenny saw him. There were dark circles under his eyes.

"Are you ill?" she asked with concern. "What's wrong?"

"Haven't been sleeping well," Jason said with a shrug.

"When was the last time you had a proper meal?" Jenny asked suspiciously. "That's it. You're coming to Seaview for dinner tonight."

"Whatever you say, Jenny," he mumbled.

They reached Dr. Smith's clinic ten minutes later. He was waiting for them.

"I went through most of Costa's records," he said. "I found more of what we saw before."

Jenny sensed there was more coming.

"One of the names seemed familiar," Dr. Smith sighed. "Eugenie Hampton. She died recently."

"How did she die?"

"I checked her death certificate," Dr. Smith said grimly. "She died of heart failure."

"I remember reading her obit," Jason said.

"Was she your patient, Dr. Smith?" Jenny asked.

"Was is the operative word," the doctor said bitterly. "I treated Eugenie Hampton for forty years. She started seeing Costa last winter."

"Any reason why?"

"He charmed her, I guess," Dr. Smith said. "Some of my patients started seeing him recently. I couldn't stop them."

"I'm guessing most of these were women of a certain age?" Jenny asked. "Did Eugenie have any chronic conditions?"

"I'm not supposed to discuss my patients with anyone," Dr. Smith reminded them. "But I can tell you this. I saw the treatment Costa was supposedly giving her. It was all wrong for her."

"So he actually gave someone wrong medicine?" Jenny asked, aghast. "But you said he was just billing the government for this extra stuff."

"Looks like he was doing more than that," Dr. Smith said. "Or there was some error in the paperwork. She saw something she was not meant to see and filled those prescriptions. Taking those drugs might have led to her demise."

"Can you prove that?"

"It will be hard to prove without an autopsy."

"Did she have any family?" Jason asked.

"Her husband lives in town," Dr. Smith said. "He's still my patient. I can give you his address."

"Let's go talk to him," Jenny said to Jason.

Peter Hampton was home when they went to see him. He was sitting out on his porch in a rocker, staring at a bird feeder that hung from an old oak.

Jason introduced himself.

"I know who you are," he grunted. "What do you want?"

"We wanted to talk to you about your wife."

"She's dead," he said. "Are you going to let me mourn her in peace?"

"We just want a few minutes of your time," Jenny pleaded.

The man paid no attention and continued staring in the distance.

"Maybe we'll come back some other time," Jason said.

He took Jenny's arm and led her back to the car.

"You are giving up?" she protested as he started the car.

"He won't talk to us right now," Jason said.

"I want to tell Adam about this guy. Why don't you drop me off there?"

Jason pulled up outside the police station a few minutes later.

"See you at seven sharp," Jenny said primly. "Bring your appetite."

Adam was immersed in some paperwork when Jenny breezed into his office.

"You have a new suspect," she declared.

Adam looked at her irritably.

"What are you blathering about, Jenny?"

"I'm talking about Gianni's murder. I just found a new suspect for you."

"Pray tell," Adam drawled.

"A woman called Eugenie Hampton died from the wrong medicine. I just saw her husband. He refused to talk to me."

"Genie's dead?" Adam sat up, surprised. "She used to be friends with my mom."

"Her husband looks devastated. Dr. Smith says she probably died from a wrong prescription. That gives her husband a motive."

"All this makes a fine story, Jenny," Adam said patiently. "But I need proof."

"Isn't it your job to get that?" Jenny shot back.

"I don't know, Jenny. Sounds farfetched to me."

Jenny stormed out of Adam's office and started walking home. She spotted Captain Charlie coming out of The Steakhouse. He was holding a small bag of food.

"Just delivered the catch," he told her. "The chef made me dinner."

"Do you know a man called Peter Hampton?"

"Aye."

"Can you find out if he came to The Steakhouse recently?"

"What are you up to, little lady?" Captain Charlie asked.

He went inside the restaurant again. Jenny tapped her foot impatiently while she waited for him to come out.

"He was here," Captain Charlie grunted when he came out. "One of the busboys told me."

"Are they sure? Do they know who he is?"

"Pete Hampton's lived here all his life," Captain Charlie quipped. "That's seventy some years you have not been here, missy. Most people around here know him well."

"What was he doing here?"

A lad walked out just then, pulling off his apron. Captain Charlie summoned him over.

"Tell her what you saw."

"Old Pete Hampton came here for dinner for Valentine's Day. It was kinda sad. We all know his wife passed."

"Was it Valentine's Day or the day after?" Jenny asked eagerly.

The lad shrugged.

"Could have been either. It was some time that weekend." He stared at Jenny for a few seconds. "I know you. You were in here with that big group. Pete was here the same day as you."

"Did he talk to anyone?"

"He was talking to that dude with the diamond earring."

The lad looked bored. He said a hasty goodbye and walked away from them rapidly.

"Does that help?" Captain Charlie asked.

"More than you know," Jenny told him, grinning from ear to ear.

She couldn't wait to talk to Adam. Jenny hurried through her dinner prep. Star had invited her new artist friend so there were six of them for dinner. Jenny made a big pot of gumbo to go around. She hoped Frank liked spicy food.

"Pete Hampton was at The Steakhouse with us," she told Adam as soon as he came home. "He was right there."

"Gianni didn't die in the restaurant, Jenny."

"But he could have been poisoned there."

"He wasn't. Trust me on that. I can't tell you any more than that now."

Jenny tried to make Jason talk during dinner. He ate a few spoonfuls of gumbo and pushed his plate away.

Jenny tried to hide her concern.

"Will you pick me up at nine tomorrow morning?" she asked him.

"Sure," he agreed.

Frank was asking Star to dinner.

"You have made me feel so welcome. I am taking you to dinner and I won't take no for an answer."

Star tried to hide a blush.

"Your aunt is so talented," he gushed, looking at Jenny. "She just started using water colors two days ago and her work is already better than mine."

"Oh Frank, stop it!" Star said, turning red.

Jimmy Parsons stared at them with a scowl on his face. It was clear he wasn't dealing well with the interloper.

Jason arrived at the café at nine the next morning. Jenny handed him a box with a giant chocolate cupcake. Jason's face broke into a smile.

"So you can still smile," Jenny teased. "Why didn't you say you wanted cake?"

"Where to?" Jason wanted to know.

Jenny told him what she had discovered the previous day.

"We are going to see Peter Hampton again. And this time I am not going to budge until he starts talking."

Peter Hampton was sitting in the same spot on his porch, staring at the bird feeder again. His brow furrowed when he spotted them.

"Didn't I tell you to clear off?" he roared.

"We need to talk, Mr. Hampton," Jenny said with her hands on her hips. "What were you doing at The Steakhouse?"

"It's a free country," the old man sneered. "I was getting a meal."

"You were doing more than that."

Peter Hampton folded his hands and looked away.

"Look, we are sorry about your wife," Jenny began.

"We were married for fifty six years," the man said. A single tear rolled down his eye. "I was supposed to take care of her."

"You couldn't have known," Jenny said gently.

"He had all those fancy certificates," Peter said. "My Genie said Dr. Smith was getting old. This Gianni fellow had access to all the latest technology. He promised he would make her sciatica go away. She believed him."

"He was giving fake prescriptions," Jenny stated. "When did you find out?"

"Not until it was too late," Peter Hampton said bitterly. "That Costa fellow said it was my Genie's fault. She couldn't read, he said. She was never supposed to take those pills."

"You went to The Steakhouse to cause a scene, didn't you?"

Peter Hampton straightened in his chair. His eyes hardened.

"I was prepared to do more than that. I was carrying a knife under my jacket. I was going to kill that bastard in the restroom."

"What happened?" Jason asked, fascinated.

He was finally beginning to act like his old self.

"I chickened out," the man said. "I couldn't do it. I couldn't kill a man in cold blood."

"Even though he was responsible for your wife's death?" Jenny pressed.

"I failed my Genie," Peter said. Tears were flowing down his face freely now. "How am I going to face her?"

"You did the right thing," Jason said, patting the man on his back.

"Did you argue with Gianni that day?" Jenny asked.

"I let him have it," Peter nodded. "He laughed at me. Said small town folks were gullible."

"Did you follow him home?" Jenny pressed.

"No Ma'am," Peter shook his head. "I went to the Rusty Anchor to drown myself in a bottle."

"Did anyone see you there?"

"Eddie Cotton did, I guess," Peter said with a frown. "And a bunch of other people in the bar. Why?"

"Never mind," Jenny said. "Mr. Hampton, can I bring you a casserole some time?"

"You are the girl from the café, aren't you? My Genie loved your waffles."

Jenny was quiet on the way back.

"You miss her, don't you?" she asked, placing her hand on Jason's.

"What happened, Jenny?" Jason asked, his eyes full of pain. "Where did I go wrong?"

"You could never go wrong, my friend," Jenny said fiercely.

"I tried calling her a few times," Jason admitted. "She won't answer my calls."

"You know how busy Kandy is," Jenny said. "Maybe she's working on some high profile case and doesn't want to be disturbed."

Jason shook his head.

"Her email clearly said we were done."

"Coward!" Jenny spit out.

She had never been impressed with Kandy's bossy personality.

"Can't you forget her, Jason?" she asked. "There's plenty of fish in the sea."

"I didn't go looking for anyone," Jason said bitterly. "She pursued me. And now she's backing out."

"It might be for the best," Jenny said with a shrug. "If she's so flighty, it's better you found out now."

"I wasn't completely honest with her," Jason said after a while. "I think she sensed that."

"What do you mean?" Jenny asked, bewildered.

"Kandy and I, we were hanging out, Jenny," Jason stuttered. "But I was, I am, in love with someone else."

Chapter 13

Jimmy Parsons walked into the Boardwalk Café. He wasn't a café regular.

"This is a surprise," Jenny said, welcoming him. "What can I get you, Jimmy?"

"I guess I'll have a cup of coffee, with cream and sugar."

"How about some breakfast? I am making waffles."

"Why not?" Jimmy shrugged.

He seemed agitated.

"Okay, out with it," Jenny said, placing a plate of waffles drizzled with her special berry sauce before Jimmy. "What's on your mind?"

"It's your aunt," Jimmy began. "Do you think she's sweet on this new artist fellow?"

Jenny burst out laughing.

"What makes you think that?"

"He's taking her to dinner tonight, to the Steakhouse, no less."

"I think she's just being polite."

"She can't stop talking about him," Jimmy grumbled. "It's Frank this or Frank that."

"She never gets to meet any fellow artists," Jenny offered. "It's just shop talk."

"I hope that's all it is."

Jimmy gazed moodily at his waffles and took a bite. Jenny took pity on him.

"She likes you, Jimmy. I know that much for sure."

Jenny decided to talk to her aunt later. The Magnolias came in and settled at their favorite table on the deck.

"You are coming to the town meeting, aren't you?" Heather asked

Jenny. "We need a good turnout."

"Are you working with Barb now?" Jenny asked.

"She needs an assistant and I am at a loose end," Heather explained. "Plus, I feel strongly about this drugs issue."

"Calling it a 'drugs issue' gives the wrong impression," Jenny said.

"Come to the town hall meeting to voice your opinion," Heather quipped. "It's an open forum. We will let everyone speak their mind."

Jenny was glad to see Heather taking an interest in something other than men.

"How was the party at your place?" Betty Sue wanted to know.

"Jenny did a great job," Molly praised. "Chris said his father likes me."

No one wanted to talk about his mother.

"I heard about your hot date," Jenny told Star. "What do you see in that guy?"

"How do you know about it?" Star asked. She looked embarrassed. "He was quite persuasive. I couldn't say no."

"Jimmy was here this morning."

"What's he doing, talking about my business?" Star asked crossly. "I need to talk to that Jimmy."

"I think he feels left out," Jenny said. "It's cute."

"Frank's just like a tourist. He'll be gone in a few months."

"As long as you don't take off with him ..."

Jenny was tossing salad for lunch when the phone rang. It was Tiffany, Gianni Costa's wife.

"You said you wanted to look at Gianni's records?" she asked Jenny. "I've put everything in a few boxes and set it aside for you. You can come and get them anytime."

Jenny told her she would come by later that day. She called Jason and asked him if he was up for a road trip.

"Who's this?" Tiffany asked as she gave Jason a once over.

"Jason lives in Pelican Cove. I rode with him today."

Jason was being his old charming self. He chatted up Tiffany.

"I was planning to leave my husband," she told Jason. "He was seeing other women on the side."

"That must have been hard on you," Jason commiserated.

"I was just a poor working girl when I met Gianni. I had nowhere to go."

"You never said you wanted to leave Gianni?" Jenny asked her.

"I put on a brave front," Tiffany shrugged. "No wife can tolerate a cheating husband. I gave him an ultimatum."

"You did?" Jenny humored her.

"He had to stop seeing this Heather girl or I was walking out."

"What did Gianni say?"

"He laughed at me. Said I was free to walk out any time I wanted."

"Did you sign any prenuptial agreement?" Jason asked.

"Jason's a lawyer," Jenny added.

"I did sign something," Tiffany said with a shrug. "But I didn't understand much of it. Gianni said I would be taken care of."

"I can take a look at it if you want me to," Jason offered.

Tiffany went in and came out with a folder.

"It's all in there."

Jason didn't need a lot of time to skim through the papers. He shook his head and gave them back to Tiffany.

"According to this, you get nothing if you leave your husband."

"Even if he cheated on me?"

"If you walk out, you don't get a penny, no matter what the reason is."

"That's not fair," Jenny said.

"Gianni said this was just a formality," Tiffany said, incensed. "I was so much in love, I didn't give it a second thought."

"What did you do later that night at the Steakhouse?" Jenny asked her.

"I was starving, but I didn't want to stay in that place for one moment more than necessary. I drove back home to Delaware."

"Alone?"

"Of course! Gianni was too busy canoodling with that tart."

"You didn't talk to Gianni at all that night?"

Tiffany shook her head.

"I'm sure he saw me there."

Jenny wanted to use the restroom. Tiffany pointed down the hallway. Jenny peeped into a powder room and walked on, taking note of the other rooms. She saw a door leading down a small path through a garden. It led to a separate building that looked like a guesthouse. Jenny went inside the bathroom and flushed the toilet. She opened a faucet for a few minutes and came out, wiping her hands.

"Do you like to swim?" she asked Tiffany. "I thought I saw a pool house."

"That's not a pool house," Tiffany pouted. "That's Gianni's clinic. It's actually a guest house."

"So he could walk to and fro between his house and workplace whenever he wanted."

"So could I," Tiffany said with a nod. "It was … convenient."

"Okay," Jenny said, standing up. "We'll get these boxes out of your way."

They stopped at a small fish and chips shop on the way back. Jenny bit into hot beer battered fish and stared moodily at the water.

"You have to convince the police that Tiffany is a suspect. That might take the spotlight away from Heather."

"Give me one reason why she's a suspect," Jason said, dipping a French fry in ketchup.

"I'll give you three," Jenny said, holding up three fingers. "Never underestimate a woman scorned. Gianni cheated on her. I don't care what she says, she must have been raving mad."

"Go on," Jason said, taking a swig of his soda.

"As you said, she didn't stand to gain anything if she left Gianni. But she inherits his entire ill gotten gains as a widow."

"And you think that was the motive? Money?"

"Money or revenge," Jenny said with a shrug."Call it what you will."

"How did she do it?" Jason asked.

"I don't know about that," Jenny said. "But she had access to Gianni's clinic. She could have ground up any combination of pills. She had plenty of opportunity."

"And how did she feed him this deadly cocktail?" Jason asked.

"I don't have all the answers," Jenny admitted. "Why not leave something for the police?"

"So she had a strong motive and she had the means," Jason summed up. "What about opportunity?"

"She was right there at the Steakhouse," Jenny cried. "She could have easily walked to Gianni's place from there."

"That does put her on the scene," Jason agreed. "Has she given any alibi to the police?"

"I don't think they ever asked her for one."

"Why is your boyfriend convinced Heather is guilty?" Jason asked. "He's known her since she was a little girl. How could he believe her capable of something so heinous?"

"You know what Adam will say," Jenny said with exasperation. "He's just doing his job."

"I'm going to talk to him about Tiffany. She can't be ruled out as a suspect."

"You're Heather's lawyer," Jenny said with a nod. "You can talk to Adam in an official capacity. He will have to listen to you."

Groups of people were walking toward the town hall when they entered Pelican Cove.

"I forgot all about the meeting tonight," Jenny said. "You are coming, right?"

She held up her hand guessing Jason was about to say no.

"It will be fun, if nothing else."

Betty Sue sat on the stage near the front of the hall. John Newbury, her estranged husband, sat next to her. Ada Newbury sat in a corner seat, glaring at the crowd. Barb Norton stood behind the podium, calling the meeting to order. Heather stood at the back with a clipboard in her hand.

The Magnolias occupied the second row. They had saved room for Jenny and Jason.

"Thank you for coming," Barb began. "We need to raise a united voice against drugs in Pelican Cove. Thank you for signing the petition. I am sure it's going to help quash this whole thing."

"Why are we here then?" someone shouted from the crowd.

"I want to make sure every opinion is heard," Barb said pompously. "Although I am acting in the interest of the town, I'm no autocrat. And we want to tell the Newburys what we are thinking and what our concerns are."

An old woman sitting in the first row struggled to her feet, leaning heavily on a walking stick.

"I hear this marivana is going to help my knees. Is that true?"

"That's right," John Newbury spoke. "Marijuana helps in pain relief. We are going to grow high grade cannabis that will be processed into pills you can take for your arthritis."

"Where are you going to sell this?" another woman asked.

"We have leased a shop on Main Street," John replied.

"Main Street is where our kids hang out," a man said. "Minor kids. This dispensary as you call it is a bad influence on them."

Another man piped up from the crowd.

"What about ground water? I hear growing marijuana can contaminate ground water resources."

People started talking among themselves. Barb Norton tried to get their attention.

"One at a time, please."

"We don't want Pelican Cove to become a drug hangout," one man roared.

"You want to teach our kids it's okay to take drugs?" another woman demanded. "What kind of example are you setting for them?"

"You are just doing this to fill your pockets," an old woman quavered.

John Newbury stood up to answer them. Someone threw a rotten tomato at him. An egg or two followed. Barb Norton tried in vain to get everyone to behave. Someone pelted her with popcorn.

The meeting pretty much derailed after that.

"What the heck was that?" Jenny asked Star on the way home. "I didn't know people here could be so violent."

"That's just your regular town hall meeting," Star laughed.

"I don't feel like cooking tonight. Let's just order in some pizza from Mama Rosa's."

"Sounds like a plan," Star said. "Will you get my favorite?"

"Chicken, jalapeno and pineapple, I know," Jenny assured her aunt. "Jimmy's started liking it too."

Star scrunched up her face at the mention of Jimmy.

"I've been thinking," she said. "I haven't spent much time with Jimmy lately."

"He's just feeling left out," Jenny said.

"Jimmy's not the kind to throw money around," Star said.

Jenny knew what she was implying. Jimmy Parsons had a bunch of cottages he rented to tourists. He didn't have any other job. Jimmy wasn't rolling in money. It hadn't mattered to Star.

"Why don't you do something simple?" Jenny suggested. "The weather's warming up. Go for a picnic on the beach. I can make up a basket for you."

"That sounds romantic," Star sighed. "You think that will make him smile?"

"You just need to convince him he's special. He's gonna love it."

"Okay then," Star said happily. "I know the perfect place for a picnic."

"Do you need any talking points?" Jenny asked saucily.

"I don't, kid," Star said, rolling her eyes. "And I won't mention Frank at the picnic."

Chapter 14

The Magnolias were all quiet for a change. Betty Sue sipped her coffee and went on knitting furiously. Molly's head was buried in a book. Heather's eyes were rimmed with red. Petunia sat staring at them, crumpling a tissue in her hands. Star walked up the café steps, holding a few canvases.

"I'm taking these to the gallery," she told Jenny. "They are from my plein air session with Frank."

Jenny tipped her head at the women and gave her aunt a pleading look.

"What's the matter, Betty Sue?" Star boomed.

"I just got back from the police station," Heather said, blowing her nose in a tissue. "They wanted to question me again."

"What?" Jenny exclaimed. "I thought they had found other suspects."

"Apparently not," Heather said. "I'm still at the top of their list."

"I need to talk to Adam," Jenny said purposefully. "I'm going over right now."

"I'm coming with you," Betty Sue declared, discarding her knitting on the table. "I need to give that Hopkins boy a piece of my mind."

"That's not necessary, Betty Sue," Jenny said, dismayed. "Let me take care of this."

"You think I'm gonna cramp your style, girl?" Betty Sue thundered.

"Of course not," Jenny hastened to calm her down. "But I have a bone to pick with Adam. It might get ugly."

"Call me if you need me," Betty Sue relented.

"Of course," Jenny assured her.

She skipped down the café steps to the boardwalk and started walking toward the police station at a brisk pace.

Nora, the desk clerk, looked up when Jenny entered the station.

"I'm the one in a bad mood today," Jenny cautioned, holding up a hand.

Nora shrugged and shook her head.

"You know where to go."

Adam was eating a late breakfast at his desk.

"Hey Jenny," he greeted her. "This quiche is delicious. Never thought of myself as a quiche man."

"When will you stop harassing Heather?" Jenny cut to the chase.

She pulled up a chair and sat down with a thud. She crossed her arms and glared at Adam.

Adam looked at her coolly.

"I'm not harassing her as you say. I'm just questioning her which is routine in an investigation."

"Didn't Jason talk to you?" Jenny pressed. "I thought we provided you with other suspects."

"I did talk to Jason. But Heather is still a suspect too."

"But why?"

"I have my reasons, Jenny. I don't need to disclose them to you."

"What about Mr. Hampton's alibi? Did you check it out?"

"I talked to Eddie Cotton," Adam sighed. "The old man was at the pub until Eddie closed it for the night. He walked him home after that. Pete Hampton wasn't feeling too good. He was sick multiple times. Eddie stayed with him. They were up almost all night. Eddie didn't go home until morning."

"That clears the old man, I guess," Jenny said reluctantly.

"I talked to him, Jenny. I know what he was planning to do that night. But it wasn't his hand that killed the doctor. I am sure of that."

"What about Tiffany? She had means, motive and opportunity."

"She also has an alibi, Jenny."

"She had access to drugs and she also had access to Gianni's house here. She could have gone there from the restaurant."

"She left The Steakhouse while we were still there. She must have reached her home in Delaware before we left the restaurant."

"How do you know that?"

"She stopped for coffee on the way. She's on camera. That's the kind of proof we cannot ignore."

"How do you know she didn't come back into Pelican Cove?"

"I don't think she did, Jenny."

"How did Gianni die?" Jenny asked Adam. "You said he was drugged but when did that happen. And how?"

"There's a reason why we haven't released that information."

"Is it because you don't have a clue yourself?"

Adam began to look frustrated.

"You're being a nuisance, Jenny. Why don't you get back to the café and let me get on with my work?"

"Heather's been crying her eyes out."

"She has nothing to worry if she's innocent."

"You've known her all your life, Adam. Do you really think she's capable of killing someone?"

"The evidence against her is pretty strong. As an officer of the law, I cannot overlook it."

"Her relationship with Gianni wasn't a secret. Tiffany admitted she knew about it too. And Heather really liked Gianni. What possible motive could she have to kill him?"

"If I had to guess, I would say revenge."

"You need to do more than guess, Adam."

"We found Heather's fingerprints on the scene, on the very glass that contained the drugs, as a matter of fact."

"Heather's been in and out of that house for the past few weeks. She must have handled many things there."

Adam rubbed his forehead with his fingers.

"She had a prescription for antidepressants."

"Haven't you listened to anything I told you?" Jenny cried. "Gianni wrote up wrong prescriptions. It was a scam he was running."

"This is a real prescription written by Dr. Smith," Adam said gravely. "Heather admitted she filled that prescription. She even has a half empty bottle with her."

"So she took the pills herself!"

"We don't know that," Adam shrugged. "Those pills match one of the drugs found in Gianni's system. Heather could have ground up those pills and added them to Gianni's drink."

Jenny sat back in shock. Adam continued his onslaught.

"Heather had free access to Gianni's clinic here. Using the argument you use against Tiffany, Heather had access to plenty of drugs."

"You honestly believe she's guilty, don't you?"

"My feelings don't matter here, Jenny. The law only looks at the evidence. Things don't look too good for Heather right now."

"My money's still on Tiffany," Jenny insisted, scrambling to her feet. "She lied multiple times. First she told me Gianni had affairs all the time and she didn't care about them. Then she said she was going to leave Gianni because he cheated on her. Based on her prenup, she wasn't going to get a penny if she walked out on him. That's why she killed him. Now she inherits his fortune. Thanks to cops like you, she's roaming free."

"Tiffany had a prenuptial agreement?" Adam asked. "I didn't know about that."

"I'm sure there is plenty more you don't know, Sheriff," Jenny said as she stomped out.

Jenny's anger subsided as soon as she stepped out of the police station. It was replaced by worry for her friend. She crossed the road and walked into Jason Stone's office.

Jason was talking to someone on the phone.

"Kandy and I were invited to a dinner party," he said stoically. "I was calling to tell them I won't be making it."

"I can go with you," Jenny offered.

"Not this time," Jason sighed. "It was for introducing Kandy to my college buddies."

"Oh."

"All well, Jenny? What brings you here at this time of the day?"

"I think Heather's in trouble," Jenny blurted out. "I just spoke to Adam."

"Did he tell you about finding her fingerprints on the scene?" Jason asked.

Jenny nodded.

"Things are not looking good, Jason. What will happen if this case goes to court?"

"I'm not a criminal lawyer, Jenny. But I can recommend one of the best persons for this job."

"Can you negotiate a lighter sentence if Heather admits she did it?"

Jason pursed his mouth.

"We should not be talking about this."

"I'm thinking of the worst case scenario here, Jason."

"I can see that. Heather's calling the shots here Jenny. She's my client, not you."

"Let me know if I can help," Jenny offered. "I'm going to keep working on this."

Jenny walked back to the café, feeling helpless. Adam had been so confident she was beginning to doubt Heather's innocence.

She spent the day feeling cranky, even snapping at a couple of tourists who wanted more salt in their soup. She had a splitting headache by the time she got home.

A couple of duffel bags lay on the front porch. Adam sat in a chair, looking at his watch and tapping his foot. Tank leapt at Jenny when he saw her, placing his paws on her shoulders.

Jenny hugged and kissed him.

"I've had a bad day, Tank," she whispered in his ear.

She finally noticed the bags.

"Do we have guests?" she questioned. "Wait a minute, has Nick turned up with some of his friends?"

Those are my bags, Jenny," Adam said calmly. "I'm going home."

"What? No!" Jenny wailed.

She stared at Adam with a wild look in her eyes.

"When did you decide that?"

"We talked about this," Adam said softly. "The contractors moved out of my house a couple of weeks ago."

"But we never talked about a date. Why today?"

"Why not?"

"You can't spring this on me, Adam. Not after the day I've had."

"I'm sorry, Jenny. The twins are coming home this weekend. I want to air the place out before that. Stock the refrigerator."

"The twins are welcome here," Jenny said in a shocked voice. "I have always loved having them here."

Adam took Jenny by the shoulders and forced her to sit down.

"This is hard for me too, Jenny. You think I want to go?"

"Then don't."

"It's not right," Adam said with a shake of his head. "I've imposed on your hospitality for too long. People are beginning to talk, and I don't like it."

"I don't care what people say."

"But I do. I feel guilty about it."

"Is this because we fought before? Is this your way of punishing me?"

"Of course not, Jenny. How can you say that?"

"Then don't go," Jenny said mulishly. "Not today."

"You are going to feel the same any time I go, Jenny. It's got to be done some time."

"I was going to arrange a farewell party for you."

"There's no need for that. I'm not going anywhere. I will probably be here for dinner very often."

Tank sensed the tension in the air. He butted Jenny in the knee, and sat down at her feet.

"Tank doesn't want to go," Jenny declared.

"He can stay here," Adam said. "I can't."

"What can I say to make you change your mind?" Jenny's eyes filled up. She was trying hard to control herself.

"Please don't be like this, Jenny. There are some things I can't do while I am still living here."

"What things?" Jenny asked, bewildered.

"You'll find out soon," Adam promised. "It's a surprise. Now dry your tears and see me off with a smile."

"You're sure you're not mad at me?" Jenny asked.

"Of course not," Adam promised. "I'll see you soon."

Adam picked up his bags and limped to his car. Tank refused to get up.

"He needs you, Tank," Jenny whispered. "Go take care of him."

Tank gave a tiny whine and followed Adam.

Jenny waved madly until Adam was out of sight. Then she felt silly. Adam was only going a couple of miles further. But she had grown used to living in the same house with him.

Star came out of the house and hugged her.

"We need a girls' night," she declared. "I'm calling the reinforcements."

Molly arrived half an hour later with Petunia in tow. Heather and Betty Sue were next.

Heather waved a bunch of DVDs in the air.

"I got all your favorites, Jenny. Start popping the corn."

"I'm making my twice baked macaroni and cheese," Star announced. "Molly's taking care of dessert."

"Banana splits with hot fudge and my special brownies," Molly promised.

"We are going to drive that Hopkins boy out of your mind, girl," Betty Sue cackled.

Jenny let her friends pamper her, trying not to think about what kind of surprise Adam had in store for her.

Chapter 15

The Magnolias were busy. Heather and Molly were assembling pimento cheese sandwiches. Star spooned crab salad on crackers and garnished them with a sprig of dill. Jenny was frosting tray after tray of cupcakes.

"I have to say, the Newburys don't do anything half-heartedly," Petunia said, bobbing her head. Her double chins wobbled as she looked around, making sure everything looked good.

"They are generous, aren't they?" Jenny said, sweeping a hand over the food. "They are paying for all this food for the whole town."

"They see it as an investment," Betty Sue snorted. "They stand to earn millions from that drug business."

There was another meeting in the town hall that evening. The Newburys had taken note of all the objections that had been raised by the people. They were going to address all those concerns.

Ada Newbury had hired the Boardwalk Café to provide refreshments for the meeting. Jenny and her friends had been busy making sure the food matched Ada's specific instructions.

The town hall was packed. People were gorging on the food. Some openly admitted coming there just for the food. A large screen had been set up. A couple of men were rigging up some kind of fancy projector. Julius Newbury, Ada's husband, stood by the side, reading from a stack of index cards.

Barb Norton called the meeting to order.

"Julius Newbury is going to answer all your questions," she said simply. "I hope you will maintain some decorum this time."

There was a smattering of applause, accompanied by a wisecrack or two from the crowd. Jenny and the Magnolias sat in the second row. Jenny had heard a lot about the uses of medical marijuana. She was eager to see what the Newburys had to say in their defense.

Lights were dimmed and the presentation started. Julius Newbury spoke well. He walked everyone through a 3D demonstration of the proposed fields and processing plant. He laid special stress on all the safety and security measures in place. A view of Main Street came up on the screen.

A murmur started going through the crowd. Julius paused the presentation and held up a hand.

"We are now going to show you the site of the dispensary itself. I know many of you have concerns about it."

The dispensary proved to be a veritable fortress. There were multiple check points to get in and get out. Employees would be scanned before they left the premises. There was no room for illicit activities.

Julius Newbury pointed to a tall, hefty man who had been standing by his side all this time. He was introduced as the security chief.

"This man has been hired to oversee the complete security of the project. Every inch of the business, whether it is the fields, the processing plant or the dispensary itself will be closely monitored by top notch security measures. The chief is here to address your concerns."

People stood up and started firing questions. The man known as 'Chief' calmly answered all of them. The crowd finally simmered down. There was a lull for a few moments. Then a woman stood up at the back.

"What about the psychological impact your drugs will have on our kids? We are teaching them it's okay to consume psychoactive drugs like cannabis? What is the message we are giving out here?"

Julius Newbury bit his lip and tried to hide his frustration.

"Your kids need to be smart enough to understand the difference. Taking a drug for a medical purpose is different from getting stoned."

"But they are too young to know the difference," another man shouted.

"That's exactly why this will never work," a voice said from the back.

"I can't discipline your kids," Julius Newbury said, turning red. "That's your job. If they are going to get into drugs, they will do it with or without my dispensary."

"What about the fields?" a woman with a baby in her arms asked. "Kids can get in there anytime."

The security chief spoke up.

"No, they can't. We have electric fences around the fields. Anyone trying to scale the fences will be electrocuted."

"You would do that to a child?" a woman asked, looking horrified.

Barb Norton stepped in before any further chaos ensued.

"We have all had our say, Julius. It's up to them now." She turned toward the crowd and pointed at Heather. "If you still want to protest this business, please sign the petition. We are going to see to it that marijuana licenses are not granted for Pelican Cove."

She looked at Julius Newbury and shrugged.

"Nothing personal, Julius."

The Magnolias helped Jenny clear up after the meeting. They took all the leftovers to Seaview for an impromptu dinner party. Jason had fired up the grill on the patio.

"The steaks are ready to go on the grill," he told Jenny.

Everyone relaxed with a drink.

"The crab salad was gone in minutes," Star said. "I'm glad we at least get to taste these pimento cheese sandwiches."

Heather's smile slipped when Adam arrived.

"Relax," he said, putting a hand on her shoulder. "I'm just here for dinner."

"It will be over soon, sweetie," Jenny promised Heather.

She wondered if she was making an empty promise. Adam stuck around after everyone had gone home. He loaded the dishwasher while Jenny put the leftovers in the fridge.

"How about a walk?" he asked.

Tank fetched a stick from the garden and dropped it at Jenny's feet.

"I guess we are going for a walk," Jenny laughed.

"What's on your mind?" Jenny asked after they had walked a quarter mile away from the house.

"More bad news," Adam said quietly. "One of Gianni's neighbors has

112

come forward. He saw Heather leaving Gianni's house at 5 AM."

Jenny stared at Adam, her fear clearly written on her face.

"That doesn't sound good."

Adam shook his head. "It places Heather at the scene of the crime. I'm sorry, Jenny."

Jenny spent a sleepless night worrying about Heather. She was so disturbed she almost burnt a pan of muffins while making breakfast.

She finally called the Bayview Inn at 7 AM.

"I need to talk to you, Heather," she burst out. "Can you come here right now?"

Heather came in ten minutes later, looking worried.

"What's so urgent, Jenny? I was serving breakfast at the inn."

Jenny led Heather out on the deck.

"We never talked about that night," Jenny began.

"I don't remember much, Jenny. I already told you that."

"That's not going to help you, Heather. Think!"

"I remember saying goodbye to all of you at The Steakhouse. Gianni wanted a drink when we got home. I had already had too much. The next thing I remember is waking up in my own bed."

"Someone saw you walking out of Gianni's house at 5 AM."

Heather looked dismayed.

"I must have passed out."

"Was anyone else there when you reached Gianni's house?"

"I don't think so. Wait, the door was open when we got there."

"Do you mean it was unlocked?" Jenny asked. "Or was it wide open?"

"I don't know. Gianni said something about changing the locks."

Jenny thought furiously.

"Changing the locks? That means whoever opened the door had a key."

"Tiffany had a key," Heather cried. "You think she was waiting for us there?"

"Tiffany left for Delaware after her little altercation with you."

"She could have come back?" Heather said hopefully.

"Speculation is not going to help us, Heather. Did you see her there?"

"I don't remember."

"That's your answer to everything."

"I've never been so drunk in my life, Jenny. And I'm paying for it now."

"Gianni was bad for you, Heather."

"I know that now, when it's too late. I guess I just latched on to him on the rebound."

"After dating a dozen other guys?" Jenny's disdain was clear. "Why were you taking antidepressants, Heather?"

"You know about that?" Heather asked.

"The police know about it too. It's another factor against you."

"I wasn't doing well, Jenny. All those guys I dated were just a ruse. I was all torn up inside. I couldn't sleep. Old Dr. Smith prescribed those pills. They were a life saver."

"Did you ever give them to Gianni?"

"Of course not," Heather denied. "He didn't even know I was taking those pills."

"When did you really find out he had a wife?" Jenny gave Heather a stern look. "Was it really at The Steakhouse?"

Heather was quiet for a while. Unfortunately, she looked guilty.

"Gianni never told me about his wife. But I was beginning to have doubts. There were small signs – scent of perfume in the air, a lipstick in the medicine cabinet. I knew there was another woman. I just never dreamed he was a married man."

"Weren't you mad when you found out?"

"I was pretty mad," Heather said, remembering. "He had been talking about taking me to the Caribbean, having a dream wedding. He was a cheat and a liar."

"Why did you fight with Tiffany at the restaurant then? She was the wife. You were the other woman, Heather."

"I don't know what came over me," Heather confessed. "And I was drunk. Less drunk than I was later, but drunk enough."

"None of these things will work in your favor," Jenny said sadly.

"Is there no hope for me?" Heather wailed again.

"Go to some quiet place, clear your mind and try to remember anything you can about that night. Your life depends on it, sweetie."

"I need your help, Jenny. You helped catch so many murderers in the past. Can't you do the same this time?"

"I'm trying my best," Jenny assured her. "Meanwhile, you need to be brave. We will try to bail you out if they take you in."

Jenny's fears proved to be true. The Magnolias were sitting out on the deck later when Adam arrived with his deputies. He arrested Heather for the murder of Dr. Gianni Costa.

Betty Sue Morse was in shock. She fainted without a word, her face falling flat on the wooden table. Star fanned her with a paper napkin while Petunia loosened the buttons at her throat. Molly was about to leave to get the doctor when Betty Sue opened her eyes. She was inconsolable.

"You need to be strong, Betty Sue," Jenny told her firmly. "I'm going to get Jason. We will have Heather back here soon."

Jason was out of town on business and unreachable. Jenny left several messages, urging him to get back to town immediately. It was afternoon by the time he came back.

"I had an idea this was coming," he told Jenny. "Don't worry, I already have the papers ready. She should be out soon."

Adam sat in his office with an inscrutable expression on his face. Jenny pushed open the door and went in, ready to give him a piece of her mind.

"Believe it or not, I'm just doing my job," he sighed. "If I don't do it, someone else will."

Jenny's anger deflated like a balloon.

"This is hard on all of us," she told him. "Dr. Smith gave Betty Sue a sedative. Her blood pressure shot up. Star is sitting by her side, keeping her company."

"Has anyone else come forward?" Jenny asked. "What about any new evidence?"

Adam shook his head. "You were looking at Gianni's old files, weren't you?" Adam asked. "Why don't you go through them again? Your out of the box approach is Heather's only hope now, Jenny."

"You are actually encouraging me to keep on digging?" Jenny asked wondrously. "That doesn't sound like you."

"What are you going to do next, Jenny?" Adam asked.

"I don't know. I'm plum out of ideas."

Chapter 16

Jenny was lost in thought as she mixed the batter for banana nut muffins. She remembered how Heather had appeared on the deck one day with Gianni Costa. He had already set up his clinic in Pelican Cove at that time.

"You found Gianni on that dating site, didn't you?" she asked Heather later that morning.

"Yes, I found his profile attractive. I didn't know he lived right here."

"Did he ever talk about his earlier life? Like where he went to college or medical school?"

"He had a bunch of certificates up on the wall in his office," Heather said with a shrug. "But I never paid much attention to them."

"I think we need to find out more about Gianni," Jenny declared. "What do his patients say about him, for example? Did any of them catch on to his scams?"

"Aren't there websites where people post reviews on doctors?" Molly asked. "Doctors have a score based on the ratings patients assign them."

"I generally check those scores before going to any specialist," Jenny nodded. "Looks like I have some work to do on the Internet."

Jenny went straight home after work that day and started her laptop. Her search yielded surprising results. Gianni had been popular with his patients. Most people had written glowing reviews about how gracious the doctor was, and how he actually listened to them. Some even went on to say he was the best doctor they had ever come across.

Jenny decided Gianni had paid someone to write fake reviews. Then she looked a bit closer. The reviews started two years ago. There wasn't a single review for Dr. Gianni Costa before that. It was almost as if he hadn't existed.

She dialed Tiffany's number.

"Hey Tiffany, got a few minutes?"

"What do you need?" Tiffany asked rudely.

She was in a bad mood.

"You don't sound so good."

"The authorities have frozen all of our bank accounts. I don't have five dollars for a cup of coffee."

"What? I am so sorry to hear that."

"What did you tell them, Jenny?" Tiffany shrieked over the phone. "What am I going to do now?"

Jenny was glad. It seemed that the authorities were pursuing other lines of investigation. That was good news for Heather.

"I'm sure it's just temporary," Jenny tried to placate her.

"Are you calling to gloat?"

"No, of course not! I had a few questions about Gianni. Do you know how long he had been living in Delaware when you met him?"

"Didn't he always live there?" Tiffany asked.

"Apparently not. Did he move there from some other part of the country?"

"If he did, he never told me about it."

"What about medical school?"

"What is this, an inquisition? There's a bunch of certificates hanging up on the wall in his clinic. I never really noticed them."

"Can you do me a favor?" Jenny pleaded. "Can you take some photos of all those certificates and send them to me? It might be important."

"Why should I do that?" Tiffany demanded. "The police confirmed my alibi for the night Gianni died. I'm in the clear."

"You won't have access to your money until the case is solved. You want that, don't you?"

"Whatever!" Tiffany said churlishly. "I guess I can take a few photos."

"Thank you. Thank you so much, Tiffany."

Jenny tapped her foot and stared at her phone every few seconds. She hoped Tiffany would send the photos right away. She didn't relish the thought of having to plead with the woman again. Jenny was just about to go out in the garden to get some fresh air when her phone pinged.

She connected her phone to her computer and downloaded the photos Tiffany had sent. Jenny was surprised to see Gianni had graduated from a prestigious medical school in the area. Why had he set up his clinic in small towns with a degree like that? He could have had a job at the finest city hospitals.

Jenny didn't have much luck when she called the medical school office. Any information about students was private. She could get a transcript if she was a prospective employer. Otherwise she had nothing.

Jenny sat on her patio, breathing in the scent of the roses, staring at the gurgling water fountain. She remembered all the alumni association meetings her ex-husband had gone to every year. She went in and opened her laptop again. She had some calls to make.

Adam grinned from ear to ear when he spotted Jenny on the beach that night. Tank was running in circles around her, nudging her with a stick in his mouth. Jenny took the stick and threw it in a wide arc. Tank leapt after it with a joyous bark.

"I didn't get any complaints about you today so I am guessing you are staying out of trouble."

"Not exactly," Jenny confessed.

She thought of the talking down she had received from some of the men she had called earlier. She decided to keep it to herself.

"I thought the twins were bent on giving me a hard time, but you take the cake, Jenny."

"I'm doing it for a good cause," Jenny said woodenly.

"So are you going to tell me about it?"

"I tried to reach some of Gianni's friends. I looked up his alumni association and called a few people. None of the people I talked to remember him."

"I have never spoken to a single person I went to college with," Adam grumbled. "I doubt any of them will remember me."

"I'm sure plenty of them will," Jenny argued. "You are not easily

119

forgettable."

"That's not the point, Jenny," Adam sighed. "Not every person is a member of their alumni association."

"My ex went to every alumni function."

"You're saying Gianni didn't."

"I don't care if he was a member," Jenny said. "I'm saying no one remembered him."

"How many people did you talk to?" Adam asked.

"Plenty," Jenny said with a grimace. "All of them were from his graduating class. None of them remembered a fellow student called Gianni Costa."

Adam was quiet for a few minutes.

"You're saying Gianni put up a fake degree in his office."

Jenny shrugged.

"He could have easily forged a document."

"I think you are shooting in the dark," Adam said bluntly. "Are you saying Gianni wasn't really a doctor?"

"I don't know what to make of it," Jenny said glumly.

"You've done all you could for Heather," Adam consoled her. "I think you should let the police do their work now. I would focus on getting her a good lawyer."

"Are you saying I should just give up?" Jenny's temper flared. "Jason would never tell me that."

"I'm not Jason," Adam said haughtily. "Don't ever confuse me for him, Jenny."

"How could I? You don't have a kind bone in your body, Adam Hopkins!"

Jenny whirled around and stomped back to Seaview. Tank followed her for a while and then turned back when Adam whistled at him.

"Gianni was a doctor alright," Jason said when Jenny visited him the next morning.

She had told him about her latest theory. Jenny had been mollified when Jason didn't reject it outright.

"Think of the scam he was running," Jason mused, scratching his chin.

He had day old stubble and his eyes were red. Jenny hoped he wasn't staying awake thinking about Kandy.

"Couldn't anyone have done it?" she asked.

"We can talk to Dr. Smith about this if you want. The scam Gianni was running required advanced knowledge about medicine and the system. Only an experienced doctor could have done it."

"Why would he put up fake credentials?"

"Because he didn't want to use his real ones?" Jason guessed.

"Wait a minute, could he have lost his license?"

"That's possible," Jason nodded. "He might have practiced in some other state before he got here."

"You won't believe it, but he has some great reviews from patients. But they only go back two years."

"What?" Jason started.

He looked at Jenny with wide eyes.

"What if it's not just the wrong medical school? What if it's the wrong person?"

"What do you mean, Jason?" Jenny asked, her heart speeding up.

"Gianni Costa could be a fake identity, Jenny. We don't know how long he was running his scams. Maybe he moved from state to state and took up a different name every time."

"New name, new credentials and new women," Jenny said softly.

"Didn't you say Tiffany came from a simple background? That's why he must have chosen her. He wanted someone who would be wowed by his money and wouldn't ask too many questions. He just wanted a wife to look respectable."

"What about Heather?"

"He needed her to build some credibility in Pelican Cove."

"Why did he get greedy, opening a clinic in two states at a time?"

Jason shrugged.

"Maybe he wanted to retire early? It's also the unique position of the Shore. He could easily live in two places at once."

"Heather dodged a bullet," Jenny said.

"We don't know what he was planning for her," Jason said seriously.

"Should we tell Adam? He's going to call this farfetched."

"Let me take care of it, Jenny. We need Adam's help to investigate further."

Jenny's phone rang, interrupting them. Her face lit up when she saw who was calling.

"It's Nick," she smiled.

"When are you coming home, Nicky?" she asked.

Jason looked on indulgently while Jenny spoke to her son. In his late forties, Jason had given up any hopes of ever being a father. But he loved watching the special bond Jenny shared with her son.

"He's coming home tonight," Jenny said happily as soon as she hung up.

Then her face clouded over. "He has something to tell me."

"Relax. I am sure it's good news."

"You will come to dinner tonight, won't you?" Jenny said briskly. "I'm going to make Nick's favorites."

"I don't want to intrude."

"Of course you won't be intruding. Star and Jimmy will be there too."

"Let me bring the wine then," Jason said.

Jenny had a huge smile on her face as she worked through her chores. She rubbed the charms around her neck, thinking of her son. She fired off a quick message to him around lunch time, warning him to drive slowly.

"Why don't you go home early?" Petunia said after they had lunch. "I can wrap up around here."

"Thanks," Jenny said.

She drove to the seafood market and picked up the catch of the day. She was planning to make Nick's favorite fried potatoes with fresh rosemary from her herb garden.

She had barely finished unloading the groceries at home when Nick arrived. He gave her a bear hug and allowed her to kiss him.

"You look scruffy," she said. "You do take a shower now and then?"

"Mom!" Nick complained. "I had a paper due today. I hit the road as soon as I turned it in."

"I'm so happy to see you, Nicky."

Jenny poured fresh squeezed lemonade in two tall glasses. She had muddled some strawberries and basil into them.

Nick drained half the glass in one gulp.

"I miss your cooking, Mom."

"Stop flattering me and tell me what you wanted to talk about."

She and Nick were sitting on a couch in the family room.

"I'm going to Europe in the summer," Nick said. "It's for a class."

"That's great," Jenny exclaimed. "You were so young when we took you there the last time. Hey, maybe I can join you when you're done."

"There's more," Nick said, making a face. "Dad's meeting me there. He's planned a road trip for the two of us."

"That's good for you," Jenny said, trying to hide her disappointment. "I'm glad your dad wants to spend some time with you."

Chapter 17

The Magnolias were enjoying their usual coffee break on the deck of the Boardwalk Café.

"Do you have any new leads?" Heather asked Jenny.

"I'm working on something."

That's all Jenny would say. She didn't want to reveal too much unless she was sure it was going to work in their favor.

"How's your little project with Barb Norton coming along?"

"Almost everyone in town has signed the petition. Over 90% of the people have said no to that dispensary. I think the Newburys are going to be disappointed."

"I feel bad for the people who really need that medicine," Jenny said. "But I guess some of the concerns people raised are real too."

Jenny packed a couple of chocolate cupcakes in a box and took them over to Jason. He loved chocolate.

"How are you, Jenny?" he asked, lighting up as he opened the box she handed over.

"Have you talked to Adam yet?" Jenny asked. "What does he say about our theory?"

"You know Adam," Jason shrugged. "He said he'll work on it. We have to give him a couple of days before we press any further."

"He's had his two days," Jenny fumed. "Time's running out."

Jason licked chocolate frosting off a fork and nodded.

"What do you want to do?"

"Let's go talk to him now."

Adam frowned when Jenny entered his office.

"I'm busy now. Come back later."

"We just need a few minutes, Adam."

She sat down and Jason followed.

"Did you find out anything more about Gianni?"

"Not yet," Adam admitted. "I'm drawing a blank."

Jenny leaned forward, her eyes shining with an idea.

"What if you ran his fingerprints? Have you done that yet? He might have a criminal record."

"Let me get back to you on that," Adam promised.

He ushered them out of his office, looking irritated. Jenny walked out, feeling hopeful.

"If Gianni was going around using a false identity, we will find that out soon enough."

"Fingers crossed, Jenny," Jason said, heading back to his office.

Jenny went back to the café. She had a big order for a birthday cake. She needed to start baking if she wanted to have the cake ready on time.

Adam came to Seaview for dinner that evening. Jenny was happy to see him. She tried to forget his boorish behavior from that morning. Adam always stressed that he wanted to keep his professional life separate from his private life. Jenny decided she would try the same. She was mad at Sheriff Adam but she was happy to see her beau Adam for dinner.

"This is like an impromptu date," Adam said, handing her a bunch of roses from the garden.

Star and Jimmy had gone out for a drive.

"It's just you and me," Jenny said with a blush. "Do you want to eat out on the patio?"

"It's kind of chilly outside," Adam said, rubbing his palms together. "I can build a fire in the pit."

They finally decided to eat in the cozy breakfast nook. Jenny lit candles and served the simple pasta dinner.

Adam dunked his crusty bread in the clam sauce and stared into Jenny's eyes.

"Do you miss having me here?"

Jenny's smile was answer enough.

"Won't be for long," Adam said cryptically.

They decided to go for a walk before dessert. Jenny went upstairs to get a wrap for herself.

"I don't want to spoil the mood but I have some more news for you, Jenny. The prints came back. They belong to a man called Joe Torres."

"What else?" Jenny asked eagerly.

"I will know more tomorrow," Adam promised.

The next day, Jenny waited impatiently to hear back from Adam. She packed some lunch for the two of them and walked over to the police station.

"I'm still working on it," Adam said, chewing on his chicken salad sandwich. "I learned a few random things but I haven't pieced it together yet."

"I'll hold on a bit longer, I guess," Jenny said reluctantly.

Heather called when Jenny was about to sit down to dinner.

"Guess who just booked two rooms at the Bayview Inn?"

"Who?" Jenny played along.

"Ann Davis and her son Ricky. They are coming here in the summer."

"So Ann wasn't kidding when she said she missed the Eastern Shore."

"Apparently not," Heather agreed. "You think they are still interested in Seaview?"

"Ann is the one who sold me the house," Jenny reminded Heather. "Keith was the one who wanted to hold on to it. But he's gone now."

"Will you invite them over?"

"I don't know, Heather, we'll see."

Jenny let Heather prattle on for some time. She was pleased to see shades of the old Heather.

"Your dinner's getting cold," Star called from the table.

Jenny giggled and hung up. She loved living with her elderly aunt. It made her feel younger and reminded her of the times she had spent summers in Pelican Cove as a teen.

Jimmy regaled them with stories of some of his tenants. With tourist season coming up, he had his work cut out for him. He fixed up all the cottages, and added a fresh coat of paint.

"Sounds like you're going to be pretty busy, Jimmy," Star said, stirring a spoon in her soup.

Jenny had made pea soup with fresh peas and mint from the garden. She paired it with lemony grilled chicken breasts in a garlic butter sauce.

"This is my usual spring routine," Jimmy shrugged. "I'm used to it."

"What do you think about taking a trip?"

"Now?" Jimmy asked. "There's no way I can get away right now."

Star said nothing and took a few bites.

"Do you need to go somewhere?" Jimmy asked a few minutes later.

"Frank had this great idea," Star hesitated. "Spring time is really beautiful in the mountains."

"But your specialty is seascapes," Jimmy pointed out. "That's what the tourists buy year after year."

"I know. But a mountain landscape would be a great addition to my work. Frank says a diverse portfolio makes the artist look more experienced."

"He would know."

"Of course he does," Star said. "He's painted mountains, deserts, canyons and beaches in every possible season. I trust his opinion."

"What are you saying?" Jimmy asked quietly.

"It's a three day trip. That gives us four or five plein air sessions. I can book a room in town and drive up into the mountains in Frank's bus every day."

"Doesn't sound like you need me there," Jimmy grumbled.

Star grasped his hand.

"Of course I need you, Jimmy. It will be fun."

"You really want to do this?" Jimmy asked.

"I've been painting the ocean and the salt marshes for years. I like the thought of trying my hand at something new."

"Let me think about it," Jimmy said.

"You're going anyway, aren't you?" Jenny asked her aunt later.

"Frank's a talented artist. I can learn a lot from him."

"Is that all?" Jenny asked. "I think you have a tiny crush on him."

Star refused to comment on that. Jenny hoped her aunt would decide not to go on the trip. She wasn't too keen on sending her off with a stranger.

Jenny spent another busy day at the café, working on a few special orders. Barb Norton came in during lunch. She tasted the chicken noodle soup Jenny placed before her and pronounced it delicious.

"What brings you here, Barb?" Jenny asked, setting down a plate of crab salad with the fat free crackers Barb preferred.

"Sit down, Jenny," Barb ordered. "Spring Fest is just a few weeks away. Have you thought about it yet?"

"I guess we'll put up something just like last time."

"You haven't signed up for it yet," Barb admonished. "I need to have your final menu by the end of the week. I am going to review all of them. I might ask you to make a few changes."

Jenny mumbled something under her breath.

"We don't want everyone offering the same thing," Barb said. "If you are working on any new recipes for the festival, arrange a tasting session in the next two days."

"That's not enough time," Jenny protested.

"Serve it at the café that day," Barb ordered. "I'm sure you can do it."

Barb gave Jenny a few more pointers about the upcoming festival while she ate her lunch.

"It's hard to choose between your cupcakes or donuts," Barb said. "No waffles. We'll have funnel cakes."

Jenny finally got a chance to eat her own lunch. Jason rushed in when she had barely taken two bites.

"Adam wants us," he said.

"Can I finish eating?" Jenny asked. "I'm starving."

"Sure. I'll join you if you have another of those." Jason looked greedily at the sandwich she was eating.

They scarfed down their food in a few minutes and started walking toward the police station.

Adam was just finishing his own lunch. He tossed everything in a trash can and turned around to beam at them.

"I have some news."

Jenny's neck muscles were taut with tension.

"Good news or bad news?"

"Relax, Jenny, this will take a while."

Adam handed over a bottle of cold water. Jenny guzzled the water and looked questioningly at Adam.

"Your hunch paid off. Joe Torres, Dr. Joe Torres, lived in a small town in New Mexico. He was arrested for medical fraud."

Jenny slammed her fist on Adam's desk.

"That's more like it. What else did you find out?"

"I talked to my counterpart over there," Adam explained, "Gianni, or Joe, whatever you call him, was one of the top doctors in the town. He had been running scams for years."

"What kind of scams?" Jason asked.

"Wrong diagnoses, double billing, there's a long list. He finally got caught. One of his patients reported him and he was arrested. But they never found enough evidence to convict."

Jenny sucked in a breath.

"He must have been tipped off."

"That's what they think," Adam agreed. "The charges didn't stick so they had to let him go. His reputation suffered though and he lost his medical license."

"That must have been a big blow," Jason said. "What did he do after that?"

Adam shrugged.

"They didn't exactly keep tabs on him. There is no record of him after that."

"So Dr. Joe Torres just disappeared?" Jenny pressed.

"Something like that, Jenny. There is no address for him in that town so all we can surmise is he went somewhere else."

"He took on a new identity," Jenny said. "But the question is, how many other identities did he have before becoming Gianni Costa."

"Does that matter?" Adam asked.

"We don't know how many people he hurt," Jenny pointed out. "If we want to find these people, we need to track down everything Gianni or Joe did."

"She has a point," Jason said, backing Jenny up.

"That's like looking for a needle in a haystack," Adam sighed.

"Are you up for the challenge?" Jenny asked him.

"We can't be sure this has any relevance to the current crime," Adam said stodgily. "It's not my job to uncover the fraud he did."

"Are you going to throw Heather under the bus just because you can't do your due diligence?"

Jenny stood with her hands on her hips and glared at Adam.

"Be careful, Jenny. I don't care for your allegations."

"Neither does Heather," Jenny snapped. "Heather may not have an alibi but I know in my heart that she is innocent."

"You're talking like the amateur you are," Adam said hotly. "Feelings don't matter in an investigation. We have to deal with hard facts."

"I will find hard facts for you, Adam Hopkins," Jenny challenged. "I will find facts you cannot ignore."

Chapter 18

"I always knew that man was up to no good," Betty Sue Morse declared. The Magnolias were huddled together on the deck of the Boardwalk Café. Coffee cooled in cups as the women mulled over what Jenny had just told them.

"What did Heather see in him?" Molly wondered out loud.

Heather sat with her hands in her lap, looking suitably contrite.

"What are you going to do next?" Star asked Jenny.

"I'm going to find out everything I can about this man, Joe Torres."

"You're a whiz at Internet research now, Jenny," Heather said meekly. "Let me know if I can help."

"I have something in mind for you," Jenny said cryptically.

Molly and Heather followed Jenny into the kitchen on the pretext of getting some food.

"What's the plan?" Molly asked, looking radiant in a new peach top.

She hadn't talked about Chris in a while but Jenny guessed the new couple was doing well.

"Heather needs to remember what happened that night," Jenny said.

Heather opened her mouth to protest. Jenny held up a hand.

"I know, I know, you were drunk! So this is what I propose. We are going to get you drunk again and try to retrace your steps. That might jog your memory."

"I promised myself I would never be that intoxicated again."

"You have to make an exception this time, Heather," Jenny said smoothly. "Your life may depend on it."

"So when are we doing this? Chris and I have a hot date tonight. We are going to Virginia Beach."

"Cancel that date," Jenny ordered. "We need you with us."

Molly agreed easily.

"You really think this idea will work?" Heather asked.

"We won't know until we try."

They agreed to meet at Seaview around 5 PM.

Jenny didn't get a chance to do her Internet research until she got home later that afternoon. She fired up her laptop and started running searches on Dr. Joe Torres. He turned out to be a popular doctor. But all the records she saw were about four years old. She started checking the social sites. Joe or Gianni appeared with a woman on his arm. There were several photos of them smiling and laughing together, at parties or at the beach. The woman was labeled as Maria or Maria Torres.

Jenny guessed the woman was his wife. The woman stopped appearing in the photos about five years ago. Jenny decided to dig deeper. She looked for other news in the region for those dates. She found some news items about a missing woman, none other than Maria Torres.

Maria had been on vacation with her husband when she disappeared. Her husband, a well known local doctor, had been devastated. The news articles printed Maria's life history. Maria had been born Maria Juanita Lopez Garcia. She had been the only child of aging parents. Her mother died when she was in high school. She had been working at the local gas company when Joe Torres saw her and fell in love with her.

A massive search had been mounted for Maria but she never came back. Many theories had been proposed. One of the theories accused Joe Torres of killing his wife and disposing of her body. It had been deemed fantastic by most people. Joe Torres was so popular in his town that no one had been willing to believe a word against him. Then he was arrested for fraud. He had been released later but the damage had been done. He lost his medical license.

Jenny couldn't find any references to Joe Torres after that. She figured he had simply relocated to another state and taken on a new identity.

Molly and Heather arrived before she had time to process all the information.

"What are we drinking?" Molly asked.

"You and I need to be sober," Jenny told her. "Heather's going to get drunk."

"Come on Jenny, we can at least have a cocktail each."

Heather chose her poison. They went into the kitchen and made strawberry daiquiris.

"Do you have something to nosh on?" Heather asked.

"You're on a liquid diet tonight, babe," Jenny teased. "Forget about food."

They watched a chick flick to while away the time. When Heather finally looked ready to pass out, Jenny drove them all to The Steakhouse.

"We are going to walk to Gianni's house from here," she told Heather.

Heather stumbled a few times but they reached the doctor's house twenty minutes later. Jenny had arranged for the door to be unlocked.

"This door was slightly ajar that night," Heather slurred.

They went in and sat down in the living room.

Heather looked around with bleary eyes.

"Gianni was sitting right there," she pointed at an arm chair. "There was a bottle on the coffee table."

"What kind of bottle?" Jenny asked.

"A fancy glass bottle full of a brown liquid."

"A crystal decanter?"

Heather shrugged. Then she sat up.

"There was a big sound, like someone banging into something."

"What did you do?"

Heather rubbed her eyes and looked at Jenny. She was beginning to sober up.

"I think I saw a shadow right there." She vaguely pointed somewhere off the living room. "And I definitely heard a sound in the kitchen."

"What did you do?"

"I told Gianni but he just laughed at me. Told me I was drunk."

"What did you do then?"

"Gianni was drinking from a glass. I grabbed it and took a sip. Then I blacked out."

"Do you remember when you woke up?"

Heather shook her head.

"I don't. Now can we please go home? This place is creeping me out."

"Let's go," Jenny agreed, helping Heather up from the couch.

They walked back to Jenny's car and got in. Jenny promised Heather a fresh pot of coffee and all the spaghetti she could eat.

Heather woke up with a headache the next morning. She went to the Boardwalk Café for breakfast. Jenny had promised her a cure for her hangover.

"Here you go," Jenny said, setting a plate of home fried potatoes before her. "Tell me when you are ready for eggs."

Heather polished off the big breakfast and sat back to enjoy her third cup of coffee.

"Did you remember anything else?" Jenny asked.

"I remember waking up," Heather replied. "It was dark outside. Gianni was sprawled on the couch."

Her eyes filled with panic when she realized what she had seen.

"Was he … he must have been …" she mumbled.

"Never mind that," Jenny soothed. "What did you do?"

"I felt nauseous," Heather told her. "The house was freezing. I realized the front door was wide open. I went out and stood there for a minute. Then I started walking home."

"Did you see anyone?"

"I don't think so," Heather shrugged. "I think I puked in some bushes somewhere."

"Did you see what time it was?"

Heather shook her head.

"I collapsed on my bed when I got home. The next thing I knew, Grandma was shaking me, telling me about Gianni."

Heather went back to the inn after that, ready to take a nap. Jenny called Molly at the library.

"How about a road trip?"

Molly managed to get some time off from the library and they set off.

"Have you called ahead?" Molly asked.

"I want to surprise her."

They reached the small Delaware town where Tiffany Costa lived. Jenny hoped she hadn't moved out yet. There was a small U-Hall outside the house and Tiffany stood by as two hefty teens loaded some furniture.

Tiffany didn't look too happy to see them.

"What are you doing here?" she asked when she spotted Jenny.

"Taking off somewhere?" Jenny asked sternly.

Tiffany shook her head.

"I'm free to go where I want. The police cleared me long ago."

"Based on a false alibi?"

Jenny folded her arms and stared at Tiffany.

"I don't know what you're talking about."

"You did stop at the coffee shop on the way out of town. But then you went back, didn't you?"

"I did no such thing."

Tiffany glared at Jenny, refusing to back down.

"Heather told me the door was ajar when she and Gianni reached home that night. Other than Gianni, you were the only one who had a key."

"That doesn't prove I used it."

"You were in the kitchen," Jenny went on. "Heather saw you."

Tiffany's nostrils flared and she looked away.

"I was looking for my bracelet," she finally admitted. "I must have dropped it in that house. It was five carats. I couldn't just let it go."

"So what? You went there looking for it?" Jenny scoffed. "Did you drug Gianni while you had a chance?"

"Of course not!" Tiffany cried. "I found the bracelet near the sink in the kitchen. I had taken it off earlier when I was doing the dishes."

"What did you see?"

"Nothing much," Tiffany said with a shrug. "Gianni was drinking whiskey from a decanter. Heather was passed out on the couch. I crept out of the living room. Gianni was too drunk to notice me. My car was parked two houses down. I got into it and drove back here."

"Did you stop anywhere on your way back?"

Tiffany answered in the negative. She had just wanted to get home and call it a night.

"So you could have been there all night," Jenny pointed out.

"Look, I'm going back home to my town. I am starting a new job next week. I want to forget I ever met Gianni."

"Good luck with that, Tiffany."

Jenny couldn't decide if Tiffany was just a victim or if she was guilty of drugging Gianni.

"What did you find out online?" Molly asked her on the way back home.

Jenny gave her a brief account of what she had learnt. They agreed Heather had escaped narrowly. Jenny dropped Molly off at the library and went to see Jason. She brought him up to date with everything she had found out.

"Let's go talk to Adam," he said grimly.

Adam Hopkins was in a bad mood again. He sat with his leg propped up on a table.

"Have you been doing your exercises?" Jenny asked him. "Your therapist can only do so much, Adam. You need to put in some effort yourself."

"Are you here to lecture me, Jenny?" Adam thundered. "What are you doing here?"

"Tiffany came back to Pelican Cove that night."

Jenny told him everything Tiffany had admitted to her. Adam didn't look convinced.

"Heather may have been present at the scene of the crime," Jason spoke. "But Tiffany was there too. They are equally innocent or guilty."

"We might have to bring Tiffany in," Adam said grudgingly.

"What about Gianni's or Joe's first wife?" Jenny asked. "Do you think he made her disappear?"

"You have been reading the tabloids," Adam told her. "There was never any proof of a crime."

Jenny and Jason walked out of the police station.

"Do you think they will drop the charges against Heather now?" Jenny asked.

"The case is not solved yet, Jenny. It's hard to say."

"Have you tried to reach Kandy again?" Jenny asked softly.

"She changed her number, Jenny." Jason sounded defeated. "I think I've tried enough. I'm done."

"Let's get your profile on that dating app Heather uses. She can show you the ropes."

"Isn't that where she met Gianni?" Jason quirked an eyebrow. "I'd rather be alone."

"You are not alone, Jason. We are all here for you."

Jason put his arm around Jenny and hugged her close. He wondered if she would ever take him seriously. He had waited too long to bare his heart.

Chapter 19

"Do you trust Tiffany?" Molly asked Jenny.

"I don't know what to say, Molls." Jenny was tired.

The girls had met for dinner at Jenny's place. Jenny had been so frustrated she had declared they needed a girls' night. Star, Petunia and Betty Sue were having their own little soiree at the Bayview Inn.

"I'm glad Grandma's not here," Heather said, taking a sip of her lemonade. "We can talk freely."

"What do you want to talk about?" Jenny asked her.

"I'm worried about her. What happens if they take me away again?"

"That's not going to happen."

Jenny's frustration was written clearly on her face.

"I haven't given up yet, Heather. I'm going to keep on digging."

"I am so sorry," Heather said with tears in her eyes. "I'm being a nuisance."

"We are here to take care of you," Molly said staunchly. "What are friends for?"

Jenny absentmindedly chewed on a piece of celery. She had hit a wall.

"Why don't we talk of something else?" she suggested. "I'm sick of thinking about Gianni. I keep going around in circles. It's not helping."

They tried to gossip about the people in town. They had talked about everyone in the next fifteen minutes.

"I need some fresh air," Heather said.

The girls moved out to the patio.

Molly shivered as some spray from the water fountain hit her.

"Do you think of her?" she asked Jenny. "Lily?"

The fountain stood on the spot where they had found the old skeleton.

"Every time I sit here," Jenny admitted. "I feel like she's waiting, asking for justice."

"Ann Davis is coming here in the summer," Heather told Molly.

"Ann was the last one to see Lily alive, wasn't she?" Molly asked. "Do you trust her?"

"I don't," Jenny said. "But I have no proof. Unless she comes forward and gives a confession, we are at an impasse."

"Looks like Lily is never going to get her justice," Molly observed.

The next day brought some surprising developments.

Adam called Jenny at the café.

"Can you come down to the station now?"

Jenny hoped they hadn't found any more evidence against Heather. Adam was waiting for her impatiently.

"Sit down, Jenny."

Adam's eyes shone with excitement. He had never been that eager to tell her anything. He pulled out a plastic evidence bag from a drawer and slapped it on the table before Jenny.

"What's this?"

"Startling developments in the Lily Davis case. They found this in the ground with the skeleton."

A ruby ring sparkled in the plastic bag. It was set in gold and had tiny diamonds surrounding it.

"Is it real?" she asked.

"Doesn't matter," Adam said. "It's a clue, Jenny. It could be vital to the investigation."

"Where was it all this time?"

"Don't know," Adam shrugged. "They must have overlooked it somehow. Doesn't matter. We have it now."

"Did it belong to Lily?"

"I don't think so," Adam said. "If it was Lily's, she would have been wearing it."

Jenny finally caught on.

"You think this belongs to the person who killed Lily?"

Adam nodded vigorously.

"That's exactly what I'm thinking."

"But we don't know who this belongs to."

"Leave it to the police," Adam bragged. "Once we find out who made it, we can easily see who ordered it."

"Do you mind if I take a picture of this?"

Adam was in a benevolent mood. He told her she could take as many pictures of the ring as she wanted.

Jenny forgot all about the ring after she got back to the café. She had two birthday cakes to bake and recipes to try for the Spring Fest.

"What about the pimento cheese sandwiches you made for that meeting?" Petunia asked. "People loved those."

"We'll see what Barb thinks about them," Jenny agreed. "I still haven't decided between cupcakes and donuts. Do you think we should make a few of each?"

"That's too much work for you, Jenny." Petunia didn't talk much most of the time but Jenny valued her advice.

"Maybe we should toss a coin," she laughed nervously.

"The people are going to love either," Petunia assured her.

Jenny was in a rare mood the next morning. She made cheese and pimento muffins along with crab omelets for breakfast. She couldn't wait to hear what the Magnolias thought of the savory muffins.

"Delicious," Molly pronounced with her mouth full. "You need to take a picture of this and put it on social media, Jenny."

"Oh, that reminds me," Jenny said, slapping the table with her palm.

She pulled out her phone from her apron pocket.

"What have you got there?" Betty Sue inquired as she looked up from her knitting.

Jenny stuck her phone in Betty Sue's face.

"Does this look familiar?"

Betty Sue's face was blank for a moment. She took the phone and adjusted her glasses. She peered at the picture with a frown. A minute later, her face cleared and an expression of incredulity came over it.

"Where…where did you get this, girl?"

"Do you recognize it?" Jenny asked eagerly.

Betty Sue was the first person Jenny went to when she had a question about the town. Betty Sue had been born there and had been around the longest. There wasn't much that slipped Betty Sue's notice in the town of Pelican Cove.

"It's a family heirloom," Betty Sue rasped. "Where did you get this?"

"Whose family?" Jenny gasped.

"The Davis family," Betty Sue said, sitting up. "This ring is over two hundred years old. It has been passed down in the family from generation to generation."

"So it's Lily's ring?"

Jenny tried to hide her disappointment.

"Are you listening to me, girl?" Betty Sue thundered. "Lily may have been born a Davis, but this ring wasn't meant for her. It was handed over to a bride coming into the family."

"What if there were many brides?" Heather asked.

"Then the oldest one got it, of course," Betty Sue snapped.

Jenny was busy making some calculations in her head.

"So you're saying this ring belongs to Ann Davis?"

"Sure does, or did," Betty Sue said confidently. "Although now that I think about it, I don't think she was wearing it last summer."

"No, she wasn't," Jenny said jubilantly.

She leapt to her feet and whirled around.

"I have to go."

"Wait a minute," Betty Sue called out. "Tell me more about this."

Jenny was already down the café steps before Betty Sue could finish her sentence. She almost jogged down the boardwalk and headed to the police station. Nora, the desk clerk waved her through.

Adam was in a meeting with a bunch of other uniformed men when Jenny burst into his office.

"How about knocking before you enter?" he asked irritably.

"It's Ann. It's Ann Davis."

"What is?"

"The ring, Adam. The ring is a Davis family jewel and it belonged to Ann Davis. Betty Sue will vouch for it."

Adam's face broke into a smile.

"Leave the rest to me, Jenny."

Jenny walked back to the café slowly, wishing for a breakthrough in Gianni's case. The Magnolias were waiting with their questions.

"That ring was found in the dirt that came with the skeleton," she told them. "Or something like that."

"What was Ann's ring doing there?" Star asked.

"That's what the police will look into now," Jenny explained. "If you ask me, it puts her on the spot."

"Why would Ann harm Lily though?" Molly asked in a puzzled voice.

"She's the only one who can tell us that."

Betty Sue's eyes had filled up.

"Lily looked up to her. She was like the older sister she never had."

"An older sister who stabbed her in the back?" Heather scoffed.

"The ring doesn't prove anything. Ann can spin any story now. I don't think she will confess after all these years."

Jenny was proven wrong.

Ann Davis unraveled like a ball of string when she saw the ring.

"She said it was an accident," Adam told her as they walked on the beach. "She didn't mean to hurt Lily."

"Why did they get into a fight?" Jenny wanted to know.

"Lily had been acting crazy," Adam explained. "Those were Ann's words. She wanted to sell Seaview for a pittance. She just wanted to get away from Pelican Cove."

"Ann wasn't ready to sell?"

"She wanted Seaview for her son."

"They fought over a piece of land?"

"That wasn't all," Adam continued. "Lily barely spoke to anyone for months. She shut herself in her room, mourning her daughter. Ann got friendly with Lily's husband. They might have had an affair."

"How dare she!" Jenny cried.

Jenny's husband had dumped her after falling in love with a much younger woman. She didn't think kindly about women who wrecked other women's homes.

"Ann didn't admit to the affair," Adam said. "She just told us they had a big argument. It got a bit violent. Ann pushed her and Lily struck her head on a stone in the garden. She died instantly."

"What if Ann was mistaken?"

"She must have tried to revive her," Adam shrugged. "We will never know that."

"So Ann decided to bury her in the garden?"

"Ann says she panicked. Ricky had watched everything from an upstairs room. Lily's son was expected back home any moment. She told Ricky to start digging."

"Didn't the son or husband notice anything amiss in the garden?"

"Ann made up that story about seeing Lily get in the car with a man. Keith was devastated when he thought his mother abandoned him."

Jenny had met Lily's son when he came to Pelican Cove. She knew he had been traumatized by his mother's actions.

"So she not only killed Lily, she also maligned her character." Jenny thought of the petite old woman she had met a few months ago. She would never have guessed she was a murderer.

"What happens now?" Jenny asked.

"Ann Davis and her son will both face charges," Adam told her.

Jenny couldn't wait to meet the Magnolias the next morning.

"I knew Lily would never turn her back on her family," Betty Sue said tersely. "Lily can finally rest in peace."

Jenny sat on the patio with her aunt, staring at the water fountain.

"Do you think it's true?" she asked her aunt. "What they say about Seaview?"

Star gave her a pained look.

"You're not thinking about that nonsense again?"

"Just think about it. Lily lost her daughter at a young age, she got herself killed, then her son got into drugs and he got himself killed. Her husband is barely alive in some senior home."

"No one can predict the future, honey," Star sighed. "You have made a beautiful home here for yourself. Try to stay happy in it."

"Here's to happy memories," Jenny nodded, clinking her cup of coffee with Star's.

Star gave her a curious look.

"I don't think you will be staying here much longer, anyway."

"What do you mean, Star?" Jenny laughed. "I'm not going anywhere."

Star looked at her niece indulgently.

"I think Adam's getting ready to pop the question."

Jenny blushed furiously.

"You do love him?" Star asked.

Jenny's eyes clouded with confusion.

"Is love enough?" Jenny asked moodily. "I loved Nick's father with all I had. Look where that got me."

"It will be different this time," Star said, patting her on the back.

"Do you approve?" Jenny asked her aunt.

"You know I like Jason more," Star winked. "But I'm with you, baby. I can't imagine being alone in this big old house though."

Jenny shook her head.

"Like I said, I'm not going anywhere."

Chapter 20

Jenny sipped her coffee quietly as the Magnolias chatted around her. Heather was giving them an update on Barb Norton's latest project. The signatures she had collected from the town people had done the job. The Newburys had not been granted the approvals they needed to set up the medical dispensary.

Heather's face was animated as she narrated what had happened. She seemed to have found a new purpose while working for Barb. But the cloud of suspicion still hung over her. Was Heather guilty after all? She had been the woman scorned.

Jenny's mind wandered as she imagined what Heather must have felt when she realized Gianni was already married. She must have been ready to bash someone's head in. Jenny chided herself for thinking the worst of her friend. There had been no new developments. The police still considered Heather their top suspect.

Jenny scratched her head and wondered what more she could do. She needed to start from scratch and go over everything with a fine-tooth comb.

"Thinking about Adam?" Molly asked with a glint in her eye.

Molly and Chris were very happy together. They felt everyone around them needed to be in a relationship.

"Come with me," Jenny said suddenly. "If you can take some time off, that is."

Molly sensed the urgency in Jenny's voice.

"Sure, Jenny, let me make a call."

Jenny started walking toward Dr. Smith's clinic.

"What are we doing?" Molly wanted to know.

"You're good at research, aren't you? I need a pair of sharp eyes."

Jenny spoke to Dr. Smith and asked for the patient records from Gianni's clinic. He pointed them to a small room at the back.

"See those four boxes?" he said. "Have at it."

"We are going to go over these again," Jenny told Molly.

"But what are we looking for?"

"Anything unusual?" Jenny shrugged. "I'm not sure, Molly. We are looking for a needle in a haystack, anything that can take the limelight away from Heather."

Jenny noticed Dr. Smith had marked some of the files. He had written remarks in the margins like 'fake diagnosis', 'wrong prescription' etc.

Molly turned out to be more efficient than Jenny. She got through a box much faster than Jenny and arranged the papers in neat piles.

"I know most of these people," Molly told Jenny. "Some are friends or acquaintances, others just sound familiar. But there's a bunch of names that don't seem to be from around here."

"They might belong to his patients in Delaware," Jenny mused. "Or they might be fictitious names. Gianni billed the government for nonexistent patients."

"What do you want to do with those?"

"Keep them in a separate pile," Jenny said thoughtfully. "I want to go through them."

The piles grew as Jenny and Molly worked through the boxes. Jenny finally turned to the pile Molly had set aside as out-of-towners. She read each file carefully, paying special attention to the names. One name caught her eye right away.

"Why does this sound familiar?" she wondered out loud. "Francis Lopez."

"Never heard of him," Molly shrugged.

The girls worked diligently for a couple of hours without much success.

"I don't know about you, Jenny, but I'm starving."

"Let's go grab a bite at the café."

They weren't in the best of spirits when they went back to the café.

"No luck?" Petunia asked sympathetically.

She placed two plates of chicken salad sandwiches before them and ladled tomato soup in earthen mugs.

"Do you know someone called Francis?" Jenny asked Petunia.

"Doesn't ring a bell," the older woman said, shaking her head. "Why don't you ask Betty Sue? She's coming here for lunch today."

Betty Sue walked in with Heather following close behind. Heather was carrying their black poodle Tootsie in her arms.

"I'll tie her out on the beach," she told Petunia immediately. "She didn't want to stay back home."

Everyone moved out to a table on the deck. Betty Sue sipped her soup and looked hopefully at Jenny.

"How's it going? Any luck?"

Jenny sighed in frustration.

"I feel I'm close, Betty Sue. But I feel I'm forgetting something."

Betty Sue had never heard of Francis Lopez either. Heather had been sitting on the café steps, playing with Tootsie. She looked up sharply.

"Isn't that the artist your aunt is going around with?"

"My aunt is not going around with anyone other than Jimmy," Jenny said sharply.

"Pay attention, Jenny," Heather pressed. "Frank Lopez? He's that new artist."

Jenny felt a chill run down her spine. She looked around at her friends.

"You think Frank Lopez is Francis Lopez?"

The ladies shrugged.

"I need to talk to Adam right away," Jenny cried, springing to her feet.

She skipped down the steps and hurried down the beach to the police station. Nora, the desk clerk, waved her through.

"Have you brought my lunch, Jenny?" Adam asked with a smile.

"Frank Lopez!" she panted. "You need to bring him in."

"Stop screaming in my ear, Jenny. I haven't had lunch yet."

"Didn't you hear what I said?" Jenny asked, putting her hands on her hips.

"You're always making outlandish demands. Now sit down and tell me what's going on."

"I think Frank Lopez is our guy. You need to bring him in right away."

"Who is he?"

"He's that new artist in town. Don't you remember?"

"And why should I arrest him?" Adam asked patiently.

Jenny launched into what she had been doing all day. She reminded him about the woman who had been Gianni's wife a few years ago.

"I think this guy is related to that girl Maria. There has to be a connection."

"Sounds farfetched to me," Adam shook his head.

"What is this Frank Lopez doing in Pelican Cove, Adam? Why is he here now?"

"We have absolutely no proof he knew Gianni."

"He was Gianni's patient. That's your connection."

Adam finally decided to humor Jenny.

"I'll send a car out to bring him in."

Jenny thanked Adam and stood up. She had decided to go confront Frank herself. Adam recognized the resolve he saw in Jenny's eyes.

"Don't do anything foolish," he called out after her.

Jenny vaguely remembered Frank talking about a house he had rented in town. Her tires spun as she raced to the address. She was looking for the trailer belonging to Frank. The house looked deserted when she got there. Her phone rang just then. It was Star.

"I'm sorry I couldn't say goodbye."

"What? Where are you?" Jenny asked, dazed.

"I'm with Frank. We are going to paint the mountains, remember? We talked about this."

"But I thought you weren't going."

"I'll be away for three days," her aunt said. "Frank's trailer is just awesome, Jenny. It has a bed and a TV and a small kitchen. I'm going to have fun."

Jenny cringed as she thought of the close quarters her aunt was sharing with Frank.

"Is Frank with you?"

"Of course he is. You don't sound too good, Jenny. Are you coming down with something?"

"I just feel bad I didn't get to say bye to you," Jenny laughed nervously. "Why don't you stop at the next rest area? I'm on my way."

"Don't be silly. I'll be back before you know it."

"No, no, I insist," Jenny said in a weird voice. "It's such a beautiful day. I'm looking forward to a nice drive."

"We're twenty miles out of town," Star said. "Can you catch up with us?"

"The trailer goes slower than a car, doesn't it? I'll be there, don't worry."

"Whatever you say, my dear." Star sounded confused but Jenny was glad she was playing along.

Jenny called Adam right away.

"You need to stop them. If I'm right, Star could be in danger."

"Aren't you getting carried away?" Adam asked.

"I'm driving out to meet them," Jenny said firmly. "You can meet me there or not. I leave it up to you."

Jenny broke the speed limit trying to reach the rest area as soon as possible. Luckily, she didn't get pulled over. A car belonging to the Pelican Cove police overtook her just as she turned into the exit lane. Adam was already out of the car by the time Jenny parked next to him. A couple of deputies stood by, waiting for a signal from Adam.

Jenny spotted Star by the vending machines and ran toward her. She flung her arms around her aunt and hugged her tight.

"Thank God, you are safe."

"What's going on, Jenny?" Star asked sharply. "Are you going to tell me why you are acting like this?"

"You'll find out soon enough."

Frank walked up, holding packets of potato chips and cans of soda.

"They didn't have the diet cola so I got regular."

He smiled at Jenny.

"You can visit with your aunt as long as you want. There's no rush."

For a moment, Jenny wondered if she was wrong about Frank.

Adam had walked up to Jenny. Frank looked at the uniformed sheriff standing before him and his shoulders slumped. He dropped the food he was carrying on a bench and held up his hands.

"I'm not sorry I avenged my daughter."

Star's eyes popped open as Adam arrested Frank and took him away.

"I'm so glad you are okay, Star," Jenny said, hugging her aunt again.

The Magnolias arrived early at the Boardwalk Café the next day. Heather was grinning widely.

"Jason just called. Frank Lopez gave a full confession."

"Tell us what happened, Jenny," Betty Sue commanded. She was looking relieved, now that Heather had been vindicated of any involvement in the crime.

"I don't have all the details," Jenny began. "This is what Adam told me at a high level. Frank's daughter Maria was married to Gianni. As far as I can tell, she was his first wife. She found out about his shady business and threatened to go to the police if he didn't clean up his act."

"So he was always crooked," Molly observed.

"Gianni promised her he would do whatever she wanted. They went on a trip after that. Maria never came back. Gianni said she walked out of the hotel room. There was a big investigation but Gianni got away because there was no evidence against him."

"Are you saying he killed that poor girl?" Petunia asked with a gasp.

Jenny nodded.

"She never surfaced anywhere else. Frank believed Gianni murdered his daughter. He hired investigators and tried hard to get Gianni convicted but he didn't succeed. Then Gianni vanished."

"How could he do that?"

"He went to a different state and took on a new identity," Jenny explained. "But he didn't change his ways. He carried out the same scams. When things got too hot, he moved and changed his name again."

"So Gianni wasn't his real name?" Heather asked.

"No, sweetie," Jenny said. "Not by a long shot."

"What do you mean, Maria was his first wife?" Star asked.

"Gianni went to small towns and wooed a local girl. He chose someone who would help him build contacts and set up his clinic. He got rid of the girl when he moved."

"So he killed more than one woman?" Heather gasped.

"That's what the police think now," Jenny told them. "We will know more after a thorough investigation."

"How did Frank know Gianni was here?" Star asked.

"Frank had been looking for Gianni ever since he disappeared. He drove around the country, following Gianni's trail. He traced him to Delaware and then to Pelican Cove. He posed as a patient and made sure Gianni was the man his daughter had been married to."

"When did he decide to murder him?" Molly asked.

"Revenge was always on his mind. Once he located Gianni, it was just a matter of when and how."

"How did he do it?" Heather asked in a hushed voice.

"That shadow you thought you saw that night," Jenny said, "that was Frank. He got into Gianni's clinic and powdered a few drugs. He added them to the whiskey decanter, knowing Gianni would probably drink from it after coming home."

"What if I had drunk from it?" Heather cried.

Jenny shrugged.

"Frank was single minded in his determination. I don't think he cared about collateral damage."

"So I almost died too?" Heather gasped.

"You had a narrow escape, girl," Betty Sue's voice boomed. "That's what comes of associating with scum."

"But he was so nice to me!"

Heather looked shocked.

"What did Frank do that night?" Molly asked, prompting Jenny to go on.

"He just stood in the shadows and watched Gianni drink from the decanter. I think he was prepared to pour it down his throat if needed."

"I don't understand one thing," Heather said. "Why did he stick around in town after that? All he had to do was get in his bus and drive away."

Jenny looked at her aunt.

"We'll never know that, I guess."

Star looked around at the group of friends gathered around the table and shook her head.

"He was a really good artist."

Epilogue

The town of Pelican Cove was busy celebrating Spring Fest. People had turned up in droves. A big marquee had been erected. Food stalls lined one side. A band was setting up on a makeshift stage on the beach.

Jenny sat among her friends, finally catching her breath after a hectic day. All the food from the Boardwalk Café had been sold. Tourists had come to the festival especially to taste Jenny's cupcakes and pimento cheese sandwiches.

"I don't know how to thank you," Heather gushed. "You saved my life, Jenny."

"You were innocent all along," Jenny said lightly. "You had nothing to fear."

Adam Hopkins limped up to the group of women. He gulped as he tried to catch Jenny's eye. Jenny had been giving him the cold shoulder for a while.

"Go talk to that Hopkins boy," Betty Sue said, tipping her head at Adam.

Jenny stood up reluctantly and took a few steps toward Adam.

"What is it?"

"Can you spare a few minutes? Please?"

The sun was low on the horizon, painting the sky in shades of orange and mauve. Jenny accompanied Adam to the beach. He was quiet while they walked away from the crowd.

"Are you going to say anything?" Jenny prompted.

Adam cleared his throat.

"You know I'm not big on words, Jenny. But I hope you know how much you mean to me."

He pulled a small gift wrapped box out of his pocket and held it out to her.

"What's this?" Jenny asked suspiciously.

"Aren't you going to open it?"

Jenny pulled off the blue satin ribbon and tore the wrapping paper. Her heart thudded a bit as she lifted the lid of the small box. A shiny key lay inside.

"Err… what's this, Adam?"

"Jenny King, you already hold the key to my heart. This is the key to my house."

Jenny's brows settled into a frown.

"I want you to move in with me, Jenny."

Jenny stared into Adam's blue eyes. She was dismayed at the hope she saw there.

"I can't do that," she said under her breath. "I'm sorry, Adam."

"Why not?" Adam asked, trying to maintain his composure.

"I am just getting settled in at Seaview. I'm not leaving it now."

"Jenny, it's just a house."

"No, Adam. It's my home. It's where I am going to spend the rest of my days."

Adam took Jenny's hands in his.

"Will you at least think about it?"

Jenny stared into the sand at her feet. She gave Adam a slight nod. Then she turned around and started walking back to her friends.

THE END

Acknowledgements

This book would not have been possible without the support of a number of people. I am thankful to my beta readers and advanced readers and all my loved ones who provide constant support and encouragement. A big thank you to my readers who take the time to write reviews or write to me with their comments – their feedback spurs me on to keep writing more books.

Muffins and Mobsters – Pelican Cove Cozy Mystery Series Book 6

By Leena Clover

Chapter 1

Jenny King sat out on her patio, sipping a glass of white wine. The fine mist coming off a gurgling water fountain sprayed her occasionally. The scent of wild roses and gardenias perfumed the air. The sky blazed in hues of orange and red as the sun went down over the ocean. A tea light flickered inside a hurricane lamp, teased by the brisk ocean breeze.

Jenny's aunt Star sat next to her, doodling something on her sketch pad.

"Can you see anything in this light?" Jenny asked her aunt.

"Enough," her aunt replied without looking up.

She was engrossed in her drawing. Star was a local artist who was famous for painting seascapes of the coastal Virginia region she called home. She had lived on the small barrier island of Pelican Cove for over forty five years. The seaside town was home to her. And now it was home to her niece Jenny.

Jenny had been married to a big city lawyer for twenty years. She had been a poster child for the rich suburban housewife who lunched with friends and threw parties to further her husband's career - until her husband introduced her to a younger model of herself. Dumped and discarded at the age of forty four, Jenny had been at a crossroads. She grabbed her aunt's invitation like a lifeline and arrived in Pelican Cove. She had worked hard to build a new life for herself there.

Suddenly, Jenny swore under her breath and brandished a fly swatter in the air. She smacked a spot on the table with gusto.

"This little thing is useless," Star told her. "We should get the electric one. These mosquitoes are getting a bit too bold."

"I never thought Pelican Cove would have so many mosquitoes."

"We are at risk alright, being so close to the marshes," Star noted. "But we manage to keep these little buggers under control."

"How?"

"The town is supposed to take care of these things," Star explained.

"Looks like someone dropped the ball on pest control this year."

"Look at me, talking about the mosquito population."

Jenny shook her head in wonder. Sometimes, she didn't recognize herself.

"What's wrong with that?" Star queried. "You know these bugs carry deadly diseases. They need to be handled."

"Let's go inside," Jenny said, getting up. "You can show me what you've been working on."

Star hugged her sketch book and covered it with her arms.

"It's a surprise. You can't see it yet."

"Just a peek?"

"No way, kiddo. Why don't you go up to bed and call that young man of yours?"

Jenny's face fell.

"I guess I can try."

Jenny had been dating Adam Hopkins, the local sheriff, for the past few months. Earlier in the spring, Adam had asked her to move in with him. At the time, Jenny was just getting settled in at Seaview, her newly renovated sea facing mansion. She had turned Adam down.

Her response had cooled things between the couple. They had gone on a couple of dates since then but Adam didn't drop in for dinner like he used to. Neither did he turn up for their late evening walks on the beach.

"You are both too headstrong," Star frowned. "One of you will have to take a step back."

"I'm not leaving Seaview any time soon," Jenny said. "It's my home now."

"You need to move past this cold war. I almost preferred to see you two fighting like cats and dogs."

"He just doesn't care anymore, I guess."

"Have some faith, Jenny. That boy loves you. You just need to spend more time together."

Star paused mid-step as they walked into the house.

"I know. You need a new crime to solve together. Nothing major — maybe something silly like a stolen bike or two?"

"Don't be ridiculous!" Jenny said haughtily as she climbed up the winding staircase to her room.

Jenny overslept the next morning. It was fifteen minutes past five when she pulled up in front of the Boardwalk Café. The building was dark. Jenny wondered why Petunia, the owner, had not opened the café. Usually, Petunia almost always arrived before her. Jenny was used to starting her day with a fresh cup of coffee and a warm hug from Petunia.

Jenny hurried through her routine, starting the oven. She mixed the batter for her blueberry muffins and added a generous amount of fresh blueberries. Her secret ingredient went in, the one that had people guessing.

Jenny had started working at the Boardwalk Café over a year ago at her aunt's insistence. The rest was history. Jenny's innate love for cooking had her creating tasty food every day, using the region's abundant seafood and fresh produce. People up and down the coast flocked to the café to sample her yummy treats.

Jenny pulled out the first pan of muffins and opened the café doors just as the clock chimed six. Captain Charlie, her favorite customer, came in. He was always the first one in when Jenny opened at 6 AM.

"Good morning," he greeted her, peering into the kitchen. "Do I smell muffins?"

"You do," Jenny said with a smile. "Blueberry muffins, your favorite."

"I like everything you cook," Captain Charlie said with a blush. He patted his slight paunch. "I have been overdoing the sweets ever since you got here."

Jenny placed two muffins in a brown paper bag and filled a large cup with coffee. She set them on the counter and glanced at the wall clock again. It was fifteen minutes past the hour. Jenny saw a few people come in and wondered when she would get a chance to call Petunia.

Captain Charlie must have read her mind.

"Where's Petunia?" he asked as he picked up his food. "She hasn't taken a day off in the past twenty five years."

Jenny felt a shudder run through her for a fraction of a second. She dismissed her apprehensions with a smile and a shrug.

"She'll be here soon, Captain Charlie. I'll tell her you were asking for her."

Jenny didn't get a chance to look at the clock again for the next hour or two. She baked a few more batches of muffins, brewed pot after pot of coffee and poached chicken for salad. She sighed with relief when her friend Heather walked into the café.

"Can you handle the register for me?" she asked. "I need to sit down for a minute."

Heather Morse ran the Bayview Inn with her grandmother. Her eyes clouded with concern as she watched Jenny take a deep breath.

"Have you had breakfast yet?" she asked with concern. "Why don't you grab a bite in the kitchen? I got this covered."

Jenny collapsed into a chair and broke a muffin into two. She popped half of it in her mouth and swallowed it without chewing. The clock chimed eight and Jenny remembered the call she needed to make. She dialed Petunia's number and tapped her foot impatiently as the phone rang several times before switching to voicemail.

Jenny walked out on the café's deck and stood with her hands on her hips, gazing at the Atlantic Ocean. The boardwalk stretched before her on both sides. The beach was almost deserted. She spotted a few tourists walking up from a parking lot, lugging camp chairs and coolers. They were clearly setting up for a day on the beach.

Jenny stepped closer to the edge and gave the beach another once over. A few benches were scattered across the boardwalk at regular intervals. She spotted a familiar orange scarf fluttering in the wind and shielded her eyes to get a better look. A lone figure sat on a bench, staring at the sea.

"What's she doing there?" she mumbled to herself.

Jenny climbed down the café's steps and strode across the boardwalk to the bench.

"Petunia!" she called out, raising her voice as she got closer.

The figure seated on the bench didn't budge.

"What are you doing out here?" Jenny asked, breaking into a run.

She was beginning to feel a bit worried.

"Aren't you cold, Petunia?"

Jenny King didn't remember what happened next. She must have screamed her head off because the few people on the beach started running toward her. Jenny's hands covered her mouth as her eyes popped open in horror. She made herself walk closer to the figure wearing the scarf. She wanted to be sure it was her friend.

Minutes passed, or hours. Sirens sounded in the distance. Jenny's body sagged as a pair of strong arms came around her and wrapped her in a tight embrace.

"Shhhh ..." Adam Hopkins murmured in her ear. "Settle down, Jenny. It's going to be okay."

Nothing was ever going to be okay again. Jenny knew that for sure. Someone had shot her friend in cold blood. Petunia Clark, owner of the Boardwalk Café, beloved resident of Pelican Cove, was dead.

Jenny wanted to fall asleep and never wake up. She barely heard Adam talking to someone. Her aunt was with her next, hugging her close.

"Let's go back to the café," her aunt soothed. "Walk with me, sweetie."

Heather and Star hovered around Jenny back at the café. Heather's grandmother Betty Sue arrived, followed by their friend Molly. The motley crew of women called themselves the Magnolias and were staunch friends. Petunia had been the quiet one, rarely speaking up but providing strong support by her mere presence.

Tears were streaming down their faces as the Magnolias sobbed unashamedly, clinging to each other.

Star had procured a bottle of brandy from somewhere. She poured two fingers in a glass and made Jenny gulp it down.

Adam Hopkins stepped into the café, followed by two deputies. He stood ramrod straight with his hands behind his back and cleared his throat.

"Jenny, you need to come with me."

"Why?" Star asked, blowing her nose in a tissue.

"I need to question her about what happened."

"What's wrong with you, boy?" Betty Sue Morse thundered. "Can't you see she's suffering?"

"I am sorry," Adam said. "Just doing my job."

Jenny stood up, wiping her tears on her sleeve.

"It's okay, girls." She looked up at Adam. "Let's go."

Adam pointed to an empty table.

"Actually, we can talk here or out on the deck, as long as we have some privacy."

Jenny shut the café doors and nodded to her aunt. The Magnolias went into the kitchen.

"Walk me through everything you did this morning," Adam ordered. "Don't leave anything out."

Jenny stared at the man who had become an important part of her life. Was she really in love with him?

She leaned forward and glared at him.

"So tell me, Adam. Are you being a jerk as usual, or are you just doing your job?"

Chapter 2

The Magnolias sat on the deck of the Boardwalk Café. The usually lively group was quiet. Jenny warmed her hands with a cup of coffee and stared at the ocean. Betty Sue's knitting needles clacked and her hands moved in a familiar rhythm as she gawked at a spot on the table. Star drew furiously in her sketch pad. Heather sat with her eyes closed and Molly held a book upside down. They were down one member and every one of them felt Petunia's absence.

"She was the kindest person I knew," Star said suddenly. "I still remember the day she took over the café."

"What did she do before that?" Jenny asked.

Star shrugged. "She came here one summer like any other tourist. I guess she fell in love with the town."

"She wasn't an islander," Betty Sue nodded. "The Boardwalk Café had been shut up for a year since the previous owner died. The next thing we know, Petunia has bought the place and is serving coffee."

"Did she have any friends other than us?" Molly asked.

"Not that I know of," Star said. "I have never seen her talking to anyone else."

"She spent most of her life here in the café," Betty Sue told them. "There wasn't a single day in the past twenty five years when she didn't open the café."

"Even for Christmas and Thanksgiving?" Jenny asked, astounded. "Didn't she celebrate it with someone?"

Star and Betty Sue shook their heads.

"She kept it open for people who had nowhere else to go."

"I miss her," Jenny said fiercely. "She gave me a chance, helped me turn my life around."

"What happens to the café now?" Heather asked.

"I'll keep running it until someone says otherwise," Jenny said. "That's the least I can do."

Jenny struggled to her feet, trying to fight off her melancholy.

"I need to start making lunch."

"I'll come and help you," her aunt offered.

"I have to get back to the library," Molly said grimly. "But call me if you need anything, Jenny."

The group dispersed and headed to their daily jobs.

Jenny chopped celery and walnuts for chicken salad. She smashed the poached chicken with a fork and started mixing the salad together as her eyes filled up. It had been Petunia's job to mix the salad. They had worked well in tandem. Jenny chopped vegetables. Petunia mixed the salad and scooped it on the bread. Jenny would add lettuce and tomato, press the sandwich together and set it on a platter.

Jenny's eyes filled up as she stuck a toothpick in the sandwich.

"You need to hold yourself together," Star said, tearing up herself.

"I don't want to," Jenny cried. "I just want her back."

"Sweetie," Star said, hugging her niece. "You know that's not possible."

"What are the police doing?" Jenny demanded. "Sitting on their behinds as usual?"

"Have you talked to Adam about this?"

"Not since that horrible day."

Jenny pulled off her apron and slammed her knife on the counter.

"I'm going to talk to him. They should have something for us by now."

"It's barely been two days," Star reminded her.

Jenny stalked out without a word. She walked briskly down the boardwalk to the police station.

"Where's your sheriff?" she hollered at the desk clerk. "I need an update on a case."

Nora, the clerk, pointed toward a closed door.

Jenny kicked the door with one foot and let it slam behind her. Adam Hopkins sat with one leg propped up on a chair. He was a war veteran who had been injured in the line of duty. His mercurial temper flared every time his leg bothered him.

Jenny and Adam both swore at the same time.

"What's wrong with you, Jenny?" Adam glared.

"You have to ask?" Jenny glowered back at him with her hands on her hips. "When are you going to get off your keister?"

"Mind what you say, Jenny," Adam warned. "What are you blabbering about?"

"I want an update on Petunia's case," Jenny said, flopping down in a chair.

"We are working on it," Adam said coolly.

"That's not good enough. I want details."

"I don't owe you any explanation, Madam." Adam's voice had dropped to a menacing whisper.

"Have you caught the killer yet? Have you identified any suspects? What are you doing to solve this, Adam?"

"I am following procedure. That's all you need to know."

"How can you just sit there with your feet up while there's a killer loose in Pelican Cove?" Jenny fumed. "Crime prevention is also part of your job, Sheriff. And judging by the crime rate here, you are not doing it."

"Thank you for letting me know."

"How dare you!" Jenny shrieked. "How dare you be so flippant when our friend just lost her life?"

"My God, Jenny. Will you stop being so hysterical?" Adam clutched his desk tightly and struggled to his feet. He looked around for his cane. "We are still waiting on the autopsy."

Jenny broke down and sobbed silently.

"Why don't you go home?" Adam said gently. "Take the day off. Let the police do their job."

"You mean let them do nothing," Jenny mumbled through her tears.

"Now, Jenny. You are too close to this. Just stay out of my way and let me do my job."

"Thank you for nothing, Sheriff!" Jenny wailed and stood up to leave.

She slammed the door again on her way out.

Five minutes later, Jenny found herself in front of her friend Jason's office. Jason Stone was Pelican Cove's top lawyer. Actually, he was the only lawyer in town. Jason had known Jenny as a teen when she visited her aunt in the summers. When Jenny came to live in Pelican Cove, Jason had been quick to renew their friendship. He had wooed Jenny along with Adam.

Jenny liked Jason's cheerful, easygoing personality but she had chosen to date Adam. She always turned to Jason in a bind though.

Jason leaped to his feet and came around his desk when he saw Jenny. He wrapped her in a tight embrace.

"How are you holding up?"

"Barely," Jenny sighed. "Tell me this is a nightmare and I am going to wake up soon and find everything as it was."

"Unfortunately, I can't do that."

Jason pulled out a bottle of juice from a small refrigerator and handed it to Jenny.

"Have the police found anything yet?"

Jenny poured out what had happened at the police station.

"Adam's good at his job. He'll get to the bottom of this."

"When?" Jenny asked.

"You know how the law works, Jenny. You will have to be patient."

Jenny went back to the café, angrier than she had been before.

The Magnolias were sitting out on the deck again. None of them had been able to concentrate on work.

"Why don't you go out there?" her aunt suggested. "Lunch is almost ready."

"It's okay," Jenny told Star. "I'll help you dish it up."

She carried a tray loaded with chicken salad sandwiches out to the deck. Her aunt followed with a tray of drinks.

Star had taken care of the lunch rush in Jenny's absence. The Boardwalk Café was the only eating establishment of its kind in Pelican Cove. Jenny knew people depended on her for their meals. She couldn't just close the café when she needed a break.

The girls were quiet as they ate their lunch.

"Yooohooo …"

Jenny cringed as she heard a familiar greeting. A short, plump woman came up the steps from the beach. She took a seat at the table and greeted everyone.

Barb Norton was a force to reckon with in Pelican Cove. She was on various committees and was always scurrying around, working on some project or the other. The older Magnolias didn't care much for her.

"I am so sorry," Barb began. "Pelican Cove has lost a valuable member."

No one said anything.

Barb went on to talk about how Petunia had been a pillar of society.

"What do you want, Barb?" Betty Sue asked between bites of a sandwich.

"I know you were all close to Petunia," Barb said. "And I know you must be grieving. Grief can be crippling. I should know. I lost a few people close to me."

"Get to the point," Star interrupted.

"You need an outlet for your grief," Barb beamed. "And I have just the thing."

"What mad project are you taking up now?" Betty Sue asked.

"You must have noticed the mosquito menace Pelican Cove is facing. Clearly, the town has failed in their pest control efforts this year. I am forming a new committee to take care of the problem."

"What's that got to do with us?" Heather asked sharply.

"The Extermination Committee needs volunteers," Barb announced. "You need something to distract you from this sordid business. I am willing to sign you all up."

"Get out," Jenny seethed. "Just get out of here and leave us alone."

"What's the matter with her?" Barb asked the others. "You do realize I am trying to help?"

"We don't need your help," Jenny said, scrambling to her feet. "We will grieve for Petunia as long as we want and any way we want. How dare you come up here and talk about some useless committee."

Barb puffed up with indignation.

"Useless? The Extermination Committee is not useless. Do you know how deadly mosquitoes can be? We are facing a possible outbreak of West Nile or Zika in Pelican Cove."

"That's fine," Star said. "But you need to leave now, Barb."

"I'm just trying to help!"

"But you're not helping," Betty Sue roared. "Go peddle your project somewhere else."

Barb Norton turned red and stomped down the café steps.

"Unbelievable," Molly fumed. "That woman is vile!"

"She's not entirely wrong," Betty Sue said.

She looked at Jenny.

"I know you have your hands full with the café. But you can't just sit around crying over what happened."

"What do you want me to do, Betty Sue?"

"Find out who killed Petunia."

"She's right, Jenny," Star said. "You have done it before. Use your skills to get to the bottom of this. It's the only way we can get justice for our friend."

"Petunia was shot with a gun," Jenny reminded them. "I have no idea why anyone would do that."

"That's exactly what we need to find out," Heather said. "I'll be your wing woman. In fact, we will all pitch in and help."

"Star and I can take care of the café," Betty Sue agreed. "You girls get busy talking to people."

"Adam won't like it."

"Since when have you done what Adam wanted?" Molly asked.

"Don't let him rule your life, Jenny," Heather added.

"We are not detectives," Jenny reasoned.

"This won't be the first time you solved a murder, Jenny," Star said grimly. "What's holding you back?"

"My friend wasn't the victim all those times," Jenny said, as a tear rolled down her cheek. "I can't be objective about this."

"That's fine," Star said. "Because this is as personal as it gets."

"She's right!" Molly and Heather chorused. "We need you on board, Jenny."

Jenny thought of the sweet old woman who had been a guiding force in her life for the past year and a half. She was just beginning to get to know her. Jenny took a deep breath as her heart filled with a new resolve. She was going to do whatever it took to catch Petunia's killer.

"Let's do this," she said, putting her hand on Heather's. Molly joined in, followed by Star and Betty Sue.

Jenny's eyes burned as she looked around at her friends.

"Best of luck to us."

Chapter 3

Jenny tried to run the Boardwalk Café by herself. She had known Petunia silently did a giant's share of work at the café. She didn't mind the extra work. But she hadn't realized how much she relied on Petunia for the little things. She found herself turning around to ask questions – how many batches of muffins to bake, how much flour to order – only to find out that she was on her own now. Petunia wasn't going to offer any advice in her soft voice.

The Magnolias clung to their routine with a tacit agreement. Betty Sue arrived at 10 AM every morning, lugging her knitting, with Heather close behind. Star and Molly completed the circle.

"Who would you say knew Petunia the best?" Jenny asked one day as they sat out on the deck.

September had brought cool breezes to Pelican Cove but it was still warm enough to sit outside without a jacket or sweater.

"She was a quiet one," Star said. "We knew her well, Betty Sue and I. We have been meeting here every morning forever."

"Even before I came back to town?" Heather asked.

Heather had been away at college and then she had worked in the city for a few years. She had come back to Pelican Cove in her late twenties.

Star nodded.

"You and Molly were in the city. My Jenny wasn't here either."

"She never talked about where she came from?" Jenny asked, surprised.

"She was from somewhere up north," Betty Sue said. "I think she was a widow."

"You think?" Heather pressed. "You don't know for sure?"

"Petunia wasn't very forthcoming about her past life," Star explained. "We realized that early on. We didn't want to pester her about it."

"You think she didn't talk about it for a reason?" Jenny mused.

172

"I always thought something painful had happened to her," Betty Sue said sagely. "Clearly, she didn't want to relive her past. And I didn't think it was my place to remind her of it."

"I get what you're saying ..." Jenny began. "But she never volunteered anything in all these years?"

Star and Betty Sue shook their heads sadly.

"Now we will never know, I suppose," Betty Sue added.

The talk turned to finding out who had murdered Petunia.

"Have you thought of how you are going to begin your search?" Molly asked Jenny.

"Well, I start with people close to the victim. In this case, that's us. I try to learn about any recent events in the victim's life, ask if the victim had any enemies."

She looked around at her friends.

"Can you think of anything out of the ordinary that might have happened this week?"

"Why was Petunia on the beach that morning?" Betty Sue asked immediately.

"And what was she doing there?" Star added. "Shouldn't she have been here at the café, helping you with the morning crowd?"

"Petunia liked to watch the sun rise over the ocean," Jenny told them. "She lingered on the beach sometimes before coming in. But she was always here before me."

"What time was that?" Molly asked, pulling out a notebook and scribbling in it.

Jenny was glad Molly was taking notes. She was too distracted to keep all the facts straight in her head.

"Well, she was here around 5 every day, or earlier. She came in before me and opened the cafe."

"So when did she watch the sunrise?" Heather asked. "Did she go out during the breakfast rush?"

"She would step outside sometimes," Jenny shrugged.

"She didn't come in at all on that day, right?" Betty Sue asked. "Do you mean to say she had been on the beach all along?"

"We don't know the time of her death," Jenny reminded them. "That's something the police will have to tell us. And it's anybody's guess when that will happen."

"Have you talked to Adam?" Molly asked.

"Not since that day," Jenny said, shaking her head. "He can call me whenever he wants."

"You know how Adam is about his job," Heather said. "Don't let it come between you, Jenny."

"Says you?" Jenny asked, rolling her eyes. "Since when did you start giving relationship advice, Heather?"

"Since I learned a bitter lesson or two," Heather shot back. "Ego has no place in love."

"If Adam loves me, he has a weird way of showing it."

"Can you be sure Petunia never came in that day?" Betty Sue asked, setting her knitting aside.

Jenny thought back for a minute.

"I didn't use my key, so the café wasn't locked. She must have come in for a few minutes, I guess."

"So she opened the door for you and then went on the beach right away? Did she do that a lot?"

"Never," Jenny told them. "Petunia brewed the first batch of coffee before I got here. And she used to prep everything for me and turn the oven on."

Jenny held up a hand when she saw her aunt lean forward to ask the next question.

"None of it was done that day. I made the coffee myself."

"I'm writing this down as an outstanding question," Molly remarked. "Why did Petunia go out that morning?"

The group broke up soon after that. Jenny had to get ready for the lunch rush. She chopped vegetables and added them to a big stock pot for making soup.

Her aunt mixed the crab salad.

"You should be at the gallery, or out on a beach somewhere, working on your art," Jenny told her.

"Hush, Jenny," her aunt said. "I am exactly where I need to be."

"How long am I going to impose on you?" Jenny asked. "I have to learn to handle everything by myself."

"Give yourself some time," Star said. "Have you thought of hiring some permanent help?"

Jenny and Petunia hired some students to help them with the summer rush. The kids were back in school.

"I haven't considered that yet," Jenny admitted. "I feel it's too soon."

"You can never replace Petunia," Star read her mind. "We all know that."

Jenny stirred the pot of soup and stared at the wall, lost in thought.

"I need to order supplies for the week ahead," she sighed.

Star pointed to a drawer.

"Petunia was a meticulous record keeper. You should find all her lists in there."

Jenny rifled through the drawer and pulled out a small notebook titled Supplies.

"It's all in here," she nodded.

Petunia had kept copious notes about what needed to be done every week of the month. There was a list of wholesalers she worked with at the back of the book with a rating for each of them.

"There's a treasure trove of information here," Jenny marveled as she pulled out more stuff from the drawer.

Her eyes fell on an appointment book.

"What's this?" she muttered.

It was a small diary with a blue leather cover. Jenny hesitated a bit before opening it.

"Have you seen this before?" Jenny asked her aunt, waving the blue colored book at her. "It looks like a planner of sorts, or an appointment diary. There's a note for a doctor's appointment here, for example. And a dentist's appointment."

"You know we don't use phones or computers to write down our appointments," Star said. "It's how we keep track of the calendar the old fashioned way."

Jenny flipped the pages furiously, searching for something.

"Did I say anything wrong?" Star asked her.

"Not at all. You just gave me a big clue."

Jenny pulled up a page and jabbed her finger at what was written down there.

She sat down next to her aunt and showed her what she had found.

"5 A. M, P/W," she said out loud. "So Petunia was planning to meet someone on the beach that day."

"At 5 in the morning?" Star asked, raising her eyebrows in disbelief.

"Give me a few minutes," Jenny said.

She flipped through the diary again, going slow this time.

"She has this appointment listed on the same day of every month," Jenny said triumphantly. "Who is this 'P/W'? Can you think of anyone?"

"I'm still trying to wrap my head around this," Star muttered. "Why meet someone at 5 in the morning?"

"I need to think about this," Jenny said.

She went out on the deck and began pacing. If Petunia had kept her appointment, she must have been at the bench by 5 AM. That meant she had been killed any time between 5 and 8.

Jenny looked up and saw a familiar figure sitting in the sand. He wore tattered clothes that had clearly seen better days. His salt and pepper beard was as dirty as his face. Jenny had been surprised to see a homeless person in Pelican Cove. The man turned up on the beach sometime in the morning and walked around all day. She would find him writing something in the sand with a stick, then wiping it off with his foot. He did that over and over again. Jenny had wondered if she should offer him anything to eat.

The man turned around and stared directly at the café. Jenny tried to ward off a sudden nervous feeling.

"Hello there," she called out. "How's it going?"

The man shrugged and looked away.

A group of people walked up to the café and Jenny went in. It was time for the lunch rush.

Star was sitting at the kitchen table, looking smug. There was a pile of blue colored notebooks in front of her.

"Look what I found in that drawer."

"Old diaries?" Jenny asked listlessly.

"Old appointment books," her aunt corrected her. "These go back five years. And all of them list the same appointment."

Jenny's eyes gleamed with interest.

"You mean Petunia was meeting someone early in the morning for the past five years?"

"At least that," her aunt nodded.

"She must have trusted this person," Jenny said thoughtfully. "You think he or she is the one who shot her?"

Star shrugged.

"We need to find this person," she said. "Only they can tell us what happened that day."

"But how do we find this 'P/W'?" Jenny asked, sounding defeated.

Jenny got busy filling lunch orders with her aunt's help. The two ladies finally sat back in the kitchen to eat their own lunch.

"Ready to call it a day?" Star asked.

"Why don't you take the car?" Jenny said. "I need to stretch my legs a bit. I will go to the seafood market on my way back."

Jenny checked the next day's menu and prepped as much as she could. She closed the café and walked to Williams Seafood Market. Her friend and Molly's fiancé Chris Williams greeted her.

"How are you holding up, Jenny?" he asked kindly.

Jenny shrugged, swallowing a lump in her throat. She had plodded through the day somehow but it was all coming back to her.

"I'll have the usual, please," she told Chris.

Chris packed a pound of shrimp and three fillets of the catch of the day.

"The catch just came in," he assured her.

Jenny took the package without a word and started walking back home.

A stream of big black SUVs suddenly passed her, stirring up a cloud of dust. Jenny stopped in her tracks, thrown aback by the onslaught. The car windows were so dark it was impossible to see inside. The lead car screeched to a stop with a spin of its tires. The other cars followed suit.

A man jumped out of the car at the front and summoned Jenny.

He was tall and wide and his gigantic belly wobbled every time he moved. He wore a dark shirt and trousers and a black leather jacket. He held out a small piece of paper and asked Jenny for directions.

"What's the holdup, Six Pac?" a high pitched voice demanded from inside.

"Just a minute, Boss!" the man yelled, snatching the paper from Jenny's hands.

"Thanks, doll," he crooned as he climbed back into the car and slammed the door.

The tires spun again and the cars sped off, leaving Jenny standing in the middle of the road, her mouth hanging open.

Chapter 4

Jenny began her day at the Boardwalk Café the next morning.

She chopped sweet peppers for her crab omelet. It was the most popular breakfast special at the Boardwalk Café. She tore off some fresh dill from a bunch and ran her knife through it.

She heard someone come into the café and went outside to take their order. Adam Hopkins stood in his uniform, his hands behind his back.

"Morning, Jenny," he greeted her. "How about a spot of breakfast?"

"Why not?" Jenny said sweetly. "This is a café, after all."

She pulled out a pad and pencil from her apron pocket and asked Adam for his order.

"I'll have whatever you are cooking," he grinned.

Jenny refused to smile back.

She went in and started cooking the omelets. She toasted some whole grain bread while the eggs cooked and put everything on a tray. She added small pots of butter and preserves. She placed the tray before Adam with a bang.

"Thank you," Adam said, picking up his knife and fork.

Heavy footsteps sounded outside. A group of men came in with much fanfare. Jenny assumed they were tourists.

A brown haired man of medium height strode into the café. He wore a three piece suit the color of butter cream. A fedora sat on his head and a cigar dangled from his lips. He was flanked by three men, all wearing neatly pressed shirts and trousers and leather jackets. Jenny recognized the man who had asked her for directions.

"There's no smoking in here," she said.

"Relax, sweetheart," the guy wearing the hat said. "It's not lit."

His high pitched voice grated on Jenny's nerves.

"Can I get you a table?" she asked.

The man in the hat held out his hand.

"Vincenzo Bellini," he offered. "Call me Vinny."

"Hello," Jenny nodded.

She was feeling mystified.

"I'm here to talk about my Ma."

"I'm sorry, but I don't know your mother."

"Sure you do," Vinny said. "She owned this café, didn't she?"

"What nonsense!" Jenny exclaimed.

The three men flanking Vinny sprung into action. Jenny found herself surrounded by them all of a sudden.

"Hey, hey, take it easy, boys," Vinny drawled. "We're just talking here."

"My Ma ran this café for twenty five years," Vinny spoke up. "I'm here to take her home."

Jenny sat down with a thud.

"Are you talking about Petunia?"

Vinny nodded.

"That's the name she went by here. But her real name was Leona."

"I didn't know Petunia had a son," Jenny explained. "She, err, didn't mention she had any kids."

"She had two boys," Vinny said in a matter of fact voice. "The other one lives in California."

Adam stood up and cleared his throat. Jenny had forgotten all about him.

"See you later, Jenny," he said meaningfully and walked out of the café.

Jenny turned back to the man called Vinny.

"How can I help you?"

"I don't need your help, sweetheart. I'm just here to take my Ma home."

"How about some breakfast, doll?" one of Vinny's posse spoke up.

Jenny finally looked at him and tried not to wince. He had a scar on his face, extending from his mouth in a line parallel to his eyes. It looked like a sneer.

Vinny let out a string of expletives.

"Smiley here's been hungry all morning. You think you can feed him something?"

"Sure," Jenny stammered. "How about a blueberry muffin?"

Jenny brought out a basket of muffins and poured fresh coffee. She made omelets for the lot. She had spotted a gun poking out from Smiley's jacket when she poured the coffee. Her hands shook when she placed the platters of food before them.

"Relax, doll," the man called Six Pac said. "We are not here to hurt you."

"Unless you whacked my Ma," Vinny laughed.

"Of course I didn't," Jenny bristled.

The men finished their food and stood up to leave. Vinny put a 100 dollar bill on the table.

"We'll be in touch," he nodded.

Jenny heard tires squealing outside and guessed the men had left in their big black cars. She pulled her apron off and almost jogged to the police station.

Adam was standing in the lobby, reading a file.

"Let's go in," he said, ushering her into his office.

"What's going on?" Jenny asked him, her hands on her hips. "Who were those men?"

Adam leaned back in his chair and put his arms behind his head.

"The mob has arrived in Pelican Cove, Jenny."

"What are you talking about?" Jenny asked, puzzled.

"Vinny 'Twix' Bellini is the scion of the infamous Bellini family."

"Infamous for what?"

"They are a mob family from New Jersey," Adam said coolly. "Enzo

Bellini is the head of the family. They call him the Hawk. He's over 85 but he still calls the shots."

"What are they doing here?"

"Didn't you hear what Vinny said?" Adam asked her. "Petunia was his mother."

"You really believe that?"

"I have been reading up on them since last night," Adam sighed. "State authorities notified us as soon as the Bellinis entered Virginia. Petunia Clark was actually Leona Bellini, Enzo's daughter and Vinny's mother."

"Are you saying Petunia was a criminal?"

Adam shook his head.

"There is no record of that. Petunia just came from a crime family. I am guessing she wanted to escape from it."

"You're saying she came to Pelican Cove to get away?"

"Looks like it."

"Why are they here? What am I supposed to do?"

"They are her next of kin," Adam said reluctantly. "I suppose they are really here to take her back."

"How can they roam around freely if they are criminals?"

"The Bellinis went legit long ago," Adam explained. "They have a string of different businesses – laundries, pizzerias, meat shops – you name it."

"They are carrying guns, Adam," Jenny burst out. "I saw a gun poking out from one guy's jacket."

"He probably has a permit for it."

"Is that all you are going to say?"

"Look. I don't think they are here to make trouble. They will be gone before you know it."

"I hope you're right, Sheriff," Jenny muttered and walked out.

She crossed the road and knocked on Jason's door.

"Jenny!" Jason greeted her with a smile. "I was just about to call you."

"Do you know what's going on in town?" Jenny asked, her chest heaving.

"The Bellinis are here," Jason said calmly.

"You knew?" Jenny exclaimed. "It's all true, then."

"I'm afraid so," Jason said with pursed lips.

"Did we know Petunia at all?" Jenny wailed. "Wait, that wasn't even her real name."

"You need to calm down, Jenny," Jason soothed. "Whatever her name, she was your friend."

"Was she?"

Jason opened a file in front of him.

"The Magnolias meant a lot to her. She left specific instructions for you regarding her last wishes."

"I don't think Vinny's going to like that."

"He doesn't have a choice in the matter," Jason said.

"How long have you been her lawyer, Jason?" Jenny asked.

"For a while. Why?"

"Who else did she hang out with other than us?"

"Honestly, the only people I have seen Petunia talking to were your aunt and Betty Sue. And the people who came into the café, of course."

Jenny told him about the man Petunia had supposedly met every month.

"That's news to me," Jason admitted. "Sounds a bit hush-hush, meeting someone at five in the morning."

"Looks like she was a pro at hiding stuff," Jenny said bitterly.

Petunia had deceived them all and Jenny wasn't happy about it.

"Don't be too hard on her, Jenny," Jason sighed. "Maybe she didn't have a choice."

Jenny returned to the café with a heavy heart. There was a mad rush at the café for lunch and Jenny barely had a minute to spare. Vinny and his posse came back for lunch. Jenny knew they had very few choices to eat out in Pelican Cove. That meant they were living somewhere in town.

Jenny talked to Captain Charlie later that day.

"I'm trying to make a list of Petunia's friends. Did you see her talking to someone in particular?"

"Your aunt and Betty Sue were about the only friends she had," Captain Charlie said. "And you young girls, of course."

"She must have had other friends in town?" Jenny persisted.

"I don't think so," Captain Charlie said. "Say. What's this I hear about some thugs claiming they knew our Petunia?"

"It's true."

Jenny gave Captain Charlie the short version. He whistled in amazement.

Jenny went to the café early the next morning. She made coffee and put a batch of muffins into the oven. Then she took a photo of Petunia and went out on the beach.

A few runners appeared at one end. Jenny stopped them and showed them the photo.

"Did you see this woman talking to anyone on this beach?"

Her first few attempts were futile. A woman walking a golden retriever seemed eager to chat.

"Everyone knew Petunia. It's a shame what happened to her."

"Do you come here often?" Jenny asked.

"Every morning, come rain or shine," the woman boasted. "This guy won't let me sleep," she said, ruffling her dog's coat. "We usually hit the beach by 5:30. Sometimes even before that."

"Have you ever seen Petunia walking around?"

"Sometimes," the woman nodded. "She used to sit on a bench, watching the sun come up."

"Did you see her talking to anyone?"

"We chatted sometimes," the woman nodded. "That is, when she wasn't hanging out with that friend."

Jenny tried to curb her excitement.

"Is he local?"

"I guess," the woman shrugged. "Must be, right? I've seen him here plenty of times."

Jenny thanked the woman and hurried back to her café. She was sure the mysterious 'P/W' did exist. Now she just needed to find out who he was.

Jenny served a few people and put a fresh batch of muffins in the oven. She stepped out on the beach again, armed with Petunia's photo.

Her queries yielded some more information this time. She could barely wait for the Magnolias.

The women were seated on the deck, sipping their mid-morning coffee.

"Guess what I found," Jenny said, her eyes shining. "I'm sure 'P/W' is a guy. Tall, dark, probably a local."

"That doesn't tell us much," Molly complained. "Could you be more specific?"

"That's all I found out," Jenny said glumly.

"Who's that?" Heather said suddenly.

She had spotted Vinny and his posse on the beach. Vinny was walking a beagle, dressed in a suit and his signature hat. The leather jackets tagged along behind him.

"Aren't they staying at the Bayview Inn?" Jenny asked.

Vinny looked up just then and waved. He came up the steps to talk to the women. Six Pac took the leash from him and scooped up the beagle in his arms.

"Howdy ladies," he greeted them. "That lawyer fella told me what my Ma wanted. I'm cool with it."

Star looked at him with interest. Betty Sue had dropped her knitting and was muttering something under her breath.

"Do you know someone called 'P/W'?" Jenny asked suddenly.

"What kinda name is that?" Vinny asked. "Never heard of him."

"Looks like your mother knew him or her."

"My Ma walked out on me when I was 17. I never saw her after that. She might have known Spiderman for all I know."

"I'm sorry," Jenny said.

"It's not your fault, sweetheart."

Vinny turned around and walked down the steps. Jenny saw him take the beagle in his arms and hug it as he walked away.

Why had Petunia deserted her family? Did it have any bearing on why someone shot her?

Chapter 5

The rays of the setting sun bathed the garden at Seaview in a golden glow. In her newly renovated kitchen, Jenny tore basil leaves and added them to the pasta salad. The fish had been pan fried in a lemon butter sauce. Star's favorite shrimp had been tossed in the same butter and sprinkled with Old Bay seasoning. It was the signature spice of the island. No meal was complete without it.

"Dinner's ready," she called out.

Star and Jimmy Parsons walked into the dining room, hand in hand. Jimmy had been better known as the town drunk for several years. His family owned the Pelican Cove light house and a small piece of land attached to it. Jenny had discovered Jimmy's feelings for her aunt. He had cleaned up his act and had been sober for a while. Star reciprocated his feelings and the two had become inseparable.

"This salad is delicious, Jenny," Jimmy complimented her.

They were halfway through the meal when Jimmy asked Jenny about Petunia.

"Any luck?"

Jenny shook her head.

"Did you know Petunia had family in New Jersey? Apparently, they are a different kind of family."

"They are living in one of my cottages," Jimmy disclosed.

Star looked at him in surprise.

"You never told me that."

"I didn't know myself," Jimmy admitted. "Some girl called me claiming to be assistant to the head of a company. Said he wanted to spend some time on the Shore. I had no idea who was going to turn up."

"So that's where Vinny is staying," Jenny muttered.

"Him and his posse," Jimmy nodded. "They paid up for two months in advance."

"Two months? What are they going to do here for that long?"

"No idea."

"Do you think this man Petunia met secretly might have been Vinny?" Jenny asked her aunt.

"What man?" Jimmy asked, cutting a big chunk of his fish.

Jenny told him about the entries in Petunia's diary.

"Someone on the beach must have seen them."

"I asked a lot of people," Jenny explained. "All I know is he's some tall, dark guy. That could be anyone."

"Don't forget 'P/W'," her aunt reminded her.

"What's that?"

"That's how Petunia referred to the meeting in her diary," Jenny told Jimmy. "We have no idea what they mean."

"They could be initials of the person," Jimmy said.

"I never thought of that!" Jenny exclaimed. "Where's the phone book? Maybe this person is listed in it."

"Shouldn't take long," Star said. "How many people have a name starting with W anyway?"

Jimmy had cleaned his plate. He pushed it away and sipped his lemonade.

"Wait a minute. I know a 'P/W'."

"What?" Star and Jenny cried together.

"Peter Wilson," he said flatly. "You know him well, Star."

"The auto shop guy?" Star scoffed. "Why would Petunia go and meet him at 5 in the morning?"

"The initials match," Jimmy reminded her.

"Who is this guy?" Jenny asked.

"Car mechanic," Jimmy said, draining his lemonade. "Has an auto shop in town – Wilson Auto Shop? You must have seen it, Jenny. It's about a quarter mile on your left when you drive off the bridge and enter

Pelican Cove."

Jenny had never noticed the auto shop.

"Petunia hid a lot from us," Jenny reminded her aunt. "Who knows what business she had with this Wilson guy?"

"Only one way to find out," Jimmy said.

Jenny was at the Boardwalk Café at 5 AM the next morning. Star arrived a couple of hours later to help her.

Jason Stone walked in after the breakfast rush had abated.

"Just the man I wanted to see," Jenny squealed.

Jason gave her a dubious smile. "What's going on, Jenny?"

"Do you know a Peter Wilson?"

"The car mechanic? Sure. Almost everyone in town knows him."

"Can you go with me to meet him?"

"Your car acting up? Why don't I take a look at it?"

Jenny shook her head.

"My car's fine. I'll bring you up to speed on the way."

Jenny packed a chocolate muffin for Jason's breakfast and handed him a large cup of coffee. She promised her aunt she would be back before the lunch rush. Grabbing another muffin for herself, she propelled Jason out of the café.

Jason munched on his muffin while Jenny explained who Peter Wilson was.

"You think he's going to be upfront with you?" he quizzed.

Jenny didn't have an answer for that.

Peter Wilson was a tall, dark haired man dressed in grease stained jeans and flannel. Jenny guessed he was a few years older than her.

He gave Jenny a curious look and shook hands with Jason.

"Something wrong with that fancy car of yours?" he asked.

"Jenny here wants to talk to you about something."

"Hi," Jenny began. "My name is Jenny King. I work at the Boardwalk

Café with Petunia."

"I know who you are," Peter Wilson nodded. "My wife loves your cupcakes. They are something else."

Jenny thanked him for the compliment.

"Do you know Petunia Clark?" she asked tentatively. "I mean, did you know her?"

"Sure," Peter Wilson shrugged. "Everyone in town knew her."

"Did you know her personally?"

Peter Wilson wiped a wrench with a dirty rag.

"What are you getting at?"

"Look. You know someone shot Petunia, right?" Jenny's voice quavered a bit but she plunged ahead. "I'm trying to find out what happened."

Peter's eyebrows shot up.

"You think I had something to do with it?"

"I found an appointment book," Jenny explained. "It says Petunia was going to meet you that day at 5 AM."

Jenny crossed her fingers behind her back while she spoke.

Peter's face crumpled.

"I was supposed to meet her, okay? But I didn't. My kid was sick. I was in the emergency room all night with my wife. That's where I heard about what happened."

"What was your meeting about?"

"It was private business," Peter Wilson shrugged again. "You don't need to know."

"Petunia's gone now," Jenny reasoned. "Look, I'm not sure how you knew her. But it looks like you had been meeting her for a while. Don't you want her killer found?"

Peter Wilson hesitated.

"I was just keeping an eye on her," he finally said. "Making sure she was alright."

"Why would you do that?"

"It's a long story," Peter said grudgingly. "I knew her way back when."

Jenny's eyes widened.

"Did you know her as Leona?"

Peter Wilson finally showed some emotion.

"Where did you get that name?"

"Vinny told me everything," Jenny said smugly. "Vinny Bellini. He was Petunia's son."

"Vinny's in town," Jason added. "Do you know him?"

"Vinny doesn't know about me, okay?" Peter Wilson burst out. "I work for the Hawk."

"Your secret's safe with us," Jenny assured him. "Why don't you tell us everything?"

"Leona, she walked out on the family one day. The Hawk, that's her papa, told me to keep an eye on her. I followed her down the coast to this little town. I been here ever since."

"So you're with the family?" Jenny asked.

Peter Wilson shrugged.

"I was twenty five when I came here. I set up this garage and stayed on. I met a local girl and married her. I never went back."

"Why were you meeting Petunia?"

"We have been meeting once a month for twenty five years," Peter said. "My job was to make sure she was doing okay. I called the Hawk and let him know how his little girl was doing."

"Petunia knew that?"

Peter shrugged.

"It was the only way the Hawk would let her live on her own."

"Why meet at 5 in the morning?"

"It was her idea." Peter shrugged again.

"Do you have any idea who shot her?" Jenny asked.

"Leona's secret was safe here. People forgot about her a long time ago."

Jenny and Jason drove back to town.

"Do you think he's a mobster too?" Jenny asked him.

"Ask your boyfriend," Jason grinned. "You should tell him about Peter."

They went to the police station and walked into Adam's office. Adam thanked them for the information.

"So Peter Wilson is part of the Bellini family? That's news to us."

"Any other updates?" she asked Adam.

"We are doing our job," Adam told her curtly.

"What now?" Jenny said when they came out of the police station.

Barb Norton waved at her from a sidewalk. She seemed to have forgotten about their earlier altercation.

"What is she up to now?" Jenny muttered to Jason.

"Do you have a few minutes, Jenny?" Jason asked. "We need to discuss something."

They went to Jason's office.

"What is it?" Jenny asked urgently.

"It's about Petunia's will," Jason admitted. "Can we talk about it now?"

"Is this about her last wishes? Maybe we should get all the Magnolias here."

"It's more than that," Jason hastened to explain. "This particularly concerns you."

"How so?"

"She left you the Boardwalk Café."

"I plan to continue working there," Jenny assured him. "As long as I'm not booted out."

"That's just it, Jenny," Jason smiled. "You own it free and clear. It's yours to do with as you please. Petunia hoped you would continue running it though."

"What?" Jenny cried. "I don't believe it. Why would she do that? She barely knew me."

"You meant a lot to her, Jenny. The rest of her estate will be settled between her sons."

"She had more money?" Jenny asked, surprised.

"Millions," Jason nodded. "It was part of her big inheritance from her father. She never touched it. Vinny and his brother get it all."

"I need a drink," Jenny said, still feeling dazed. "What am I going to do with the café, Jason?"

"Just keep working your magic," Jason laughed. "And keep supplying me with chocolate cake."

Jason pulled out a chilled bottle of water from the refrigerator and handed it to Jenny.

"I would much rather have her by my side," Jenny said softly.

"I know," Jason said, squeezing her trembling hand.

The midmorning sun warmed her back as Jenny walked back to the café, feeling guilty about benefiting from her friend's death. She thought about selling the café and donating the money to charity. But she loved the Boardwalk Café. She could picture herself working there for years, baking sweet treats, making chocolates and feeding locals and tourists healthy, wholesome meals.

Jenny struggled with her thoughts as she fried shrimp for the lunch special. She generously sprinkled them with seasoning and assembled the po'boy sandwiches that were so popular. She put two sandwiches in a brown paper bag and went out on the deck. Her eyes scanned the beach, searching for a familiar figure.

The man stood at the water's edge, drawing something in the sand with his stick.

"Hello there," Jenny called out, walking toward him.

The man stared at her through hooded eyes.

Jenny offered him the brown paper bag.

"I am trying out a new recipe. Why don't you tell me how you like it?"

"I don't take charity," the man mumbled.

"It's not charity," Jenny said hastily. "You'd be doing me a favor. I really need some feedback."

The man peered into the bag suspiciously. He pulled out the roll, bursting with crunchy fried shrimp. He stared at it longingly.

"Please," Jenny said. "I need your help."

The man took a small bite and chewed slowly. He took a bigger bite and wolfed the sandwich down in two minutes.

"It's good," he said. "A bit spicy."

"I'll tone down the spice then," Jenny agreed.

The man was pulling out the second sandwich.

"Are you from around here?" she asked. "I'm new in town myself."

"Came here for a job," the man offered reluctantly.

"Me too," Jenny said. "Where's your family?"

"Up in the mountains," the man mumbled.

"My son lives away from me too," Jenny volunteered. "I miss him."

The man laughed suddenly. He had finished eating the sandwich. He thrust the brown paper bag in Jenny's hands. He picked up his stick and gave her a salute.

Before Jenny could say anything else, the man turned his back on her and started walking away. He scratched something in the sand with his stick and rubbed it off with his foot, muttering to himself.

Jenny realized she didn't even know his name.

Chapter 6

The Magnolias had gathered on the deck of the Boardwalk Café.

"We need to send our girl off in style," Betty Sue ordained. "Spare no effort or expense."

"Petunia left clear instructions about what she wants," Star reminded her.

"We'll do all that," Jenny nodded. "And we'll throw her the biggest party this town has ever seen. Right here at the Boardwalk Café."

"That's a great idea, Jenny," Molly said eagerly. "How can I help?"

"We'll have a party alright," Heather said emphatically. "But what about finding out who shot Petunia? Have you made any progress at all, Jenny?"

Jenny told them about meeting Peter Wilson.

"Adam says his real name is Fabio Lombardi. He was being trained as a capo or something before he dropped everything and came here."

"So he gave up a fancy career in the mob to come look after our Petunia?" Heather asked.

"Sounds like it," Jenny agreed.

"Does he have a gun?" Molly asked. "Why couldn't he be our shooter?"

"He was more like a bodyguard, remember?" Jenny said. "And he has an alibi. He was in the hospital all night, taking care of his sick kid."

"Bummer," Heather said. "That would have been too easy."

"Does anyone benefit from Petunia's death?" Betty Sue asked. "Isn't that what you always look for, Jenny?"

"You're right, Betty Sue. Jason told me Petunia left all her money to her sons."

"So that goon Vinny benefits?" Molly asked.

"He's not going to kill his mother for a few dollars," Star dismissed.

"She walked away from him," Jenny mused. "And it's not just a few dollars, Star. Jason said it's in millions."

"Maybe you should talk to him," Betty Sue said grimly.

Heather and Molly jumped up.

"We are coming with you, Jenny."

"He's living in one of Jimmy's cottages," Jenny said. "It's barely a mile out."

Jenny told them to settle down. She assembled some sandwiches for lunch and made sure Star could handle the crowd by herself.

Vinny walked into the café just as they were getting ready to leave.

"Hello sweetheart," he said, smiling at Jenny.

Vinny was dressed in another cream colored suit, with his signature hat perched jauntily on his head. His three companions wore their uniform of dark clothes and leather jackets. Jenny figured they spent more on their wardrobe than she did.

"I was just coming to see you, Vinny," Jenny said.

"It's my lucky day," he smiled. "How about a spot of lunch? We are starving."

Jenny led them out on the deck.

"I would kill for this view," Vinny drawled.

He laughed heartily when he saw the expression on Jenny's face.

"Relax, I'm joking."

Six Pac, Smiley and the third man sprawled on the chairs around Vinny. Jenny had learned he was called Biggie. He was barely five feet tall and weighed under a hundred pounds.

Chowder was on the menu that day, with tomato mozzarella sandwiches. Vinny tucked a napkin under his chin and started on his soup. He waved a hand at Jenny.

"What did you want to talk about?"

"Jason told me Petunia left you a lot of money."

Vinny shrugged.

"A little bit. Why?"

"How do I know you didn't shoot her for the money?"

Vinny put the spoon back in his soup. His eyes had turned hard.

"You think I killed my Ma?"

"You could have," Jenny said boldly. "Where were you that day between 5 and 8."

"I was up in Jersey sleeping next to my wife," Vinny said coldly. "Not that I owe you any explanation."

Smiley spoke up.

"You got some guts, lady."

"A few million dollars is a lot of money," Jenny mumbled.

"You know how much money I got?" Vinny asked her with a smile. "I have billions, in this country and offshore. I don't need the money."

"Maybe you had a grudge against her," Jenny shrugged.

"For the last time, lady, I didn't whack my Ma."

Vinny slurped the last of his soup and picked up his sandwich.

"Someone told me you are some hotshot detective. Is this all you got?"

"Money is generally a big motive," Jenny persisted.

"That lawyer told me my Ma left you this café," Vinny said. "How do I know you didn't pull the trigger?"

"I would never do that!" Jenny said, sucking in her breath. "I loved Petunia. She gave me a chance when I had nothing."

"Okay," Vinny said, nodding his head. "So you and I both had nothing to do with it. Let's agree on that, shall we?"

Jenny found herself nodding her head.

"I want you to find out who shot my Ma," Vinny continued. "Name your price."

"I don't want money," Jenny said, scandalized. "I want justice for Petunia."

"Okay then," Vinny said. "Just let me know if I can help."

Vinny and his goons stayed on the deck for the next couple of hours, eating pie and drinking coffee.

Jenny walked to the police station as soon as they left.

"Any updates?" she asked Adam. "Do you have any suspects yet?"

"One or two," Adam said, looking at her thoughtfully.

"Who is it?" Jenny asked. "Her sons inherit millions from her death. You think they have a part in this?"

"Her sons are already rolling in money," Adam told her. "I don't think a few millions would make a difference."

"So money wasn't the motive?"

Adam shrugged.

"Hard to say."

"What do you mean, Adam?"

"Don't you inherit the café?" he asked.

Jenny's face changed color as she processed what Adam had said.

"You think I had something to do with it?"

"I don't think that, Jenny. But since we are talking about motives …"

"I had a generous divorce settlement. I don't need the money."

Adam leaned forward, twirling a pencil in his hand.

"You spent most of it on buying that monstrous house of yours. The café is an unexpected windfall. Admit it."

"Of course it's unexpected," Jenny cried. "You think I knew this was going to happen?"

"The Boardwalk Café is an asset you can bank on for the rest of your life."

"You know what I earned at the café last year?" Jenny asked. "Nothing! That's because I didn't take any pay. The café was barely breaking even. In fact, I put up some capital to help Petunia out."

"Did you disagree with the way Petunia was running the café?"

"No. Why are you asking all these questions?"

"You changed the menu, didn't you? Did Petunia agree with your ideas?"

"She was a bit hesitant at first, I guess," Jenny said honestly. "But she saw how popular my food was getting. She was the one who suggested we revamp the menu."

"You're sure you didn't have any arguments with her?"

"Where is all this going, Adam?" Jenny asked, frustrated. "Why are you giving me the third degree?"

Adam sighed.

"The police are looking at you as a person of interest, Jenny."

"That's ridiculous!"

"Is it?" Adam asked. "You stood to gain by Petunia's death. You were right there at five in the morning. And you were very familiar with Petunia's routine."

"I don't have a gun."

"That's the only thing in your favor."

"You don't really think I am guilty?"

"I'm just doing my job, Jenny."

Jenny's gaze hardened as she folded her arms.

"I guess I better go get a lawyer then."

"That's a good idea," Adam agreed.

Jenny walked out without another word.

Molly was waiting for her at the Boardwalk Café. She jumped up as soon as she saw Jenny.

"Can we talk?" she asked urgently.

"Sure, Molly," Jenny said, taking her hands in hers. "What's the matter?"

Molly burst into tears.

"It's so unexpected. I don't know what to do."

"Calm down and take a deep breath," Jenny ordered. "I'm making some chamomile tea for us."

Jenny brewed tea while Molly paced in the tiny kitchen.

"What's going on? Why are you so nervous?"

Jenny took Molly by the shoulders and made her sit down.

"Tell me everything," Jenny said gently, adding honey to their tea and placing a cup before Molly.

"I think I'm pregnant!" Molly blurted.

"That's wonderful news, Molly," Jenny said, her eyes shining with pleasure. "That's the best thing I have heard in the past few days."

"How could this happen, Jenny?"

"Do I really need to tell you that?" Jenny joked. "Have you told Chris yet?"

"No. And I'm not going to."

"Why not?"

"It's too soon, Jenny. We haven't talked about starting a family. I don't even know if he wants kids."

"Of course he wants kids," Jenny argued. "He's young and single. He's never been married. Why wouldn't he want children of his own?"

Molly considered that for a moment.

"It does seem logical," she agreed. "But what if he's mad at me for this?"

"Chris is a sensible young man," Jenny said firmly. "He's going to support you through this. I'm sure."

"We just started seeing each other," Molly mumbled.

"You love him, don't you?" Jenny asked.

"This is a big decision," Molly said, shaking her head. "I am not sure what I want myself."

"I think you should discuss this with Chris."

"I don't want him to influence me either way. Maybe I should sit on this for a while."

"Is that fair to him?"

"I don't know, Jenny," Molly said, finally taking a sip of her tea.

Jenny talked with Molly some more, forcing her to calm down. Heather burst into the café, slightly out of breath.

"I called her," Molly told Jenny.

Heather collapsed in a chair.

"Sorry I'm late. I was helping Grandma with laundry."

"Molly has some news," Jenny smiled. "Tell her, Molly."

Heather clapped her hands in glee when she heard.

"That's fantastic! Why don't you look happy, Molls?"

"She's still processing it," Jenny explained. "I was dazed for days when I found out I was pregnant with Nick."

The girls talked for a while, trying to cheer Molly up.

"Are you coming to the town hall meeting tonight?" Heather asked them. "Barb's forming her mosquito committee."

"You mean she was serious about that whole extermination thing?" Jenny asked.

"Of course," Heather laughed. "Barb's always serious about her projects. She is asking for volunteers."

"I have my hands full at the café," Jenny said.

"That won't matter to Barb," Heather told her. "I'm sure she will rope you in one way or the other."

"That sounds ominous."

"No one in this town has ever escaped from Barb's clutches."

Jenny was tired from her long day but she forced herself to get started on the next day's prep. An hour later, she went home, her mind in turmoil. Her aunt made her famous baked macaroni and cheese for dinner.

"Where's Jimmy?" Jenny asked.

"He's having dinner with some friends tonight," Star said

diplomatically.

Jenny knew that was code for a support group meeting.

"Jimmy's doing good, huh?" she asked her aunt.

Star blushed and nodded.

"Have you finalized the menu for the memorial?" she asked.

"Why don't we talk about it now?" Jenny offered. "We need all Petunia's favorite dishes. She loved my crab puffs, and the tiny pimento cheese sandwiches. We'll have fish and chips from Ethan's Crab Shack. I'll make a few salads."

"What about desserts?"

"Cupcakes and the chocolate berry cake she liked."

"People will bring food, you know," Star warned. "Get ready for a lot of casseroles."

"Have you made a guest list?"

"Oh honey," Star said sadly. "We don't need a guest list. The whole town will turn up."

"What about Vinny?"

"I expect he will turn up too," Star said.

"I can't believe she's gone," Jenny said, fighting back tears. "How are we going to survive without her?"

Chapter 7

A big black SUV with dark windows screeched to a stop in front of the Boardwalk Café. A short, skinny man wearing a red track suit and a white fedora stepped out. He tottered into the café, followed by a tall, beefy man dressed in a leather jacket. The old man sat at a window table. His companion stood behind him.

Jenny greeted the man with a smile.

"What can I get you?"

"You must be Jenny," the old man said. "Sit down."

Jenny stared back at him, mystified.

"The boss wants you to sit," the tall man repeated.

Jenny pulled out a chair and sat down.

"I'm Enzo Bellini," the old man said.

He spoke in a soft voice, almost a whisper. Jenny had to lean forward to hear his voice.

"Oh," Jenny said. "Did you know Petunia?"

The man nodded.

"She was my daughter."

His hand shook as he picked up a salt shaker and played with it.

"I know all about you," Enzo nodded. "You were good to my baby girl."

"You have it all wrong," Jenny said. "She was good to me."

"I got updates from my man here," Enzo said. "He talked to my girl every month."

"Thanks for coming for her funeral," Jenny said. "I know you probably wanted to take her home with you."

Don Enzo pulled out a cigar from his pocket. The man standing behind him lit it for him. Jenny didn't dare to tell him about the No Smoking rule.

"Don't know what she saw in this place," Enzo said. He used a string of profanities to describe the place. "But this little bitty town was home to her."

"You must have missed her all these years."

"How about some coffee?" the old man whispered, puffing on his cigar. "I hear you can bake a cake or two."

Jenny leapt up and went inside. She made a fresh pot of coffee and placed some cupcakes on a plate. She took them out to the old man.

Enzo's hand trembled as he picked up the coffee cup. Some of the dark liquid spilled over.

"I have the Parkinson's," he told Jenny. "It's supposed to get worse."

Jenny guessed the old man was well into his eighties. He was in quite good health, considering.

"Tell me about Petunia," she urged.

"Never liked that name," Enzo spat. "What kind of darn fool name is that? Her name was Leona. She was as strong and brave as a lion."

"Was she your only child?"

"The only one who gave me grandkids. My sons died long ago."

"Must have been hard to see her go."

Enzo shrugged.

"Leona, she had a mind of her own. She married young but she never liked the family business."

"What did her husband do?"

"He was my capo," Enzo said.

Jenny decided she needed to look up some mob lingo.

"Kind of like a manager," Enzo explained, guessing her thoughts. "He got gunned down."

"Oh!" Jenny stared back at Enzo, wide eyed.

"All in a day's work," Enzo said with a shrug. "Leona said it was the last straw. She wasn't having any more of it."

"How did she come to Pelican Cove? Did you know anyone here?"

"She got into the car and started driving. She trusted this guy called Fabio. He was her husband's right hand man. I made him follow her. He told me she had stopped in some small seaside town."

"It's not that far from Jersey," Jenny mused.

"It's far enough," Enzo cackled. "I bought her a house and this café. Told Fabio to stay back here and keep an eye on her."

"Did you come visit?"

Enzo shook his head mournfully.

"She didn't want to talk to me in those days. Then I got busted. Spent twenty years in the slammer. I made Leona promise me something. She gave monthly reports to Fabio. He told me how things were going with her."

"What about her kids?"

"Leaving them was the hardest thing she ever did. She wanted them to go with her but they both refused. They were old enough to say what they wanted."

"So Vinny and his brother grew up without a mother?"

"They were already grown. Vinny was 17 when my Leona left. Baby — that's Charles, Vinny's brother - was 15."

"So there's no reason why Vinny would have a grudge against Petunia?"

"That boy is a complete idiot," Enzo hissed. "I don't trust him. I don't trust him at all."

"You think he shot Petunia?" Jenny asked with a gasp.

Enzo whistled through the gap in his teeth. "He could have. Vinny has a temper. He shoots first and asks questions later."

Jenny wondered how much she could believe the old man.

"Did Vinny know Petunia lived here in Pelican Cove?"

Enzo looked puzzled.

"I don't know."

He struggled to stand up and swayed on his feet. The henchman behind him caught him by the elbow and steadied him.

"Thank you for being there for my daughter," Enzo said to Jenny. "I won't forget it."

He shuffled out slowly and walked toward his car. The car had been running all this time with headlights on. It rolled forward as soon as Enzo slammed the door, spewing smoke in the atmosphere. Jenny stood staring after it.

"What are you staring at?" Heather tapped her on the shoulder.

"Heather!" Jenny exclaimed with a start. "I didn't see you come in."

"I'm here to assist with lunch."

"Thanks, I could really use the help."

Jenny stirred a pot of minestrone soup while Heather spooned crab salad on slices of bread. The aroma of fresh baked chocolate chip cookies wafted through the kitchen. Heather arranged two sandwiches on a plate and took a photo.

"That's for Instagram," she told Jenny. "You need to let people know you are still serving crab."

"Social media is the last thing on my mind right now," Jenny confessed.

"I know," Heather winced. "But don't forget you have a business to run, Jenny. This café is Petunia's legacy. We need to keep it alive and flourishing."

"When did you get so smart?" Jenny joked.

"I dropped the ball this past year," Heather said seriously. "I fought with Grandma, neglected the inn and dated one deadbeat after another. I'm turning over a new leaf now."

"Good for you," Jenny praised. "So what's the plan?"

"The inn hasn't been doing well," Heather shared. "I need to rebuild our brand and drum up more business. That's the first thing on my agenda."

"That's a great idea, Heather," Jenny said solemnly. "Let me know if I can help."

"I might take you up on that," Heather nodded. "We will continue to serve breakfast from the Boardwalk Café. That's not going to change. In fact, I am going to advertise it in our new brochures."

"Why don't we offer a discount to your guests?" Jenny asked eagerly. "50% off to guests of the Bayview Inn. That will help us both build business."

"Alright!" Heather crowed, giving Jenny a high five. "Now, if only we could get rid of these mosquitoes."

"You sound like Barb Norton," Jenny laughed.

"She has a point, you know," Heather said. "We had two guests check out yesterday because of the mosquitoes. Said they didn't come here to get Zika."

"That's crazy!" Jenny moaned. "Does that mean we should go volunteer for Barb's committee?"

"Didn't you hear? Barb has already dispatched her minions. They are going to inspect gardens and yards and report to her."

"Report what?"

"I guess we'll know soon enough," Heather laughed. "Barb's not going to be quiet about it."

Jenny breezed through the lunch rush with Heather's help. She packed a couple of sandwiches and cookies in a basket. It reminded her of how Petunia used to pack lunch for her and Adam. Jenny walked to the police station, hoping Adam hadn't eaten yet. She hadn't called ahead for a reason.

"Is that for me?" Adam smiled when he saw the basket on her arm. "I'm starving."

"Let's eat," Jenny nodded, unpacking a couple of plates.

She unwrapped the sandwiches and opened a packet of chips. Adam tore the plastic wrap off a dill pickle and munched on it.

"How was your meeting with the don?" he asked.

"You know about that?"

"Don Enzo or the Hawk is the head of the Bellini family. Of course we are keeping a close eye on him."

"He looks like a harmless old man."

"This harmless old man has confessed to multiple heinous crimes."

"You don't think he would harm his own daughter?"

Adam shook his head.

"He has a strong alibi. We checked."

"Have you learned anything new?"

"We found the type of gun used to shoot Petunia," Adam told her. "It's an advanced type. I'm sure no one in Pelican Cove owns that kind of a gun."

"Does that mean she was shot by a tourist?"

Adam was quiet. Jenny talked out loud as she ate her lunch.

"Why would a tourist do that? What motive would they have to kill Petunia?"

"You hit the nail on the head," Adam agreed. "I admit I am stumped."

"Would a mob man own that kind of gun?" Jenny asked.

"They might," Adam said. "And there's one person in town that fits the bill."

"Who is it?"

"Peter Wilson," Adam said reluctantly. "Or Fabio Lombardi. Do you know he was called The Triggerman back in the day? He was training to be a capo. He is rumored to have gunned down a dozen men once. But nothing was ever proven."

Jenny thought of the tall, quiet man she had met in the auto shop. She trembled as she imagined him holding a gun and shooting someone.

"He seemed pretty normal."

"As far as we know, Wilson gave all that up. He's been living on the straight and narrow all these years."

"So you don't suspect him at all?"

"He would have been my top suspect," Adam sighed. "But plenty of people saw him in the emergency room. He never left the building. There's no way he could have been at the beach between five and eight that morning."

"What about Vinny?" Jenny asked. "He says he was at home with his wife."

"Guys like Vinny don't get their hands dirty, Jenny. They hire people."

"What about those guys who follow him around? Six Pac or Smiley? They all carry guns."

"We are checking their alibis now."

"I wonder why Petunia's other son hasn't come here yet."

"Charles Bellini?" Adam asked. "He left the business long ago, just like Petunia. He's a school teacher out in California."

"We are not getting anywhere," Jenny said, sounding defeated. "What if it was a tourist who was just driving through town? We will never find him."

"He will slip up somewhere," Adam promised. "We will catch him then."

"Are we meeting later tonight?" Jenny asked shyly. "It's been a while since you came for a walk on the beach."

"I've been busy," Adam said curtly. Then he gave her a wink. "But I might be heading home early tonight."

Jenny walked out of the police station, reflecting on how they seemed to have no tangible leads. Were they ever going to find out what happened to Petunia?

She decided to take the scenic route back to the café. A familiar figure squatted on the beach, scrawling something in the sand with his stick. Jenny ventured closer and greeted him.

The man stared back at her with eyes the color of the ocean.

"Hello there," she said. "You never told me your name."

"Mason," the man mumbled.

"I'm Jenny. Would you like a crab sandwich? I miscalculated and now I have plenty left over. I'll be eating them all week if you don't help me out."

"If it's no trouble," the man said, staring at his feet.

Chapter 8

Another sunny day dawned in Pelican Cove. The Magnolias stuck to their routine, silently coming to terms with their grief.

Star crumbled a blueberry muffin with her fingers and looked around at her friends. Molly was buried in a book and Betty Sue was busy knitting. Heather was fiddling with her phone as usual. Jenny stared at the ocean, a sad look in her eyes.

"Have you talked to any more people about that day?" Star asked her.

Jenny shook her head.

"The only people I talked to were regulars, people who go for a run or walk on the beach in the morning. But that doesn't include any tourists who might have been staying in town at that time."

"What about that camera?" Heather said, pointing at a spot on the roof. "Have you checked the footage for that day?"

Jenny's eyes grew wide as she turned to look up at the roof.

"I forgot all about it."

The Boardwalk Café had been the target of vandalism a few months ago. Adam had insisted they install security cameras at the front and back of the café. The camera captured a small portion of the beach adjoining the café on both sides.

"I am surprised the police haven't been here for those tapes," Molly said.

"Do you think we'll find something?" Jenny asked eagerly.

"Only one way to know," Heather said dryly. "Does that thing come with a tape of some kind?"

"Petunia insisted we get the best system available," Jenny said soberly. "It's state of the art. Uploads the video online, I think. I read the manual when we first got it but now I forgot all about it."

Heather sprang up and walked closer to the wall. She peered up at the camera and fed something into her phone.

"Give me a minute," she said. She looked up a few minutes later. "This should come with a recorder. Do you have a DVR like box somewhere? Something that looks like a DVD player?"

"I think so," Jenny said uncertainly. "Let's check in the office."

The office was nothing but a small closet that housed a computer and other knick knacks. Petunia had used the space for doing accounts and keeping track of inventory. Jenny had hardly ever gone in there, assuming it was Petunia's private domain.

Heather pointed to a black box that sat on a shelf.

"Looks like it's already hooked up to this screen."

She clicked a few more buttons and an image showed up on the screen. It was the beach at the back of the café.

"This shows footage for the past few days," Heather explained. "When do you want to go through this?"

"No time like the present," Jenny said.

Molly, Jenny and Heather squashed into the tiny office and held their breaths as the camera rolled.

A woman walking a dog came into view.

"That's the woman I spoke to," Jenny cried. "I recognize her."

The camera had captured all the people who came into range.

"Is that all you have?" Jenny asked Heather in a defeated voice. "I already talked to these people."

"We checked the camera for one day before and after, just in case. I'm sorry, Jenny. This is all we have."

Molly seemed thoughtful.

"This camera only captures a certain portion of the beach, right? And the bench Petunia sat on is to the right. What about people who might have approached the bench from the other side?"

Heather caught on immediately.

"You need to check if anyone else uses security cameras," she told Jenny. "Talk to the other store owners."

"That sounds like a plan," Jenny said hopefully. "Wanna go with me?"

Molly and Heather both eagerly accepted. The girls were back at the Boardwalk Café half an hour later, looking disappointed.

"Any luck?" Star and Betty Sue asked.

"None of them have surveillance cameras," Jenny groaned.

"I could have told you that," Betty Sue said stiffly. "But you went off without saying a word to us."

"Most people don't lock doors around here, sweetie," Star reasoned. "They would never think of mounting security cameras."

"Petunia got spooked by that attack on the café," Betty Sue said. "That's the only reason she went for that doohickey up there. That and because you wanted to impress that Hopkins boy."

"That's not true," Jenny objected.

Star and Betty Sue ignored her.

"I wonder why Adam hasn't advised everyone on Main Street to go for a security system," Heather cribbed. "Just imagine … if there had been a camera mounted on every shop, we might have caught Petunia's killer red handed."

"Forget the cameras," Star said. "Did you talk to the people who own these shops? Maybe they saw someone suspicious?"

"I talked to some of them," Jenny told her. "There's one guy I haven't talked to. Remember that little snow cone place by the big parking lot? It was closed when I went by."

"That place might be shut up for the season," Star told her. "It's owned by a couple who live in the city. They have a cottage here. They open that store when they live here in the summer."

"I think they are still around," Molly spoke up. "Chris and I got a snow cone from there just yesterday."

"I'll go there later today," Jenny promised the women.

The Magnolias were taking turns helping Jenny at the café. It was Star's turn to stay in and help with lunch.

Jenny was making barbecued chicken wings with potato salad. It could get messy but people loved it. She grilled some corn on the cob and slathered it with her special herbed butter.

Vinny and his posse came in and sat out on deck. They ate double helpings of everything and asked for dessert. Jenny took half a strawberry cheesecake out to them.

Vinny kissed his fingers with a smacking sound.

"My Ma knew what she was doing. Your food is just yum."

"Thanks," Jenny said with a shrug. "Your mother was very nice to me."

"Any luck finding out what happened?" Vinny asked. "Hey, you meet some wise guy who won't talk, just let me know. The boys will make sure he opens up."

"I'll keep that in mind," Jenny promised.

Jenny prepped for next morning before she closed the café for the day. She walked to the snow cone shop, praying she could talk to the owners. The little kiosk was closed again. A man sat on the floor, leaning against it, reading a book. He sat on a sleeping bag which had seen better days.

"Any idea when they might open?" she asked him.

The man looked up at her and shook his head.

"Reckon they are gone for a while."

"Do you come here often?" Jenny asked him.

He gave a slight nod and went back to reading his book.

Jenny inched a bit closer to the man.

"Can I ask you a few questions, please?"

"I don't want any trouble," the man said slowly. "I'm just sitting here reading a book."

"You can sit here as long as you want," Jenny said hastily. "I don't mind that."

The man quirked an eyebrow and waited for her to go on.

"There was an incident here a few days ago," Jenny began.

"You talking about that old woman who got shot?"

"You know about that?" Jenny asked in a rush.

"Was right here, wasn't I?" the man said. "Heard a woman screaming her head off. Got up to see what was wrong. Turns out there's a dead woman sitting on that bench over there."

"Were you here the night before that?"

"I don't sleep here, lady," the man dismissed. "Got here a bit after five. I like to catch the first rays of the morning sun."

"Did you see anyone else around here?"

"A man was leaving around the time I got here."

"Can you describe him?" Jenny asked eagerly, holding her breath.

The man shook his head.

"Not really. I just saw his back. He got into a car and drove away."

"Did he come from the beach?"

"No idea," the man shrugged.

"What kind of car was he driving? Did you notice the tags?"

"I was barely awake," the man reasoned. "It was some kind of dark car. A sedan, I think. That's all I can tell you."

"Were there any other cars in the lot?"

"I don't think so," the man said. "Can I read my book now?"

Jenny thanked the man for his time.

"Why don't you come to the Boardwalk Café sometime? Lunch is on me."

The man's face broke into a smile and he agreed readily.

Jenny walked home, trying to process what the man had told her. Her heart thudded when she realized he might have spotted the murderer.

Jenny and Star spent a quiet evening at home, watching television. Jenny pulled herself out of bed at four thirty the next morning and got ready to go to the café.

The Boardwalk Café seemed lonely without Petunia's presence. Trying to drum up some inspiration, Jenny decided to mix things up for breakfast. She made a batch of blueberry banana muffins with sliced almonds.

"On the house," she told Captain Charlie when he came in for breakfast. "It's a new recipe I'm trying."

"Anything you bake is going to be good for me," he told her.

A couple came in and sat at a window table. The man was dressed in khakis and a light blue shirt. The woman wore a dress Jenny knew cost three figures.

They ordered the breakfast special. The man buried his head in a newspaper and the woman looked around with a sneer on her face.

Vinny and his guys came in for breakfast. Vinny gave a start when he spotted the couple. He walked up to the man and slapped him on the back.

"Didn't know you were coming, Baby," he roared.

The man dropped his newspaper and looked up at Vinny.

"Of course I came," he said. "She was my mother too."

Vinny summoned Jenny to the table.

"Have you met my brother, sweetheart?" Vinny asked, pulling up a chair and sitting between the couple.

The woman looked at him as if he was vermin. Vinny ignored her.

Jenny greeted the man seated at the table. Outwardly, he was nothing like Vinny. But there was a clear family resemblance. They both had a cleft chin and brown eyes the same color as Petunia's.

"You look a lot like your mother," Jenny told him.

Heather came in with an empty basket on her arm.

"Sorry I'm late." She pulled out a tray of muffins from the oven and started placing them in the basket.

"What's going on outside?" she asked, peeping out of the kitchen. She clutched Jenny's arm when she spotted the couple. "See that woman? She was here before."

"In the café? You must be mistaken, Heather. She just came in with her husband."

"Not in the café," Heather said, wide eyed. "In Pelican Cove."

"Are you sure? That guy is Vinny's brother. The woman's his wife, I guess."

"What's their name?"

"Bellini, of course. Why?"

"That's not the name she gave me."

Jenny stared at Heather with her hands on her hips.

"You must be mistaken. Charles was just telling Vinny they came in last night."

"That Charles guy did check in last night," Heather confirmed. "But the wife was in town before this. I'm telling you she stayed at the inn. She checked in with a different name though."

"That doesn't make sense."

"Wait till you hear the rest," Heather said under her breath. "She was here when Petunia got shot. She was right here in Pelican Cove, under an assumed name."

Jenny's eyes gleamed in triumph.

"That's a whole new can of worms, Heather."

Chapter 9

Adam Hopkins was engrossed in some urgent paperwork. Jenny sat in his office at the police station, tapping her foot impatiently.

"How much longer, Adam?" she burst out.

"Unfortunately, I don't work for you," he told Jenny curtly. "Come back later or wait till I finish what I'm doing."

Jenny chose to wait.

Adam finally pushed aside the stack of files and gave a big yawn.

"What have you done now, Jenny? Why are you here?"

"I have a witness," Jenny said eagerly. "He might have seen the killer leave the scene of the crime."

"Does this witness have a name?"

"I guess," Jenny said. "I didn't ask him."

"What does he do?"

"He was sitting in that big parking lot, reading a book."

"So you are relying on the word of some transient who could be anywhere right now."

"I think you'll find him at the same spot," Jenny persisted. "Right by the snow cone shop."

"That little hut?" Adam asked sardonically. "That's closed for the season."

"You don't have to go in there. You have to talk to the guy who sits outside."

"Okay. What did this guy say?"

"He saw someone get into a car that morning. Don't you see? This guy could be our shooter."

"What kind of car was it?" Adam asked.

"He didn't say," Jenny admitted. "It was dark. He thinks it was a sedan."

"That's slim, Jenny. What am I supposed to do with this information?"

"Follow up," Jenny shrugged. "Isn't that what the police do? Spread your net wider, Adam. I am sure someone else must have seen that car that morning."

"I'll look into it, Jenny," Adam sighed. "No promises though."

"I understand," Jenny nodded sadly.

Adam leaned forward and looked into her eyes.

"What are you doing tonight? How about getting dinner somewhere?"

Jenny's heart skipped a beat. Adam had asked her to move in with him a few months ago. He had been curt with her after she refused. They hadn't been on a proper date since then.

"I can manage that," she said. "Will you pick me up at home?"

"You're on," Adam said, trying to hide a smile.

Jenny hurried back to the café. Star and Heather were assembling sandwiches in the kitchen.

"Who's that grin for?" Heather asked immediately. "Tell me, quick."

"I'm having dinner with Adam."

"Finally!" Star exclaimed, rolling her eyes. "Looks like that boy is coming to his senses."

"Just roll with it," Heather advised. "Stay away from taboo topics."

"I'll try," Jenny agreed.

She dressed carefully that evening, not sure where her relationship was headed. Was it just dinner between friends, or did Adam want to pick up where they left off. She wished he had given her a hint.

Adam arrived on time, dressed in a sports coat. Jenny was glad she hadn't worn jeans. He was wearing his favorite shirt, one she had bought for him. She had chosen it for its color, the exact shade of blue as his eyes.

"Have fun," Star called out merrily. "I won't wait up."

"We are going to Virginia Beach," Adam told her. "There's a new seafood restaurant on the boardwalk. It's getting rave reviews."

"Sounds great," Jenny said enthusiastically.

"We haven't gone out in a while," Adam explained. "I wanted this evening to be special."

Jenny slipped her hand in his and clutched it tight. Adam was a grouch most of the time but he did manage to surprise her sometimes.

They talked about the weather and their kids. They were both careful about avoiding painful topics.

Jenny enjoyed the drive over the Chesapeake Bay Bridge-Tunnel. The road was busier than usual with the last of the summer tourists.

The hostess led them to a table on the beach. Adam ordered Jenny's favorite local wine along with the shrimp cocktail. The food lived up to the hype. They both got the blackened fish and watched the people walking by. Vinny waved at her from a table at the other end. Enzo sat next to him, wearing a blue tracksuit, puffing his cigar. Charles was the third person at the table.

"Looks like a family dinner," Jenny noted.

Smiley and the other guys occupied a table adjoining Vinny's.

"Forget about them," Adam said. "This is our night."

"What do you want to talk about?" Jenny asked.

Adam pulled out a tiny box from his pocket. He handed it to Jenny.

"What is it?" Jenny asked with bated breath.

"Open it," Adam smiled.

Jenny flipped the box open and felt herself relax. The box held a pair of pearl earrings.

"They are beautiful," Jenny breathed. "But what's the occasion? It's not my birthday or anything."

"I wanted to do something special for you," Adam said.

"You know you don't have to buy me expensive gifts, Adam," Jenny said frankly.

"Do you like them?"

"Of course I like them. They are cute."

"Then they are yours," Adam said.

He took Jenny's hands in his and kissed them.

"I missed you, Jenny."

"I missed you too," Jenny said quickly.

"Let's not fight about anything. I don't care where you live. Your house, my house. You have a place in my heart, Jenny King."

Jenny felt her eyes fill up.

"Don't make me cry, Adam Hopkins."

"Never," Adam said, shaking his head. "I want to make you happy for the rest of your days."

"Just be yourself, Adam," Jenny whispered. "That's enough for me."

They ordered baked Alaska for dessert and shared it, feeding each other.

"Shall we go for a walk here?" Adam asked, offering Jenny his arm.

Jenny blushed and nodded. She wished she could stay in that moment forever, without thinking about the other things going on in her life. But Vinny's presence was a stark reminder of what had happened to her friend. She wasn't going to give up until Petunia's killer was behind bars.

Jenny had a spring in her step as she entered the Boardwalk Café the next morning. A smile tugged at the corner of her mouth as she relived the evening she had spent with Adam. She made a special streusel topping for the muffins and chatted animatedly with her customers.

Molly and Heather teased her mercilessly. Star and Betty Sue laughed at their antics.

"I'm going to be a bridesmaid soon," Heather crowed.

"Don't get ahead of yourself, girl," Jenny said shyly.

She was wearing the pearl earrings Adam had given her.

Barb Norton huffed up the café steps and flopped into a chair.

"You're coming tonight, aren't you?" she asked. "No excuses."

"What are you doing now, Barb?" Betty Sue asked.

"Pelican Cove has a big problem," Barb announced. "No wonder we are battling this mosquito menace. We are going to address it all in tonight's meeting."

"There's a town hall tonight?" Heather asked. "Great. I have been working on some off-season discounts at the Bayview Inn for the locals. I want to talk about them at the meeting."

"We may not have time for frivolous stuff," Barb dismissed. "See you later, girls."

Barb declined Jenny's offer of coffee and muffins and went on her way.

"I'm sure this has to do with those inspections," Molly said.

She turned out to be right.

Most of the town had flocked to the town hall meeting. People didn't look too pleased to be there. Jenny decided Barb had managed to browbeat all of them into attending.

Barb tapped on the mic and called for attention.

"You have been negligent, Pelican Cove. You have all been negligent."

A murmur rose through the crowd. A wisecrack or two followed and everyone began laughing.

"This is not funny," Barb said. "The Extermination Committee inspected every garden and yard in town. Their results are very disturbing."

"Get on with it, Barb," Betty Sue bellowed from the front row.

"60% of the people in town have standing water. Some of you have bird feeders overflowing with water, others have gutters full of rain water … and the ponds and ditches. These are breeding grounds for mosquitoes."

"What do we do now?" someone asked.

"We need to spray the town," Barb said. "But we don't have funds. I am open to any fund raising ideas."

Jenny tuned out Barb's voice and thought about Petunia. There hadn't been a single positive development in the case. Were they missing something obvious?

She thought of the woman staying at Heather's inn. Jenny decided to talk to her the next day.

Laura Bellini helped her by coming in for breakfast by herself the next morning. She ordered the crab omelet with a smirk and sat drumming her fingers on the table.

"We need to talk," Jenny announced.

"Is that a small town thing?" the woman sneered. "Talking to every customer?"

"Petunia meant a lot to me," Jenny said curtly. "You are her son's wife, aren't you?"

The woman gave a slight nod.

"Why did you check into the Bayview Inn under a false name?"

The woman's smile slipped. She looked around fearfully and placed a finger on her lips.

"Can we keep that between us? Please?"

Jenny noticed how Laura's posture changed. She was on edge.

"Why did you do it? Tell me everything."

Laura cut a piece of her omelet and chewed it slowly. Her eyes narrowed as she looked at Jenny.

"Tell me how you knew my mother-in-law."

"I am new in town," Jenny said. "I was at a loose end, looking for work. Petunia took me in. She was good to me."

"Wait. Are you that woman who inherited this café?" Laura asked. "Charles told me some upstart woman had sweet talked his mother into it."

"I didn't ask for it," Jenny told her. "I had no idea she was going to do that."

"She talked about you a lot," Laura said. "Said you were like the daughter she never had."

"When did you talk to Petunia?" Jenny asked, surprised.

"When I came to town earlier this month," Laura Bellini explained.

"Why did you come here, exactly?"

"You know what my husband does?" she asked Jenny.

"I hear he is not part of the family business," Jenny said haltingly.

"He's a teacher!" Laura exclaimed with disgust. "He's a teacher in the public school system. You know what that job pays? A pittance."

"But your husband is rich, right?" Jenny asked.

"His grandpa wrote him off when we moved to California. I have to scrimp and save when his family is rolling in billions."

"That must be hard on you," Jenny commiserated.

"Darn right it is," Laura swore.

She had the family habit of using plenty of expletives in her speech.

"I want a better life, you know," Laura said, pulling a cigarette out of her purse.

"There's no smoking here," Jenny said quickly.

"Relax," Laura snapped. "I'm not going to light it."

She placed the cigarette between her lips and mumbled under her breath.

"I want a better life," she repeated, pulling the cigarette out of her mouth. "I want to drive a better car. I want to wear good clothes. I want our kids to go to a private school."

"You have kids?" Jenny asked in awe. "Did Petunia know she had grandchildren?"

"She knew," Laura said softly. "She walked out on the family a long time ago."

"Why did you think she would talk to you?"

"I was here to beg for money," Laura confessed. "It was like a last resort. I didn't tell Charles where I was going. I wasn't even sure she would agree to talk to me. That's why I used a false name."

"What did she say?" Jenny asked.

"She asked me how much I wanted," Laura said with wonder. "All that tension I was feeling was for nothing. She offered me a cool million. Told me to buy something nice for the kids. One million dollars. Can you believe it? I've never seen that kind of money."

Another string of profanity followed.

"That's just the tip of the iceberg, though, isn't it?" Jenny asked. "Your husband inherits several million dollars now that she is gone."

Chapter 10

Sun worshippers lined the beach behind the Boardwalk Café, sprawled on colorful beach towels. The weather was a balmy eighty degrees. Pelican Cove remained an attractive choice for tourists even in September.

Molly sat on the café's deck with a frown on her face, surrounded by the Magnolias.

"This is great news," Star was saying. "Why haven't you told us before?"

"A baby," Betty Sue said softly, her needles clacking as she knit a blue colored scarf. "That's exactly what we need."

"Ask her if she has told Chris yet though?" Heather interrupted. "What does he feel about this?"

"I talked to Chris," Molly told them.

"And?" Four voices chorused.

"He wants to get married right away."

"Excellent," Star boomed.

Jenny added her congratulations.

"I knew that boy would do the right thing," Betty Sue thundered.

"But I don't want to," Molly burst out. "At least, not this way."

"What do you mean, Molls?" Jenny asked.

"I have been married before," Molly reminded them. "It turned out to be a mistake. I don't want to get carried away this time."

"You love Chris, don't you?" Heather asked suspiciously.

"Of course I do," Molly said vigorously. "But does he love me enough?"

"What nonsense!" Star exclaimed. "I've seen how that boy looks at you."

"You already met the parents," Heather reminded her.

"I don't want a shotgun wedding," Molly said, warding them off. "This way, I am forcing his hand. I will never know if Chris really loves me. Or rather, if he loves me enough."

Jenny guessed what Molly was trying to say.

"There are no secrets between us, Molly," she said. "I think it's best if you clear the air."

Star and Betty Sue gave each other a knowing look.

"What's going on?" Heather asked, mystified.

"Molly thinks Chris might still have feelings for you," Jenny said flatly.

"What?" Heather asked, wide eyed. "That's ridiculous."

Heather and Chris had been a couple for several years. Everyone knew they had an understanding. A year ago, Heather had decided to date other people. She paraded one guy after another before Chris. He had decided Heather wasn't coming back. He fell in love with Molly, Heather's gentle, soft spoken friend.

"I know he still cares about you," Molly persisted. "And he worries about you."

"Chris and I have known each other since third grade," Heather said. "I hope we will always be close. But he's not in love with me now, Molly. Trust me."

Jenny noticed how Heather avoided saying anything about her own feelings.

"He's very excited," Molly finally said with a smile. "He insists on going with me to the doctor."

"Chris will make a wonderful father," Jenny assured her. "Don't overanalyze things, Molly."

"I guess I'm being silly," Molly said grudgingly. "I'm lucky to have him."

"She's already getting emotional," Star cackled. "She'll be puking her guts out in a few days."

"I didn't have any morning sickness at all," Betty Sue shared. "Don't worry, Molly. We'll take care of you."

"I know you will," Molly said tearfully. "You're the best friends a girl could ask for."

They huddled together for a group hug. Star voiced what everyone was thinking.

"I can't believe she's gone."

"She's alive in our heart," Betty Sue sniffed. She blew her nose in a lace handkerchief and looked at Jenny. "Do you have any suspects at all?"

Jenny looked beaten.

"Every person I talk to seems to have an alibi."

"What about that boy who goes around wearing that ridiculous hat?"

"Vinny? He inherits millions. But he was home in New Jersey the day Petunia was shot."

"Don't these people hire hitmen?" Star said.

"That's true. But I don't think Vinny had anything to do with it."

"You're not crushing after this mobster, are you?" Heather giggled.

Jenny silenced her with a glare.

"I think Peter Wilson could have done it."

"That car mechanic?" Star asked. "All those times I took my car to him, I never knew he was in the mafia."

"Peter Wilson was meeting Petunia that morning," Jenny reminded them. "He knew exactly where she was going to be at a certain time."

"What's his alibi?"

"He was in the hospital with a sick child. I suppose he could have crept out for a few minutes. But Adam is sure he was there all the time."

"What about that couple staying at our inn?" Heather asked.

"Laura Bellini," Jenny nodded. "She was here to ask Petunia for money. I don't trust that woman."

"Is that all you have done until now?" Betty Sue complained. "What about finding someone who was on the beach that day?"

"I did talk to some beach walkers," Jenny said. "They couldn't tell me much. But this guy in the parking lot sounds more promising. I am going to follow up that lead."

A familiar voice trilled in the background.

"Yooohooo …" Barb Norton called out, puffing up the café steps.

"Why are you here, Barb?" Star asked curtly.

"We need funds for the aerial spraying of the town," Barb wheezed. "Surely you heard that at yesterday's meeting?"

"Go on," Betty Sue said reluctantly.

"I have an idea. We are going to impose fines on people who have standing water or ponds on their properties. They have directly contributed to the mosquito menace. So they should be the ones who have to pay."

"Are you out of your mind?" Betty Sue cried. "You can't fine people just because they haven't cleaned out their gutters."

"I can," Barb beamed. "I went through town regulations. And I found the legal loophole which allows me to levy those fines."

"People are not going to like it," Heather said.

"You are one of those people," Barb said maliciously. "That lily pond you have is a breeding ground for the deadliest mosquitoes."

"Can't you raise money any other way?" Jenny asked.

"I'm glad you asked," Barb said. "I am thinking of a bake sale. I will need your help with that."

"I'm already stretched thin, Barb," Jenny protested. "I don't think I can contribute much this time."

"We'll see about that," Barb said.

She stood up and pointed a finger at Betty Sue.

"My volunteers are printing up notices as we speak. You have three days to pay the fine. Otherwise you will have to pay double."

"What …" Betty Sue sputtered. "You're out of control, Barb!"

Barb Norton gave them a jaunty wave and walked down the beach.

"She's going to come to a sticky end one of these days," Star said.

"Mark my words."

"I'm not paying any atrocious fines," Betty Sue declared. "I don't care what Barb says."

The Magnolias dispersed after that.

Star insisted on staying back to help Jenny. A man came into the café an hour later. Star was at the counter.

"Can I help you?"

"I'm looking for someone," he mumbled. "A lady told me I could come here for lunch."

Jenny came out of the kitchen just then. She recognized the man who had been reading in the parking lot.

"I got this," she told her aunt.

She greeted the man and showed him to a table. She was back with a big bowl of chicken noodle soup.

"Grilled cheese sandwiches for lunch today," she told him. "Is that okay?"

The man nodded, looking hungrily at the soup. He picked up his spoon and began eating. Jenny kept an eye on him. She was back with a hot crispy sandwich oozing melted cheese.

"You're a good cook," the man told her. "This soup is just like the one my grandma used to make. She always had soup on the stove in the fall."

"I'll pack some more for you," Jenny said.

"I remembered something," the man said suddenly.

"Is this about the man you saw in the parking lot?" Jenny asked eagerly.

"No. But it's about the car. It had a big dent on one side. And some kind of sticker on the back window."

"Good catch," Jenny beamed. "That's a huge help. Thanks so much."

The man blushed.

"Someone told me the woman who died was your friend. Just trying to help."

"I appreciate it," Jenny said. "You are welcome here anytime."

Jenny handed him a brown paper bag when he got up to leave. She had added a container of soup and some muffins from that morning. She hoped he would get at least one more meal out of it.

Jenny had just turned her back to go into the kitchen when a familiar voice called out to her.

"Jason!" she exclaimed in delight. "I was going to call you."

"My 2 PM cancelled," he said. "Thought I would enjoy a leisurely lunch at my favorite café."

Star came out and hugged Jason.

"Jenny hasn't eaten yet either. Why don't you two sit out on deck? I'll get your lunch."

"You're looking chipper today," Jenny observed as they ate their soup.

Jason shrugged.

"It's a beautiful day and we are lucky to be alive and kicking."

Jason had been dealing with a bad breakup. Jenny realized he was finally coming out of his shell.

"Ready to put on your sleuthing cap?" she asked.

"Bring it on," Jason nodded.

Jenny told him about the man in the parking lot and what he had seen.

"We need to figure out where that car went," Jason said thoughtfully. "Why don't we go to the parking lot after lunch?"

They drove down Main Street in Jason's fancy car. Jenny relaxed in the heated seats. She had forgotten how comfortable they could be.

Jason made a right first. It took them back toward the Boardwalk Café. Jason drove past the cluster of stores. The road wound across town for a mile before ending in a cluster of homes. They were expensive properties right on the water with their own private docks. Jason and Jenny could see a boat tied to many of them.

"This is a dead end," Jason said. "Let's go the other way."

They turned around and drove past the parking lot. The road stretched on for a couple of miles and eventually merged on the bridge that connected the island to the main shore.

"What about those lanes we saw?" Jenny asked, referring to a couple of turnoffs they had encountered.

Jason obliged her by driving down the lanes. Both of them were deserted and ended in a small clearing of sorts.

"Looks like he drove out of town," Jason mused.

"How can you be so sure?"

"I'm just speculating, Jenny," Jason admitted. "He couldn't have gone back into town. He could have gone into one of those lanes to hide. But why would he do that? He would want to get out of town as soon as possible."

"If only someone saw where that car went …"

"We can check security cameras," Jason told her. "They might have recorded the car driving by."

"I spoke to some store owners around the café," Jenny told him. "None of them have cameras."

"The Newburys have cameras," Jason said suddenly. "Remember that warehouse we passed? It belongs to them."

"Will they give us access?" Jenny asked.

"They can't refuse," Jason said.

He pulled up at the warehouse a few minutes later. The security guy on duty recognized him. Jenny explained what they were looking for.

"I can't give you access without getting approval," he said.

"We just want to look," Jenny told him. "If we find something, I will go talk to Julius Newbury myself."

Jenny and Jason squashed into the cramped security office and waited for the man to pull up the relevant footage. There had been no cars on the road that morning.

"How is that possible?" Jenny wailed. "Where did the car go?"

"He could have parked the car in the woods and walked somewhere," Jason suggested. "He's had plenty of time since then to go back and move the car."

"We are never going to find him," Jenny said in a defeated voice.

"We can't do more than this, Jenny," Jason reasoned. "Let the police handle it."

"I told Adam about this," Jenny said soberly. "He ticked me off."

"So we'll talk to him again. My gut tells me this car is important, Jenny. We need to find it anyhow."

Chapter 11

Jenny finished serving breakfast at the Boardwalk Café and walked to the police station with her fingers crossed. She wanted to get an update from Adam. She had no idea how forthcoming he would be. It all depended on his mood.

"Anything new?" she asked, taking a seat before him.

Adam was struggling with a bottle of pain pills. Jenny unscrewed the bottle and handed him two pills.

"Nothing much to share," Adam told her. "At least, nothing I care to tell you, Jenny."

"How kind," Jenny said, her voice dripping with sarcasm.

"You can leave now."

"Not so fast, Adam. Have you run a background check on Charles Bellini?"

"The other son? He's a middle school teacher. Teaches English and history, I think."

"And his wife?"

"What about her?"

"Does she have a job? What does she do?"

Adam hesitated.

"We haven't given her much importance."

"Maybe you should," Jenny told him. "She's devious. She stayed at the Bayview Inn under an assumed name."

"Who told you that?" Adam asked.

"Heather did. And Laura Bellini told me so herself."

"When was this?"

"She was right here the day Petunia died," Jenny said triumphantly. "What do you think of that?"

Adam leaned forward with interest.

"I did not know that. Good work, Jenny."

"I guess we have Heather to thank for the heads up."

Jenny told Adam about her conversation with Laura Bellini.

"If she had anything to hide, she wouldn't have come back here," Adam mused.

"She could be stupid," Jenny offered. "Or overconfident."

"You don't like her, I guess."

"She said some nasty things about Petunia."

"You can't let that cloud your judgment," Adam advised. "Laura as a person is not on trial here."

"You're right, I guess," Jenny admitted.

"Am I seeing you later tonight?" Adam asked. "Tank misses you."

Tank was Adam's yellow Labrador. He had traveled with Adam on his various deployments. Tank and Jenny had taken a shine to each other. When Jenny's husband had cruelly retained custody of her own aging dog, she had been heartbroken. Tank had filled the void a bit.

"I miss him too. Why don't you let him visit? Let him stay at Seaview for a few days. Star and I would love to pamper him a bit."

"I'm sure he will love that," Adam smiled.

Neither of them talked about Adam coming to stay. Adam had spent a few months at Seaview when his own home was being renovated. He wanted Jenny to move in with him after that but she had refused to leave her home. Jenny didn't know how they would ever move past that issue.

"You are sure the police have made no progress?" Jenny wheedled. "Why don't you throw me some scraps, Adam?"

"You're relentless, aren't you?" Adam shook his head in wonder.

"I plan to badger you until you give up and spill the beans."

Adam gave a deep sigh and leaned back in his chair.

"We might have something," Adam said reluctantly. "Most people have talked about a white guy wearing a hooded jacket. He was seen around the beach."

"Where on the beach?" Jenny pounced.

"Near the bench," Adam admitted.

"What else? Did they notice the color of his hair? Anything else?"

"There wasn't much light so it's hard to say. They did mention seeing some kind of picture on the back of the jacket."

"You mean like a logo?"

"A drawing or a graphic of some kind. This is where it gets distorted. One person says it looked like a skull. Another said it looked like a big bird."

"An eagle?" Jenny asked thoughtfully.

"More like a turkey."

"What else?"

"We have been looking around for a man wearing that jacket."

"What if he was a tourist?" Jenny asked with a frown. "He must be long gone."

"Question is, what was this guy doing on the beach so early in the morning."

"Could he be the one who got into the car and drove away?"

"No idea, Jenny," Adam said.

He banged a fist on the table, looking frustrated.

"I knew Petunia longer than you, Jenny. You think I don't want to find out what happened to her? I'm doing everything I can to find her killer."

Jenny patted his hand.

"I know you're good at your job, Adam. I trust you."

Jenny dragged herself back to the café. Star was stirring a big pot of soup for lunch.

"How's the chili?" Jenny asked.

"Just yum," Star said, tasting some with a spoon. "I measured out the ingredients for the corn bread."

"I'm going to start mixing it," Jenny said. "Let me grab a cup of coffee first."

"Are you going to add jalapenos?"

Jenny nodded, thinking of her son Nick.

"Nicky loves my jalapeno cornbread," she said wistfully. "He's been eating it since he was six. He never complained about the heat."

Jenny rubbed a tiny gold heart shaped charm hanging around her neck on a chain. Her son Nick had gifted her a charm every year for Mother's Day. She wore them around her neck now, close to her heart. They provided the only tangible connection she had with her child.

"When is that scamp coming home?" Star asked. "Have you talked to him recently?"

Jenny shook her head.

"I haven't told him about Petunia. She adored him."

"You should call him, Jenny," Star said. "He needs to know."

Jenny and her aunt talked about how Nick was growing up to be a fine young man. Jenny pulled the first batch of corn bread out of the oven. She cut a generous piece and broke it in half. She offered it to her aunt.

"Delicious," Star said, fanning her mouth. "Better save some for us. You're going to run out of this in no time."

Jenny smiled and ladled chili into a big soup bowl. She garnished it with some chopped green onions and shredded cheddar cheese. A dollop of sour cream went on top. Jenny placed a piece of corn bread on one side and began taking pictures.

"For the Internet?" her aunt asked.

There was a commotion of sorts outside. Jenny heard raised voices and ran to see what was happening.

Barb Norton sat at a table, her chest heaving. One side of her face was caked with mud. A tiny trickle of blood flowed down her forehead.

"Barb!" Jenny cried. "What happened to you?"

"I was attacked," Barb wailed dramatically. "That's what happened. In broad daylight, no less. What's this town coming to?"

Star had come out of the kitchen behind Jenny.

"Calm down, Barb," she said. "You are going to blow a gasket."

Barb's red face turned purple.

"I'm not going to calm down," she cried. "I almost lost my life."

Jenny poured water in a glass and made Barb drink it.

"I'm making tea," she said. "Why don't you come into the kitchen and tell us what happened?"

"Call your boyfriend," Barb commanded. "I want to file a complaint."

"I can call the police from the kitchen," Jenny assured her. "Let's take care of you first."

Barb's story was simple enough. She had been walking on the road, going to the library. She didn't know what hit her. She blacked out and when she came to, she was lying in a ditch by the side of the road. A man walking by had helped her up.

"First Petunia, now me. Do you think someone is targeting older ladies?"

Jenny didn't have an answer for that. She called Adam at the police station and told him what had happened.

"He's coming here," she told Barb.

Adam arrived ten minutes later, looking grim. Barb bombarded him with a string of questions.

"Let me ask the questions, please," Adam said. "You do want me to write up a report?"

Adam learned that Barb had been walking on a lonely stretch of road. She hadn't seen anyone else.

Jenny spotted a bump at the back of Barb's head. She hadn't noticed it before.

"You need to go to the doctor, Barb," Jenny said. "Get checked out."

Adam offered to drive Barb to the emergency room at the hospital. She agreed readily.

"What do you think of that?" Jenny asked her aunt after they left.

Heather rushed in just then, waving a piece of paper in the air.

"I want to kill Barb Norton!"

"Apparently, you are not the only one," Jenny said.

Heather barely heard her.

"Just look at this, Jenny. Look at how atrocious this fine is that she is asking us to pay."

Jenny took the paper from Heather and gasped as she saw the amount at the bottom of the page.

"What is this for?"

"According to her, the Bayview Inn has contributed to the mosquito menace. This is her way of punishing us for it."

"It does sound a bit much," Jenny agreed.

"That's not all," Heather continued in an incensed voice. "She wants to destroy our lily pond. My Dad and I dug that pond when I was little. It's not just a pond, Jenny. It has memories attached to it."

"Are you the only one who got this kind of notice?" Jenny asked.

"I bet we got one too," Star said drily. "Barb's going to take objection to your water fountain. I'm sure of it."

"That fountain's not going anywhere," Jenny said stoutly.

She looked at Heather.

"Well?"

"These notices have been served all around town," Heather said. "She's even sent one to the Newburys. Ada was on the phone with Grandma."

The Newburys were the richest people in town. They considered themselves a notch above the rest.

"She has guts. I'll give her that."

"She's being idiotic," Star said flatly. "There are other ways to raise money. I think Barb Norton has gone too far this time."

Jenny's eyes widened as she processed her aunt's words.

"You don't think she was attacked because of these fines?"

Star shrugged.

"You can only push people so far."

Heather was looking puzzled. Jenny explained what had happened.

"No way," Heather said. "The people of Pelican Cove don't go around attacking each other."

There was a flurry of footsteps outside and a figure in a leather jacket peeped in.

"Boss wants his lunch."

"I'll be out in a minute, Smiley," Jenny said.

"You know those mobsters by name?" Heather asked, rolling her eyes.

"Do you think one of them might have hit Barb?" Star asked.

Jenny gave it some thought.

"I don't think Vinny cares about the mosquitoes."

She served the chili into bowls and placed the cheese and onions on small plates. She cut big pieces of corn bread and served them on a platter.

Vinny took one bite of the chili and smacked his lips appreciatively.

"This is so good! You sure know how to cook."

"I'm planning the menu for Petunia's memorial. Is there something you want to add?"

"Ma liked those tiny meatballs on a stick," Vinny said. "She made them for all our birthdays."

"I didn't know that," Jenny told him. "I'll put them on the menu."

She looked at Vinny and debated what she was going to say next.

"Petunia didn't say much. Was she always that quiet?"

"She might have acted like a mouse. But she had the heart of a lion. She knew what she wanted and she went after it."

Jenny brought out plates of tiramisu. She had never served it in the café before.

"It's your mother's recipe," she told Vinny. "She had written it down at the back of a diary."

"This is our Nona's recipe," Vinny said after he had tasted it. "Our grandmother's. Ma was making this the day our Pa got whacked."

Jenny understood why Petunia had never made it again.

Chapter 12

Molly came up the steps of the café and sat down with a sigh. She put her feet up on a chair and dug into a warm muffin. Star and Betty Sue exchanged a knowing look when Molly reached for her second one.

"What?" she pouted. "I'm just hungry."

"And you're eating for two," Betty Sue said, her eyes gleaming. "When do you go to the doctor?"

"Tomorrow. Chris is going with me."

"Of course he is," Betty Sue said. "That there is a responsible boy. He'll do right by you, Molly."

"I am able to take care of myself and my baby," Molly protested. "I don't need to be taken care of."

"Okay, okay." Star held up her hand. "We know you girls like to think you can do everything alone. And that's admirable. But be happy you have a guy like Chris."

"I am," Molly said emphatically. "Why do you think I am in love with him?"

She blushed prettily and picked up her cup of coffee.

"Switch to ginger ale," Betty Sue said. "That's better for you."

"I can't imagine giving up coffee," Molly said stoutly.

"Who's giving up what?" Jenny asked, coming out with six steaming hot muffins on a plate.

Heather was right behind her.

"Pumpkin and cream cheese muffins," Jenny announced. "I am trying these out for the fall menu."

"Mmmm …" Molly moaned as she bit off a big chunk from one. "These are delicious. I love the cinnamon, and is that ginger I taste?"

Star and Betty Sue added their compliments.

"Who's the sixth one for?" Betty Sue asked.

Her face fell as soon as she asked the question. The mood around the table changed instantly.

Just then, a commotion broke out on the beach.

"What's going on there?" Betty Sue boomed.

The Magnolias lined the deck and watched the drama unfolding on the beach.

Two men faced each other. Both of them held an aggressive stance.

"That's Peter Wilson," Jenny said with a gasp.

"Who's that ruffian standing before him?" Star asked. "Never seen him before."

Jenny peered at the unkempt man wearing an oversized coat. His face was smudged with dirt or soot and his hair was in total disarray.

"That looks like Mason," Jenny said.

"And who is that?" Betty Sue demanded.

"How do you know him?" Heather wasn't far behind.

"I don't, really. He's just a guy who hangs out on the beach."

"Hush, girls," Molly interrupted. "Can you hear what they are saying?"

Peter Wilson was waving his hands in the air, clearly disturbed about something. He jabbed a finger in the other man's chest and pushed him. Mason pushed Wilson back.

A crowd had begun to gather. People stood in a circle a few feet away from the two men, watching them intently.

Suddenly, Mason pulled something out of his coat pocket. It glinted in the sunlight.

"Oh my God, is that a gun?" Heather shrieked.

The Magnolias huddled together, struck speechless.

Peter Wilson took a step back. Mason held the gun in both hands and pointed it at Peter Wilson's chest. The crowd had begun to step back. Mason whirled around and pointed the gun to his right. A woman in the crowd grabbed her child and clutched him tightly.

Mason threw back his head and laughed. Every eye on the beach was trained on him now. He turned around again and pointed the gun at someone else.

"Let's go inside," Star said under her breath. "Start walking back very, very slowly. Do you hear me, girls? Don't make any sudden movements."

For once, Heather listened without any arguments and started inching back inside.

"Wait," Molly said. "That Wilson guy's saying something."

They saw Mason give a nod and put the gun back in his coat. He began walking away. The crowd parted to let him pass.

A few minutes later, Mason was out of sight.

"I think he's gone," Molly said.

Betty Sue had collapsed in her chair. Her brow was drenched in sweat. Jenny felt some beads of sweat on her own lip. They had almost been in the line of fire. Anything could have happened if the man had started shooting.

"What was that?" Star asked, sitting down with a thump.

No one spoke a word.

"That man is your friend?" Betty Sue thundered. "You need to be more careful, girl."

"He's not my friend," Jenny argued. "I've just seen him on the beach here. He walks around, scribbling something in the sand. I thought he might be hard up so I offered him a meal."

"I advise you to stay away from that man," Star said strongly. "You need to be more circumspect, Jenny."

"Shouldn't we report this?" Molly asked.

"Of course," Jenny agreed. "I'm calling Adam now."

She went into the kitchen and called the police station.

"Jenny!" His voice was laced with urgency and a good amount of fear. "Are you alright? All of you? I hear someone just pulled a gun on the beach."

"We are fine," Jenny assured him. "I was just calling to report that."

"We got multiple reports," Adam told her. "Some people even came in and demanded action."

"Are you going to arrest that man?"

"We'll bring him in for questioning. But I'm guessing he's long gone."

Jenny told him everything she knew about the man.

"Stay away from him in the future," Adam warned.

Jenny went back out. The Magnolias had calmed down a bit. A few groups of people came into the café and Jenny was kept busy for the next hour. Heather helped her serve the customers.

"Sit down," Star said when Jenny went out to the deck again.

"I don't agree with them," Molly said.

"What are you talking about?"

"Getting a gun," Betty Sue said. "You saw what just happened. You need to get a gun to protect yourself."

"I don't believe in guns," Jenny said flatly. "I'm surprised you are saying this, Betty Sue."

"My grandpa taught me how to shoot when I was eight," Betty Sue said. "I went hunting with him when I grew up. There was a rifle up on the wall in our living room, ready to greet any intruders."

"So what? We should all whip out our guns and shoot at each other?" Jenny asked, incensed.

"The town's changing," Star said. "We have more transients than we ever had before. There's nothing wrong in being prepared."

Jenny said nothing. Her aunt had a point.

"Look what happened to Barb Norton," Betty Sue continued.

"She had a close call," Star reminded Jenny.

"Did we find out who attacked her?" Heather asked. "I still think it was because of those ridiculous fines she imposed."

"She's not completely wrong," Betty Sue said grudgingly. "Mosquitoes and pests carry deadly diseases. We had a really bad outbreak one year, back in the 70s. It was the Rocky Mountain Spotted Fever. People died because of it."

"West Nile and Zika are bad too," Jenny noted. "Surely the people understand that? Barb might be a bit overzealous sometimes, but it's all for a good cause."

"Why did someone bash her on the head then?" Heather demanded.

"Do you think it was a prank?" Molly asked. "Kids from the high school having some fun?"

"Barb is too well known around town," Star said. "She probably knows most of the kids and their parents."

"How is Barb doing?" Jenny asked. "Has she recovered from the shock?"

"Today's the last day to pay the fines," Heather said. "And there's another meeting at the town hall tomorrow. Barb will be there alright, ready to pounce on people who haven't paid up."

The Magnolias dispersed soon after. Jenny was making chicken parmesan sandwiches for lunch. She stirred her homemade tomato sauce and seasoned it the way Petunia had taught her to. Heather had brought some fresh oregano and thyme from the inn's garden.

Vinny and his boys arrived and went to sit out on the deck. Jenny placed steaming sandwiches before them, smothered in melted mozzarella.

"How you doing, sweetheart?" Vinny asked her. "I heard someone pulled a gun out there today?"

Jenny assured him she was fine.

"You want me to set you up with a piece?" he asked.

"A piece of what?" Jenny asked, bewildered.

Smiley, Six Pac and Biggie burst out laughing.

"Never mind," Vinny said. "Someone comes bugging you, you let Vinny know. Alright, sweetheart?"

Jenny hoped Vinny was just grandstanding. She didn't want to think about the alternative. She pasted a smile on her face and served them big slices of chocolate cake.

Enzo Bellini arrived a few minutes after Vinny left. He was dressed in a blue tracksuit. He wore his signature fedora and chewed on his cigar.

"Fabio came to see me," he said to Jenny.

Jenny needed a few seconds to remember Fabio was none other than Peter Wilson.

"Who's this punk with a gun, anyway?" Enzo whispered. "I told Fabio to keep an eye on you."

"That's not necessary," Jenny protested.

"He's always taken care of the café. I don't see why that should stop now."

"Petunia …" Jenny stuttered.

"My girl thought a lot about you," Enzo wheezed. "You are family now. And Enzo Bellini takes care of his own."

"Thanks," Jenny said shakily.

She wasn't sure what the old man expected from her.

Back home, Jenny spent the evening in her garden, admiring her roses as the sun went down over the horizon.

Dinner was a lively meal, with Jimmy and Star talking about a trip they wanted to take.

"Weren't you planning a trip to the mountains?" Star asked her.

"That was last year," Jenny said. "We never made it there. Adam hasn't said anything about a trip this year."

"Maybe we should all go together," Jimmy suggested.

"Talk to Adam about it," Star whispered, giving him a nudge.

Jenny rolled her eyes and ignored them. She was feeling stuffed after a lavish meal of crab cakes and oven baked fish. But she forced herself to lace up her walking shoes and go out for her walk.

Tank came bounding up after she had barely taken a few steps. She hugged him tight and pulled a battered tennis ball out of her pocket. She flung it in a wide arc, smiling as Tank leapt after it.

She finally looked up and met Adam's gaze.

"What a day, huh?" he breathed. "I'm so glad to see you are fine."

"Apparently, there's more than one person looking out for me."

"What does that mean?" Adam asked.

Jenny laughed and told him about Enzo's offer. Adam swore under his breath.

"You're getting a bit too close to these people."

"That's not all," Jenny said. "Betty Sue wants me to keep a gun at the café."

"No, no, Jenny." Adam shook his head vehemently. "That's not a good idea."

"Relax," Jenny cooed, taking his hand in hers. "I have already told them I am against the concept. I don't believe in violence."

"It's real," Adam said seriously. "But the café is full of civilians most of the time, including kids. Not a good place for guns."

"I know you can protect me, Adam," Jenny said. "The police station is less than a block away."

"Speaking of … who do you think has a license for an automatic?"

Jenny quirked an eyebrow and waited for Adam to continue.

"Laura Bellini, the teacher's wife."

"What does she want a gun for?"

"I'm going to find out," Adam said grimly. "I'm meeting her tomorrow to talk about it."

"Does she carry it around?"

"We don't know where the gun is. The local police in California are looking for it now."

"Can you prove she brought it to Pelican Cove the last time she was here?"

"We need to find the gun first. Once we have it, we can run all kinds of tests on it. We'll know if it was fired, for example."

"Do you think it's going to be that simple?" Jenny asked.

Her gut told her Laura Bellini was not a killer.

Chapter 13

Jenny was having lunch with Adam at the police station.

"I'm stuck, Adam," Jenny sighed. "I'm hitting a wall wherever I look."

Adam speared some more pasta salad on his fork and heard Jenny out. But he said nothing.

"How many people have you talked to?" he finally asked.

"I talked to people close to Petunia," Jenny said, counting off her fingers. "I am still not sure about Peter Wilson. But he has no motive and he also has the strongest alibi."

Jenny paused to take a bite of her chicken sandwich. Adam hadn't scowled or barked at her since she came in. She hoped his good mood would prevail. She had crossed her fingers behind her back and proceeded to pump him for information.

"The same applies to her sons, Vinny and Charles. They have alibis and no possible motive."

Jenny frowned as she pulled the lid off her salad container.

"I don't trust Laura Bellini though."

"Who else?" Adam asked.

"Actually, there is no one else. I'm going around in circles, evaluating the same people. I feel I am missing something. What about that man in the jacket?"

"We haven't made much progress with that," Adam said evasively.

He wolfed down the last piece of his sandwich and wiped his mouth with a paper napkin. He was looking forward to eating the apple pie Jenny had brought along. She had baked it with the first apples of the season.

"Why don't you let me talk to those people? They might remember something more."

"Sure. They hid the real story from us. They are just waiting for you to come along, right?"

"Don't be sarcastic, Adam. What do you have to lose?"

In Jenny's experience, people were naturally intimidated while talking to the police. She encouraged them to talk about anything, often ending up with relevant information which everyone had missed.

"I'm willing to try anything at this stage," Adam said, sounding dejected.

He wrote a few names on a notepad and tore the paper off, handing it to Jenny. He had added notes about where Jenny would find them.

Jenny went to the seafood market to shop for dinner. Chris Williams was nowhere to be seen. She realized Chris and Molly had their doctor's appointment that day. Her face broke into a smile. A baby would bring new life with it. Jenny looked forward to being an aunt.

"Do you remember the first time you met her?" Jenny asked Star that evening.

They sat out on the patio at Seaview, sipping wine before dinner. Roses and gardenias perfumed the air, their scent mingling with the salty breeze coming off the ocean.

Star had a faraway look in her eyes.

"It was on that rocky beach on the south side of town. I had set up my easel there to paint a commission. It was a cold, windy day. The wind caught one of my rags and I ran after it. Petunia was sitting behind a rock, staring out at the sea."

"Was she crying?"

Star thought a bit and shook her head.

"I think she was sad though. I asked her if she was new in town. She told me she needed a fresh start in life. I told her she had come to the perfect place."

"What did you do then?"

"I invited her home for coffee. She said she needed to keep busy. I told her how the town needed a decent diner."

"Was the café closed at that time?"

Star nodded.

"The previous owner, Millie, had died two years ago. Her son tried to run it for some time after that but he couldn't handle it. The café had been shut up since then."

"So she just bought the café?"

"She must have," Star said fondly. "The next thing I know, Petunia is serving coffee and making soup. She asked me to think of a name for the café because it had been my idea."

"And you thought of naming it the Boardwalk Café?"

"They were just building the new boardwalk at the time. It was supposed to be a big draw for the tourists. I thought Boardwalk Café sounded better than Millie's. Millie was gone anyway. Petunia loved the name. I painted the first sign for the café, you know."

"And you have been friends ever since?" Jenny asked, suddenly missing the warm, motherly woman who had never doubted her.

"We started meeting for coffee every morning," Star said wistfully. "Betty Sue asked if she could join us. Heather had just come to live with her. In a way, she was starting a new life, just like Petunia."

Jenny wondered if she would still be that close to Molly and Heather twenty five years later. At least she hoped to be.

"Petunia wasn't just my friend," Star said, her eyes welling with tears. "She was my sister. You need to find out who killed her, Jenny."

Jenny rubbed Star's arm, her gaze hardening with resolve.

"I'm doing everything I can," she promised. "How would you like to join me tomorrow? I am talking to a few people who might have seen something."

"Count me in," Star said.

They went in for dinner, leaning on each other.

Jenny sat out on the deck of the Boardwalk Café the next morning. She had asked Heather to come in and help her with breakfast. She had already baked a few batches of muffins and made crab salad for lunch.

"I need to talk to a couple of people today," she explained. "I'm hoping they will have some information for me."

Star sat next to Jenny, drawing something in her sketch pad. A woman came into view, walking a golden retriever. Jenny recognized her.

"Hello there," she waved.

The woman smiled uncertainly, pulling at the dog's leash to make him stop.

Jenny skipped down the café steps and ran the few steps to the woman.

"Can we talk? Please?"

"Sure," the woman shrugged. "Haven't I talked to you before?"

Jenny invited her to sit on the deck. She offered her some coffee.

"No, thanks. I only drink green juice in the mornings."

Star knew the woman well. They talked about a book club they both belonged to. The woman seemed to forget her hesitation after that.

"So what can I help you with?"

"It's about Petunia," Jenny began. "I hear you saw someone wearing a hooded jacket. Can we talk about that, please?"

The woman told Jenny what she already knew.

"Was there anything odd about that man? Anything that might have stood out?"

"All I remember is there was some kind of drawing on the back of that jacket. It was a bit frightening."

"Can you describe it?" Star said. "Let's see if I can come up with a sketch."

The woman's memory wasn't very clear. Star encouraged her to share any tiny detail she could think of. Star's fingers flew over her sketch pad as the woman talked. Finally, Star held up her pad.

"Was it something like this?"

Jenny's face crumpled when she saw what Star had drummed up. The picture didn't make any sense at all. The bottom part of it looked like a face or a skull. Feathers stuck out of the top, making it look like a bird of sorts.

The woman shook her head when she saw the drawing.

"That's not it." She shook her head. "Except for the feathers. You got that part right."

"Was it a bird of some kind?" Jenny asked.

"I just remember the feathers," the woman repeated.

Her dog began barking his head off.

"I need to go," she said apologetically. "I'm here almost every morning in case you have more questions."

Jenny thanked her for her time and waved goodbye.

"This looks ridiculous!" Star groaned as she stared at the picture.

"We have one more person to talk to," Jenny said. "Let's go."

Jenny started her car and drove down half a mile to a gas station. A kid was working at the counter. He looked barely out of school. Jenny guessed he was eighteen or nineteen.

"I have a break coming up," the kid told them. "Can you wait until then?"

Jenny and Star sat in Jenny's car, fiddling with the radio until the kid came out. His name was Skinner and he was a high school dropout.

Skinner admitted he had noticed a man loitering around. He hadn't seen his face clearly because of the hooded jacket.

"You said there was some kind of picture on the back of the jacket?" Jenny asked hopefully. "Can you tell us about it?"

"It was weird, dude. Like a turkey coming to get ya."

"Can you describe it?" Star asked, pulling out a sketch pad. "I'm going to try and draw it."

Star's picture turned out to be a bird which looked very much like a turkey.

"You got the feathers right," the kid said. "There was something else. Like pirate stuff."

"You mean a skull?" Jenny asked eagerly.

"What's that funny hat Captain Sparrow wears?"

"A tricorn?"

Skinner shook his head.

"I don't know, dude. It wasn't anything I had seen before."

Jenny knew when she was beaten. She thanked the kid and drove back to the café.

"That was a waste of time," Star grumbled.

"They were both sure about the feathers."

"That doesn't make sense at all, Jenny."

"I am going to do some research on that," Jenny said stoutly as they drove back to the cafe.

Jason came to pick up lunch.

"I'm going to the mainland for an appointment," he told Jenny. "Can I get you something?"

Jenny shook her head absent mindedly.

"How about some Chinese food from your favorite place in town?" Jason smiled. "Looks like you're in a funk."

"I'm stumped," Jenny admitted. "And Chinese takeout sounds perfect for dinner. I'll bake some brownies for dessert."

"Now you're talking," Jason said, giving her a high five. "Don't worry, Jenny. We'll talk about it when I get back. Can you hold the fort down until then?"

Jenny nodded. She always felt better after talking to Jason.

They made short work of the takeout Jason brought home. Jenny warmed the brownies and scooped generous portions of vanilla ice cream to go with them. She poured her special hot fudge on top and added a handful of chopped hazelnuts.

"I might have to run an extra mile tomorrow," Jason said, "but I'm digging into this tonight."

"Did you see those?" Jenny asked, pointing to the drawings Jason had been looking at. "Do they make any sense to you?"

"What are they?"

Jenny brought him up to speed.

"My guess is it could be a logo of some kind."

"I thought that too," Jenny said. "But who puts a skull on a logo? A tattoo parlor? A biker gang?"

"A gang!" they both cried together.

"Dial back a bit," Jenny exhaled. "What are you really saying, Jason?"

"I think we are getting ahead of ourselves," he said. "Have you looked this up online?"

"Not yet. I was planning to do that after dinner."

"Let's do it, then."

Star and Jimmy decided to sit out on the patio. Jenny sat with Jason at the kitchen table, running searches on skulls and feathers.

Jason told her about some forums frequented by private investigators.

"They are pretty cool about sharing information. Why don't you give them a brief description of what Star came up with? Add that it could be some kind of logo."

Jenny registered herself on a couple of websites and posted her question.

"Now what?" she asked Jason.

"Now we wait," Jason said. "Do you want to watch a movie?"

Jenny wanted to watch Downton Abbey reruns. Jason readily agreed.

"You're the best, Jason!" Jenny exclaimed, giving him a hug. "What would I do without you?"

Jason hugged her back and planted a kiss on her forehead. He held her by the arms and stared deep into her eyes.

"If I have my way, Jenny King, you'll never have to find out."

Chapter 14

Jenny's laptop pinged just as the second episode of Downton Abbey came to an end. She got up eagerly to check it out.

"A guy in Atlanta believes it could be a gang logo," she told Jason.

"Can he be more specific?" Jason asked.

Jenny pursed her lips.

"That's all he says."

The computer pinged again.

"Oh wait. Someone else is writing a reply to my question. He calls himself TopNJPI."

Jason stifled a yawn.

"What does this one say?"

"He says the feathers sound familiar. He wants me to send him a picture."

"Do it."

Jenny looked around for Star's drawings. She had shoved them in a kitchen drawer. She clicked a photo with her phone and sent it on.

Jason came and sat next to Jenny. They waited impatiently for the man to respond.

Jenny read his reply off the screen.

"He says the feathers make him think of a local Jersey gang."

"A biker gang?" Jason asked quizzically. "Is this guy sure?"

Jenny typed furiously, talking with a man she had never met or heard of before.

"He is asking me to look up the Purple Rooster gang."

Jason pulled out his phone and started typing. Jenny did the same with her computer. They looked at each other at the same time.

Jason showed her the picture he had pulled up on his phone.

"It does look a bit like Star's drawing," Jenny said grudgingly. "But it's not the same."

"Nothing matches other than the feathers," Jason said.

Jenny started pulling up information on the Purple Rooster gang.

"Oh my!" she exclaimed as her mouth fell open. "The Purple Rooster is a street gang in New Jersey."

"What do they do?"

"They are involved in all kinds of illegal activities, mostly drugs. But that's not all, Jason."

"Get on with it, Jenny."

"They are connected to some big crime family."

"That's not uncommon," Jason said.

"This family is supposedly at war with the Bellinis."

Jenny and Jason were both speechless.

"You don't think this gang came here to kill Petunia?" Jenny asked haltingly. "She walked away from that life a long time ago."

"But she was still a Bellini," Jason said softly.

He tapped his fingers on the table.

"This is too big for you or me, Jenny. You need to take this to the police."

"What about Vinny? Shouldn't I tell him first?"

"There's no telling how he will react to this," Jason warned.

"This is all speculative," Jenny argued. "I think we should talk to Vinny first."

"Do you have his number?"

Jenny nodded.

Vinny offered to meet her somewhere. Jenny reluctantly invited him to Seaview.

"Do you know what you're doing?" Star asked.

"I'm doing it for Petunia," Jenny said.

Vinny arrived with Enzo in tow. Enzo was wearing another track suit. Vinny was dressed in a cream colored suit tailored to perfection. Both men wore white colored fedoras. Six Pac and the guys stayed outside with the car.

Jenny didn't waste any time in showing Vinny the drawings.

"What's this, sweetheart?" Vinny asked, chewing on his cigar. "Some kind of art project?"

Jenny told them about the man in the hooded jacket.

"I did some digging. I think he was from the Purple Rooster gang."

Vinny and Enzo both threw back their heads and laughed.

"What do you know about the Purple Roosters?"

"Nothing," Jenny admitted. "But I thought this picture looked like their logo."

"The feathers are a bit familiar," Vinny conceded. "But they are not purple."

"Aren't you fighting with that gang?" Jenny asked.

Vinny and Enzo looked at each other.

"Not anymore," Enzo said. "I had a beef with those boys thirty years ago. But I made up with them when I was in prison."

"Wait. Are you thinking the Purple Roosters whacked my Ma?" Vinny asked.

Jenny was beginning to feel embarrassed.

"It was just a thought. I have no other suspects."

"They wouldn't dare put a hit on my girl," Enzo whispered. "But since you brought it up, I am going to ask around."

"Did many people know Petunia was living in Pelican Cove?"

"Most people thought she was dead," Enzo whispered. "I let them think that. It was easier than answering questions about what happened to her."

"Do you think Peter Wilson, err Fabio, could have told anyone about Petunia?"

Enzo looked at her coldly.

"My men are loyal to me, girl. I trust Fabio with my life. I trusted him with my baby girl's life. He took care of her all these years."

Vinny and Enzo ate Jenny's brownies before they went back.

"What do you think, Jason?" Jenny asked. "Was someone taking care of an old grudge?"

"Why wait so long to do that? Petunia lived here without incident for twenty five years."

Something Enzo had said niggled at Jenny.

"What if this person was unable to track her down?"

"You mean what if he or she was in prison."

"Is that too farfetched?" Jenny frowned.

"It does seem fantastic at first." Jason narrowed his eyes. "But it's not farfetched, Jenny. I have heard of stranger things in court."

"How did this person find Petunia? She hadn't talked to any of her family members since she came here."

"Peter Wilson!" they both exclaimed together.

"He was her only link to her old life," Jenny said in triumph. "His alibi doesn't help him here. What if Peter Wilson told someone about Petunia?"

"I think you might have something there, Jenny," Jason nodded. "But this is bigger than you can handle."

"I will go to the police station first thing tomorrow morning," Jenny promised. "They can question Wilson about this."

Jenny went up to her room after bidding Jason goodnight. She hoped her latest theory would lead them to the killer. She was saddened by the thought of Petunia being the victim of some old feud. She tossed and turned under the covers, waiting impatiently for the sun to rise.

Star accompanied Jenny to the café the next morning. She wasn't used to early mornings. Jenny forced her to sit down and put her feet up after she had yawned nonstop for fifteen minutes.

Jenny poured her a fresh cup of coffee.

"You didn't have to come in with me. I have to learn to handle everything myself."

"This work is too much for one person," Star argued as Jenny mixed the muffin batter. "You can't work in the kitchen and serve the customers at the same time."

"What if I ask them to serve themselves?" Jenny thought out loud. "I can just set everything out on a couple of tables."

"You need to think seriously about hiring some help, Jenny."

"I know that," Jenny said. "Just not yet."

Adam came in for breakfast.

"We have a lot to talk about," Jenny told him as she served him the breakfast special, a three cheese omelet with spinach and sundried tomatoes.

"You want to talk here?" Adam asked.

"No. Let me take care of the breakfast rush. I'll see you at the station."

Heather came in to help. Jenny packed some fresh oatmeal raisin cookies in a box and walked to the police station. She handed the box to Nora, the desk clerk.

"Just what I needed," Nora said happily.

"No cookies for me?" Adam teased when she entered his office.

"Too much sugar is not good for you," Jenny kidded.

She told Adam about the gang logo first.

"The Purple Rooster gang used to be notorious," Adam told her. "But they have fizzled out in the past few years. Their leader was killed and most of the older members went to prison."

"So you don't think they could have a hand in this?"

"The Bellinis don't think so, do they?"

Jenny shook her head.

"Can you double check, just in case?"

"This is out of my jurisdiction, Jenny. But I'll put some feelers out."

Jenny continued her theory about old feuds.

Adam's eyebrows shot up.

"That's one line of investigation we haven't pursued."

"Do you think there's any substance to it, though?"

"If it was a gang hit, we may never find out who did it, Jenny."

Adam had turned serious.

"We are hitting a wall wherever we turn," Jenny said in frustration.

"I know your efforts helped us solve some murders, Jenny. But things don't often work that way."

Jenny turned to Peter Wilson.

"He was the only one who knew Petunia's real identity," Jenny stressed. "He has to be involved in this somehow."

"These fellows are generally pretty loyal," Adam mused. "I don't see Wilson going against his boss. He has his own family to think about."

"That's all I have," Jenny sighed. "But none of this helps."

"We are doing all we can, Jenny. Don't give up yet."

"Have you checked Laura Bellini's finances?" Jenny asked suddenly.

She told Adam about the million dollars Petunia had given her.

"There's something else about Laura," Adam said reluctantly. "Police didn't find the gun registered to her."

"You think she ditched it?"

"She said it went missing."

"She has to be lying, Adam."

"Laura said she reported her missing gun long before coming to Pelican Cove."

"The first time or the second time?"

Adam was apologetic.

"We are still following up on that."

Adam's phone rang. Jenny caught a few random words as the person on the other end let loose a tirade. Adam apologized repeatedly. Jenny stared at him in amazement. She had never seen him so subdued before.

Adam hung up the phone and rubbed his eyes with his hands.

"That was Barb," he sighed. "She's not happy."

"How is she?" Jenny asked with genuine concern.

"Recovering nicely, judging by her energy."

Barb Norton was well known for making absurd demands of everyone. But Jenny knew she was justified this time.

"She wants to know why we haven't caught her attacker yet," Adam disclosed.

"Why haven't you?"

"We don't have a single eyewitness," Adam growled, frustrated. "It's almost like some phantom figure hit her and disappeared in thin air."

"Just like Petunia," Jenny said softly.

She sat straighter, her eyes growing wide as a sudden thought hit her.

"What if the two incidents are related? Could someone be targeting older women?"

"I don't think so, Jenny," Adam dismissed.

"Why not?" Jenny argued. "They were both the same age. They were both the same height and build although Petunia's hair was darker."

"Stop right there, Jenny," Adam warned. "I have too many things to work on already. I don't want you to start a panic in town with these silly theories."

"It's not silly," Jenny said coldly. "I think it's worth thinking about. It's not like you have any tangible leads, anyway."

"I can't stop you, Jenny. Do what you want."

"Let's not fight, please," Jenny urged.

Adam's voice turned softer.

"That's the last thing I want to do, Jenny."

"Why don't you come to Seaview for dinner tonight?" Jenny wheedled. "I'm making enchiladas. Bring Tank with you."

"Sounds like a plan," Adam smiled. "We'll get dessert."

"Are the twins coming here for fall break?"

"Probably," Adam said. "I plan to make it worth their while."

"Planning something special?" Jenny asked.

Adam hid a smile but said nothing.

Jenny set a brisk pace back to the café, enjoying the pleasant weather. She decided it was a good time to call her son.

"When are you coming home, Nicky?"

"Looks tough, Mom," her son said, breaking into a coughing fit. "I have too many classes this time."

Jenny knew her son always started coughing when he was lying. She wondered what he was hiding this time.

"Are you and the twins stirring up trouble?" she asked suspiciously.

Her son and Adam's twins went to different colleges but they talked to each other regularly.

"Of course not, Mother," Nick said, starting to cough again.

Jenny smiled all the way back to the café. She could be patient when needed. She guessed Adam had a surprise for her. Maybe there was still some hope for them.

Chapter 15

A crisp breeze blew over the ocean the next morning, signaling the arrival of fall. On the deck of the Boardwalk Café, the Magnolias stared with amazement at Molly, their coffee forgotten.

"What do you mean, you were mistaken?" Heather cried. "How is that possible?"

Molly blushed.

"You know …"

"How did you find out?" Jenny asked gently, placing a hand on Heather to calm her down.

"At the doctor's," Molly said. "It was so embarrassing."

"Was Chris with you?" Heather asked.

Molly nodded.

Betty Sue leaned forward in her chair, her knitting needles clacking in a fast rhythm.

"You do know how these things are supposed to happen?" she asked Molly.

Molly looked like she was about to burst into tears.

"Begin at the beginning," Star ordered. "I think I am missing something here."

"It's all pretty straightforward," Molly shrugged. "Chris and I went to our doctor's appointment. It was my first appointment for the baby. Turns out I am not pregnant. I never was."

All the women at the table looked sorry.

"I was knitting this for the baby," Betty Sue said, holding up something fluffy in a peach color.

"How did Chris take it?" Jenny asked.

"He was disappointed. So was I."

"What now?" Star wanted to know.

"This whole misunderstanding forced us to consider parenthood," Molly admitted. "I was very impressed by how Chris reacted to it."

"Chris Williams is a good man," Betty Sue sighed.

For the past twenty years or so, she had believed he would marry her granddaughter Heather.

Jenny knew Molly hadn't been very sure about how committed Chris was to her.

"Do you trust him now?" she asked Molly.

"I trust him more," Molly said diplomatically. "I know he is going to be a good father."

"So when are you planning a family?" Star laughed. "For real, this time."

Molly blushed prettily.

"Soon."

"Let them get married first," Jenny nudged her aunt. "Have you thought about setting a date?"

Earlier that year, Chris and Molly had started wearing promise rings.

"Don't you want a proper engagement first?" Star asked.

"We are talking about it," Molly told them.

"I think you should just elope," Heather winked.

"No, thanks!" Molly said firmly. "This might be my second wedding, but I want to do it right."

Jenny secretly looked forward to planning Molly's wedding. She had come to love Molly like a sister, and she hoped to be in the wedding party.

Jenny spotted Vinny walking on the beach, accompanied by his posse. Molly followed her gaze.

"How's your search going, Jenny?" she asked.

"I have a lot of theories," Jenny admitted reluctantly. "But there is no proof to support any of them."

"You just haven't found it yet," Star said encouragingly. "Keep looking, sweetie."

"I almost forgot," Jenny exclaimed. "Jason and I are meeting Adam in a few minutes."

Jason stepped out on the patio just then. He greeted the Magnolias and looked inquiringly at Jenny.

"Ready to go?"

Jenny pulled off her apron and nodded. They went down the steps to the beach on their way to the police station.

"Do you think Adam will agree?"

Jenny was feeling doubtful about their mission.

"What does he have to lose?" Jason quipped.

Adam wasn't too happy to see them.

"I have a long day ahead of me, Jenny. What are you two doing here?"

"We have a request," Jason said. "We want access to the traffic cameras."

"Why?" Adam asked, tapping his pencil on the desk.

Jenny reminded Adam about the car in the parking lot.

"I am almost sure the killer escaped in that car. We need to find out where it went."

"The cameras might have caught the tag plates," Jason said hopefully. "Who knows? We may even get a glimpse of the driver."

"Okay," Adam said grudgingly. "I am only doing this because I need a break in the case. But you will have to watch the tapes here."

Jason and Jenny agreed readily.

"How are we going to do this?" Jenny asked.

One of the techs at the police station helped them. They decided to focus on the road around the parking lot. They chose a time slot of 5 to 8 AM, the approximate time of Petunia's death.

"We should watch for a dark sedan with a dent around the trunk."

It was slow work. Nora, the desk clerk, came around to chat with

Jenny. Jenny made some polite conversation. They drank the sour coffee Nora offered. Jenny took one sip and set it aside.

"I don't see any cars matching the description," Jason said after some time.

He was beginning to look frustrated.

"Let's widen the search," Jenny suggested.

Jason was staring at one camera which showed a gas station.

"You think that guy might have gone in here?" he wondered.

They decided to look at all the cars going into the gas station. None of the cars stopping at the station matched the description of the car they were looking for.

"What's that kid doing there?" Jason asked, pointing at a figure. "He seems to be in and out of that door a lot."

"That must be Skinner," Jenny said. "He works at the gas station. He does a lot of odd jobs in addition to managing the cash register."

Jenny grew bored as the tapes rolled slowly. She yawned and that set Jason off.

"Hold it," Jenny cried suddenly.

She was pointing to something on the screen.

"What's that? That right there?"

Jason paused the picture and peered at the screen.

"Looks like the same kid."

"What is he wearing?" Jenny asked in a hushed voice.

"A jacket?"

"Look at the back of the jacket, Jason," Jenny said.

"Hmmm … looks like something's printed on the back."

Jenny made Jason zoom in to the picture. She could make out a few feathers.

"Wanna bet it's the same jacket?" Jenny banged a fist on the table. "That little creep. He lied to us."

"Hold it, Jenny. What are you blabbering about?"

Jenny explained her theory to Jason.

"Let's go talk to him," Jason said, leaping up.

Jenny's cell phone rang when Jason was driving to the gas station. It was Adam.

"What's going on? Where did you rush off all of a sudden?"

Jenny gave him the condensed version.

"Turn around right now!" Adam ordered. "You are not going there alone."

"Jason is here with me."

"You are both crazy. What if this kid is really the person we are looking for? He could have a gun."

"Relax!" Jenny said. "I've met that kid. He's harmless."

Adam became more incensed.

"You don't know that, Jenny. Please stop the car immediately. Let me talk to Jason."

"Jason says we can handle it."

"Stop right now, or I will arrest you both for messing with police business."

"Don't be such a grouch, Adam."

Jenny hung up the phone.

"What did he say?" Jason asked her.

"That's just Adam being Adam."

A police car with flashing lights and a blaring siren overtook them two minutes later. It pulled into the gas station's parking lot ahead of Jason. Adam stumbled out, leaning on his cane. He looked ready to burst.

"That was quick," Jenny said glibly.

"I'll deal with you later, Jenny." He turned toward Jason. "Let me do the talking."

"Fine by me," Jason shrugged.

The kid working at the gas station came out to see what was happening.

"This is Skinner," Jenny introduced him.

"Do you work here?" Adam asked.

The kid looked like he was about to bolt.

"I ain't done nothing wrong," he said sullenly.

"No one's saying you did," Adam snapped. "I need to ask you a few questions."

The kid shrugged.

"I got nothing to hide."

"You remember what we talked about?" she began. "You told us you didn't know the guy in the hoodie."

"So what?"

"We saw you wearing the same jacket later that day," Jenny said. "How did you get it if you didn't know that man?"

The kid's eyes filled with fear.

"I found it in the dumpster. I swear."

"You better not be lying, son," Adam said sternly.

"I'm not lying. I found it in the dumpster out back. It was a windy day and I was feeling cold. So I wore it."

"You picked it up from the trash?" Adam asked.

Skinner was defensive.

"I don't go dumpster diving. But there was nothing wrong with that jacket. Can't be too picky, you know. I don't even make minimum wage."

"I think he's telling the truth," Jenny said supportively.

"Thank you for your opinion," Adam said coldly. He turned toward Skinner. "We will need to look at your security cameras."

"You have to talk to my boss," the kid said. "But we don't have any cameras near the dumpster."

"Are you sure?" Adam asked.

"There's a camera out back but it's broken. The dumpster's out of its range anyway."

Adam asked a few more questions but he had to let the kid go.

He stalked back to his car and left without a word.

"Looks like he's really mad at you, Jenny."

Jason drove to Ethan's Crab Shack for lunch. Ethan was Adam's twin. He had the same imposing height and deep blue eyes but the similarities ended there. The deeply etched laugh lines around his face were a testament to his cheerful personality.

Ethan greeted her with a hug.

"Haven't seen you in a while, Jenny."

Jason ordered the special of the day, which was an assortment of fried fish and crabs. Ethan brought up a platter loaded with hand cut fries and hush puppies. Jenny couldn't wait to dip them into his special tartar sauce.

"I'm sorry I wasted your time."

"What are you talking about?" Jason acted surprised. "I had a wonderful day."

"We hit another wall," Jenny said gloomily.

"We did find something," Jason reminded her. "So far, we had only heard about that jacket. Now we know it did exist. That means the man is real too."

"You're right," Jenny said, cheering up.

"What happened to the car, though?" Jason mused. "That's a big puzzle."

Jenny bit off a piece of fried flounder. It melted in her mouth.

"I'm losing hope, Jason. I don't think we are ever going to find out the truth."

"Don't give up yet, Jenny. We just have to keep looking."

"How is that grumpy brother of mine behaving?" Ethan boomed as he set bowls of peach cobbler before them.

Jenny rolled her eyes.

"He just threw a fit. Would you believe it?"

"That's his way of showing his love," Ethan laughed.

Jenny felt her cheeks burn.

"Has he always been like this?"

"He's changed a lot since he met you, Jenny," Ethan assured her. "For the better."

Jenny thought of Ethan's words as she walked on the beach after dinner. A big hairy body almost toppled her.

"Tank! You adorable darling! I missed you."

She patted the big dog and scratched him under his ears. Tank butted her in the knee and sat down in the sand.

Adam stood in the shadows, looking at her with a guarded expression.

"I was hoping to run into you."

"Me too," Adam said, clearing his throat.

They walked for a while, Tank running in circles around them, wagging his tail.

Jenny wondered if Adam expected her to apologize.

"I am sorry, Jenny," he said suddenly.

He pulled her close to him and hugged her tightly.

"You scared the hell out of me."

"I'm fine, Adam. See?"

"What if that kid had pulled out a gun?"

"People in Pelican Cove don't own guns. You told me so yourself."

"But someone does have a gun, Jenny. Someone who shot Petunia in cold blood."

"Thank you for worrying about me," Jenny said softly.

"Of course I worry," Adam said. "You are the light of my life, Jenny King. What would I do if anything happened to you?"

Chapter 16

The Magnolias were sitting out on the deck, having their mid-morning coffee break. The café had been unusually busy for breakfast and Jenny was exhausted.

"We ran out of muffins," she explained as she set out some cookies with the coffee. "Why don't you all stay on for lunch?"

"You have enough on your plate without us crowding you," Molly said. "I wish I could help you more, Jenny. But I can't get away from my desk at the library."

"Heather and Star are both pitching in," Jenny said gratefully. "I don't know what I would do without them."

"Petunia was a quiet one, wasn't she?" Star said.

"But she did the lion's share of work around here," Jenny spoke up. "She was always there, telling me what to do next. I need to make all those decisions now and I am not good at them."

"You will learn," Betty Sue consoled her. "What other option do you have?"

"Petunia always spoke up when it mattered," Molly pointed out. "She wasn't afraid to voice her opinion."

Jenny closed her eyes and leaned back in her chair.

"I miss her so much!"

"We all do, sweetie," Star said, stroking her back.

Barb Norton puffed up the steps of the Boardwalk Café, scratching her arm.

"How are you, Barb?" Betty Sue asked solicitously. "Have you recovered from that bump on your head?"

Barb assumed the air of a martyr.

"It's the price I pay for what I do."

Heather giggled.

"Stop tittering at my plight, young lady. Hasn't your grandma taught you better?"

"Leave my girl alone," Betty Sue snapped. "What do you want?"

"Did you get my letter about the fines?" Barb's tone was acerbic. "Hardly anyone has paid up."

"You can't penalize people just because they have some water in their bird feeders," Star scoffed. "Get real, Barb. No one is paying those ridiculous fines."

"How do you propose we deal with these mosquitoes then?" Barb asked, scratching her neck now.

Her arm and neck had both turned red.

"Stop scratching, Barb!" Betty Sue hollered. "You're making it worse."

"These little bloodsuckers keep biting me."

"They must like you a lot," Heather grinned.

Jenny took pity on the woman.

"Would you like a cookie, Barb?"

"I want more than one. How about five dozen?"

"Huh?" Jenny was bewildered.

"I am putting together a bake sale," Barb said. "It's the only way to raise money for the extermination."

"I'm sorry I can't help you this time."

"But I am counting on you, Jenny. Pelican Cove is counting on you."

"I'm up to my ears in work, Barb. Plus I still have to plan Petunia's memorial. There's no way I can squeeze this in."

"Petunia would never have turned her back on me," Barb said cagily.

"That's below the belt, Barb!" Star exclaimed.

"Take that back!" Betty Sue cried.

Heather and Molly watched on with their eyes wide.

Jenny caved.

"Two dozen cookies, Barb. That's it. Any kind I choose."

"That'll be just fine, dear," Barb smiled. "Don't forget the meeting tonight, girls. I will see you there."

"Does she ever get tired of these meetings?" Molly groaned.

"She just likes to boss people around," Star quipped.

"She was right about Petunia," Jenny sighed. "How can I ever live up to her?"

"You are doing good, kid," Star assured her. "She would be proud of you."

The other women agreed with Star. They tried to cheer Jenny up. She thought they were just being kind.

"Any luck watching those cameras?" Heather asked.

"We watched the traffic cams in town yesterday," Jenny told her. "Didn't find much."

"I admire your patience. You must have looked at every camera in town."

"What was that?" Jenny asked suddenly. "Heather, you are brilliant!"

She ran inside and called Jason.

"I just thought of something. What are you doing right now?"

Jason invited her to come over.

"Can you handle the lunch crowd again?" she asked her aunt. "Soup's almost done. I already mixed the chicken salad."

Star assured her she would be fine. Jenny hurried to Jason's office. She apologized for disturbing him.

"I don't have anything on my calendar," he assured her. "Just some paper work. You know I'll do anything to get out of that."

Jenny tried to curb her excitement.

"This might be nothing," she began. "But something Heather said got me thinking."

"Go on," Jason encouraged her.

"We looked at the tapes at the police station. But what about other cameras in town?"

"Didn't you already talk to some store owners? I thought no one in Pelican Cove used security cameras."

"Those were places along the beach," Jenny nodded. "But there's another camera we can look at."

Jason looked blank.

"The gas station!" Jenny exclaimed. "Remember what that kid Skinner said about the camera at the back?"

"It wasn't working?"

"Right. But I'm sure they have more cameras around the front."

"That does seem logical," Jason said. "Want to go check them out?"

Jenny was relieved to find Skinner working at the gas station.

"We want to look at your security cameras."

"Weren't you here yesterday?" he asked sullenly. "I told you the camera at the back was busted."

"How many more cameras do you have?" Jason asked.

The kid shrugged.

"A few, I guess."

Jenny and Jason went out and walked around the little store. Jenny squinted in the bright noon sunshine, trying to spot the cameras.

They counted four more. Jenny pointed to a camera mounted near the entrance to the parking lot. The road directly led to the dumpster at the back.

"We don't need the dumpster camera," she said eagerly. "Our man would have to enter from somewhere right? Any of these cameras might have caught him."

Jason agreed with her theory. They went back inside.

"We want to look at your tapes."

"It's all set up in that little office at the back," he said. "I'm not allowed to go in there."

"Do you want me to call the Sheriff?" Jason asked. "He can come here with a warrant and seal your place."

"Take it easy, mister," the kid complained. "I don't want to lose my job."

He pulled his phone out of his pocket and tapped some keys. He thrust the phone in Jason's face.

"That's my boss. Why don't you call him and sort it out. Keep me out of it, okay?"

Jason started dialing the number.

"I didn't tell you about the cameras," Skinner reminded him.

Jason stepped outside and Jenny followed him.

The gas station owner turned out to be a guy Jason knew well. Jenny folded her hands and leaned against a wall, waiting for Jason to get on with it. Jason got to the point after five minutes of small talk.

"We went to high school together," Jason told Jenny when he hung up.

"Not hard to believe, considering you know everyone in town."

"He knows Adam too," Jason explained. "And he knew Petunia well."

"What about the cameras?" Jenny was getting impatient.

"He says we have full access. We can look at any footage we want. He's going to call the kid and let him know."

The phone rang inside just as Jenny pushed the door open. Skinner gave some brief replies and hung up.

"I'm supposed to let you in there," he grumbled.

He pulled out a big bunch of keys from a drawer and ambled to the back. A small door lay hidden behind stacks of merchandise. The kid tried a couple of keys before he found the right one.

"Can you figure this thing out?" he asked, pointing at a computer on a tiny desk. "Just holler if you want something."

Jenny was feeling parched.

"Actually, I could use some coffee."

"I can ring it up for you," Skinner nodded.

Jenny glanced at a half full flask sitting on a warmer and decided to pass. She filled two cups from an automatic coffee machine. It was sweeter than she preferred but at least it didn't taste bitter.

The office at the back was barely bigger than a closet. Jason pointed to the tiny chair. Jenny squeezed into it, hugging her knees together. Jason stood behind her with his back against the wall.

Jenny started the computer and waited for it to boot up. The desktop had a folder titled 'security footage'. She clicked on it to find a bunch of folders arranged by week. Each folder contained a file for a particular day.

"This looks well organized," Jason said.

They pulled up the file for the day in question. The picture was slightly grainy at first.

"That's before sunrise," Jason noted.

They skimmed through the whole tape without much luck.

"What exactly are we looking for?" Jason asked. "A dark colored sedan?"

"What if the man just walked in for a drink or something? He may have parked his car somewhere else."

"Run the video again, Jenny. We'll focus on the people this time."

Jenny's stomach growled.

"Oops," Jenny apologized. "I had a light breakfast today."

"Hold on," Jason said.

He went out into the store and came back a few minutes later, clutching a bunch of snacks. Jenny chose an energy bar and bit off a big chunk.

"Thanks."

Jason started munching on some potato chips.

They peered at the people entering and leaving the store. Jenny grew frustrated after an hour had passed.

"This is a big waste of time."

"We have looked at a couple dozen people," Jason agreed.

"None of them walked to the back of the store," Jenny noted. "I don't see how that jacket appeared in the dumpster. Unless it was there all along?"

"That's not possible," Jason pointed out. "Our man was seen wearing it that morning, remember?"

Jenny suddenly jabbed her finger at the screen.

"What's that?"

A disheveled man was pushing a shopping cart ahead of him. It was filled with some boxes and knick knacks. A dark colored cloth lay on top.

"Can you zoom in on that?" Jason asked.

Jenny fiddled with the mouse and enlarged the portion showing the cart.

"Do you see those feathers?" Jenny exclaimed. "That's our jacket."

"What's it doing in that cart?"

"Do you know who that man is?" Jenny asked Jason.

"Looks like a hobo, Jenny, or someone down on his luck."

Jenny reversed and forwarded the video, training her eyes on the man with the cart. He came out of the store carrying something wrapped in paper. He wheeled his cart to one end of the parking lot and sat down.

"That looks like a hot dog," Jenny said, as the man on the screen unwrapped the object he was carrying.

He ate the hot dog very slowly, as if savoring each bite. Then he just sat on the ground, staring into the distance.

A figure came out from the store and walked toward the man with the cart.

"That's the kid," Jason said, stamping his foot to get some circulation going.

Their mouths dropped open as they watched the screen.

"I don't believe it!" Jenny yelled. "That little creep!"

Jenny and Jason rushed outside to the cash register. Skinner was packing some stuff into a backpack.

"Where do you think you're going?" Jenny cried.

Skinner looked up with a pained expression.

"Home? My shift's over."

He nodded at a young girl who was coming in.

"You lied to us," Jason said sternly.

"You didn't find the jacket in the dumpster," Jenny seethed.

"Okay, okay, calm down. I took it from some guy."

"Do you realize this is a murder investigation?" Jason fumed. "I could have you arrested for obstruction."

"I don't want no trouble," Skinner said, holding up his hands. "I liked the jacket so I took it."

"Do you know where the man got it?"

"No idea. I just took it and he didn't say a word."

"Did you see where he went?" Jenny asked.

"Sorry," Skinner said, shaking his head. "Never saw him again."

"Would you recognize him if you saw him?" Jason asked.

"I don't think so. I didn't really look at him."

Chapter 17

That evening, Jenny sat alone in the Rusty Anchor, Pelican Cove's one and only pub. She was waiting for Adam. She saw a lot of familiar faces around her and waved at a couple of them. But she didn't get up and go talk to anyone.

Eddie Cotton, the bartender and pub owner, placed a glass of wine before her.

"What's got into you, Jenny? You seem quiet."

Jenny's eyes filled up.

"I'm trying everything I can to find Petunia's killer. But I can't seem to catch a break."

"If anyone can do it, Jenny, you can," Eddie said loyally.

Jenny thanked him for his kindness. Adam finally entered the pub. He was out of uniform.

"Sorry I'm late," he said, taking a seat. "I wanted to go home and change."

They were going out to dinner after drinks.

"Where do you want to eat, Jenny?" Adam asked solicitously.

"I don't care," Jenny said. "We can pick up a pie at Mama Rosa's and go home."

"Are you still thinking about that jacket?" Adam asked.

Jenny and Jason had gone to meet Adam from the gas station. He had been impressed by what they had discovered. He was going to look for the man with the shopping cart.

"My men are scouring the nearby towns for that man," Adam assured her. "We tried to get his picture off that video."

"It's probably another dead end," Jenny said darkly.

"Don't lose hope yet, Jenny," Adam comforted her. "We'll get there."

Jenny didn't have the heart to face Vinny the next day. He came to the café twice every day. He greeted Jenny and asked after her. He relished whatever food she put before him. He didn't say much but Jenny found his silence suffocating. She felt he was waiting for her to work her magic and catch the killer.

Star and Betty Sue, the older Magnolias, sat out on the deck. Betty Sue was busy knitting something with lavender yarn.

"What about Barb's grandson?" Star asked.

"The one in Florida?" Betty Sue scoffed. "He's barely out of school."

"Not that one," Star said. "I mean her niece's son. He used to spend his summers in town."

"The one who wears those fancy suits and works in New York?" Betty Sue asked, her eyes gleaming. "He might work. Do you know how old he is?"

"He must be thirty at least," Star said.

"That's younger than my Heather."

"Age doesn't matter anymore," Star quipped. "I think these modern girls prefer younger boys."

Betty Sue puffed up in protest.

"What is the world coming to? That wasn't how it was in my day. Beaus were a lot older than girls. They had to be."

"What are you two up to?" Jenny asked, bringing out a fresh pot of coffee.

Molly had some extra work at the library and she couldn't get away for a break.

"We are just talking," Star said, clamming up. "The usual gossip, you know."

"Where's Heather?"

"Heather's out walking Tootsie," Betty Sue said. "She should be here any minute."

Tootsie was the Morse family poodle and was heavily pampered by Heather and Betty Sue.

"So you're talking about Heather," Jenny winked.

"Betty Sue's trying to set her up with a suitable boy," Star burst out.

Betty Sue muttered under her breath.

"Heather wants to focus on the inn," Jenny told them. "She doesn't have time for men."

"That's what worries me," Betty Sue nodded. "She's almost thirty five. Is she ever going to settle down?"

"All in good time," Star shrugged.

"I don't get it, Betty Sue," Jenny protested. "Just a few weeks ago, you were worried Heather was going out with the wrong kind of men. Now that she's finally sworn off them, you want her to start dating again?"

"I want her to date the right kind of man," Betty Sue cried.

"Someone like Chris, you mean?" Jenny smirked.

"Better than him," Betty Sue said. "Heather's pretty and smart. She runs a business almost singlehandedly. She needs a man who can recognize and respect her abilities."

"I agree with that," Jenny nodded. "But where is she going to find someone like that in Pelican Cove?"

"Who are you talking about?" a voice spoke in Jenny's ear, making her jump.

"Heather!" Jenny exclaimed. "When did you get here? And where's Tootsie?"

"Back home playing with her toys. What are you ladies up to?"

"You're late, Heather!" Betty Sue complained. "It's time to get back to the inn."

"Actually, Heather," Jenny said. "How about a drive?"

"You know I'm your wing woman," Heather grinned. "Just point the way, Captain."

Jenny looked inquiringly at her aunt.

"Go," Star said. "I got the café covered."

"Lunch is ready," Jenny promised. "And I won't be long."

Jenny drove toward the gas station.

"What's the plan?" Heather asked.

"It's a bit silly," Jenny admitted. "I am hoping to run into that man with the cart."

"You think he might be at the gas station again," Heather deduced. "Fingers crossed, then. You never know."

Jenny parked her car and cracked a window open. Heather got out to get some snacks. Skinner came out of the store and waved at Jenny.

Heather and Jenny worked through two big packets of fried, salty stuff and guzzled sodas.

"I have to go in," Jenny said.

"I've been keeping an eye out for him," Skinner told her. "I know how badly you want to talk to him."

Jenny gave up some time later and drove back to the café. She dropped Heather off at the Bayview Inn first.

"Adam rang for you," Star told her just as she entered. "He wants you to go to the police station right away."

Ignoring her yearning for a sandwich, Jenny turned around and started walking to the police station.

"What is it?" she asked, bursting into Adam's room.

"We rounded up all the transients we found in the area. I think we might have found the man with the cart."

"Can you take me to him?"

"Would you be able to recognize him?"

"I haven't actually seen him," Jenny reminded Adam. "I saw him on tape just like you did."

Adam took her to a big one-way mirror and pointed to a bunch of men standing on the other side.

"They can't see you. Take your time, Jenny."

Jenny's gaze picked out the man right away.

"That's him," she said, pointing. "The man in that faded black shirt."

Adam spoke to one of his deputies. The men filed out one by one until the man Jenny had picked remained.

"Let's go in," Adam said.

Adam talked to the man. He seemed skittish and wouldn't answer any questions.

"We are not here to hurt you," Jenny spoke kindly. "We just need your help."

The man looked up and stared at her.

"We saw you at the gas station at the edge of town a few days ago. You were pushing a shopping cart."

The man shrugged.

"Do you remember that?"

"I walk around a lot," he finally said. "Lost track."

"There was a jacket in your shopping cart. The kid from the gas station took it from you."

The man grew disturbed. He talked about how he had been cold for a while.

"Where did you get that jacket?" Adam asked sternly. "Did you steal it?"

The man cowered, clamming up again. No amount of cajoling would make him speak. Adam threatened to arrest him.

Jenny stood up and went out. Adam followed her reluctantly.

"He's scared out of his wits," Jenny glared, her hands on her hips. "Can't you see that?"

"You need a firm hand with these people, Jenny," Adam growled. "Don't tell me how to do my job."

Ten futile minutes later, Adam came out again.

"We'll have to let him go. We have nothing to hold him here."

Jenny stood outside the police station, waiting for the man to come out. She saw him shuffle out of a side door.

"Hello," she called, walking up to him. "Can we talk a bit?"

"I didn't do anything," he said.

"I know that," Jenny said. "I'm not going to hurt you."

The man stared at her uncertainly.

"Let's walk away from here," Jenny suggested.

She led him out of sight of the station.

"My name is Jenny." She held out her hand.

The man hesitated. Then he grasped her hand in a tight grip and shook it.

"I run the café over yonder," Jenny told him. "The Boardwalk Café? I can get you something to eat."

"I don't know," the man said.

"My friend died here on this beach," Jenny said. "She was sitting on a bench over there and someone shot her."

The man's eyes filled with terror.

"Do you know anything about it?"

The man inched a few steps away from her.

"I know you didn't do anything. But I thought you might remember seeing someone. Anyone."

The man slowly shook his head.

"It's that jacket, you see?"

Jenny waited a few minutes for the man to say something. He was looking bewildered.

"Will you let me know if you remember anything? Come to the café when you are hungry. I mean it. I'll fix you up."

"Can I go now?" the man trembled.

Jenny nodded, trying to hide her disappointment. She was sure the man held some information which would be valuable to them. But she had no idea if she would ever see him again.

Back at the café, Star took one look at Jenny and ordered her to sit down. She placed a bowl of chicken soup before her, along with a turkey and cheddar sandwich.

"I'm taking an executive decision. We need a spa night."

Jenny wasn't sure she deserved to let her hair down but she went with the flow.

Heather and Betty Sue arrived at Seaview with Tootsie. Heather was carrying a basket in her arms.

"I have samples from local spas," she said. "I'm trying them out for the inn."

Heather had a bunch of new ideas to drum up business for the Bayview Inn. One of them involved a DIY spa weekend where groups of friends could hang out, giving each other makeovers.

Jenny picked up a lavender sugar scrub. Another small pot was labeled coffee mask.

"These look interesting, Heather."

"Why would someone spend money to stay at the inn?" Betty Sue grumbled. "Wouldn't they spend it at the spa?"

"We are giving them a homely atmosphere where they can unwind with their friends," Heather explained. "The spa doesn't give them that. Many women are intimidated by the sterile environment."

"I agree with Heather," Jenny said, backing up her friend.

Molly arrived, holding a brown paper bag full of avocadoes.

"We are making my special avocado honey mask," she told them. "What are we eating?"

"Calzones from Mama Rosa's," Jenny told her. "And I'm hoping you will make your special brownie sundaes."

Molly pulled out a Tupperware container full of brownies from her bag.

Inevitably, the talk turned to Jenny's investigation.

Betty Sue spoke up. "The one question I can't answer is why Petunia. She never talked back to a seagull. Why kill her, that too in such a heinous manner?"

"It must be connected to her past," Star said. "She led a blameless life since she came to Pelican Cove."

"Are you saying she wasn't blameless when she lived back in Jersey?" Jenny asked.

"We don't know what kind of a person she was," Molly said. "She might have ruffled a few feathers. Or her husband did."

"Or her father?" Star asked darkly.

"So you are all sure Petunia's death has something to do with her mob family?" Jenny asked, looking around at each of them.

"That's the only logical explanation, Jenny," Heather said. "We don't have any other motive."

"So she always had a mark on her head?" Jenny asked them. "She just managed to evade it for twenty five years."

Chapter 18

Jenny parked her car outside the Boardwalk Café the next morning. Although the fall weather had produced some chilly mornings, it was a pleasant enough walk. But Jenny had taken to driving in since Petunia's accident.

The spa night had been good for all of them. The ladies had decided to sleep over at Seaview. They had given each other facials and watched movies until past midnight. Betty Sue and Heather had taken advantage of no guests at the inn. They were enjoying a rare opportunity to sleep in.

Jenny had promised them a grand breakfast at the café.

Jenny spied a figure sleeping against the café wall, huddled under a torn blanket. A shopping cart stood at one side, stuffed with trash bags. A gallon of water was tucked in between the bags. A faded camp chair was placed on top. A small one-eyed teddy bear sat on the folding shelf, giving Jenny a doleful stare.

Jenny didn't have the heart to wake up the man. She went in and started her daily routine. Soon, the café was filled with the aroma of fresh brewed coffee and muffins baking in the oven.

Jenny chopped onions and peppers and started beating eggs for omelets. Captain Charlie, her favorite customer, came in and rang the tiny bell on the counter.

"Good Morning," Jenny greeted him. "Is it six already?"

"Dreaming about that young man of yours?" Captain Charlie teased.

Jenny had in fact been thinking of Petunia. She shook her head and placed a tall cup of coffee on the table.

"Muffins are coming right out."

Captain Charlie commented on the man sleeping outside.

"Seeing a lot of homeless men in town this year," he said.

"Where do they come from?"

"Anywhere, I guess. They are just down on their luck, looking for a square meal and a place to rest their head."

"Do you think they are violent?" Jenny asked.

"Very few of them are," Captain Charlie told her. "Some of them come from good backgrounds. They weren't always hobos."

Jenny thought about Captain Charlie's words long after he left. The breakfast rush had her scurrying around. The Magnolias came in around 8 AM.

"Crab omelets all around," Heather said, peeping into the kitchen. "Need some help?"

"I got this."

"Did you know there's a scary looking man sitting outside the café?"

"Are you talking about the man with the shopping cart?" Jenny asked. "Is he awake?"

"He's sitting up," Heather nodded. "Staring at the ground."

Jenny decided to check on the man after she served the Magnolias. She crossed her fingers and hoped it was the man from the gas station.

Twenty minutes later, she was standing outside the café, looking around for the man. The shopping cart lay against the wall. A neatly folded blanket lay on top of the trash bags. But the man was nowhere to be seen. Jenny looked around, beginning to feel frustrated. She didn't want to miss the opportunity to talk to the man. She walked around the café to the beach on a hunch. The man sat in the sand in a camp chair, staring out at the sea.

"Hello," Jenny called out.

He looked up and gave her a gap toothed smile.

"How about some coffee?"

The man shrugged and stared at her feet.

"Do you want to come inside?"

He stood up and folded his chair. He followed Jenny, carrying the chair in one hand. He put it in his cart when they reached the front.

"Do you like crab?" Jenny asked him. "I am making crab omelets."

The man shrugged again.

Jenny had spoken to the man the previous day so she knew he could talk. She guessed he was a man of few words.

Jenny showed him to a table near the window. He seemed comfortable in the café. She brought out a big platter, loaded with a three egg omelet, toast, juice and a flask of coffee.

"I'll be around if you need anything," Jenny told him.

She watched him from the kitchen. He took his time buttering his toast. Then he picked up his knife and fork and ate his omelet in small bites. Someone had definitely taught him the right table manners. Jenny remembered Captain Charlie's words. Her homeless guy must have come from a good life.

"More coffee?" Jenny asked him when he had eaten everything on his plate.

"Thanks," the man finally spoke.

"Did you like the food?" Jenny asked earnestly.

"Best I have eaten in a while," the man conceded. "Are you a trained chef?"

"Trained in the school of life," Jenny smiled.

"I thought about where I got the jacket," the man said. "It was somewhere around here, on this beach."

Jenny tried to curb her excitement.

"Was it lying somewhere?"

The man looked thoughtful.

"I don't think so. A man gave it to me."

He pointed a finger to his forehead.

"Memory's not what it used to be. It all runs together."

"Take your time," Jenny encouraged him. "There's no rush."

"I was sitting on the beach in my chair. This man was walking around. He hung out here a lot, just like me."

"Do you remember what day it was?" Jenny asked.

291

"A few days ago," the man said. "Don't remember the exact day."

"Can you describe the man?" Jenny asked.

She wanted to ask if he was a hobo too. The man must have guessed what she was thinking.

"He was scruffy," he said thoughtfully. "But I don't think he slept on the beach, know what I mean?"

"That's a big help," Jenny said, thanking the man. "Did he say why he gave you the jacket?"

"Didn't ask," the man muttered. "Kind of threw it away without a backward glance. It was a perfectly good jacket."

The man stood up to leave. Jenny told him he was welcome at the café anytime. She packed a few muffins in a brown paper bag and handed it to the man.

"Thank you for your help."

"Good luck," the man nodded and left.

Jenny stood at the café door, waving goodbye as he pushed his cart down the street.

Jason Stone came up the street and hailed Jenny.

"Got any breakfast left? I'm starving."

"You won't believe who that was!" Jenny beamed with excitement as she set a loaded plate before Jason.

"Why did the guy throw away the jacket?" Jason asked, raising his eyebrows.

"He wanted to get rid of it, of course!"

"We can agree it was deliberate."

"It also means this wasn't an accident," Jenny said. "The guy ditched the jacket to avoid suspicion."

Jason cut off a big bite of omelet and wolfed it down.

"We always come back to the same point, Jenny. It was a man on this beach. Now who do we know who was definitely going to be here?"

"This homeless guy said the man was scruffy. He wasn't exactly a hobo but he wasn't normal either."

"Do you know anyone who fits that description?" Jason quizzed.

Jenny sat down before him, glad to rest her feet.

"You know what? I do!"

Jenny thought of the man who used to walk up and down the beach.

"There was a man here," she told Jason eagerly. "I spoke to him once or twice. He used to walk around here all the time, writing something in the sand."

"Writing what?"

"I don't know," Jenny said. "He used to scribble something with a stick and wait for the waves to wash it off."

Jason rolled his eyes.

"Where is this man now?"

"Haven't seen him in a while," Jenny said thoughtfully.

"Did he talk to anyone other than you?"

Jenny didn't have an answer for that. They talked about how they could look for the man. Jenny decided to talk to some of the beach regulars, like the woman who walked her dog every day.

Barb Norton came in, followed by a small mousy woman. She commandeered the biggest table in the café and sat down, setting a big pile of files down with a thud.

"I'm putting you down for five dozen chocolate cupcakes," Barb began, pointing a finger at Jenny. "And five dozen each of oatmeal raisin and lemon cookies."

"What are you talking about, Barb?" Jenny asked, bewildered.

"The bake sale?" Barb reminded her. "The Extermination Committee is holding one day after tomorrow. You would have known that if you had come to the last town meeting."

"But that's impossible," Jenny cried. "I told you I can't bake more than two dozen cookies."

"You have plenty of people to help you," Barb scowled, staring suggestively at Jason.

"I'm getting out of here," Jason mumbled.

"Sit down!" Barb ordered. "I'm not done with you."

"I'm no baker," Jason protested.

"Spread the word," Barb ordered. "Call clients up and down the coast. Get them here for the bake sale."

"Is that really going to help, Barb?" Jason asked. "How much money can you possibly raise selling cookies and cakes?"

Barb pulled out a sheet of paper from her file. Jason's eyes widened when he read what was on it.

"You can't possibly …"

"Leave that to me," Barb snapped. "You just focus on getting people here."

"Jason will do that," Jenny said, "but I can't contribute any more this time, Barb. I am already pushing the envelope here."

"You are one of us now, Jenny," Barb wheedled. "Don't you want to do your bit for the town?"

"The Boardwalk Café has always done its bit for the town," Jenny said firmly. "But I am sitting this one out. I have more important things to do."

"You're just blowing me off, girl. I won't forget this."

"Why are you harassing them, Barb?" Betty Sue Morse boomed. "Still yapping about those mosquitoes?"

"Someone has to do right by this town," Barb said pompously.

"You just manage to get everyone riled up," Betty Sue said.

The older women argued over past events where Barb had thrown her weight around. Jason crept out silently. Jenny went into the kitchen, clutching her head.

"Are they still at it?" Heather asked gleefully.

She was chopping celery for the chicken salad.

The lunch crowd began trickling in as soon as Barb left. Jenny thought the day would never end. She forgot all about the man on the beach until dinner that night.

They had a simple meal of grilled fish and salad. It was a cool evening so they chose to sit in the cavernous family room at Seaview. Jenny closed her eyes and let herself be lulled by the sound of the ocean.

"We need to plan Petunia's memorial," Star reminded her. "At least finish planning the menu."

"I want to make all her favorites," Jenny said. "Vinny told me she liked those tiny cocktail meatballs."

Star looked surprised.

"I never knew that. She went along with pretty much everything."

They talked about Petunia for some time. Jenny's heart was heavy. She forced herself to go out for her walk.

She ran into Adam and Tank a few minutes later. Tank put his paws on her chest and licked her face.

"Get down, Tank," Jenny laughed. "Get down."

Adam smiled at her. Unlike Jason, Adam wasn't into impromptu hugs. Jenny was getting used to his standoffish nature.

"You remember that foliage trip we talked about last year?"

"We never made it," Jenny said.

"Why don't we go this weekend?" Adam asked eagerly. "I checked the foliage cam. The leaves are in peak color. It will be a beautiful drive."

"Are you serious?" Jenny asked.

"Of course. Skyline Drive is really beautiful this time of the year. We'll have a good time, Jenny."

"How can you be so insensitive, Adam?" Jenny glowered. "I haven't even buried my friend yet. Her killer is roaming around scot free."

"But ..."

Adam bit his lip and looked away.

"No matter what I do, I can't seem to please you, Jenny."

"I appreciate the thought, Adam," Jenny said, swallowing a lump. "It's just not a good time for me right now."

"You mean it's not a good time for us!"

Chapter 19

It was a windy day at the beach. A middle aged man helped his two toddlers build a sand castle. A young couple waded into the ocean waves, hand in hand. Out on the deck of the Boardwalk Café, the Magnolias sampled the cinnamon apple muffins Jenny had baked that morning. She was trying out a new recipe for autumn.

"How's that Hopkins boy treating you?" Betty Sue asked Jenny.

Jenny had spent another sleepless night, agonizing over what she had said to Adam.

"He wants us to go away for the weekend," Jenny told the Magnolias.

The frothy waves of a high tide crashed against the shore. The Magnolias were enjoying their second cup of coffee.

"That sounds romantic," Heather sighed.

"It's callous, that's what it is," Jenny bristled. "I told him that."

Star and Betty Sue shared a look.

"You have to get on with your life, Jenny," Star said gently. "We all do."

Molly took Jenny's side.

"We all grieve at our own pace. I think Jenny's right."

"You might be pushing him away," Star warned. "He's already miffed because you didn't move in with him."

"I finally have a place I can call my own," Jenny said.

She had been a model wife for twenty years. Her husband had kicked her out one fine day. Jenny had vowed she would never give another man the opportunity to treat her like that again. When her divorce settlement came through, the first thing she had bought herself was a house. She intended to grow old in it, with or without a companion.

"You said it yourself, Star. We have to plan Petunia's memorial."

"We are all going to pitch in for that," Heather said. "If you want to spend a romantic weekend in the mountains, we will understand."

"Time and tide wait for no one," Betty Sue said heavily. "Petunia would want you to be happy, Jenny."

Jenny felt hemmed in from all sides.

"I'll think about it," she sighed.

Later, Jenny closed the café for the day and walked to Jason's office. She had remembered something and she needed his advice.

"Howdy Partner!" Jason greeted her.

"Am I disturbing you?"

"Not at all. I just finished up some paperwork. I do have court tomorrow, though."

"That man I was talking about yesterday," Jenny burst out. "He's the one who pulled that gun."

"Gun? How do I not know this?"

"This guy was arguing with someone for a long time and he suddenly pulled a gun out of his pocket. He ran off before anyone could report it."

"Who was he fighting with?"

Jenny's hands flew to her mouth.

"How could I forget that? It was Peter Wilson."

"The auto shop guy?"

"Yes! The guy Petunia was supposed to meet on the beach that fateful day."

"How is he connected to the man with the gun?"

"I don't know."

"But surely he knows the guy if he was fighting with him?"

"Let's find out."

Jenny didn't know where Peter Wilson lived. Jason told her that wasn't a problem.

"He must be at his shop. Let's go over there right now."

Jason pulled out his car and they reached Wilson's Auto Shop a few minutes later.

Peter Wilson recognized Jenny. He came over to greet them.

"Any new leads?" he asked hopefully.

"Not really," Jenny said. "But I have a few questions for you."

Peter smiled encouragingly.

"Remember the guy on the beach who pulled a gun on you?"

"Mason?"

Jenny turned toward Jason and groaned.

"That's right. I completely forgot his name was Mason."

"What do you want with him?" Peter Wilson asked.

"How is it that you know him?" Jenny asked. "Does he work for you?"

"No, he doesn't," Peter said. "He doesn't have a job as far as I know."

"Is he new in town?" Jason asked.

"Came here a few months ago," Peter nodded. "The Newburys hired him. But they let him go."

"Why?"

Peter Wilson shrugged.

"No idea. He wasn't a big talker."

"What were you fighting about that day?" Jenny asked curiously.

"I offered him a job," Peter explained. "Nothing big, just washing and detailing cars that come in here. He turned it down."

"That was nice of you," Jenny said. "Why did he pull a gun on you?"

"Said it was beneath him," Peter Wilson shrugged. "Accused me of working for his wife."

"Wife?"

"I'm as clueless as you are. Maybe the Newburys can tell you more."

Jenny and Jason thanked the mechanic and went back to their car.

"The Newburys are everywhere!" Jenny exclaimed. "They really do have a finger in every pie, don't they?"

"We'll have to go talk to them," Jason said. "Do you want to call ahead?"

The Newburys were the richest family in Pelican Cove. Rumor had it their riches came from sunken treasure. Ada Newbury considered herself a notch above the people in town. She didn't lose any opportunity driving it home.

"Ada will probably be too busy for us. I have an idea though."

Jenny asked Jason to make a pit stop at the Bayview Inn. She needed Betty Sue's help. Betty Sue and Ada were staunch rivals. Betty Sue's ancestor had been the original owner of the island. It had been called Morse Isle then. In addition to her impeccable heritage, Betty Sue was married to John Newbury, the head of the Newbury family. Although long separated, Jenny knew the couple held each other in high regard.

"You are saying Ada knows this man with the gun?" Betty Sue asked.

"He's connected to the Newburys," Jenny explained. "We want to find out more."

Betty Sue called John Newbury and made sure he would be on hand to meet Jenny.

Jason drove up a hill toward the Newbury estate. Jenny watched the red, yellow and russet leaves on the trees and thought of Adam. She was sure she had done the right thing, refusing to go on the foliage trip.

"Penny for your thoughts," Jason said, his face stretched in a smile.

Jenny noticed the deeply etched laugh lines in Jason's face and the crinkles around his eyes. Jason's emotions were clearly written on his face. He seemed to be recovering well from his breakup. Jenny was glad to see shades of her old friend in that smile.

"Just enjoying the view," Jenny blushed.

"Me too, Jenny, me too," Jason winked.

Jason pulled up before a pair of massive iron gates. The guard in the small cabin spoke to someone with a walkie talkie and waved them through.

Jenny recognized the old housekeeper who let them in. She showed them into a cozy sitting room.

John Newbury stood up to greet them. He was a spry old man in his eighties, with a shock of thick white hair. Jason knew him well.

Ada Newbury sat stiffly in a wingback chair. She gave Jenny a slight nod.

A maid brought in a tea service. Jenny offered to pour the tea. Jason picked up a tiny cucumber sandwich and popped it in his mouth. John Newbury made some small talk. Ada glanced at her watch a couple of times.

"Feel free to leave any time, Ada," John said. "We don't want to hold you up."

Ada's nostrils flared but she said nothing.

John waited until Jenny took a few sips of her tea.

"What brings you here, dear?" he asked. "Betty Sue said it was urgent."

"Thank you for seeing us at such short notice," Jenny began.

Jason picked up a shortbread cookie from a tray and nodded.

"Do you know a man called Mason?"

"Mason Bush?" John asked. "We hired him as chief of security a while ago. But we had to let him go."

"May I ask why?"

John set his cup down and sighed.

"We hired him for the dispensary project. But it never materialized."

The Newburys had proposed setting up a medical marijuana farm and dispensary in Pelican Cove a few weeks ago. The town had strongly protested the idea. The outcry against the whole project had been so effective that the Newburys had failed to get the required licenses from the government. The project was scuttled before it got started.

"I am sorry about that," Jenny said sincerely. "I think it might have helped some people."

John shrugged.

"It wouldn't have worked without the town's approval."

"What happened to this guy after you fired him?" Jason asked.

"He was a good worker," John said. "Was in the military, you know. We offered a generous pay package and a house to live in. He moved his family here from somewhere in the mid-west."

"So he wasn't local," Jenny murmured.

"He was excited about living in a beach town," John said. "His life went downhill after we let him go. His wife left him and filed for divorce. She wouldn't let him talk to the kids."

"But it wasn't his fault he lost the job?" Jenny asked.

"That's right," John said. "But the wife blamed him."

Jenny told him about the man she had seen wandering on the beach.

"I had no idea things were that bad!" John exclaimed. "We gave him a good severance package. I even offered to act as a reference."

"Would you say he was violent?"

John hesitated.

"Honestly, I never interacted with him much. My staff shortlisted him and interviewed him. I just saw him a couple of times when we had those meetings in town."

Ada spoke up.

"He escorted me a couple of times. He was quite jolly. He talked about his wife and kids all the time. Showed me a photo he carried in his wallet. But he changed overnight."

"How do you know that?" Jenny asked.

"I saw him walking around in town after we let him go," Ada told them. "He was unshaven. His clothes were streaked with mud. And I think he was drunk. He was swaying on his feet, muttering to himself."

"Did you talk to him?"

"I don't talk to riff-raff," Ada dismissed.

"Why are you asking so many questions about this man?" John wanted to know.

"He pulled a gun on someone down at the beach one day," Jenny explained. "He might be violent."

John Newbury couldn't hide his shock.

"I'm going to notify security about him immediately. Thanks for bringing this to my attention."

Jenny and Jason said goodbye.

"That was helpful!" Jenny complained as she settled in the car.

"Look on the bright side," Jason soothed. "We know the man's name. Adam can take it from here."

"Didn't Ada say the man was drunk?" Jenny asked a few minutes later. "Do you think he might have gone to the Rusty Anchor?"

Eddie Cotton, the proprietor of the Rusty Anchor, was quite good at remembering people. If Mason Bush had ever been to the pub, Eddie would know.

Jason drove to the Rusty Anchor, Jenny clinging on to the slight ray of hope she felt.

Her phone rang. It was John Newbury.

"Did I leave something behind?" Jenny asked.

"I remembered something," John said. "I called the office to double check before calling you."

"What is it?" Jenny asked, trying to curb her impatience.

"We provided a house for Mason Bush. He moved into it with his family. According to our severance package – I told you it was generous – he can stay there for two months after being let go."

"What does that mean, Mr. Newbury?"

"He's still living in that house," John said. "I made sure he hasn't turned in the keys."

"Do you have the address?" Jenny asked with bated breath.

She motioned Jason to pull the car over.

"Can you write this down?"

"Give me a second," Jenny breathed, pulling an envelope out of her hand bag. She fished around for a pen. "Okay, tell me."

Jenny wrote the address John Newbury provided. She thanked him before hanging up.

She waved the envelope before Jason, her eyes shining with excitement.

"I know where he lives!"

Chapter 20

"Why don't you tell Adam about this?" Jason asked as he fed the address in the GPS.

"Let's go see if he's really living there," Jenny said.

Jason started driving and headed toward a set of houses by the water.

"This place seems familiar," Jenny said. "Have we been here before?"

Jason frowned and tried to think.

"Remember when we were tracing that car's route? One road led out of town. The other one led to a group of houses near the water."

Jenny nodded.

"This is where it led? I think we are getting warmer."

The address turned out to be a ranch style bungalow with a small dock at the back. A speedboat was tied to the dock. Jason parked in front of the house and they got out. The fading evening light cast long shadows as they stared at the house.

"Why don't you stay behind me, Jenny?"

"Don't be ridiculous!" Jenny exclaimed.

A car backfired just then and Jenny felt something whiz past her ear.

"Get down, Jenny," Jason cried. "He's shooting at us."

They ducked behind Jason's car. A couple more shots rang out.

"Do you think it's time to call Adam now?" Jason asked.

Jenny was already dialing her phone.

An engine sputtered to life just then. Jenny peeped from behind the car to see the boat speed away from the shore, leaving a frothy wake.

"He's getting away!" she cried, jumping up. "Do something, Jason!"

"What can I do?" Jason shrugged. "I don't see another boat here."

The speed boat was a mere speck by then.

"Jenny!" a voice crackled through Jenny's phone. "Hello, Jenny! Are you there?"

Jenny plastered her cell phone to her ear.

"He got away, Adam. Where are you? You need to get here soon."

Adam rattled off a string of questions. Jenny calmed down enough to explain that Mason Bush had escaped using a boat.

"I'll be there in five minutes!" Adam said before hanging up.

Jenny leaned against Jason's car, frustrated.

"I'm sure they will catch him," Jason consoled her.

"But is he our man?" Jenny wanted to know.

"He shot at us," Jason said. "He also fled the scene. So he must be guilty of something."

"Do you think he's just crazy?"

"Be patient, Jenny," Jason reasoned. "We'll find out soon enough."

A police cruiser arrived in a cloud of dust and screeched to a stop. Adam hobbled out, leaning on his cane.

"I called the Coast Guard," he told them. "They have patrol boats out on the water. Now tell me everything from the beginning."

Jenny began with what the man with the shopping cart had told her.

"You sat on this all this time?" Adam fumed.

"I told you about the man with the gun," Jenny said. "But you never brought him in."

Jason stepped in.

"Stop fighting, you two. What do we do next?"

"We wait," Adam said. "Why don't you two go home now?"

Jenny realized Adam was right.

Two days later, the Magnolias gathered at the Boardwalk Café, eager for the latest update.

Jenny brought out a plate of fresh blueberry muffins. Star was right behind her with a pot of coffee.

Betty Sue barely glanced at the food.

"So? Was it him? Tell us what you know."

Jenny sat down and poured herself a cup. She gave her friends a watery smile.

"Mason Bush confessed last night. He fired the shot that killed Petunia."

"Why?" Betty Sue cried. "What did she ever do to him?"

Jenny felt the weight of her pent up emotions.

"It was a mistake."

The Magnolias started speaking at once. Jenny felt their outrage. She had been battling the same feelings since the previous night.

"What do you mean, Jenny?" Heather's question filtered through. "Was he just shooting his gun off on the beach?"

"He wanted to kill someone," Jenny said, stressing the last word. "It wasn't Petunia though."

"I'm guessing there is more to this story," Star said. "Start at the beginning, Jenny."

"Mason Bush was a decorated soldier," Jenny started. "He retired from the army and started looking for a job. He got one worthy of his qualifications."

"Is that when the Newburys hired him?" Molly asked.

Jenny nodded.

"The dispensary project was going to be big. Mason was hired as security chief. He had a bunch of people reporting to him. Unfortunately, the project fell through. The Newburys didn't have any need for him so they had to terminate his employment."

"Didn't he look for another job?" Heather asked.

"He must have. But he had a streak of bad luck. His wife left him. She took the kids. What's more, she refused to let him meet them."

"All because he lost that job?" Betty Sue asked.

"That part is not clear," Jenny shrugged. "Maybe they had some other differences. But Mason hit an all time low."

"Is that when he started roaming around like a homeless guy?" Molly queried.

"He was never homeless, really. He had a severance package and a house to live in. He probably had a pension too. He was just depressed."

"What does that have to do with our Petunia?" Star glowered.

"I'm coming to that. Mason started playing the blame game. He figured the town was responsible for him losing his job. And then he remembered the person who was at the forefront in all those protests."

"Who?" All voices yelled together.

"The person who made sure the Newburys didn't get the necessary licenses for their project. The person who saw to it that the project got scuttled."

"Barb Norton," Betty Sue said under her breath.

"Barb Norton?" Molly and Heather cried.

Jenny gave a deep sigh.

"Mason wanted revenge. He decided the only way he would get it was by killing Barb."

"What happened on the beach that day?" Star asked.

Jenny paused to recollect what Adam had told her.

"Mason couldn't sleep. He was walking on the beach when he saw Petunia sitting on that bench. She was the same height and build as Barb. And she was wearing a scarf that looked a lot like something Barb has."

"He thought she was Barb," Star said, welling up.

Jenny nodded.

"He pulled out his gun and shot her. He said he didn't give it much thought."

"He must have fled the scene though, huh?" Heather asked. "He didn't come forward when the police were making their inquiries."

"I guess his survival instincts kicked in when he realized what he had done. He drove his car out of the parking lot. He had done a survey of the town's security systems. He knew about the traffic cameras. He parked his car in the woods and just walked home. He retrieved his car later."

"What about that jacket?" Molly asked. "Wasn't that what led you to him?"

"Mason realized the jacket might put him on the spot. He handed it over to a man on the beach."

There was a stunned silence as the Magnolias digested the story.

"It's not fair!" Molly wailed indignantly. "So Petunia's only fault was she was in the wrong place at the wrong time."

"We have to send her off in style," Betty Sue said in a heavy voice, dabbing her eyes with a lace handkerchief. "Pretty much all we can do now."

Jenny and the ladies banded together to fulfill Petunia's last wishes. She was cremated and her ashes were scattered at sea, the girls saying their final goodbye as they stood on the deck of Captain Charlie's boat.

Jason covered Jenny with his jacket and held her as she cried her eyes out.

Petunia had approved a memorial. The Magnolias got busy planning a grand party. The whole town was invited. Jenny made all her signature dishes, ones Petunia had loved. There were crab puffs, and pimento cheese, chocolate cupcakes and strawberry cheesecake. Jenny made tiny meatballs using a recipe she found in Petunia's diaries.

The Boardwalk Café wore a festive air the day of the memorial. Any tourist might have mistaken it for a happy occasion. But the moist eyes and bittersweet expressions on the women's faces told a different story.

Adam stood close to Jenny with a protective arm around her shoulders.

"Let's get away somewhere," Jenny said.

"You mean now?" Adam asked.

"Not now. Tomorrow. Later. I'm beginning to suffocate here, Adam. I want some time away from here."

"Okay," Adam agreed. "Where do you want to go?"

"Enough with the questions," Jenny snapped, leaving Adam bewildered.

Heather pulled Jenny aside and hissed in her ear.

"What is she doing here?"

Barb Norton had arrived, wearing her usual pompous expression.

"She's got some gall, coming here," Star bristled, coming to stand beside Jenny.

Mason Bush had confessed to attacking Barb in the street. The police told her how he mistook Petunia for her and shot her. Barb hadn't been seen around town after that. Everyone hoped she would go visit her daughter in Florida for a few days.

"I'm asking her to leave," Heather seethed.

Betty Sue had sidled up to them.

"It's not her fault," she sighed. "Let her pay her respects."

Barb walked up and opened her arms. She hugged each of them.

"I am so sorry," she said sincerely. "I know that doesn't change anything. I am going to miss Petunia."

"It's not your fault," Betty Sue said again. "Thank you for coming here, Barb."

Jenny gritted her teeth and spoke about the weather.

A screech of tires sounded outside. A stream of big, black SUVs with dark windows came to a stop outside the café. The Bellinis had arrived.

Vinny and his cohorts got out of one car. Vinny wore a dark suit and a dark fedora. Enzo Bellini stepped out of the second car, wearing a black track suit with his signature white hat. Charles and Laura stepped out of the third car. They made a grand entrance into the café.

Enzo pumped Jenny's hand and thanked her profusely.

"Thank you for catching my baby girl's killer."

Vinny had spotted the meatballs-on-a-stick. He popped one in his mouth and walked toward Jenny.

"Great party, sweetheart! Thanks for doing this."

"Thank you for coming," Jenny muttered, feeling overwhelmed.

She wondered why the Bellinis were still hanging around Pelican Cove. Vinny answered her unspoken question.

"Had to tie up some loose ends ... we are getting out of town after this party."

"Your mother would be glad you came," Jenny told him.

Vinny looked around the packed café.

"Our Ma had a good life here. Are you going to keep the café going?"

Jenny nodded.

"I love this place. You don't mind Petunia left it to me?"

"Not at all. You take care of this place for her."

He pulled out a card from his pocket and handed it to her.

"Call me if you need anything. We take care of our own."

He tipped his hat and wished her good luck. He walked out, flanked by his three men.

Jenny and her friends began tidying up the café. The party moved to Seaview, Jenny's seaside house.

Jason took drink orders from everyone. Adam sat next to Jenny, peering at her with concern.

"I'm not going to break, Adam," Jenny grumbled. "Relax!"

"I know it was a tough day," he said, rubbing Jenny's palm. "But you handled it well."

Heather raised her glass in a toast.

"To Petunia ... may she rest in peace."

Everyone raised their glasses and toasted their dear friend.

"To Petunia."

Star sat up suddenly.

"I almost forgot, Jenny."

311

She went inside and came out with a big sketchbook.

"These are just some designs I have been working on."

Jenny opened the book curiously, and gasped when she saw the drawing inside.

"You talked about sprucing up the café," Star explained. "I thought you might want a new logo."

Jenny stared at the lifelike caricature of Petunia juxtaposed next to some pretty lettering.

"I love it," Jenny squealed, handing the sketchbook to Heather.

Everyone wholeheartedly approved the new logo.

Adam's phone rang shrilly, making Jenny jump. He stood up and walked into the next room to take the call.

Jenny was the only one watching when he came back.

"What's the matter?" she asked, dreading his reply.

"That was the station," Adam said, dumbfounded. "Mason Bush is dead. He was found stabbed in his cell."

Epilogue

The car climbed into the mountains, following the serpentine road. Tall firs towered over them, ablaze in vivid tones of yellow and orange. There was a riot of color wherever Jenny looked.

"Skyline Drive stretches over a hundred miles in the Blue Ridge Mountains," Adam told her.

Jenny had finally caved and agreed to go on the foliage trip with Adam. She fought against the happiness bubbling inside her. Wasn't it wrong to feel such joy when she had just lost her close friend?

"You up for a small hike?" Adam asked, clutching her hand tighter and planting a feather light kiss on her forehead.

They had been holding hands since they left Pelican Cove. Adam had refused to let go. Jenny thought it was romantic. Her heart beat in anticipation of what was coming next.

Adam parked near a trail head and they got out. Adam packed some snacks and drinking water in a backpack and slung it over his shoulder.

"It's about three miles to the falls but they should be worth it," he told Jenny.

Jenny set a leisurely pace as they walked down the trail. They passed a few hikers on the way. They heard the falls before they saw them.

Adam helped Jenny onto a rocky ledge that provided a good view of the waterfall. Jenny looked down on the water, drinking in the beauty of the scene.

She heard a throat clear and whirled around instinctively. The sight before her took her breath away, more so than the churning water below.

Adam Hopkins was down on one knee, holding up a tiny box. He popped it open, making Jenny's eyes go wide and her mouth drop.

"Will you marry me, Jenny King?"

THE END

Acknowledgements

I can't believe this is the sixth book in the series. I have been overwhelmed by the positive response and encouraging emails that are pouring in. I owe thanks to a lot of people – beta readers, advanced readers, family, friends – above all, my readers who take the time to leave reviews or write to me telling me how much they like Pelican Cove.

I am grateful for all the support and encouragement. I hope you keep it coming because it motivates me to write more.

Thank you from the bottom of my heart.

Parfaits and Paramours – Pelican Cove Cozy Mystery Series Book 7

By Leena Clover

Chapter 1

Jenny King maneuvered her van around a steep curve and climbed over a small hill. She was still in awe of this exclusive part of Pelican Cove. The island's wealthy residents had their estates in this part of town. Sprawling mansions, extensive grounds and private beaches were the norm here. So were sparkling swimming pools and an army of domestic staff.

"Can you turn the heat on, please?" Jenny's friend Heather Morse asked with a shiver.

Spring had come early to Pelican Cove, bringing warmer days. Flowers were beginning to bloom along Main Street, promising a riot of color in the coming weeks. But the temperature dropped as the sun crept closer to the horizon. A large mosaic of pinks and mauves was scattered across the March sky, heralding sunset.

Jenny fiddled with the temperature knob and muttered an oath. The van was a relic, rarely used unless Jenny had any deliveries or catering jobs. Jenny didn't remember the last time she had paid for a full tank of gas for the rundown vehicle.

"We're almost there, Heather," she said in a chiding tone. "I told you to wear a warm sweater."

"Why don't you fix the heat?" Heather asked with a pout. "At least get an estimate from the auto shop."

"I did that," Jenny sighed. "I need to replace the thermostat. It's going to cost more than this pile of junk is worth."

The two friends bickered as the sky darkened and the sun set on the horizon.

"Give it a rest, Heather," Jenny pleaded. "I need to catch my breath before Ada Newbury launches her list of complaints."

Ada Newbury was one of the richest women in Pelican Cove. The Newburys belonged to an elite class of the island's population, the Pioneers. Their ancestors had come to the island hundreds of years ago and had been one of the first settlers. People still murmured about how the Newburys had become rich overnight, thanks to sunken treasure. But no one could deny that the Newburys were now rich as Croesus.

"She won't," Heather dismissed. "She loves your food. Why do you think she's paying double to have you cater this party?"

Jenny's face broke into a smile. Her life had taken an unexpected turn. She couldn't believe people from far and wide came to Pelican Cove to visit her café and gorge on her delicious food.

Jenny King had been a suburban soccer mom for most of her life. One day, her husband of twenty years had come home with devastating news. He was going out with a much younger girl who was now in the family way. He asked Jenny to clear out.

Jenny had sought shelter on the remote island of Pelican Cove. Her aunt, Star, had welcomed her warmly and opened her house and heart to Jenny. After letting her mope and sulk for a few weeks, Star had cajoled Jenny into starting work at her friend Petunia's café. The rest, as they said, was history.

Jenny had started working her magic in the kitchen and now the whole town of Pelican Cove was singing her praises. People lined up to taste her food. Jenny didn't disappoint, coming up with delicious new recipes every few days, using the area's abundant local produce and fresh seafood.

She had built a new life for herself on the island. She had made lasting friendships and found something she had never imagined she would have in her life again. Jenny King was in love.

Instead of settling into the mid forties' drudgery she thought was her lot in life, Jenny was writing a new chapter in her life.

"Do you think we have enough food?" Jenny asked Heather worriedly.

Ada Newbury had been too busy to go over the menu with Jenny. She had just wanted it to be fresh and modern. Jenny wondered what that meant. She just hoped the dishes she had come up with would pass muster with the old harridan.

"Everyone's going to be licking their fingers, Jenny," Heather said loyally. "Just wait and see."

Jenny pulled up outside a set of massive iron gates. A security guard came out of a small cabin and waved at them.

"Are you from the Boardwalk Café?" he asked. "You are late."

He spoke curtly into his phone and the gates swung open.

"It's two minutes past six," Jenny cursed. "Plenty of time to set up."

Ada Newbury was throwing a party for her grandson. He was recently engaged to a girl from the city. Their impending nuptials were the talk of the town. No expense was being spared and the locals were vying for an invitation to the country club extravaganza the wedding promised to be. Ada had arranged the party in lieu of a wedding shower. She called it a meet and greet for both sides of the family.

Jenny drove her van to the back of the house. A marquee had been set up on the lawn and linen covered tables stood ready for the food. A life sized ice sculpture depicting an embracing couple graced the centre of the lawn. Fairy lights were woven through the trees and large paper lanterns swayed in the breeze.

"This place looks beautiful," Jenny gushed.

"Ada hired a party planner from the city," Heather supplied. "The planner works with a city based caterer but Ada stuck to her guns. She wanted your food for this party."

A tall, slim woman stepped out on the porch before Jenny had a chance to reply.

"You're late," she complained. "I hope you got everything?"

"Don't worry, Mrs. Newbury," Jenny hastened to assure the woman. "It's all under control."

"It better be," Ada snapped. "The guests arrive at seven."

She turned toward Heather.

"Your grandmother is here. We are having tea in the parlor."

Heather's grandmother and Ada Newbury were staunch rivals. Betty Sue Morse was formidable even in her eighties. She had been married to John Newbury, the older of the Newbury brothers. Amicably separated, she still blushed every time she came across the dapper old man.

Betty Sue was the descendant of the island's founder. It had been called

Morse Isle then. Her family had originally owned the island. She was the fourth generation descendant of James Morse who had travelled south from New England with his family in 1837. He had bought the island for $125 and named it Morse Isle. He built a house for his family on a large tract of land. Fishing provided him with a livelihood, so did floating wrecks. He sent for a friend or two from up north. They came and settled on the island with their families. They in turn invited their friends. Morse Isle soon became a thriving community.

Being a barrier island, it took a battering in the great storm of 1962. Half the island was submerged forever. Most of that land had belonged to the Morse family. A new town emerged in the aftermath of the storm and it was named Pelican Cove.

Betty Sue had retained the Morse name even after her marriage. Heather was the last Morse on the island. Single at thirty five, she was a source of constant worry for her grandmother. Betty Sue wasn't ready to let the Morse bloodline end with Heather.

The Newburys and their money could not compete with Betty Sue's pedigree. She made sure Ada knew that every time they met.

"I'm going to help Jenny set up here," Heather told Ada.

Ada shrugged, the look she directed at Heather full of disdain.

"Don't forget you are a guest here, Heather," she said, giving Jenny a withering look.

"She's right, Heather," Jenny said hastily. "Why don't you go meet Betty Sue? I can take it from here."

Heather mouthed a brief apology as she followed Ada inside the house.

The food was being served buffet style. Jenny worked quickly, aided by some of Ada's domestic staff and stood back to admire the lavish spread. She had taken different tastes into account and believed there was something for everyone.

The guests started trickling in at seven.

Ada leaned on a short, stocky young man with cobalt blue eyes. Jenny surmised he was the grandson.

Heather sipped cold soup from a small glass and sighed with pleasure.

"These gazpacho shots are genius!"

Jenny smiled proudly and looked around. Guests were exclaiming over the food, smacking their lips and going for seconds.

Ada walked over to Jenny.

"Do we have any crab dip?" she asked.

Jenny pointed toward a chunky dip resting in a sourdough bowl. It nestled on a platter with an assortment of crackers.

"Brandon loves it," Ada said, walking toward it.

She didn't bother to introduce Jenny to her grandson. Jenny was the help after all.

"That's Brandon," Heather whispered in her ear. "He's got a big job in the city, aide to some senator. His parents are proud of him."

"Where are they?" Jenny asked, looking around.

She had never set eyes on Ada's offspring before.

"Brandon's parents are on a world tour," Heather told her. "They have been on a cruise for six months. They are expected back before the wedding."

"And where's the bride?"

A short brunette with highlighted hair and violet eyes walked up to Jenny just then. Jenny found herself smiling back as the girl beamed at her. Jenny secretly admitted she envied the girl her youth and beauty.

"Your food is simply super," the girl gushed. "I can't have enough of that beer boiled shrimp. That cocktail sauce has just the right zing. And the caprese bites and the olive tapenade! A couple of my friends are vegetarian and they are amazed at all the veggie options. They thought they would have to starve here, you know."

Jenny thanked the girl politely.

"Meet the bride," Heather said, hugging the girl. "Kelly, this is my friend Jenny. She's the genius behind this whole spread."

Kelly popped a pimento cheese sandwich in her mouth and wiped her hand before extending it toward Jenny.

"I'm Kelly Fox," she said simply. "This is a wonderful party. Brandon's grandma is so cute, isn't she?"

Jenny stifled a smile. No one had ever called Ada Newbury 'cute'.

"She wanted the best for you," Jenny nodded. "I hope you enjoy your wedding shower."

A tall, brown haired man walked up to Kelly and put an arm around her. His other hand held a glass of champagne. He threw back his drink and picked up a canapé from a tray.

"This is delicious," he said.

"Hummus and cucumber bites," Kelly read off the label. "Please tell me you are going to cater my wedding too."

"Who's this hunk?" Heather asked with a wink, staring at the tall and attractive stranger.

"Oh," Kelly cried. "Where are my manners? This is Binkie, my cousin. I'm an orphan, you see. I grew up in foster homes. Binkie is the only family I have here."

They chatted with Jenny and Heather and tasted everything on the buffet.

"Those turkey and avocado wraps are to die for," Binkie sighed. "You have a gift!"

"Save room for dessert," Jenny warned them. "We have banana mascarpone parfaits, and chocolate chip marshmallow cookies with ice cream."

Betty Sue Morse came over and chatted with Jenny.

"You've done a fine job here, girl," she said approvingly. "That crab dip is better than mine. And the shrimp is cooked just right."

Brandon came over with a ravishing beauty on his arm. She was shorter than Kelly but equally attractive. Her hazel eyes picked up the green in her dress and her carrot hair glistened in the soft light. Jenny was surprised the bride and groom weren't plastered to each other.

"Did you make those pimento cheese sandwiches?" the girl asked Jenny. "They are so yum! Everything is. I'm taking plenty of photos."

"Hello Megan," Heather said stiffly. "Didn't know you were in town."

"Brandon's getting married," Megan said brightly. "I wouldn't miss it for the world."

Chapter 2

A sunny spring morning dawned in Pelican Cove. Jenny had arrived at the Boardwalk Café at 5 AM. She baked her signature muffins and assembled a dozen parfaits. Jenny's baking had taken a toll on her. She had gained at least twenty pounds in the two years since she had started dishing out her treats at the cafe. Personally, she preferred this slightly plump version of herself. She was certainly happier than she had been when she agonized over every leaf of lettuce she consumed. But she needed to fit into a wedding dress soon. This desire had inspired her to come up with healthier food options at the café. She was still experimenting with the perfect recipe for a berry yogurt parfait. Initial response had been encouraging.

Jenny's aunt Star arrived at the café around eight, looking sleepy. She guzzled a big cup of coffee and shooed Jenny out of the kitchen.

"Aren't you getting late? Don't give that shrew any more reason to yell at you."

Jenny needed to go back to the Newbury mansion to collect her stuff.

"I feel bad, making you work on a Saturday."

"Don't be silly," Star dismissed. "Most of the food is already prepped. I can handle the café for a couple of hours."

Jenny got into her van and hummed a tune as she drove down the familiar road. She wondered when the party broke up the previous night. She had stuck on until nine the previous evening, refilling the food as needed. Her work was done once she finished serving the dessert.

"You may go now," Ada had told her curtly. "Come back tomorrow morning to clear up."

Jenny took the hint and drove home to rest her aching feet. She had spied Heather chatting with the bride in the distance. Heather was going to drive home with her grandmother.

The security guard in the cabin didn't come out this time. The iron gates opened and Jenny drove through, smiling back as the guard waved at her.

Jenny was relieved to see she didn't have much to do. Ada's staff had done the bulk of the work. Her large serving trays and dishes had been washed and dried and stacked on a table. All she needed to do was load the stuff in her van and be on her way. She looked around for her giant punch bowl and spotted it under the table.

Heather came out on the porch.

"Need a hand with that?"

"Heather!" Jenny exclaimed. "Did you stay over?"

"Grandma and I were right behind you. Brandon invited me for breakfast. He wants to properly introduce me to Kelly."

"You hardly need an introduction from what I saw."

"Kelly's a friendly soul," Heather nodded. "We hit it off last night. But Brandon sounded so eager. I'll let him show her off."

Brandon came out of the house. His face lit up when he saw Jenny.

"Your food was amazing. Kelly can't stop raving about it."

Jenny thanked him politely and took her leave.

"Why don't you stay for breakfast?" Brandon asked. "Kelly wants to talk to you about catering the wedding."

"Your grandma might have some other plans for that," Jenny said.

"Don't worry about Grandma," Brandon said confidently. "I can bring her around."

"Please stay," Heather pressed. "It will be fun."

Jenny knew Ada Newbury wouldn't be pleased. She hesitated.

"Why isn't Kelly here yet?" Heather asked Brandon. "Looks like she had a little too much champagne."

"Kelly's an early riser," Brandon said with a frown. "I'm going to call her."

He pulled a cell phone out of his pocket and turned around, jabbing some buttons on the screen.

"It's ringing," he explained.

A tall, strapping young man came running from the beach. Jenny sensed the panic in his coal black eyes. He came to a stop before Brandon and began gesticulating with his hands.

Brandon stared back at the youth in confusion.

"Get a grip, man!" Brandon exclaimed. "What's wrong with you?"

The man pointed somewhere behind him and started walking back.

"I guess he wants us to follow him," Heather muttered.

The youth whirled around and looked pleadingly at Heather.

"You wait," he stuttered.

He looked at Brandon.

"Come with me."

Brandon shrugged and began following the guy.

Heather raised her eyebrows and stared at Jenny.

"Who is he?" Jenny asked.

"The gardener?" Heather mused. "How would I know?"

A shout went up somewhere in the foliage behind Jenny. There was a flurry of footsteps and Brandon ran up to them, white in the face.

"It's Kelly," he cried, collapsing on the lawn.

He clutched his head in both hands as he stared wild eyed at Heather.

"She's dead. My Kelly's dead."

Ada Newbury came out on the porch.

"What's the commotion?" She gave Jenny a piercing look and stared at her grandson. "Why are you sitting on the grass, Brandon? Get inside. Cook's poaching the eggs for your Eggs Benedict."

Jenny found herself taking over. Ada refused to believe her grandson. She grabbed Heather by the hand and started walking through a gap in the trees. Jenny realized there was a small path there she hadn't noticed before. Heather and Ada were back a few minutes later. Heather gave a slight nod as she stared at Jenny. Jenny pulled out her phone and called the police.

Heather told her how they had found Kelly floating in the pool, face down. There was no doubt she had been dead for a while.

A wail of sirens sounded in the distance and grew louder as they approached the Newbury's mansion. The cook was coaxing Ada to drink a cup of tea. Jenny sat on a delicate chair with spindly legs, feeling out of place in the ornate parlor.

A tall, uniformed man came into the room, leaning on a cane. Jenny's heart sped up as she gazed into his piercing blue eyes. Adam Hopkins was the sheriff of Pelican Cove. He was also Jenny's betrothed. After a rocky courtship, Jenny had finally agreed to marry Adam the previous autumn. Six months later, they still hadn't set a wedding date.

"What are you doing here, Jenny?" Adam asked with a frown.

"I can't believe this is happening again," Ada Newbury wailed.

A stranger's corpse had been discovered on the Newbury estate several months ago.

"Did you know the deceased?" Adam asked stiffly.

He took his job seriously and was firmly in cop mode.

"Of course I did," Ada snapped. "My grandson was going to marry that girl."

"Where is he, by the way?"

Brandon had locked himself in his room. He had been inconsolable.

"That poor boy," Ada sobbed.

"When was the last time you saw this girl?"

Adam launched into a series of questions. Jenny knew the drill. Adam would be merciless in his questioning. He was just doing his job.

Adam let Jenny go after a few cursory questions. He warned her not to gossip about what had happened.

"Surely you know me better than that?" she fumed.

It was hard to keep anything secret in Pelican Cove. The Magnolias were waiting for Jenny back at the Boardwalk Café. This was a motley group of women Jenny had grown fond of. She would lay her life down for one of them. Betty Sue Morse was the unopposed leader of the pack. Jenny's aunt Star was the most free spirited member of the group. Heather and Molly were the youngest. The Magnolias had suffered a shock the previous year when Petunia, their kindest member, had been struck down. They were still grieving for her. Petunia had left the Boardwalk Café in Jenny's care and she was doing everything she could to live up to her friend's legacy.

"Heather called," Betty Sue told Jenny, her hands busy knitting a canary yellow scarf.

"Is it true?" Molly asked, her eyes popping out of their Coke-bottle glasses.

Tall and scrawny, Molly worked at the local library and was hailed by her friends as one smart cookie.

"Do you know what happened?" Star asked Jenny.

Jenny looked thoughtful.

"That girl was brought up right," Betty Sue stated. "She asked after my arthritis. She even brought a wrap for me from inside."

Jenny remembered Kelly was an orphan. She wondered if anyone would grieve for her. She remembered the tall, handsome man who had been hanging around her. He had a funny name.

The Magnolias decided to stick around at the café until Heather got back. Jenny worked through the lunch crowd, trying to keep herself from calling Adam. He didn't appreciate personal calls when he was busy on the job.

"Time to have lunch," she told the Magnolias as she brought out a big platter of sandwiches.

The Magnolias sat on the deck of the café, overlooking the Atlantic Ocean. The bright sunlight was a bit deceptive as a cold wind whipped Jenny's tresses around her face.

The ladies were quiet as they munched on Jenny's chicken salad sandwiches. There was a big sigh of relief when they spotted Heather walking along the boardwalk toward them. She jogged up the café's steps and collapsed in a chair with a thud.

"I'm starving!" she complained. "I never had that breakfast."

Jenny fixed a plate for her while the others bombarded her with questions. Heather warded off their questions while she took a few bites. Then she delivered the shocking news.

"Ada Newbury has been arrested."

"That's outrageous!" Betty Sue declared. "Looks like your young man is up to no good again, Jenny."

"What was she arrested for?" Star asked Heather, ignoring Betty Sue.

"Kelly's murder."

"Isn't it too soon to say that?" Molly asked.

"Apparently not," Heather explained. "The police have decided that Kelly was murdered. And they think Ada had the strongest motive."

"That's a bit hasty, even for Adam," Jenny said reluctantly.

"Ada wasn't too fond of Kelly," Heather told them. "I think most of the staff knew that. She thought Brandon was marrying someone beneath him."

"So what's new?" Star asked, rolling her eyes. "Ada thinks everyone is beneath the Newburys."

"That's not a strong enough motive," Molly agreed.

"Adam must have had his reasons," Jenny said, coming to his defense.

"Does Julius know?" Betty Sue asked, referring to Ada's husband.

"Julius is out of town. He was going to call Jason when I left. I think Jason will bail her out soon."

Jason Stone was the one and only lawyer in Pelican Cove. He had known Jenny as a teen, when she had spent summers on the island visiting her aunt. He had tried to woo Jenny when she came to live in Pelican Cove again. Jenny was very fond of Jason but he hadn't made her heart race like Adam did. Jason still flirted with her at every possible opportunity and Jenny took it in her stride.

"Did you talk to that girl yesterday?" Star asked Jenny curiously.

"She was sweet," Jenny nodded. "And so pretty. No wonder Brandon fell for her."

Star exchanged a glance with Betty Sue.

"She was there," Betty Sue nodded cryptically. "The shameless hussy."

"Come on, Grandma," Heather grimaced. "That's all water under the bridge."

"What are you guys talking about?" Jenny asked them.

"Just some gossip," Heather dismissed. "Pay no heed, Jenny."

"Are they talking about Megan?" Molly asked.

"Isn't that the redhead Brandon was walking around with last night?" Jenny asked. "Who is she?"

Chapter 3

Betty Sue clammed up at Jenny's question. Molly began to look uncomfortable. Heather took pity on Jenny and spoke up.

"Megan Patterson used to be Brandon's girl friend."

Jenny's mouth hung open.

"He seemed pretty friendly with her last night."

"Megan dumped him," Heather explained. "I wonder if Brandon still has a thing for her."

Jenny's opinion of Brandon took a nosedive.

"You don't say? Did Kelly know about their past?"

Heather shrugged.

"How would I know?"

Betty Sue rushed to Brandon Newbury's defense.

"Brandon's a good boy. He turned out pretty well, considering."

"Why don't you tell her the whole story?" Star suggested.

"Ada and Julius adore Brandon," Heather supplied. "Ada as good as raised him. He spent a lot of his childhood here."

"What about his parents?" Jenny asked.

"They like to travel," Betty Sue grunted. "They are off gallivanting in some little known country most of the time. They never had time for Brandon."

"What does this have to do with Megan?" Jenny asked, wondering if there was a point to the conversation.

"Megan's grandparents live here too," Star explained. "She did some of her schooling here. She was a popular girl, head of the cheerleading squad and all that."

"So Megan and Brandon met years ago?"

"They are childhood sweethearts," Heather sighed. "It's hard to forget that kind of history."

"What does this Megan do?" Jenny asked.

"She lives in the city," Heather explained. "I have no idea what she does. No one knows what went wrong between her and Brandon."

"They must have made up though," Molly spoke. "Why would he invite her otherwise?"

"Ada threw last night's party, remember?" Betty Sue said. "Maybe Ada invited Megan."

"Let me guess," Jenny smirked. "Ada actually likes this girl?"

"She's besotted by her," Heather corrected. "Very few people can gain Ada's favor. Megan's one of them. She's always been welcome at the Newbury mansion."

Jenny wondered if Ada had been trying to mend fences between Megan and Brandon.

"What sort of man is Brandon?" Jenny asked. "Would he leave Kelly in the lurch if Megan went back to him?"

"Men!" Star spat. "Who can predict what they will do?"

"Brandon's not like that," Heather argued. "He really loved Kelly."

"Where did he meet her?" Jenny asked.

"We were going to talk about that this morning," Heather said. "I guess we won't be doing that anymore."

"Speaking of weddings," Betty Sue said. "When are you setting a date, Jenny?"

Jenny couldn't control the blush that stole over her.

"I haven't thought about it yet."

"You have had six months to think about it," her aunt reminded her. "You have to stop dilly dallying now."

"I can't wait to be a bridesmaid," Heather hinted.

"I thought Chris and Molly might beat me to it," Jenny said, trying to divert attention from herself.

Molly obliged them by turning red. She was dating Chris Williams, a young local realtor. Molly and Chris had exchanged promise rings a few months ago, instead of engagement rings. They both wanted to be completely sure of their commitment to each other before assigning any labels to their relationship.

"We are not in a hurry," she said quickly. "I think you and Adam should take the plunge first, Jenny."

Heather looked at them irritably.

"You are both one of a kind. You know what I would be doing if I was in your place? I would be knee deep in wedding magazines and stuff, planning the wedding of the century. And here you can't even set a date."

"Don't forget, Heather," Jenny said gently. "Adam and I have both been married before."

"So have I," Molly reminded her.

Neither of their marriages had ended well.

"So what?" Heather rolled her eyes. "This is a new beginning for both of you. Forget those losers you were married to before. Adam and Chris are some of the finest men you could ever meet."

"I fully agree with that," Jenny said with a laugh.

"What's holding you back then, sweetie?" Star asked, looking worried.

Jenny rubbed the tiny gold heart shaped charm that hung around her neck. She did that whenever she thought of her son Nick. Nick had gifted her a gold charm every Mother's Day ever since he turned eight. Jenny wore them all on a chain now. They provided her a tangible connection with her son whenever she thought of him.

"What does Nick feel about this?" Molly asked, picking up on Jenny's thoughts.

"We've never really discussed it," Jenny confessed.

"It's high time you did," Star quipped. "Nick is a grown man. He just wants you to be happy."

Jenny humored the Magnolias as they pestered her about her wedding. The group finally broke up when Molly got up to get back to the library. Heather and Betty Sue returned to the Bayview Inn to prepare for the arrival of their new guests.

Star stayed back to help Jenny.

"When are you going to hire some help?" she asked Jenny. "You've been running the café singlehandedly for over six months now. It's taking a toll on you."

Jenny barely heard her aunt. She had been ignoring her aching back and sore feet for several weeks now. She couldn't explain why she hadn't hired some permanent staff for the café. The truth was she still missed her friend Petunia. Hiring someone else felt like she was replacing her. Jenny couldn't imagine doing that.

Jenny drove home as the daylight waned early under a cloudy sky. Her phone rang moments after she collapsed on the couch in her great room.

It was Adam, asking her what kind of food she fancied that evening. She had completely forgotten their dinner date.

Jenny showered and slipped into her trusty little black dress. She wished she had something new and bright to wear. Maybe she needed a shopping trip with the girls.

Adam was right on time. Jenny had a hankering for Mexican food. Adam drove to a small Mexican restaurant in a neighboring town.

Adam was in a sober mood.

"She was barely 25, Jenny," he moaned, referring to Kelly Fox. "She had her whole life ahead of her."

"Are you sure she didn't drown by herself?" Jenny asked hesitantly. "The champagne was flowing freely last night."

"I'm sure," Adam said. "We'll know more after the autopsy. But I am pretty sure someone killed that girl."

"But why?"

"That's what I have to find out."

Adam took a hefty bite of his taco and chewed thoughtfully. Jenny recognized the grim determination in his eyes.

"She seemed very happy," Jenny supplied. "Who wouldn't be? Brandon Newbury is supposed to be a great catch."

"Ada Newbury didn't like her," Adam said flatly. "Almost every member of their staff told me that."

"Did they have an argument or something?"

"Ada warned her off. Told her no good would come of marrying Brandon."

"Is that why you arrested her?"

"I didn't arrest her, Jenny," Adam sighed. "You have to stop listening to the grapevine. I just brought her in for questioning."

"Why does she need a lawyer then?" Jenny pounced. "You are hiding something from me."

Normally, Jenny's statement would have produced an outburst from Adam. But he had mellowed a bit since their engagement.

"I don't have to tell you everything I know, Jenny," he said with a smile. "I can't. It's part of an ongoing investigation."

"How did you zero in on Ada so quickly?" Jenny pressed. "Doesn't she have an alibi?"

Adam and Jenny parried back and forth, Jenny trying hard to squeeze as much information as possible from Adam. They shared a caramel flan for dessert and Adam took her to their favorite beach. Jenny forgot all about the Newburys as she held hands with Adam. They walked silently in the bright moonlight, enjoying each other's company.

Jenny started the next day with a smile on her face. She beamed at her favorite customer, the first in line when she opened the Boardwalk Café for business every morning. Captain Charlie gave her a knowing look.

"How's that young man of yours?" he asked. "I hear he hasn't thrown a tantrum in three full days."

Adam Hopkins was known for his irascible nature. Everyone believed Jenny had succeeded in taming him.

"Adam's fine, Captain Charlie," Jenny sighed. "Are you going to try one of my yogurt parfaits today? You need to start eating healthy."

Captain Charlie agreed to try Jenny's fancy breakfast, provided he could still eat his muffin. Jenny packed a blueberry muffin for him along with the berry parfait.

Most of the café's customers turned out to be like Captain Charlie. They went for the parfait only after they had their fill of muffins and omelets, treating the parfait as dessert.

"Does anyone here understand the concept of a low calorie breakfast?" Jenny wailed.

"I don't see why you are complaining," Star laughed. "More business for you."

"I thought I would help build some healthy habits," Jenny said reproachfully.

"That's a noble thought," Star said sagely. "But it ain't happening here, Jenny. The people in this town are set in their ways. You should know that by now."

After a dozen more customers chose a crab omelet over the parfait, Jenny had to admit her aunt was right. Jenny brainstormed about how she could make her parfaits more attractive.

"What if I add toasted coconut, or pecans?"

"Or chocolate chips?" her aunt suggested naughtily.

The Magnolias arrived at ten for their daily coffee break. Heather and Molly dutifully ate a parfait each while Betty Sue stuck to her muffin.

"You might be getting a visitor today," Heather told Jenny.

A long, black car pulled up outside the café just then. A uniformed driver got out and opened the back door. Ada Newbury stepped out, resplendent in a silk dress and a thick strand of pearls. Her head was held high and her expression was as haughty as ever. She stepped into the café and walked out on the deck.

"You there," she called out, snapping her fingers at Jenny.

Jenny didn't appreciate being insulted in her own café. She stood her ground, barely budging an inch.

"What can I do for you, Mrs. Newbury?"

"We need to talk."

Jenny invited her to pick an empty table. Ada's lips curled in an expression of disgust. She pulled out a lace handkerchief from her purse and placed it on a deck chair. She sat down gingerly, flicking a speck of dust off her sleeve.

Jenny sat down before Ada and folded her hands. She raised her eyebrows questioningly and waited for Ada to speak up.

"Your young man has gone berserk."

Jenny was silent, waiting for Ada to say more.

"He thinks we killed that silly girl."

"Did you?" Jenny asked.

"How dare you!" Ada fumed. "Brandon was in love with her."

"But you didn't like her, did you?" Jenny asked.

"She was a nobody," Ada spat. "Brandon could have done so much better."

"Looks like you don't have to worry about her now," Jenny said with a shrug.

"How I wish that were true," Ada said.

Her posture seemed to crumple and she suddenly looked frail and old.

"Why are you here, Mrs. Newbury?" Jenny asked. "Are you here to complain about the food at the party?"

Ada looked pathetic as she leaned forward and grasped Jenny's arm.

"I need your help. Find out who killed that girl. I will pay you anything you want."

"I'm not a detective," Jenny protested. "And I don't want your money."

"Then take pity on me," Ada pleaded. "I'm innocent. I may have disliked that girl, but I didn't do anything to harm her."

"I can't guarantee anything," Jenny sighed.

Ada's voice wavered as her eyes bore into Jenny's.

"Just promise me you'll look into it."

Chapter 4

Adam and Jenny were having an old argument. Adam was incensed as he cut into his eggs.

"I don't see why you have to be involved this time."

"Ada Newbury needs my help. She personally came over here and begged me to help her."

"That's convenient," Adam jeered. "Have you forgotten how that woman treats you most of the time? What about the way she snubs your aunt?"

"I know all that. And I am also sure she won't change even if I manage to bail her out of trouble."

"Then why are you bending over backwards, meddling in police business?"

"Don't forget I have helped you out in the past," Jenny said. "And I don't meddle. You do your thing. I'll do mine."

"Things are different now, Jenny. People know about us. They will assume I tell you everything about the investigation."

Jenny let out a snort.

"You're not giving out any state secrets, Adam. And here I thought you were worried about my safety."

Adam had the grace to look a bit guilty.

"Of course I worry about you. I haven't forgotten all those close calls you have had in the past couple of years, Jenny. What would I do if something happened to you?"

Jenny poured a fresh cup of coffee for Adam and rolled her eyes.

"You're making too much out of this."

Adam shook his head in disgust. He and Jenny agreed about most things. But he couldn't curb her sleuthing. Jenny called it helping people. He called it poking her nose into someone else's business.

"Time to go," Adam said, pushing his chair back and struggling to his feet.

He was a war veteran who had been injured in the line of duty. He had a pronounced limp and needed a cane most of the time. His recent therapy had led to a lot of improvement though. He was secretly hoping to get through his wedding without the cane. It was supposed to be a surprise for Jenny.

Jenny waved goodbye to Adam and went inside. She hadn't told him about her plans for the day.

Star was chopping vegetables in the kitchen.

"I will get the soup started before I leave," Jenny told her. "I should be back in time for lunch."

She started sautéing vegetables in a knob of butter.

"Are you going alone?" Star asked.

Jenny nodded. She usually took Heather along with her for moral support. But she had to stop being in awe of the Newburys at some point.

Bright blue skies studded with fluffy white clouds brought a smile to Jenny's face. Watery sunlight bathed everything in a soft glow as Jenny drove to the Newbury estate. She handed over a bag of muffins to the security guard at the gate. He thanked her profusely, looking surprised.

A maid ushered Jenny into the opulent living room. Jenny stood in the center of the room, looking around, wondering where to sit.

"Are you going to stand there all day?" Ada Newbury griped, snapping at Jenny as she came in.

The maid entered with a tray loaded with tea things. There was a three tiered stand with tiny cakes and cookies, and a big kettle of tea.

Ada poured tea for them and added milk and sugar to Jenny's cup. Jenny wasn't sure if Ada remembered how she took her tea, or she just assumed.

"Try the shortbread," Ada said. "It's our cook's specialty."

Jenny obliged her and bit into the buttery, crumbly cookie.

"Let's talk about Megan," she said.

Ada looked surprised.

"Did you invite her to the party?" Jenny cut to the chase.

Ada nodded.

"Did Brandon ask you to do that?"

"I don't think he knew Megan was in town."

"I'm guessing you had something to do with that too," Jenny asked.

"Megan is such a sweet girl," Ada sighed. "She and Brandon always got along like a house on fire."

"But Brandon was seeing someone else," Jenny reminded her. "He was engaged to Kelly."

"Megan used to be here all the time, running after Brandon. She would come here after school. They would do their homework together and beg Cook for more fruit cake."

Ada sounded wistful as she reminisced about years gone by.

"What did you hope to achieve by inviting Megan?"

"Megan works in the city too," Ada said. "I told her to come down to Pelican Cove this weekend. This was her last chance if she wanted to win Brandon back."

Jenny was confused.

"I heard she was the one who left Brandon."

"Girls are fickle at that age," Ada dismissed. "I think they had a lovers' tiff. Megan must have thought Brandon would beg her to take him back. I think her plan backfired."

"Do you know this for a fact or are you just guessing?"

Ada's face slipped into a familiar haughty expression.

"I have seen a lot more of life than you have, young lady. That girl loves my Brandon. I am sure about that."

"So you were hoping that she and Brandon would get back together this weekend?"

Ada was silent but Jenny had her answer.

"What about the wedding? I thought it's all planned out."

"Plans can be canceled," Ada said harshly. "Marriage is for life. You know what they say, marry in haste, repent at leisure." Ada gave Jenny a calculating look. "I'm sure you have first-hand experience with it."

Nasty Ada was back.

"I was happy with my husband," Jenny said lamely, then gave up.

Ada Newbury would probably hold her responsible for her philandering husband.

"Never mind that," Ada quipped. "Brandon completely forgot how happy he was with Megan. He needed a reminder."

"So you asked Megan to come to Pelican Cove. Was she in on your plan to drive a wedge between the happy couple?"

Ada shrugged.

"Megan's a smart girl. I was sure she would figure it out."

"Was Brandon surprised to see Megan at the party?"

"He was overjoyed. I can tell you that. He clung to her all evening."

Jenny remembered how she had mistakenly thought that Megan was Brandon's betrothed. Brandon may not have been in love with her, but he clearly still adored her. They must have remained friends even after their breakup, Jenny mused. Maybe they had continued to meet. They did live in the same city.

"What did Kelly think about it?"

"I don't know. I was hoping she would be angry."

"Did you think she would create a scene?" Jenny probed.

Ada blushed.

"She hid her reaction, whatever it was. She seemed cool with Megan. I can't understand these youngsters. In my day, I would never have tolerated an interloper. I would have gauged her eyes out."

Jenny realized the opposite had happened.

"Kelly is the victim here, Mrs. Newbury," she reminded Ada. "Not Megan. Looks like you don't have to worry about Brandon marrying

Kelly now."

"I didn't want her dead," Ada sighed. "I just wanted her to leave my grandson alone."

"Why didn't you like Kelly?" Jenny asked, genuinely curious. "She was pretty enough."

"The Newburys can trace their roots back to the Mayflower. Who was this girl, an orphan? She had no idea who her family was."

"No one cares about that stuff now," Jenny said gently.

"We do," Ada said stiffly. "Bloodlines matter to us."

Jenny couldn't hold herself back.

"I suppose Megan has an impeccable bloodline."

"She'll do. She's not a Pioneer, but her family has lived here since the 19th century."

"Did you ever give Kelly a chance?" Jenny asked, exasperated. "She might have been a really nice person."

Ada didn't bother to reply.

"Do you think Megan was capable of harming Kelly?" Jenny asked.

"She didn't need to," Ada replied. "You were here. You saw how besotted Brandon was with her. Megan would have charmed her way into his heart anyhow."

"When did Megan go home that night?"

Ada wasn't sure. She had retired to her room around nine thirty, a few minutes after Jenny herself left. The party was in full swing at that time. Everyone had imbibed a bit too much by then. Jenny remembered seeing Megan giggling over something Brandon said.

"Where is Brandon?" Jenny asked. "Is he staying here with you?"

"Of course," Ada snapped. "This is his home."

"How is he handling this?"

"That poor boy! He hasn't come out of his room since yesterday."

Jenny realized she would have to talk to Brandon some other time. She didn't relish speaking to him in front of Ada anyway.

"Have the police contacted you again?" Jenny asked.

"The sheriff called just before you got here," Ada told her. "That girl died sometime around midnight. Someone bashed her head in, it seems."

Jenny wondered if Kelly had already been dead when she was pushed into the pool. She would have to beg Adam for more details.

"Can you think of anyone who might have wanted to harm Kelly?" she asked Ada.

Ada shook her head.

"I barely knew the girl. Honestly, I didn't make an effort to get to know her."

Ada's brow furrowed and she muttered under her breath. "She could have died somewhere else."

"I'm sure she didn't choose to be killed on your property, Mrs. Newbury," Jenny said lightly.

Ada paid no attention to Jenny's sarcasm. She suddenly leaned forward in her chair.

"I had a feeling about her, you know."

"You mean, like, an intuition?"

Ada's face hardened.

"She was wrong for my Brandon. She would have hurt him, I am sure."

"You do realize Kelly is the victim here?" Jenny said mildly.

"That doesn't mean she was blameless."

Ada seemed intent on painting Kelly as the villain. Jenny tried to get her to focus on the problem at hand.

"We need to figure out who had a grudge against Kelly," Jenny said patiently. "Who, other than you, hated her enough to take her life?"

Ada looked at her watch and stood up.

"We'll have to continue some other time. I have a golf lesson at the club."

"You play golf?" Jenny asked, surprised.

Ada Newbury didn't look like she would voluntarily break a sweat.

Ada's face lit up at the question.

"I never took an interest in golf, until a few weeks ago. We have the best golf pro at the country club. He says I have a natural flair for the game."

Jenny had once been an avid golfer herself. Her husband had insisted she learn the game so they could play couples' golf and hobnob with his rich clients. She reflected over how much her life had changed since then. She didn't miss the forced socializing but she yearned for a good game.

"I love golf," she said eagerly. "How about a friendly round sometime?"

Ada was kind in her dismissal.

"I'll think about it."

"I need to talk to everyone who was working here on the night of the party," Jenny told Ada, getting back to business.

"Just make sure you don't take them away from their duties," Ada warned.

"I will also need to talk to Brandon," Jenny reminded her.

"Brandon will contact you when he is ready," Ada said. "I will make sure of it."

"We'll talk again," Jenny nodded, taking her leave.

Jenny drove back to the Boardwalk Café, going over her conversation with Ada in her mind. She didn't think she had made any progress that day.

Jenny started helping her aunt make lunch as soon as she reached the café. Star had marinated the shrimp based on Jenny's instructions. Jenny's stomach rumbled with hunger as she fried the shrimp for po'boy sandwiches. She slathered her homemade tartar sauce on soft white rolls and thought about her next step.

She decided to talk to Megan. Now that Kelly was dead, Brandon was single again. Megan definitely had a lot to gain by Kelly's death.

Chapter 5

The Magnolias were assembled in the kitchen of the Boardwalk Café. Jenny had woken up to a light drizzle and grey skies. The rain picked up after 9 AM, promising a wet day. The café's deck was soaked and Betty Sue had grudgingly agreed to sit inside.

"How well do you know this Megan?" Jenny asked Heather.

"I used to babysit her," Heather replied. "And we all know each other on the island."

"Her grandmother is in my knitting circle," Betty Sue added. "The Pattersons are a well respected family in Pelican Cove."

"Why is that important?" Jenny asked. "You sound just like Ada."

"Breeding will tell," Betty Sue said. "You youngsters don't realize it."

"I need to go talk to Megan," Jenny told them. "Can one of you come with me?"

Molly couldn't get away from her desk at the library.

"You know I'm your wing woman," Heather said eagerly. "When do you want to go?"

"Give me half an hour," Jenny said.

She spent some time prepping for lunch. Star assured Jenny she could assemble the crab salad sandwiches when needed.

Heather knew where Megan lived and she also knew her phone number. Jenny made sure she was available to talk to them. The rain started coming down in torrents just when they got into her car.

Heather called out the directions. Jenny drove carefully, squinting at the water logged road. One of her wiper blades was broken and her car was due for an oil change. She had taken much better care of her vehicles when she lived in the city. Although she barely drove two miles a day now, her car was beginning to exhibit some wear and tear.

"What kind of person is Megan?" Jenny asked Heather. "Does she tend to fly off the handle?"

"Megan's a friendly girl," Heather said. "Don't be fooled by that red hair."

"She has quite a presence," Jenny nodded.

"She's always been popular," Heather told Jenny. "She kind of takes over everything. But people still like her."

Megan welcomed them with a wide smile and led them to a sun room that looked out on a beautiful garden.

"I'm here to help you any way I can," Megan said before Jenny had a chance to speak up. "Poor Brandon! He was crazy about Kelly."

"What did you think about her?" Jenny asked.

"Kelly was a sweetheart."

"You sound as if you knew her."

"Kelly and I got along really well," Megan explained. "We met a few months ago in the city. Brandon introduced us."

Jenny couldn't hide her surprise.

"You knew Brandon was engaged?"

"Of course," Megan said without any guile. "Brandon and I have been friends since we were barely out of braces. He tells me everything."

"Wasn't that odd?" Heather interrupted. "You two were an item after all."

Megan laughed. She sounded genuine.

"So what? We parted amicably. I always want the best for Brandon."

"Who invited you to the party?" Jenny asked her. "Did Brandon know you were coming?"

"He didn't. Kelly and I wanted to surprise him."

"Wait. Kelly knew you were coming?" Jenny couldn't hide her surprise. "I thought Ada Newbury invited you to the party."

"She's a dear, isn't she?" Megan gushed. "I let her think that. Kelly had already told me about the party."

"You spent a lot of time with Brandon there."

"It was just like old times," Megan said wistfully. "We caught up with all our friends."

"Kelly must have felt left out," Jenny suggested.

"Kelly didn't mind," Megan said confidently. "She wasn't clingy. Not like some girls I know."

Heather had been tapping her foot impatiently while Megan spoke. She interrupted them suddenly.

"Wait a minute, Megan. Are you actually saying you were friends with Kelly?"

Megan shrugged.

Jenny picked up the conversation.

"Looks like you knew Kelly Fox well enough. What kind of a person would you say she was?"

Megan thought for a minute.

"I'm no judge of character. She seemed like a regular gal."

"Why would someone want to kill her?"

Megan looked stricken.

"Kill her? Are you saying someone deliberately murdered her?"

Jenny couldn't believe Megan was that naïve.

"You do live in Pelican Cove?" Heather asked Megan. "How do you not know this?"

"I've been busy catching up with work since yesterday," Megan said lightly. "I haven't really talked to anyone."

"What kind of job do you have in the city?" Jenny asked politely.

"I'm a publicist," Megan said proudly. "I have a long roster of clients who always need something. They keep me on my toes."

She looked at her watch.

"I have a video call with a client in half an hour. I really need to prep for it."

"Just a few questions more," Jenny smiled. "When did you leave the party?"

"Frankly, I have no idea!" Megan sighed. "I think I went a bit overboard with the champagne."

"How long did the party go on?"

Megan pursed her mouth, shaking her head from side to side.

"I can't tell you that either. But there were a few people milling about when I left."

"What about Kelly?" Jenny asked. "When did you last see her?"

"Kelly was having the time of her life," Megan said. She narrowed her eyes as if she was trying to remember what had happened at the party. "I remember telling her I was leaving. She wanted me to stay a bit longer."

"Did you?" Heather asked.

"I might have. I started to leave a couple of times. But then I stayed on. My memory is really hazy on that point."

"Do you know anyone who might have wanted to harm Kelly?" Jenny asked Megan.

Megan shook her head.

"I didn't know much about her personal life. She was friendly but she didn't share much about herself. I thought it might be because she didn't have a family. I didn't want to pry."

Jenny couldn't think of any more questions to ask the girl.

"So it was just a regular party ... you didn't notice anything unusual."

"Not really," Megan said, getting up.

Heather and Jenny took the hint.

"Thanks for talking to us, Megan," Jenny said with a smile. "Will you call me if you think of anything else?"

"Sure," Megan nodded. "I know the party ended in disaster. But I really enjoyed your food. I could go for that crab dip any day."

"You should go to the Boardwalk Café," Heather told her. "Jenny cooks something different every day."

"Oh yeah," Jenny said. "Come over to the café any time. I'll make you anything you like."

Jenny and Heather went over their visit on the way back to the café.

"Don't you think she's a bit too chirpy?" Jenny asked.

"You think it's all an act?" Heather quirked an eyebrow. "This is how Megan is. She gets along really well with people."

"Maybe she just told us what we wanted to hear."

"Do you think she was lying, Jenny?"

"I know Megan belongs to a different generation," Jenny said, swerving to avoid a puddle. "But surely the world hasn't changed that much? Friends with Kelly? I don't buy that."

"She could have been leading us on," Heather mused. "But why would she do that?"

"To hide the truth, of course," Jenny said. "I say she hated Kelly. I am ready to wager anything on that."

"How are you going to prove that?" Heather asked.

Jenny didn't have an answer for that. Heather continued thinking out loud.

"Do you think she had a motive?"

"I think so," Jenny said. "Now that Kelly's out of the way, she has a straight shot at Brandon."

"Don't forget she broke up with him."

"She might have realized her mistake after she lost him. I saw how possessive she was of Brandon at the party. She was a woman on the prowl, make no mistake."

"You may be right," Heather relented. "But I don't think she needed to kill Kelly to get Brandon back. Have you looked at Megan? She can bewitch any man in a five mile radius."

"Don't be ridiculous!" Jenny threw back her head and laughed.

Heather joined in. Jenny called her out on her tendency to exaggerate.

"But seriously," Heather said, "she has a silver tongue to match those looks. It's a lethal combination."

"She doesn't really have an alibi," Jenny pointed out. "And she's not ready to commit to when she left the party."

"Have the police questioned her yet?" Heather asked. "She will have to give them some concrete answer."

"Adam might get more out of her," Jenny agreed.

Megan would have to give an accurate account of her movements to the authorities. There would be repercussions if she lied to them. Jenny wondered if Megan had been spinning a yarn all along. Had she sweet talked Jenny into believing what she wanted her to believe?

"Who's next on your list, Jenny?"

"Brandon Newbury."

"I'm sure Brandon's innocent," Heather said. "And I'm not just saying that because we are related. Brandon couldn't hurt a fly."

"I want to talk to Ada's staff too. They will open up more if you are with me."

"We don't have too many bookings at the inn this week. I'm not busy."

"Great. Am I missing anyone else?" Jenny asked.

"You already talked to Ada," Heather said, counting off her fingers. "Megan and Brandon are the major players. Aren't you forgetting Kelly?"

"She can't talk to me, Heather," Jenny smirked.

Heather punched her in the shoulder.

"What do you know about Kelly, huh?"

Jenny realized what she had been missing. She clicked her tongue in annoyance.

"How could I forget that? We definitely need to find out more about Kelly. I'm going to do some basic online research tonight."

Jenny dropped Heather off at the Bayview Inn and headed to the Boardwalk Café. Her aunt had assembled a tray of sandwiches and was already serving them to the lunch crowd. Soup was simmering on the stove. Jenny pulled on an apron and joined her aunt, shrugging off her fatigue.

Jason Stone came in just as the café emptied. Tiny droplets of water streamed down his face. He wiped his face with a white linen handkerchief and smiled broadly at Jenny, opening his arms wide for a hug.

"How's my favorite café owner today?"

Jenny hugged him back.

"You need to dry your hair," she said.

She grabbed a bunch of paper towels from a table and led Jason out to the deck. Jason obliged her and dried his hair sheepishly.

"What a day! We have two more days of this infernal rain. I can't wait for the sun to shine again."

"My garden needs this rain," Jenny said. "I'm looking forward to a great flowering season."

Jason asked Jenny to join him for lunch.

"Go ahead, sweetie," Star said. "You gotta eat."

"What about you?" Jenny asked her aunt.

Star was an artist who painted seascapes of the surrounding region. They were popular with the tourists. She had put her work on hold to help Jenny at the café. Jenny knew her aunt was burning the midnight oil to keep up with the demand for her work. She was worried about her health.

"I'm going to grab a sandwich and eat it on my way home," Star told her.

"No way," Jenny protested. "Eat with us. You can go paint up a storm after that."

Star relented.

"How's that old grouch treating you?" Jason asked, taking a jab at Adam.

"Very well, thank you very much," Jenny said, making a face. "What about you? Are you seeing someone?"

Jason's face clouded over. He laughed nervously, trying to look stoic.

"I'm too busy to date," he told them. "I have so many pending cases, I am working 12 hour days to get through them."

Star gave him a knowing look. She knew Jason still had a thing for Jenny. Unfortunately, it didn't look like they had a future together.

Chapter 6

Jenny and Heather were back at the Newbury estate. Heather exclaimed in delight the moment they stepped into the parlor.

A tall, stout man with a shock of white hair held his arms out to Heather. Heather ran into them and hugged the man tightly.

"How are you, munchkin?" the man asked.

Robert Newbury was Heather's grandfather. He and Betty Sue had been separated for decades.

"When did you get back home?" Heather asked him.

"Last night," Robert answered. "What's the matter with you kids? I leave town for a couple of days and you manage to land in hot water."

"You know," Heather murmured. "How is Brandon?"

"Still crying his eyes out. I don't blame him, of course. There are some times in life when a man should not be ashamed of showing his emotions."

"We were hoping to talk to him," Jenny spoke up.

"You remember my friend Jenny?" Heather asked her grandpa. "She's helping us find out what happened to Kelly."

Robert's face fell.

"That Kelly. She was a sweet girl. She was good for Brandon."

Jenny noticed how his opinion was diametrically opposite to that of Ada's.

"We are here to talk to the staff," Heather told her grandfather. "Can I catch up with you later?"

"Stay for lunch," Robert urged. "Cook's making fried chicken with all the fixings."

Heather promised him she would think about it. Jenny curbed an urge to giggle. She couldn't imagine Ada Newbury inviting her to eat lunch with the family.

Heather led Jenny down a long passage. She pushed open a door and entered a cavernous kitchen. A large woman wearing a chef's hat and a soiled apron around her wide girth stood with one arm on her hip, frying chicken. Her face broke into a broad smile when she looked up and spotted Heather.

"Hey baby girl! Come taste some bread pudding. I made that special brandy sauce you like."

Heather greeted the old woman with a hug. She breathed in the aromas of the different pots and pans on the cooking range. She promised they would stay for lunch. The cook spooned some warm pudding into a bowl and made them taste it. It was buttery and gooey, loaded with plenty of plump black raisins. Jenny wondered if the old cook would share her recipe.

Cook's expression changed once Heather had eaten a few spoonfuls of pudding.

"Are you here for Brandon? That poor boy! Maybe you can coax him to eat a bite."

"I do want to talk to Brandon," Heather nodded, sharing a glance with Jenny. "But we were hoping to talk to you first."

The cook narrowed her eyes and trained them on Jenny.

"Girl, you playing Nancy Drew again?"

"Mrs. Newbury needs my help. I am going to try and find out what happened to Kelly."

"She didn't deserve to die," Cook said, wiping her eyes on her apron. "She was so sweet. She made Brandon happy."

"Can we talk to you about that night?" Heather asked.

"I was off duty that night," the old woman said. "Your friend here took care of all the food."

"But you were helping serve the food, weren't you? I think I remember seeing you out in the courtyard."

"That's right."

"When did you last see Kelly?"

The cook's face clouded over. "I don't exactly remember. I brought her some of my leftover pot roast from the kitchen. She said she loved the spread you had put out but she was hankering for some of that roast from lunch."

Jenny figured Kelly was just buttering up the old cook. She had no idea why the young girl would do that. Either she was really good at heart or she had an ulterior motive. Or maybe she really liked pot roast. Although Kelly had been fawning over Jenny's food, she hadn't really seemed like a gourmand.

"What time was that?" she asked.

"Around nine," the cook answered. "That was before she had that fight with the missus."

"Do you know what that was about?" Heather asked curiously.

The cook was an old employee and apparently didn't think twice before speaking her mind.

"That woman doesn't need a reason to talk someone down. You know that!"

"Did Kelly stick around after her altercation with Ada?" Jenny asked.

"She seemed fine after that," Cook said, her admiration for the girl clear in her tone. "I don't know how much longer she stuck around though. I went to my quarters after ten. The party was still going strong at that time."

Jenny needed to establish what Kelly had been up to between the hours of ten and midnight.

"What about Megan? You know who Megan is, don't you?"

The cook frowned.

"That girl is trouble. She means no good, I can tell you that."

"How so?" Jenny asked.

"She's got her eye on Brandon. She was fixing to break those two up."

"Did Megan and Kelly talk to each other?"

The old woman bobbed her head up and down.

"Yes Sir! They said they were like sisters. You know that Megan's a smooth talker. She had Kelly believing whatever spurted out of her mouth."

"Was Megan here when you left?" Jenny asked the cook.

The woman didn't remember that.

"We were hoping to talk to some of the other people who were working that night."

A couple of girls came into the kitchen just then. They were both wearing staff uniforms.

"You can talk to them," Cook warned Heather. "But don't take too long. I have to start serving lunch soon."

She looked at the girls who were standing at a counter, stacking dishes.

"This lady wants to talk to you about the night of the party," Cook said, nodding toward Jenny. "There is no need to be afraid. Just tell her what you saw or heard."

Jenny introduced herself. They already knew who Heather was.

The girls had seen Ada argue with Kelly. They had also noticed how friendly Megan and Kelly had seemed to be.

"How long were you working that night?" Jenny asked them.

"We were here until the food ran out," one girl answered. "Most of the guests had left by that time."

"When was that?" Heather asked immediately.

"Sometime after 11," the other girl said. "I wasn't wearing my watch but I heard the big clock inside the house chime."

"Can you tell me who was still hanging around?"

One of the girls shook her head. The other hesitated.

"It's hard to say," she finally said. "Brandon was in and out of the house. Megan had left earlier but then she came back."

"What was Kelly doing?"

"Kelly was drunk," the first girl said and giggled.

"She wasn't that drunk," the other girl objected.

"So Brandon, Megan and Kelly were still at the party after 11," Jenny asked again.

She thought this timeline was important so she wanted to be sure of the facts.

A gong sounded somewhere in the distance.

"Time to start serving lunch," Cook said, suddenly snapping to attention.

She clapped her hands, bursting into a flurry of activity as she began plating the food. She pointed at the girls and started barking orders.

"You take the potatoes and green beans, and you, take the apple sauce and the rolls. I will bring out the chicken."

She looked at Heather and Jenny apologetically.

"Don't you go anywhere without tasting my food."

Jenny thanked the cook and reluctantly stepped out of the kitchen.

"What next?" she asked Heather.

"Let's go find Brandon."

Heather peeped into the dining room to make sure Brandon wasn't at the table. She took Jenny's hand and led her to a different part of the house.

Heather banged on the door insistently when her gentle knocks didn't produce an answer. The door finally burst open and Brandon stared out at them, bleary eyed. Jenny could barely recognize him.

"We need to talk," Heather said, rushing into the room. "What's that smell?"

Jenny realized Brandon was still dressed in the same clothes he had been wearing at the party. Heather marched him into an ensuite bathroom. He reappeared a few minutes later, his face freshly scrubbed and his wet hair finger combed. Heather had dug out a fresh shirt for him.

"I'm sorry for your loss," Jenny said softly.

"I should never have come here," Brandon said bitterly. "We should have eloped, had a wedding in Vegas or something."

"You can't change what happened, B," Heather consoled him. "We have to move on. Jenny here is going to help find out who hurt Kelly."

"That won't bring her back."

"You're right," Heather agreed. "But it might keep your grandma from being arrested for a murder she didn't commit."

"Grandma never liked her," Brandon told them. "Apparently, Kelly wasn't good enough to be a Newbury."

"Do you think she was capable of harming her?" Jenny asked.

"Of course not!" Brandon said indignantly. "What kind of question is that?"

"Are you willing to talk to me?" Jenny asked him. "We need to figure out what happened that night."

Brandon sat down at the edge of the bed and waved his hand toward a couch set against the wall. Jenny accepted the silent invitation and sat down.

"What do you want to know?" Brandon asked, rubbing his eyes.

"When was the last time you ate something?" Heather demanded, noting the circles under Brandon's eyes.

He gave her a vague look. Heather stood up to leave.

"You can call the kitchen from here," Brandon said weakly. "But I'm not really hungry. I just want Kelly back."

Heather picked up the phone and pressed the code for the kitchen. She asked them to send food and coffee to the room.

"Where did you meet Kelly?" Jenny asked Brandon, hoping to ease into the conversation.

"At a party ... we hit it off."

"So it was love at first sight?" Jenny smiled.

"I was smitten," Brandon nodded. "I asked her out right away."

"Were you seeing Megan at that time?"

Brandon gave a snort.

"Megan had dumped me weeks ago. I had been mooning over her. But I forgot all about Megan when I went out with Kelly."

"When did you see her last on the night of the party?"

"Around 11 PM?" Brandon wasn't sure.

There was a knock on the door. A maid appeared with a tray of food. Heather forced Brandon to eat while Jenny took him through her set of questions. Nothing new came out of it. Brandon and Kelly had met Megan in the city. The girls seemed to get along well. Brandon hadn't realized he had spent more time with Megan at the party than he had with Kelly. According to him, he was just being a good host.

Jenny and Heather made a detour to the kitchen before they left. The fried chicken was pronounced perfect and Jenny begged the cook for the recipe.

"He's devastated," Heather remarked as Jenny drove back down the hill into town.

"What happened to Brandon's guests?" Jenny asked. "Are they still in town?"

Heather had the contact information for a couple of Brandon's friends. She had met them at the party. She pulled out her phone and forwarded the info to Jenny.

"Are you going to call them now?" Heather asked.

"No time like the present," Jenny said, pulling up in front of the café.

Jenny went in and called Brandon's friends, armed with her usual questions.

"Brandon may be grieving now," one of them said. "But all was not well. There was trouble in paradise."

"Oh?"

Jenny crossed her fingers, wondering what the man on the phone was about to reveal.

"Kelly was having an affair. At least Brandon thought she was."

Chapter 7

Jenny shared what she had learned from Brandon's friends with Heather the next morning. The two friends talked as they worked in the kitchen at the Boardwalk Café.

Jenny browned onions in a pot. She was trying out a new recipe for shrimp curry. Locals and tourists loved her food and she kept them happy by coming up with monthly specials. She had regularly cooked curry when she lived in the city and had once attended a class where they taught how to make authentic Indian curry. Over the years, Jenny had broken down the recipe into something simple that used regular grocery store ingredients.

"Do you believe this guy?" Heather asked her.

Heather was peeling garlic, a task she didn't relish at all.

"Hard to say," Jenny said, scraping the brown bits at the bottom of the pan where the onion was beginning to stick. "But there's no smoke without fire."

"Was he just being nasty?"

"Kelly's gone," Jenny reasoned. "Why would this guy want to smear her name?"

"Maybe she snubbed him," Heather shrugged. "Or, he's just stirring up trouble, having a laugh."

"That sounds mean."

"Yeah, but people do that, Jenny."

When Brandon's friend talked about Kelly having an affair, Jenny hadn't known what to think. He hadn't volunteered many details, just that Brandon suspected Kelly. Had Brandon intended to go ahead with the wedding? Or was he just biding time, trying to find out what Kelly was up to. Jenny reluctantly admitted that this gave Brandon a motive. Had he and Kelly had a fight about it? A fight that ended in Kelly landing in the pool?

"We need to go check out that pool," Jenny said to Heather. "Do you know where it is?"

"It's about fifty yards from that courtyard where we had the party. I used to go there a lot when I was a child."

"How does one get there?"

"It's on Ada's property, Jenny. You have to go through their front gate."

Ada Newbury had extended an open invite to Jenny. This kind of generosity was unheard of from Ada. Jenny assumed she had made an exception since her neck was on the line.

Jenny called ahead to let Ada know about her visit. Ada had to go out somewhere but she assured Jenny the security would let her in.

"How much more garlic do you need?" Heather grumbled.

Jenny looked at the small pile before Heather.

"That's enough. You can start peeling the ginger now."

Heather groaned and muttered through the process. The Magnolias arrived for lunch. They were the first group Jenny wanted to try out her recipe on. Star and Molly pronounced it delicious. Betty Sue declared it was too spicy.

Heather took a photo of the dish and posted it on social media.

Jenny and Heather set off after lunch. They breezed through the security gate and parked in front of the house.

Heather pointed to a paved path that wound through a clump of bushes.

"We can directly walk down to the pool. Do you want to do that?"

Jenny nodded her assent and set off at a brisk pace. The path took them around the house and beyond the courtyard. A couple of minutes later, Jenny turned a corner and stopped in her tracks.

A good sized building stood before her. A large pool with shimmering blue water lay inside a fancy enclosure. Plush cabanas with lime green cushions lined the pool on one side. Patio furniture with cozy sitting areas was arranged on the far side. There was a solid structure that looked like a pool house. It had a covered porch with a granite topped bar running along one wall. Jenny spotted another smaller pool in the distance. She guessed it was a hot tub.

"This is the pool complex," Heather said. "It used to be just the pool when I was younger. Ada turned it into this fancy thing a few years ago."

"How do we get in?" Jenny asked.

"I guess we open that door?" Heather pointed.

The door they spotted turned out to be locked. Jenny spotted a tiny button on one side. She pressed it, wondering if it was a doorbell of sorts. Her guess turned out to be right.

A tall, black haired youth with mussed hair ambled out on the covered porch. He wore a pair of sweat pants and nothing else. Heather and Jenny couldn't help but stare at his washboard stomach and six pack abs. Jenny recognized him as the guy who had found Kelly.

He gave them a wide smile and pressed some switch on the wall. The door slid open. The young man beckoned them over.

"Hello ladies," he beamed. "I'm Enrique. I take care of the pool."

Heather introduced them.

"Do you live here?" Jenny asked curiously.

"At the moment, yes," Enrique nodded. "Why don't you come in?"

Enrique opened a refrigerator and pulled out a few cans of soda. He offered them to the girls.

"I'm sure the boss won't mind," he grinned.

Jenny flipped the top off a can of ginger ale and took a big gulp. She was thinking about the locked door they had come through.

"Do people always ring that bell when they want to come in?" she asked.

Enrique shook his head.

"There's a digital access code. You have to enter it in a panel that's mounted by the side of the door."

"And how many people have that code?"

"Just the family, mostly. The boss is pretty stingy about handing it out.

She doesn't like the staff using the pool."

"Isn't the pool already on private property?" Heather spoke her mind. "What's the need for all this security?"

Enrique shrugged.

"Like I said, the boss doesn't like anyone else using it. The maids used to take a dip all the time when they didn't have this whole enclosure. The missus didn't like that."

Jenny leaned forward and spoke softly.

"I'm sure they all know the code, eh?"

Enrique laughed readily.

"It's hard to keep it a secret," he nodded. "That's why they change it every week."

"That's too much!" Heather exclaimed.

"The boss gets what she wants," Enrique noted.

Jenny asked the question that had been rolling around in her mind.

"Did Kelly have the code?"

"I don't know," Enrique said. "Kelly was staying at the country club. There was no reason for her to have the code, unless someone gave it to her."

Jenny looked at Heather.

"So Kelly either had to have the code or someone let her in."

They both turned their heads around and stared at Enrique.

"Don't look at me," he said. "I didn't do it."

"Where were you the night of the party?"

"Right here," Enrique said. "Sleeping in my bed."

"You didn't see Kelly come in?"

"I didn't see or hear anyone," Enrique said. He looked sheepish. "I sneaked into the party and stole a couple of drinks from the bar." He looked down at the floor and muttered something. "Okay, I grabbed half a bottle of tequila. I was pretty drunk."

"You do realize there was a murder here that night?" Heather burst out. "How could you sleep through it?"

Enrique stretched his arms above his head and yawned.

"I didn't know there was going to be a murder here. I would have stayed awake if I knew."

Jenny realized Enrique was a smooth talker.

"Did you know Kelly?" Jenny asked.

She didn't get a straight answer.

"I saw her around here a couple of times," Enrique said.

"Did anyone else come to the pool that night?" she asked.

"I told you, I was fast asleep."

"What happens when someone enters the access code to get in?" Jenny asked. "Do you get some kind of indication inside?"

"I hear a beep," Enrique told them. "If it's during my working hours, I come out here."

It turned out that Enrique also acted as a lifeguard during the day. It was his job to keep an eye on whoever was using the pool and be ready to offer assistance.

"Are you allowed to have visitors?" Jenny asked.

"No visitors!" Enrique shook his head. "The boss will fire my ass if I bring a girl here. And I'm not allowed to mingle with the maids either."

"That's a tough deal," Heather sympathized.

Enrique shrugged.

"It could be worse. I'm not complaining."

Jenny decided she wasn't going to get any more information out of Enrique. She wanted to take a stab at talking to Brandon again.

She walked back to the main house with Heather. Heather walked across the patio and opened a screen door.

"Ada doesn't like this," she giggled. "But she's not home."

A maid saw them and came over.

"Madam has asked you to go into the parlor."

It turned out Ada Newbury was home after all. She was wearing a snazzy outfit Jenny recognized as the latest in women's golf apparel.

"I just got back from my golf lesson. We were having tea."

Jenny looked around and realized there was someone else in the room. A deeply tanned man with a mane of light brown hair sat in a wing chair near the fireplace. His long legs were stretched out before him and his tawny eyes were busy giving Jenny a once over.

"This is Zac," Ada said. "He's my golf coach."

Her cheeks turned pink while she introduced the man.

"Zac Gordon," the man drawled. "Like Ada said. I'm the golf pro over at the country club."

"I love golf," Jenny volunteered. "I'm a bit rusty, though. Haven't played a round in a while."

Zac sat up a bit.

"Come see me at the club. I'll fix you up right away."

"The country club is members only," Ada butted in. "It's not for everyone."

Zac winked at Jenny.

"Don't worry about that."

Ada clucked impatiently and motioned the girls toward a couch.

The girls took a seat. A couple of maids came in with tea and snacks. Jenny wasn't keen on talking about anything related to Kelly in the man's presence. Ada forced her hand.

"Did you have any more questions for me?"

"I wanted to take a look at the pool," Jenny explained. "I didn't realize it was a restricted area."

Ada waited until the maids left the room.

"The staff takes undue advantage. They took midnight dips in the pool. Some of the girls even brought men over. I had to get that enclosure built."

"We met Enrique," Heather supplied. "He told us about the access codes."

"How many people know those codes, Mrs. Newbury?" Jenny asked.

"Just the family," Ada said. "I make sure of that."

"How do you think Kelly got in there? Did Brandon give her the code?"

Ada turned red.

"He shouldn't have. Kelly wasn't family."

"What are you saying?" Heather burst out. "Brandon was going to marry her in just a few days."

"He wouldn't have gone ahead with the wedding," Ada said suddenly.

Jenny didn't know whether to believe Ada. Was it just wishful thinking on her part? Did she have a concrete plan to split up the couple? Why was she so confident of getting Kelly out of the way?

"Brandon's broken up over Kelly," Heather observed. "I think he loved her a lot."

Jenny steered the question back to the access codes.

"The important thing here is how Kelly got into the pool house."

Zac Gordon spoke up, shocking Jenny with his assertion.

"That pool boy let her in, of course."

"Enrique? Why do you think that?"

"They were having an affair," Zac said with relish. "Kelly was two timing Brandon, seeing the pool boy on the side."

Ada didn't look surprised.

"Did you know about this?" Heather asked her.

Ada's mouth twisted in disgust.

"That girl was not right for my Brandon."

Zac Gordon was looking pleased with himself. Jenny asked the question uppermost in her mind.

"Wait a minute, Zac. How did you know Kelly?"

Chapter 8

Adam and Jenny were having dinner at Seaview, the three storied ocean facing house Jenny now called home. Adam brought a bottle of the local wine Jenny liked. They started their meal with crab cakes and caught up on what Jenny had been up to.

Jenny told Adam about meeting Enrique.

"Who is this Enrique?" Adam asked, simmering with anger. "He didn't come forward when we interviewed all the staff."

"He wasn't working at the party," Jenny explained. "Maybe that's why his name never came up."

"I'm going to talk to him first thing tomorrow."

"He looks like a player," Jenny said with a smile.

She wanted to talk to Enrique herself.

The next morning, Jenny arrived at the café at 5 AM and started prepping for the day. Star came in around eight and helped Jenny serve breakfast. The Magnolias came in after the crowd thinned.

"Ready to hit the road?" Heather asked Jenny.

"I'm ready," Jenny nodded.

The girls were going back to talk to Enrique.

Jenny hated to impose on Star all the time. She promised to be back in an hour and set off with Heather.

The girls took the path that led to the pool house. They rang the bell again, waiting for Enrique. There was a click as the door unlocked. Jenny took it as an invitation to enter and went in. She walked around the pool and went to the covered porch, calling out for Enrique. He didn't look too happy when he came out. Jenny was relieved to see he was fully dressed this time.

"I didn't know you had a uniform?" Heather remarked. "It suits you."

"Everyone working on the estate has to wear one," Enrique said with a shrug. "Are you here for a dip in the pool?"

"Can we do that?" Heather asked, surprised.

"I don't see why not," Enrique said. "You are on the list."

"What list?" Jenny asked.

"The list of people who can come in here," Enrique said in a bored voice. "Looks like this lady here is some relation of the Newburys."

Heather actually was a Newbury, although she didn't use that name.

"Grandpa must have added my name," Heather surmised. "I haven't been here in ages though."

Jenny gazed at Enrique.

"Did you talk to the police?"

"They were just here," Enrique grumbled. "Grilled me for an hour. I told them the same thing I told you. I slept right through that party."

"You're sure you didn't let Kelly in?"

"100%."

"How well did you know Kelly?"

"I met her when she came to the pool once or twice with Brandon. She was the friendly kind. Not stuck up like some of the boss's guests."

"You hit it off, huh?" Jenny asked.

Enrique took a deep breath.

"What are you suggesting?"

"Were you having an affair with Kelly?"

Enrique threw back his head and laughed.

"You can't be serious."

"Just answer me, Enrique," Jenny said, refusing to back down. "Were you and Kelly having an affair?"

"Of course not!" Enrique said irritably. "What gave you that idea?"

"I heard you were," Jenny persisted. "Why would someone say that?"

"I don't know ... to get me in trouble?"

"Come on," Jenny cajoled. "You can talk to me. I know how pretty

Kelly was. I know how a young buck like you would be attracted to her."

Enrique looked over his shoulder.

"Kelly wasn't just pretty, okay? She was friendly too. She didn't mind chatting with the help."

"So you flirted with her a bit?" Jenny smiled.

She wanted Enrique to get comfortable with her.

"It was the other way around," Enrique said. "Kelly came on to me. I had to push her away a couple of times."

Jenny didn't have trouble imagining that. Enrique was the male version of a hot swimsuit model.

"You didn't find her attractive?"

Enrique gave his usual shrug.

"I'm not blind, lady. But she was the boss's girl. I would be out on my hide if I so much as looked at her."

Jenny decided to give him the benefit of the doubt.

"She must have felt snubbed."

"She backed off. I didn't think too much about it."

Enrique sounded sincere. Jenny wondered if Adam had been able to get more out of him.

The girls went back to the Boardwalk Café.

Jenny made a batch of shrimp curry for lunch. She had tweaked the recipe after taking feedback from the Magnolias.

Adam came to the café for lunch.

"I hear you visited the pool boy?" Jenny asked as she placed a platter of rice and curry on the table.

Adam pursed his lips.

"Nothing ever stays secret in this town."

Jenny laughed as she spooned some curry on Adam's plate.

"There is no gossip involved this time. I have it from the horse's mouth."

"You met Enrique again?" Adam asked, leaning forward.

Jenny told him about her latest trip to the Newbury place.

"I hope you were not alone."

"Heather went with me," Jenny said. "But that's beside the point. Why can't I go alone? I can take care of myself."

"Will you listen to me this time?"

"Don't be so controlling, Adam. Enrique is just a harmless boy. He's the same age as Nicky."

Adam ate a bite and sat back. He complimented the food.

"I ran a background check," he said reluctantly. "That harmless boy as you call him was almost convicted."

Jenny sat down with a thump.

"What did he do?"

"He molested a girl," Adam said bluntly. "At least, that's what he was arrested for. But the charges didn't stick."

"Do you know why?"

"The girl refused to testify. Rumor is he threatened her."

"Wow!" Jenny exclaimed. "Was it a local girl?"

"She was local alright. She was a year younger than him. They dated for a while."

"They dated?" Jenny was curious. "Could it have been a lovers' tiff?"

She grudgingly admitted to herself that Enrique must have charmed her. She found it hard to believe he was capable of doing anything wrong.

Adam slapped a hand on the table.

"That's exactly what the girl said later. She said they had a falling out and she wanted to get back at him. But she later realized it wasn't the right thing to do. So she dropped the charges and Enrique got away."

"Or he was really innocent," Jenny said stoutly.

"All I'm saying is, be careful around this guy."

"Fine," Jenny said. "I'll keep that in mind. Now tell me how you like the curry."

Adam had cleared his plate while they were talking. He asked for seconds.

"You have another winner, Jenny. This shrimp curry is perfect. It's spicy and exotic but so familiar."

"Is it too exotic for Pelican Cove?"

"Give us some credit," Adam said. "I know we like our down home favorites but we do appreciate variety. And the tourists are going to love it too."

Jenny was pleased. She served herself some of the curry and dug in.

"Who's your top suspect?" she asked Adam after a while. "Is Ada off your list now?"

"You know I can't discuss that with you, Jenny," Adam sighed.

"It all depends on the motive, doesn't it?" Jenny continued. "What did anyone gain by killing a sweet young girl like Kelly?"

"Money?" Adam said reluctantly.

"I don't think so," Jenny said. "Kelly was an orphan and she had a regular office job. She was definitely marrying up. I don't think she had a dime to spare for anyone."

"We didn't find much in her room, other than a few clothes and make-up. No jewelry."

"What about a phone?" Jenny asked suddenly. "She must have had a cell phone. Everyone has one."

"She did have a phone," Adam nodded. "The techs are looking at it."

"Did you go through the phone?" Jenny asked.

"Not yet. Why?"

"That phone could have a lot of answers. Can I have a look at it please?"

"Nice try!" Adam snorted. "That phone is part of the evidence. You won't get anywhere near it."

"Did you find it near the pool?" Jenny asked.

Adam didn't reply.

"If you didn't find it near the pool, it's not really part of the crime scene, is it?"

"It's part of Kelly's personal effects at the very least," Adam said.

"Who gets access to that stuff?"

"Her family, I guess," Adam said.

"She doesn't have any," Jenny reminded him. "Brandon might be her next of kin since he was her fiancé. What if Brandon puts in a request for that phone?"

"Okay, stop," Adam said, holding both his hands up. "What do you want?"

"I just want to look at the phone for a few minutes," Jenny said with a smile. "I won't take it out of your sight. In fact, we can look at it together."

"What do you hope to achieve by this?"

"I won't know until I look."

Adam arranged to meet Jenny in a couple of hours. Jenny served the last customers of the day and closed the café. She walked to the police station, feeling excited. She had a strong intuition that Kelly's phone would point them in the right direction.

Adam sat in his office, staring at a phone encased in a plastic bag. He told Jenny to sit down.

"I'm as curious as you are," he said. "Let's get this show on the road."

He pulled on a pair of gloves and picked up the phone. The battery had discharged. Adam pulled a charger from a drawer and plugged the phone in. The voice mail icon came on.

"Looks like she has a lot of messages."

Jenny had walked around the desk to stand behind Adam. She peered at the phone over his shoulder. She asked him to press a bunch of keys and read off the screen.

"Who's Paula?" she asked Adam. "Have you come across anyone by that name?"

Adam declined.

"Looks like Kelly was quite friendly with this person. She's called her multiple times a day and messaged her several times in an hour."

Kelly had called Brandon too. Adam pointed it out.

"Of course she called Brandon. They were engaged, weren't they? And look, there's a call to Megan."

"So what does this prove?" Adam frowned. "Kelly liked calling people?"

"That's what kids do these days," Jenny reminded him. "Remember Nick and the twins?"

She was referring to her son and Adam's twin girls. They had met in Pelican Cove and established a rapport almost instantly. They texted each other several times a day. Jenny complained Nick called the twins more often than he called her.

"What are you saying?"

"This generation needs to share everything. They text their friends every time they sneeze or poop. Kelly was doing the same."

"I still don't get it," Adam said.

"Whoever this Paula is, she meant a lot to Kelly. She must have been her go-to friend. The one person Kelly wanted to tell everything."

"We need to find out who Paula is," Adam said, catching on.

"That's right," Jenny said.

"I don't think there was anyone by this name at the party," Adam said, going through a list on his desk.

"You're right," Jenny agreed. "I don't remember meeting anyone by this name either."

"If this Paula was such a good friend," Adam mused, "why wasn't she at the party?"

"Maybe Paula is code for something else," Jenny said. "Or someone else."

"That sounds farfetched," Adam said.

"Not really," Jenny said, reluctant to give up on her theory. "It could be a nickname."

"So how do you propose to find this Paula?" Adam asked.

Jenny pulled up Paula's number in Kelly's address book and pressed the call button. The call went to voicemail.

"Looks like this phone is switched off."

"What now?" Adam asked.

"I'm going to talk to Brandon. If Kelly was so close to this Paula, Brandon must surely know her."

Chapter 9

The spring sun bathed Pelican Cove in bright light. A cool ocean breeze made people keep their sweaters on. The sunlight wasn't strong enough to warm the skin. The Magnolias braved the weather and sat out on the deck at the Boardwalk Café.

Betty Sue carried on with her knitting, pausing only to take a sip of her coffee. Jenny brought out a tray loaded with tiny parfaits.

"I took your advice," she told her aunt. "These parfaits have layers of shaved chocolate. Why don't you try one and let me know if it tastes good?"

Heather walked up the boardwalk, tugging her black poodle Tootsie along with her. She tied Tootsie to a post and bounded up the stairs.

"I'll have one of those," she said, picking up a parfait cup.

"How's your investigation coming along?" Betty Sue asked Jenny.

"That's a big word," Jenny winced. "I'm just trying to figure out what happened."

"Did you try calling that number again?" Heather asked, referring to the number Jenny had found in Kelly's phone.

"The phone's still switched off," Jenny said. "It's highly suspicious."

Betty Sue and Star wanted to know what the girls were talking about. Jenny explained how Kelly had frequently been in touch with a girl called Paula.

"I think it belongs to a man," Betty Sue said.

"Why do you say that?" Jenny asked, surprised.

"It's a code, girl. We used to do that all the time."

"Huh?" Heather sat up. "You had a cell phone?"

Betty Sue rolled her eyes.

"Don't be ridiculous, Heather!"

She took a deep breath and stared at the ocean. Her voice turned softer.

"I was young once. There was this boy my Daddy didn't like. We, my friend Lily and I, gave him a name. We called him Ruth. We used to talk about him all the time and no one was the wiser. My Daddy thought Ruth was a girl who lived on the other side of town."

"Betty Sue! You sneaky devil!" Star laughed.

"So you think Paula is a guy?" Jenny asked Betty Sue.

"I don't agree," Heather said. "Times have changed, Grandma. It's perfectly okay to be friends with a guy. It's not taboo anymore."

"And Kelly wasn't a teen staying at home with her parents," Jenny reasoned. "She was an independent woman who lived alone. She could talk to anyone she wanted to, guy or girl."

"Cheating on your beau is still frowned upon though, right?" Betty Sue asked.

"You didn't spend much time with Kelly," Heather told Betty Sue. "She was very friendly. She must have been like that with everyone."

Jenny was lost in thought. She was thinking about the repercussions of Kelly having an affair.

"Remember what Brandon's friend said?" she spoke up. "What if Kelly was seeing someone behind Brandon's back? He wouldn't like that."

"You think Brandon knew?" Heather asked. "Why was he going ahead with the wedding, then?"

"I can't answer that," Jenny said. "We need to talk to Brandon."

Was Brandon the vindictive kind, Jenny wondered. What if he had caught Kelly with another man? Would he harm Kelly in a fit of anger?

Heather and Jenny set off for the Newbury estate after lunch. Brandon was sitting out in the courtyard, staring in the distance. Jenny sat before him and waited for him to speak.

Brandon sighed heavily after a few minutes.

"I miss her. What am I going to do without her, Heather?"

Heather patted his hand but said nothing.

"What time did you turn in on the night of the party?" Jenny asked.

"10, 10:30?" Brandon looked at her blankly. "I don't remember."

"When was the last time you talked to Kelly?"

"We barely talked during the party," Brandon said bitterly. "Megan was here and we were catching up with old friends. Kelly was hanging out with Binkie."

"That was kind of odd," Jenny observed. "Many people thought you and Megan were the happy couple."

"What people?" Brandon asked, sounding angry.

"I could use a drink," Jenny said, getting up. "Do you want something?"

"I can ring for sweet tea," Brandon said.

"It's okay," Jenny told him. "I'm going inside anyway. I'll let the kitchen staff know."

She went into the house, leaving Heather with Brandon. The house was quiet inside. Jenny wondered where Ada was. She pushed open the kitchen door. The old cook sat at a small table with her feet up on a chair. She looked sleepy.

"Hello," Jenny greeted her. "I'm Heather's friend. I was here a couple of days ago …"

"I know who you are, missy," the cook interrupted her. "How can I help you?"

"I'm trying to determine everyone's whereabouts the night of the party," Jenny explained. "How long was the staff around, do you know?"

"Most guests left by ten," the cook said. "Some of the young ones still hung around, I'm sure."

The door opened and a maid came in. Jenny remembered she had been serving food at the party. She repeated her question.

"I was around for a while after ten," the maid said evasively.

"This is between us," Jenny assured her. "I am not going to report you to Mrs. Newbury."

The maid hesitated.

"The missus went in around 9:30. The courtyard was empty by 11."

"How long did you stick around?" Jenny asked.

"My boyfriend came over," the girl said reluctantly. "I picked up a bottle of wine from the bar and we sat out in the garden, drinking."

"Did you see anyone walking toward the pool?" Jenny asked eagerly.

"We weren't really paying attention," the girl said. "If you know what I mean …"

Jenny knew what she meant.

"You didn't see a single person out in the courtyard after 11?"

"I didn't say that," the maid said. "Brandon came out around 11:30. I saw him from the corner of my eye."

"Do you think he saw you?"

The girl shrugged.

"We were standing in a dark corner, so maybe not."

"Where did he go?"

"I don't know," the girl said. "He was there one minute, then he was gone."

"But you're sure you saw him?"

The girl nodded emphatically.

Jenny spoke to the cook.

"Can we have some sweet tea, please?"

"Sure," the cook drawled. "I'll send someone out there, don't worry."

Jenny walked back to the courtyard. Brandon had a frown on his face as Heather chatted with him.

"I'm parched," he said, looking up at Jenny. "What's taking them so long?"

"You told me you turned in around ten the night of the party," Jenny said, taking a seat.

"And?"

"It looks like you came out of your room around 11:30. You were seen walking around here."

Brandon was looking bewildered.

"What were you doing out here, Brandon?" Jenny asked. "Were you looking for Kelly?"

"I don't know what you are talking about."

"Did you know Kelly was going to be at the pool? Did you arrange to meet her there? Maybe the two of you wanted to take a midnight dip."

"Kelly wasn't staying here," Brandon said, rubbing his forehead. "She had a room at the country club."

"You could still have met her at the pool house," Jenny pressed.

"But I didn't," Brandon said.

"What were you doing out here so late at night?"

"I don't know," Brandon pleaded. "I honestly don't know. I must have been walking in my sleep."

"That's convenient," Jenny muttered.

"Since when do you sleep walk?" Heather asked.

"It started a few months ago," Brandon told her. "I do it when I am stressed about something."

"What did you have to stress about?" Heather scoffed. "You were marrying the love of your life."

"I don't know, Heather," Brandon whined. "I don't control it."

Jenny didn't believe the sleepwalking theory. She was sure Brandon had just made it up on the spot.

"Were you following Kelly?" she asked softly, leaning toward Brandon.

"Why would I do that?" Brandon cried.

"Look, we think Kelly might have been having an affair. Did you know about it?"

"Kelly would never cheat on me," Brandon protested. "She was a good kid."

Jenny looked at Brandon, trying to read his mind. She didn't believe he was that ignorant.

"Kelly sent a lot of messages to someone," Jenny told Brandon. "Did you notice she was using her phone a lot?"

Brandon seemed to hesitate a bit. Then his face crumpled.

"You're right. Kelly might have been having an affair."

"What made you suspect her?"

"It's like you said," Brandon explained. "She was on the phone a lot, even when she was with me. I even joked about it. She said it was a friend who was in distress. She needed to hold her hand."

"That's possible," Jenny nodded, considering what Brandon said. "But not probable. If she was so close to this friend, why didn't she introduce you to her?"

"That's what I thought too," Brandon said bitterly.

"If you suspected Kelly, why were you going ahead with the wedding?" Heather asked.

"I was hopeful," Brandon said. "I thought maybe she was having a last fling."

"You're saying you would have been fine with that?" Jenny asked incredulously.

Brandon clutched his head and groaned.

"I have a headache. Can we talk later?"

He stood up and started walking inside.

Jenny and Heather talked about what had happened on the way back.

"I'm sure he's lying," Jenny declared. "He's hiding something."

"I believe Brandon," Heather said supportively. "He was hopeful in spite of his suspicions. That's a man in love."

Jenny dropped Heather off at the Bayview Inn and stopped at Mama Rosa's, the island's pizzeria, on the way home. She was feeling exhausted and was in no mood to cook dinner. She ran into Jason.

"Hey Jenny!" he greeted her.

They chatted while their order was getting ready.

"Are you eating pizza every night?" Jenny admonished. "Why don't you cook something simple at home?"

"Cooking for one is a chore," Jason said. "Most days, I'm too tired anyway."

Jenny extended a dinner invitation and made Jason order a salad with his pizza.

That night, Jenny thought about Jason as she walked on the beach. Jason had been recovering from a bad breakup for the past year. She wanted him to be happy. Even though she had chosen Adam over Jason, she cared deeply for him. Deep down, she felt a bit guilty for turning him down.

Dark clouds lined the horizon when Jenny stepped out of her house the next morning. The sky was overcast and a chilly wind whipped Jenny's hair around. She headed to the Boardwalk Café and started getting breakfast ready.

Jenny pulled out a pan of freshly baked banana nut muffins just as the clock struck six. The phone rang before she had a chance to open the café doors. It was Jason.

Jenny rushed to Jason's house, praying that everything was alright. She had been unable to make sense of Jason's gibberish. He had been hysterical and Jenny had promised to go see him right away.

Jenny scrambled out of her car a few minutes later. Jason was standing out on the porch, white in the face. He held a pink colored bundle in his hands. He stood there dumbly, staring at Jenny.

"What's wrong, Jason?" Jenny cried. "What's going on?"

Jason held his arms out to Jenny.

"Emily," he mumbled.

"Speak up, Jason."

A wail arose from the bundle before Jason had a chance to say anything.

"This is Emily," he said, staring at the bundle in his hands. "Emily Stone."

Jenny's eyes widened as she realized what Jason held. She gently eased the bundle out of his arms and stared down at the chubby infant. A pair of brown, almond shaped eyes stared back at her. The baby gurgled and waved a fist in the air, demanding attention.

"Where did she come from?" Jenny asked softly, looking up at Jason.

Chapter 10

Jenny bustled through the breakfast rush at the Boardwalk Café. After grabbing a cup of coffee and a muffin for herself, she made a batch of her banana caramel parfaits. Heather arrived right on time to taste them.

Heather dug into the delicious treat as Jenny dialed the number she had been calling for the last couple of days. She muttered an oath when the standard recording came on. The phone was still switched off.

"Any luck?" Heather asked with her mouth full.

"I'm beginning to think someone chucked this phone into the ocean."

"You may be right," Heather said seriously. "You need Adam's help here."

"I'm going to talk to him," Jenny said, her mouth set in a firm line. "Are you sticking around here?"

Heather nodded.

"Grandma will be here soon. You go ahead. I will keep an eye on things here."

Jenny walked the couple of blocks to the police station, hoping Adam wasn't too busy. The front desk was deserted and Nora, the desk clerk, was nowhere in sight. Jenny knocked on Adam's door and went in.

Adam sat with his leg propped up on a chair.

"Is your leg bothering you again?" Jenny asked with concern.

"No more than usual," Adam said with a shrug. "What are you doing here, Jenny?"

"I tried that number again," Jenny said, pulling up a chair. "No response."

"You don't give up, do you?"

"You need to trace this number, Adam. Find out who it belongs to."

"Are you trying to tell me how to do my job?" Adam asked, suppressing a grin. "You know better than that, Jenny."

"All I'm saying is, this phone is important. It could be our biggest lead."

"Our?"

"Whatever," Jenny snapped. "This Paula person was close to Kelly. We need to hunt her down so we can talk to her."

"I agree with you this time," Adam said. "I'm already on it."

"Will you let me know when you learn something?" Jenny asked.

"I can't promise that," Adam said honestly. "It's all part of my investigation. I'm not obligated to share any information with you, Jenny. You on the other hand, are."

Jenny stood up in a huff and stalked out. Adam was very particular about keeping his professional life separate from his personal one. She just wished he would cut her some slack once in a while.

Jenny took the scenic route back to the café, going over everything she knew about Kelly so far. She spotted a few familiar faces on the beach and waved at them. A bright cornflower blue sky stretched above her with not a single cloud in sight. Many tourists seemed to have taken advantage of the fair weather and were beginning to arrive on the beach.

Jenny spotted the Magnolias sitting out on the deck of the Boardwalk Café and her face broke into a smile. She picked up her pace, eager to join the lively discussion that seemed to be on.

"What do you say, Jenny?" Betty Sue asked as soon as she spotted Jenny coming up the café's steps. "Can Jason take care of Emily?"

Jason Stone and his baby girl Emily had become the talk of the town. Jason had told Jenny the whole story after he had come out of his initial shock. There wasn't much to tell. His doorbell had rung early in the morning. He opened the door to find a baby on his doorstep. His baby.

There was a small note tucked in the baby's blanket. It was from Kandy, a city lawyer who had unceremoniously dumped Jason and disappeared from his life. As it turned out, Kandy had been pregnant. She decided she wanted to have the child on her own. A few months after Emily was born, Kandy had come to a new decision. There was no room for a baby in her life. She had left the baby on Jason's doorstep, probably believing he would take care of her.

Jason had come out of his daze after a day or two. He was overjoyed. In his late forties, Jason had given up all hope of ever becoming a father. Emily was a gift he cherished with all his heart. His aunt Linda had taken one look at the baby and declared she was 100% Stone. Jason had turned his home office into a nursery.

The old biddies in town wondered how a single man, a confirmed bachelor, could raise a child on his own. But Jenny believed in Jason.

"Of course he can," she said supportively. "He's going to be the best father you ever came across."

"But can he do it alone?" Molly asked. "You know what they say. It takes a village to raise a child."

"And we have that village here," Jenny said brightly. "I have signed up for babysitting duty. I can't wait to wrap that little munchkin in my arms."

"Jason's out of town a lot," Star reminded Jenny. "Who's going to take care of the baby then?"

"He can hire a full time nanny," Heather said.

"Or he can reduce his workload," Jenny said. "I'm sure Jason will figure it out."

"It's been a while since I bounced a baby on my knee," Betty Sue sighed. "I wouldn't mind looking after that little one sometime."

"I'm not changing any diapers," Heather groaned, wrinkling her nose. "But I can play with her."

"I can read her a story," Molly joined in.

The group broke up after a while and Jenny started making lunch. Two hours later, she collapsed into a chair in the kitchen, exhausted.

The café had been busy and they had sold out of everything.

"I saved a sandwich for you," her aunt said, pulling out a plate covered in plastic wrap from the refrigerator. "There's half a cup of soup left."

Jenny took a big bite of the sandwich and warmed the soup in the microwave. Something had been niggling at the back of her mind all day. The fog in her mind cleared suddenly and she almost choked on her sandwich. Star patted her on the back as she started coughing.

"What's the matter, sweetie?"

"How could I forget that?" Jenny chided herself and cleared her throat.

"Why don't you finish eating first?" her aunt suggested calmly.

Jenny took a couple of minutes to finish chewing her sandwich.

"Ada had an argument with Kelly on the night of the party," she explained. "I was going to talk to Ada about it but I completely forgot."

"You can do it now," Star said.

"Do you want to go with me?" Jenny asked.

Ada Newbury was a snob. She only talked to a small bunch of people in town. Star wasn't one of them.

"I have no wish to be insulted by that monster," Star smirked. "You go ahead."

Heather was busy working at the inn so Jenny set off for the Newbury estate on her own. The security guards waved her through, and the maid who greeted her at the door led her into Ada's parlor.

Ada's mouth twisted in a grimace when she saw Jenny.

"Have you considered calling ahead?" she asked haughtily. "I'm afraid I have a golf lesson in fifteen minutes."

"We need to talk," Jenny said, ignoring Ada's thinly veiled rebuke.

"I'll be back in a couple of hours. You can wait here until then. But it might be better if you came back with an appointment."

Jenny sat down on a sofa and looked up at Ada.

"Do you want to find out what happened to Kelly?" she asked calmly. "I don't have to do this, Mrs. Newbury."

Ada rolled her eyes and sat down opposite Jenny.

"I suppose I can cancel my golf lesson."

She picked up a phone and dialed someone. She turned her back on Jenny and talked softly into the phone. She hung up a couple of minutes later.

"I postponed my appointment," she explained. "I'm lucky my coach agreed to move some things around."

Jenny got to the point.

"People saw you arguing with Kelly on the night of the party. Can you tell me what that was about?"

"Just wedding stuff," Ada said.

"Can you be more specific?"

"Brandon doesn't know about this," Ada said softly, looking over her shoulder.

"I'll try to keep this to myself."

"That girl wasn't right," Ada complained, back in form. "I was giving her the wedding of a lifetime. A poor orphan like her, getting married at the country club? Any other girl would have been grateful."

"What did Kelly do?"

"She didn't want the club wedding. She was happy with a civil ceremony. She wanted me to take the money I would spend on the country club wedding and give it to her."

"But why?" Jenny asked, perplexed.

"She said she needed it for a down payment on a house, the house she and Brandon would live in after they got married."

"That's not a bad idea," Jenny shrugged.

"Brandon already has a place of his own," Ada dismissed. "There was no need to go buy another house."

"Didn't Kelly know that?"

"Of course she did," Ada cried. "I think she just wanted my money. She would have taken the money and run."

Jenny wondered if Kelly had been that calculating.

"Leaving Brandon at the altar?" Jenny asked.

"I wouldn't put it past her," Ada said strongly.

"I need to find out more about this argument," Jenny told Ada. "I'm going to talk to a few more people."

"Do that," Ada said curtly. "And call before coming next time."

Jenny wandered through the house, hoping to run into some of the staff that had been working the night of the party. She gravitated toward the kitchen. The cook greeted her like an old friend.

"Got more questions for me?" she asked.

"It's about the fight Ada had with Kelly. I want to find out more about it."

The cook picked up a wall mounted phone and pressed a button. She asked the person at the other end to come into the kitchen. Jenny guessed it was an internal line.

Jenny recognized the maid who walked into the kitchen a few minutes later.

"This is about the night of the party," Jenny began. "You saw Mrs. Newbury arguing with Kelly, right?"

"Those two were ready to gauge each other's eyes out," the girl said with a grin.

"Do you know what happened?"

"It was about money," the girl said, climbing up on a tall stool next to the big kitchen island. She picked up a carrot from a pile and started peeling it. "I think the boss wanted her to go away and leave Mr. Brandon alone."

Jenny could imagine Ada doing that.

"Are you sure about that?"

The girl became defensive.

"Kelly was saying she didn't care about the money. She just wanted to make Brandon happy."

"What else?"

The girl's voice dropped as she leaned toward Jenny.

"The boss got all red in the face. Told Kelly she better listen to her or else. Then she pushed Kelly."

"I can't imagine Ada doing that," Jenny said skeptically.

"Talk to the others," the girl said. "They will tell you the same thing."

Jenny spent the next hour talking to other members of Ada's domestic staff. All of them had watched the altercation between the two women. Each of them had their own theory about what the fight was about. They all seemed to agree on two things. Money had been mentioned. And Ada Newbury had pushed Kelly.

Jenny felt confused on the drive back home. She knew Ada was a snob and loved talking down to people she didn't consider her equals. Jenny could well imagine Ada looking down her nose at Kelly, calling her names. She could even imagine Ada offering the girl a bunch of money to leave Brandon alone. But was Ada Newbury capable of physically assaulting someone?

Chapter 11

Jenny had a surprise waiting for her when she got home. Her son Nick sat dozing on the sofa, his feet up on the coffee table.

"Nicky!" Jenny cried joyfully. "When did you get here?"

She had no idea he had been planning a visit home.

Nick sat up and rubbed his eyes. His youthful face broke into a smile. He leapt up and wrapped Jenny in a tight hug.

"I missed you, Mom," he said. "I just wanted to spend some time with you. Is that okay?"

"Of course it's okay," Jenny said, planting a kiss on his cheek. "You don't need permission to come home."

"You sure I'm not upsetting any weekend plans?" Nick asked with a grin.

"Don't be silly," Jenny dismissed.

Nick was a junior in college. He wanted to be a lawyer like his father.

"Why didn't you warn me you were coming?" Jenny asked as she walked into the kitchen. "I would have stocked up on your favorite stuff."

"I'm not here for the food, Mom," Nick grinned. "I mean, not just for the food," he said with a wink. "Whatever you cook is going to be great."

Jenny inspected the refrigerator, noting its meager contents.

"How about meatloaf for dinner?" she asked. "We will get fresh fish at the market tomorrow."

Star arrived and exclaimed over Nick.

Dinner was a lively meal, with Nick regaling them with anecdotes of his campus life.

Jenny and Nick sat out on the patio later, sipping coffee. The salty air was a bit chilly, but pleasant enough to sit outside. A large stone water fountain gurgled a few feet away and a gibbous moon rose in the sky.

"How's Adam?" Nick asked his mother. "Is he behaving himself?"

Jenny punched her son in the arm.

"Don't get fresh."

"Seriously, Mom," Nick said. "Is he treating you well? I know he tends to fly off the handle sometimes."

"You don't have to worry about that," Jenny assured him. "Adam's changed a bit. For the better."

"I'm glad to hear that," Nick nodded, sounding decades older than twenty. "When are you getting married?"

Jenny blushed.

"We haven't set a date yet. What's the rush?"

"You know you have my blessing?" Nick asked her. "I'm with you whatever you decide to do. You can dump the guy or marry him tomorrow. It's your call."

"I'll keep that in mind," Jenny said lightly. "Now let's talk about your grades."

Nick groaned and launched into a lengthy explanation of why he had dropped one class and was barely scraping through in another.

Jenny woke before the sun rose the next morning. She had a big smile on her face as she got ready to go to the café. Having her son home really made her happy. She drove to the café as the sky lightened and an orange glow crept over the horizon.

Adam surprised her by coming to the café for breakfast. Jenny stood by his table as he tucked into his crab omelet.

"Have you found anything new?" she asked, topping up his coffee.

"I have," Adam nodded. "We got back Paula's phone records."

Jenny waited for Adam to go on. He ignored her and got back to eating his omelet.

"What do the records say?" Jenny asked, refusing to back down.

"They belong to someone called Paula Briggs, okay?" Adam said, sounding exasperated. "And the phone was in the vicinity of Kelly's phone."

"So whoever Paula is, she wasn't far away," Jenny summed up.

She thought over the different people she had met at Ada's, focusing on girls she had seen Kelly talking to. She immediately thought of Megan. Could Kelly have been talking to Megan?

Jenny didn't voice her suspicions to Adam. She was sure he would forbid her to do anything. She planned her next move and sat down to have a cup of coffee with Adam.

"Does Jason really have a kid?" Adam asked.

"He sure does. You have to meet Emily. She's the cutest baby you ever saw. We should all have dinner sometime."

Adam muttered something under his breath.

"Kind of weird, huh?" he said, looking dazed. "At his age."

"What's wrong with his age?" Jenny demanded. "Jason's going to make a great dad."

Adam finally left. Jenny rushed to the phone and called Heather.

"Can you come over?" she asked.

The two girls headed to Megan's. Jenny purposely didn't call ahead. She didn't want to give Megan any time to prepare herself.

Megan seemed a bit tired. She didn't look too happy to see them.

"You were around Kelly a lot, weren't you?" Jenny asked directly.

"We were both at the same party," Megan said. "Just like you."

"Were the two of you up to something?"

"We were planning to go shopping in the city," Megan said, looking bewildered. "Didn't we talk about this before?"

"What I mean is, were you hiding something from Brandon?"

"Why would I do that?" Megan asked wearily. "Brandon is my friend, not Kelly."

Heather tried to help Jenny.

"What she means is … maybe Kelly wanted to surprise Brandon or something. She could have asked for your help. You see what we are getting at?"

Megan shook her head.

"Kelly and I didn't talk about Brandon at all. We just discussed some girl stuff. Fashion, work stuff, life in the city …"

"So you two hit it off?" Jenny murmured.

Megan shrugged.

"I guess you could say that. I thought I made a new friend. It gets pretty lonely in the city, you know, living on your own. It's hard to find someone who understands what you are going through." Megan's voice sounded hoarse with emotion. "Doesn't matter now. Kelly's gone."

Jenny and Heather took their leave. Megan made it clear she was happy to see them go.

"What do you think?" Heather asked as soon as they got into the car. "Was she lying?"

Jenny said nothing for a while.

"Could Megan and Kelly have been plotting something together?"

"Like what?" Heather asked, raising her eyebrows. "I don't believe Megan would ever do anything against Brandon."

"Don't forget she was a woman scorned," Jenny reminded her. "We don't know what happened between them. Maybe they had a really bad breakup."

"You haven't seen Megan mooning around Brandon like I have," Heather argued. "She's had her eye on him for years. It's easier to believe she was working on getting him back."

"So you don't think she was really friendly with Kelly?"

"Would you be?" Heather asked. "Brandon is the love of her life. Why would she want to go shopping with the woman who's taken her place?"

Jenny was quiet while she processed what Heather said.

"Maybe I'm looking at it all wrong," she said. "What if Megan was hounding Kelly? Forcing her to do something for her?"

"We'll never know that now," Heather pointed out.

"The whole idea is farfetched anyway," Jenny sighed. "We need to talk to Brandon."

"Let's go see him now," Heather said. "Star can take care of the café."

"She's been helping me a lot lately," Jenny said. "She barely has time to paint. I feel bad, imposing on her so much."

"She's doing it because she loves you," Heather said.

Jenny reflected over her good fortune. When her husband left her for another woman, she had been alone and forlorn. Coming to Pelican Cove had been the best decision of her life. She had reconnected with her aunt and met the Magnolias. The group of women provided a strong support system for Jenny and she felt touched by their unconditional love.

Jenny called the café on her cell phone and spoke to her aunt. She drove to the Newbury estate, hoping Brandon would be in a better mood.

Both girls heaved a sigh of relief when they learned Ada Newbury was out. The maid led them out to the beach. Brandon was out for a run. They could see him in the distance.

"Looks like he's getting back to normal," Heather said.

Brandon spotted them and waved. They waited until he jogged up to them. Brandon picked up a towel from a chair and wiped the sweat off his face and hands.

"Nice day for a run," he said, picking up a glass of juice and draining it in a gulp.

The maid came back with a tray loaded with refreshments. Brandon played the gracious host and insisted they taste the assortment of cookies before them. Jenny sipped the freshly squeezed lemonade and felt energized.

"What brings you here, ladies?" Brandon asked.

"More questions," Jenny said. "I hope you don't mind."

"You can ask me anything you want." Brandon was solicitous. "I hope you will find out what happened to Kelly. It won't bring her back but at least it will give me some closure."

"It's about Megan and Kelly," Jenny explained. "Did you find it odd that they got along so well together?"

Brandon looked surprised.

"Why would I?" he asked. "Kelly knew Megan before she met me."

"What?" Heather and Jenny cried out together.

"I met Kelly at a party thrown by Megan," Brandon said. "We hit it off right away. Megan had already dumped me at that time, so I was free to see whoever I wanted. We went on our first date the next day, Kelly and I."

"Did you ever ask Megan how she knew Kelly?"

Brandon shook his head.

"Never thought about it."

Heather chatted with Brandon for a while and the girls took their leave.

"Back to Megan's?" Heather asked as Jenny started the car.

Jenny nodded grimly. She tried to remember all the questions she had asked Megan. Had she ever asked Megan when she first met Kelly?

Megan didn't hide her displeasure when she opened the door and saw them standing outside.

"What now?"

"We just have some follow-up questions," Jenny said, refusing to back down. "You can talk to us or talk to the police."

"You can't threaten me like that," Megan said angrily. "And I don't mind talking to the police. I have nothing to hide."

"Let us come in, then," Heather soothed.

Jenny didn't waste any time.

"When did you first meet Kelly?"

"Didn't we already talk about that?" Megan asked with a frown.

"Tell me again."

"Brandon introduced us. I don't remember the exact date. It was a Sunday and we met for brunch."

"You are sure you didn't know her before that?" Jenny pressed.

"That's not what Brandon says," Heather burst out. "He says you introduced them."

"Impossible," Megan exclaimed. She stared back at Jenny. "Did Brandon really say that?"

Jenny thought back to their conversation with Brandon, trying to remember his exact words.

"He said he met her at a party you threw."

Megan sighed with relief and laughed nervously.

"Oh! That doesn't mean I knew her."

"Can you explain what you mean by that?" Jenny asked.

"I'm a publicist," Megan began. "I host a lot of parties for my clients. Most of them are high profile people from different walks of life. My job is to invite a selected group of people who can be seen and photographed with my clients. I need to create the right vibe and sometimes I need a crowd of people. I hire people who produce this crowd, youngsters working in the city who like to party. They just come for the free booze. I rarely get to talk to these people."

"You are saying Kelly was one of these freeloaders?"

"She might have been," Megan said emphatically. "My point is, I don't know all the people who come to my parties. Not unless I have invited them myself."

Jenny marveled over how ironic the situation was. Megan had unwittingly played a part in bringing Brandon and Kelly together.

Chapter 12

Jenny scooped some mashed avocado on slices of smoked turkey and squirted her special chipotle mayo on top. She folded the wrap and set it on a platter.

Star tossed pasta and diced vegetables in fresh basil pesto.

"Did you post the turkey wraps on Instagram?" she asked Jenny. "The tourists are going to love them."

"You think so?" Jenny asked, furrowing her brow.

Jenny's creative recipes had made the Boardwalk Café a roaring success. But she was still hesitant before introducing any new items on the menu.

"Didn't you want to talk to Adam?" Star asked. "Why don't you go now?"

Jenny made a few dozen wraps and put them in the refrigerator. She grabbed two wraps and a small container of salad for Adam and walked to the police station.

Pelican Cove was enjoying another warm, spring day. Jenny gazed up at the sky and closed her eyes, breathing in the salty air.

A big pile of files littered Adam's desk. He didn't look too happy to see Jenny.

"Isn't it early for lunch?" he asked, spying the basket Jenny carried on her arm.

"You can eat it later," Jenny told him. "I'm going to put this in the refrigerator out in the galley."

"Thanks, Jenny," Adam smiled. "That's kind of you."

Jenny stood her ground.

"Is there anything else?" Adam sighed.

"Do you have Kelly's phone records?" Jenny asked. "We never talked about them."

"And we are not going to," Adam snorted. "I have a busy day ahead,

Jenny."

Jenny took the hint and walked out of Adam's office. The phone records would have to wait.

The Magnolias had arrived for their mid-morning break by the time Jenny got back to the Boardwalk Café.

Betty Sue stared at something while her hands moved in a rhythm, knitting something green. Molly barely paid attention to the book in her hand. Heather was busy snapping pictures on her phone. Jenny wondered what the women were so engrossed in.

Then she noticed her aunt. Star held a bundle wrapped in pink in her arms.

"Is that Emily?" Jenny squealed as she ran up the café steps.

She looked down at the baby her aunt held and made kissing noises. The cherub gurgled and looked back at her with large brown eyes.

"Emily's spending some time with us," Star said. "Jason is running some errands."

The baby let out a cry, signaling she needed to be changed. Jenny took her inside and clumsily changed her diaper. She hadn't done that since her son grew up.

Emily sat in her stroller, chewing her fists, drooling and smiling at the Magnolias.

Jenny poured coffee for everyone and brought out a plate of muffins.

"Is Ada treating you well?" Betty Sue asked Jenny. "You let me know if she gets too hoity toity. You are doing her a favor. Don't you let her forget it."

"Don't worry about me, Betty Sue," Jenny assured her. "I'm not bothered about Ada."

"Found anything new?" Molly asked.

Jenny shook her head.

"I don't seem to have any clear leads."

"That pool boy is highly suspicious," Heather said, setting her phone aside.

She had clicked a few dozen pictures of the baby.

"Who, Enrique?" Jenny asked. "Why do you suspect him, Heather?"

"Have you looked at him?" Heather asked, fanning herself. "He's so hot it's got to be a crime."

Betty Sue cleared her throat and looked flushed.

"Didn't he say he was sleeping the night of the party?" Molly asked.

"That's what he says," Heather nodded. "But do we really believe him? He's the only person who could have let Kelly into the pool house."

"So you think he's been lying to us all this time?" Jenny asked.

"Why not?" Heather asked. "You have no reason to trust him, Jenny."

"Say he let Kelly in that night," Jenny said. "What do you think happened?"

"They fought over something?" Heather said. "This Kelly seems like a loose character. Maybe she came on to Enrique and he snubbed her. Or it could have been the other way around. What if Enrique got fresh with Kelly?"

Jenny continued Heather's line of thought.

"They had a tussle. Enrique pushed Kelly into the pool. Or she could have slipped and fallen in herself."

"Why didn't he pull her out?" Molly asked.

"He didn't realize she was drowning?" Jenny spoke out loud. "He might have walked away and never realized what was happening behind his back."

Heather's face darkened as she thought of the alternative.

"Or he stood there and let Kelly die."

"That would make him a cold blooded murderer," Jenny said with a shudder. "Why would Enrique do that?"

"Revenge?" Star offered. "Didn't you say Kelly rejected his advances?"

"That's just one of my theories," Jenny sighed. "Enrique insists it was the other way round."

"He could have been working for someone else," Heather offered.

"You mean like a hired killer?" Jenny asked. "This is beginning to sound fantastic."

The baby had fallen asleep while the women talked. Star covered her with an extra blanket, making sure she was warm enough.

"What if Ada Newbury hired the pool boy to kill that poor girl?" Star asked.

Jenny's mouth dropped open.

"She wouldn't go that far," she said hoarsely.

Betty Sue was shaking her head from side to side, too shocked at Star's suggestion to say anything.

"She does have a motive," Molly offered. "We know Mrs. Newbury wasn't happy with the wedding. Clearly, she didn't want her grandson marrying Kelly."

"We know she tried to bribe Kelly," Heather mused. "Maybe she didn't stop there."

"I am sure Ada was fast asleep in her bed at midnight," Betty Sue insisted.

She and Ada were staunch rivals and rarely saw eye to eye. So the Magnolias were surprised to see her defend Ada.

"You have given me an idea," Jenny told Betty Sue. "I never asked Ada about her alibi."

"Let's go talk to her now," Heather said eagerly.

"Hello ladies!" a cheerful voice hailed them from the boardwalk.

Jason Stone walked up, holding a few grocery bags in his hands. He came up the café steps and rushed to the baby's stroller.

"Shhh …" Star said, placing a finger on her lips.

"Isn't she an angel?" Jason gushed.

He set his bags down and collapsed into a chair. Jenny offered him a muffin.

"I'm too tired to eat," Jason groaned. "In fact, I'm exhausted."

He tipped his head at the baby in the stroller.

"This little lady's been keeping me up at night."

"Have you thought of getting a nanny?" Betty Sue asked.

"I'm not too keen on that," Jason said. "I want to take care of her myself."

"We are here to help," Star said, patting him on the arm.

Jason let out a big yawn. He told them how he had driven around Pelican Cove for hours the previous night with Emily in her car seat.

"She would nod off while the car was moving, and start crying as soon as the car stopped."

"Nick was like that," Jenny said, remembering. "I used to wear a hole in the carpet, walking him around the house. He would start wailing the moment I set him down."

They talked about Emily for a few minutes. Jason finally stood up and headed home with his baby.

"Shall we go now?" Heather reminded Jenny.

"Let's make sure Ada's home," Jenny said.

Ada was expected back home in an hour. Star forced them to stay back and have lunch before they went out.

"Ada won't like being questioned," Heather said as they drove into the hills where the Newbury estate was situated.

"When does she like anything I say?" Jenny shrugged. "I need to ask the tough questions."

Ada Newbury was entertaining her golf coach in the parlor.

"We just got back from a lesson," she enthused. "Coach says I am improving a lot."

She looked admiringly at the tall man who sat sprawled in a delicate chair.

"She's really been working on her swing," the man spoke. "I wish all my students were that dedicated."

"Zac, right?" Jenny greeted the man. She turned to look at Ada. "Can I have a word with you, Mrs. Newbury?"

Ada looked longingly at the golf pro.

"Zac has to leave for another lesson."

Zac Gordon stood up and stretched himself. He patted Ada on the shoulder and took his leave.

"What brings you here today?" Ada asked tersely.

Jenny was direct.

"We never talked about your alibi. What were you doing around midnight the night of the party?"

"What do you think I was doing?" Ada shot back. "I must have been in bed."

"Were you?" Jenny asked.

"Of course I was," Ada said.

"Can someone vouch for it?"

"Julius is out of town," Ada said, referring to her husband. "I was alone."

"Are you ready to swear you never left your room that night?" Jenny asked.

"You're out of line," Ada scowled. "Are you actually suspecting me?"

"You did have a motive," Jenny pointed out. "And you argued with Kelly that night."

"That doesn't mean I'm guilty," Ada said.

Jenny didn't back down.

"I'm not saying you are. I just want to know where you were that night, and what you were doing."

"I don't want to talk about it," Ada said.

"As you wish," Jenny said with a shrug. "But you're holding me back."

She walked out of the house with Heather close behind. One of the maids came hurrying out while they were getting into the car. Jenny didn't recognize her.

"Are you the one who's asking questions about the party?" the girl asked.

"What's up?" Jenny asked, nodding affirmatively.

"You know Enrique, the pool boy?" the girl asked. "I saw him on the beach just when the party was winding down."

"But …" Heather butted in.

Jenny held up her hand, warning Heather to stay quiet.

"What was he doing there?"

"He was drinking," the girl said. "Must have filched a bottle from the bar."

"Was he alone?" Jenny asked.

"He was, at first. Then Mr. Brandon's girl walked up to him."

"You mean Kelly?" Jenny asked. "The girl who died?"

"That's right," the maid nodded. "Enrique was shaking his head while he talked to her. Then he laughed at her. She stomped off."

"What time was this?" Heather asked.

"Some time after 11," the girl said. "At least that's what I think. But I'm not sure."

"Thanks for letting us know," Jenny told the girl.

The girl smiled shyly and hurried back inside.

Jenny and Heather stared at each other, speechless.

"I told you not to trust that stud muffin," Heather burst out. "So he's been lying to us all this time."

"I don't know, Heather." Jenny was skeptical. "How do we know it's not the maid who lied to us? I mean, where was she all this time? Why did she come forward now?"

"You have a soft spot for that pool boy," Heather said, rolling her eyes. "He's worked his magic on you, hasn't he?"

"Don't be ridiculous," Jenny snapped. "I'm just trying to be objective."

"Doesn't look like that to me."

The girls bickered over whether the pool boy was guilty or not on the way back to town.

"One thing's odd," Jenny said, trying to calm down. "Kelly seems to have had an argument with multiple people. She fought with Ada. Now we learn she fought with the pool boy. She was sending all those messages to Paula. What in the world was this girl up to?"

"Don't forget she was probably having an affair too," Heather said vehemently. "I'm starting to believe Ada. Kelly wasn't kosher. She was bad for Brandon."

"It's beginning to look that way," Jenny agreed. "But did Brandon know the truth about Kelly?"

Chapter 13

The Boardwalk Café was packed. Tourists and locals sat elbow to elbow, enjoying Jenny's lunch special.

"I'm not a curry fan," Barb Norton, a short, stout woman said. "But I could eat this shrimp curry every day."

Jenny hurried from table to table, making sure everyone was well looked after.

"Allow yourself a pat on the back," Star beamed. "This shrimp curry is going to make you famous."

"More famous than she already is, you mean," Heather said.

She had posted pictures of Jenny's special shrimp curry on social media. Fans of the Boardwalk Café had called for reservations, not wanting to miss the limited time item on the menu.

"You might have to make this curry a regular feature," Betty Sue said. "And why not? We have access to the freshest shrimp."

Jenny drank in all the praise with a smile on her face. Her mind was whirling with other thoughts. Ada Newbury was still under suspicion. The police hadn't made much progress, and neither had she. Jenny wondered what the missing link was.

She hadn't had much help from Adam. She had tried to make him talk when they went out for dinner the previous night. But Adam didn't have much to say. He had admitted he was stumped. They needed a break and soon.

Jenny thought about what to do next and remembered Kelly's phone. Were the police still waiting on her phone records? She would have to talk to Adam again.

Adam Hopkins himself walked into the café a few minutes later.

"What are you doing here?" Jenny asked in surprise.

"This is your moment of triumph," he said, planting a kiss on her forehead. "I wasn't going to miss it."

Jenny's eyes widened in surprise. Adam wasn't fond of showing affection in public. A stranger looking at them wouldn't know they were an engaged couple.

"You've already tasted the curry!" Jenny exclaimed.

She had cooked at least a dozen test batches until she perfected her recipe.

"Who says I can't enjoy it again?" Adam asked with a smile.

Jenny led him out to the deck. It was a beautiful spring day in Pelican Cove. Warm afternoon sunshine bathed the tables. The air smelt salty and the breeze blowing over the ocean was cool and pleasant.

"One shrimp curry coming up," Jenny said cheerfully.

"Why don't you join me?" Adam asked, when Jenny brought out his order herself.

"Why don't you get started?" Jenny asked apologetically. "I need to be out front for a little while more."

"I'll be waiting," Adam said, picking up his fork with gusto.

Jenny accepted many compliments from her customers and promised them she would make the shrimp curry a weekly feature.

Star and Heather pushed her out on the deck after the crowd thinned.

"Go sit with that young man of yours," Star said. "And grab a bite to eat."

Adam's face lit up when Jenny sat down before him.

"I have some news," Adam said, scraping the last bit of rice and curry from his plate.

Jenny waited while he savored his mouthful. She crossed her fingers and waited for him to speak.

"Kelly's phone records came back," Adam said, dabbing his mouth with a tissue. "We already know who she was calling or talking to. I was more interested in finding out where she has been."

"What did you find?" Jenny asked, holding her breath.

"Her phone was in the same location as Paula's several times."

"We need to find out who Kelly was with both before and during the party," Jenny said. "Who did she spend a lot of time with apart from Brandon?"

Neither of them had an answer for that.

"We have hit a wall again," Adam said, getting up.

Jenny saw Adam off and started helping her aunt clear up.

"What's that frown for?" Heather asked, drying dishes with a towel. "Did you and Adam have a fight again?"

"I'm thinking of Kelly," Jenny admitted. "We need to find out more about her life in the city."

"Only one way to do that," Heather said with a grin. "Go to the source."

"Are you angling for a road trip, Heather?" Jenny asked, rolling her eyes.

"Think about it. It's been ages since we had some fun. We can do some sleuthing and hit that Mexican restaurant you like so much."

"What about Molly?"

"She's getting off early today," Heather informed Jenny. "It's the perfect day for a trip to the city."

Heather called Brandon and asked him for Kelly's address in the city. Kelly had shared an apartment with two other girls. Jenny knew the area well.

Molly was excited when they picked her up.

"This trip is long overdue," she said as she climbed into Jenny's car.

The girls cranked up the radio and sang at the top of their voices as the car sped across the miles. The sun was just setting as they entered the city. The roads were clogged with commuters heading home. A pink haze shrouded the city and restaurants filled with people meeting for drinks or dinner.

"I'm starving," Heather complained.

"Didn't you have two helpings of the curry?" Jenny teased. "Let's get to work first, ladies. You gotta sing for your supper, you know."

Getting to Kelly's apartment took them longer than expected. Jenny drove through a pair of imposing gates and parked before the leasing office. A young man was busy mowing the lawn. He pointed out Kelly's apartment building. It was a two storied structure with eight units. Kelly's turned out to be the one at the back on the second floor. Jenny pressed the doorbell and hoped someone was home.

"Who are you?" a heavily made up girl asked as she opened the door a crack.

Jenny eyed the tiny gold dress she wore, too low at the top and too high at the bottom. She was very obviously dressed to go out and party.

"Is this Kelly's apartment?" Jenny asked.

The girl nodded and narrowed her eyes suspiciously.

"We are Kelly's friends," Jenny explained. "We wanted to grab something from her closet."

The girl's eyes widened as she connected the dots. She finally opened the door and invited them in.

The apartment was clean and well furnished. The girl pointed to a closed door situated to the right of the living room.

"That's Kelly's room. She shared it with another girl."

"How many girls live here?" Heather asked.

"It's a two bedroom apartment," the girl bragged. "There's four of us on the lease. We rent out our couch sometimes."

Jenny, Heather and Molly stared at the girl.

"This place is expensive!" the girl said defensively. "Everyone knows that."

Jenny agreed with the girl and talked passionately about rising apartment rents. Heather and Molly went into Kelly's room and started rooting around in her closet. Heather took her time, giving Jenny a chance to talk with the girl.

"How long did you know Kelly?"

"We've been roomies for a couple of years," the girl replied. "But we hardly saw each other."

"Oh?"

"I work the night shift," the girl explained. "So does another girl who lives here. That's why we didn't step on each other's toes. We were hardly here at the same time."

"So you never met Brandon?" Jenny asked innocently.

"Who's Brandon?" the girl asked.

"Her fiancé."

"Kelly was a sly one, wasn't she? She ditched the tall hunk."

"Was Kelly dating someone?" Jenny asked.

The girl assumed a knowing look.

"Tall, dark haired hunk with a six pack. You could bounce a ball off those abs."

Jenny tried to visualize Brandon Newbury. The kindest person wouldn't call him tall. He certainly didn't have a flat stomach.

"Did she introduce this tall guy as her boyfriend?"

"He spent a lot of time here," the girl said suggestively. "Behind that door, if you know what I mean."

"Did Kelly break up with this guy?" Jenny asked curiously.

"I couldn't say either way," the girl said with a shrug. "Look, we weren't that close. Kelly kept to herself."

"Do you know this guy's name?" Jenny asked.

"His name was Paul, although Kelly called him something else. It was a silly nickname. I don't remember."

Heather and Molly came out of the room, holding a couple of dresses.

"Thanks for letting us in," she told the girl.

"Where is Kelly's funeral?" the girl asked. "Me and the other girls might try to make it."

Jenny noted the girl's phone number and promised to send her the details.

Heather and Molly declared they were dying of thirst.

"I want a tall frozen margarita," Molly sighed. "With plenty of salt on the rim."

"I thought you were driving," Jenny groaned.

"No way," Heather and Molly both cried out.

Jenny agreed to be the designated driver under protest.

"You can still have something frozen," Molly consoled and yowled when Jenny punched her in the shoulder.

The girls had started on their second basket of chips and salsa when Heather finally mentioned Kelly.

"Did you learn anything new?"

"I'm not sure what I learnt," Jenny said, scooping up some guacamole with a warm tortilla chip.

She told the girls about the tall, handsome guy who Kelly had been going around with.

"Brandon's good looking but even I wouldn't call him tall," Heather declared. "Does this confirm Kelly was two timing Brandon?"

"Looks that way," Jenny nodded. "But who is this mysterious tall guy?"

"Did you get his name?" Molly asked.

"The girl said he was called Paul," Jenny said.

Then she clamped a hand on her mouth and stared at the girls.

"Paul, Paul-a. It's like Betty Sue said. Paula is actually a man."

"It can't be that obvious," Heather said, shaking her head.

The waitress brought over their order. The girls had opted for different types of enchiladas. Heather cut into the melted cheese and argued with Jenny.

"So Kelly was calling and messaging this guy in front of Brandon? And he never caught on?"

"We know this Paula person was in Pelican Cove," Jenny said, her food forgotten. "Who could it be?"

"Didn't you mention Kelly was hanging around with some guy on the night of the party?" Molly asked, swallowing a big bite.

She had never met Kelly since she hadn't been invited to the party. But she had a strong memory and she remembered the girls talking about how Brandon and Kelly had both spent the evening with other people instead of each other.

"That was her cousin," Jenny dismissed.

Then she thought again. Could it be?

"Is it possible?" she asked out loud.

"You don't think Binkie was her boyfriend?" Heather asked, alarmed.

"Think of how she was clinging to him that night."

"Surely she wasn't that shameless?" Heather cried. "You're saying she paraded her boyfriend around at her own wedding party? Right in front of the man she was supposedly going to marry?"

"He was supposed to be her cousin," Jenny said slowly. "Why would anyone suspect them?"

Heather ate a big bite and put down her fork.

"He was quite handsome," she said. "And tall. Much taller than Brandon. And Binkie can't be his real name."

"So Binkie and Paul are the same," Jenny summed up. "And he was either Kelly's ex or she was still seeing him on the side."

"Do you think Brandon knew about him?" Heather asked, feeling sorry for her cousin.

"I hope not," Jenny sighed. "It gives him a very strong motive."

Chapter 14

Jenny primped before the mirror, excited about her dinner date with Adam. He was taking her to a new restaurant in a nearby town.

Star sat in a chair in Jenny's room, looking at her indulgently.

"Are you going to talk about setting a date?"

"I told you, we are not in a hurry," Jenny said, fastening a diamond stud.

"That boy needs a nudge," Star said. "He won't make a move on his own."

Star ignored her niece's protests and decided to drop a few hints when she saw Adam again.

"Whatever you do, don't talk about the murder," Star advised. "Don't spoil the mood."

"What mood is that?" Jenny asked with a laugh.

"Try to be more romantic, Jenny," Star clucked. "Stay away from hot button issues."

"There is no such thing," Jenny said patiently.

"Of course there is," Star protested. "Don't talk about Jason, for instance."

"Why not?" Jenny asked, surprised.

"The whole town knows Jason is in love with you," Star sighed. "Adam knows it too, Jenny. And he's jealous."

"That's silly," Jenny said. "I chose him, didn't I?"

"I still think Jason is the better man for you," Star said hopefully.

Star was very fond of Jason Stone. She had tried to push her niece toward the jovial, kind hearted lawyer but Jenny's heart had chosen Adam, the cranky, brooding sheriff.

"No more of that, Auntie," Jenny warned.

"You're spending too much time with Jason," Star continued. "People are beginning to talk. Adam's noticed it too."

"I'm spending time with Emily," Jenny said. Her face lit up as she thought of Jason's baby girl. "Adam knows I am in love with that sweet baby."

"What about her father?" Star asked, quirking an eyebrow.

Jenny ignored her aunt and ran a brush through her hair. The doorbell chimed below and she skipped down the steps, looking forward to her date.

Adam stood outside the door, carrying an armful of red roses. Jenny put them in a vase and took Adam's arm. The moon was rising over the ocean, lighting up the sky as they drove out of town.

"How was your day?" Jenny asked Adam. "Anything interesting happen?"

"Let's not talk about work," Adam said.

Jenny agreed readily. The next three hours passed pleasantly. Jenny enjoyed a chardonnay from a local winery and dug into her lobster ravioli with gusto. Adam declared the spaghetti and meatballs he had ordered were the best he had ever eaten. They had passion fruit gelato for dessert. Jenny sighed happily as she sipped her coffee. Adam had a rare smile on his face.

Jenny was drowsy on the drive back home. She barely paid attention when Adam started talking about Kelly.

"I think this clears Ada Newbury."

"What? What was that?" Jenny asked, snapping awake.

"Paul Briggs is a more likely suspect."

"Who's Paul Briggs?" Jenny asked, stifling a yawn.

"Haven't you heard anything I just said?" Adam asked.

Jenny admitted she might have dozed off. She blamed it on the excellent meal they had just indulged in.

"We brought Paul Briggs in for questioning today," Adam began again. "He says he is Kelly's ex-boyfriend but I believe they were still seeing each other."

"That's Binkie, right? The guy who was parading as Kelly's cousin?"

"You knew about that?" Adam asked.

"I wasn't sure until now. Why didn't Kelly break it off with Brandon if she was still involved with this guy?"

"It was all part of their plan," Adam explained. "They were going to dupe Brandon."

"How?"

"He was sketchy about the details. But they were playing a long game. I think Kelly was going to marry Brandon and then divorce him a few days later, getting a big settlement or alimony."

"Not very original," Jenny offered.

"No," Adam agreed. "Briggs readily admits he was planning to con Brandon. But he is emphatic about being innocent of Kelly's murder. First of all, he loved Kelly and he wouldn't dream of harming her. More importantly though, she was his meal ticket. Their big pay day depended on the success of this plan."

"Exactly!" Jenny said eagerly. "But what if Kelly changed her mind?"

"She got greedy?"

"Think about it. She came here and saw the Newbury estate. She realized how rich Brandon really was. Why wouldn't she want it all for herself?"

"That would leave this Briggs guy in the lurch."

"So you can't rule him out completely."

Adam banged his hand on the steering wheel and exclaimed in frustration.

Jenny patted his arm.

"Ada's motive looks really weak now, doesn't it? Can I tell her she's in the clear?"

"Go ahead," Adam said grudgingly. "I'm going to focus on these three men now. Brandon, Paul and that pool guy."

Jenny told Adam about Enrique's fake alibi.

"I'm not surprised he lied," Adam said. "I believe he is capable of doing anything for money."

Jenny wasn't ready for the evening to end. She suggested a walk on the beach and Adam readily agreed. They strolled hand in hand, enjoying the fair weather. Jenny told Adam she was watching Emily the next morning.

"You don't mind, do you?" she asked Adam, watching his face for any sign of aggravation.

"You're spending a lot of time with Jason," Adam said woodenly.

"Jason and I will always be friends," Jenny said. There was a note of censure in her voice. "Emily's just a baby, Adam."

"Better than traipsing around, getting into trouble," Adam muttered. He cleared his throat and said meekly, "I didn't know you liked babies."

"Of course I love babies. Who doesn't? And Emily is such a dear. She hardly ever cries."

Adam deftly changed the topic. They had reached an unspoken truce by the time they got back to the house. Jenny spotted Jason's car in the driveway and rushed in.

Star was pacing the living room, carrying Emily in her arms. Jason sat in an armchair, looking frazzled. Jenny noticed he was dressed in pajamas.

"What's wrong?" she burst out. "Is Emily sick?"

Star widened her eyes and shook her head, warning Jenny to be quiet.

Adam had come in after Jenny. He took in the whole scene at a glance. He tipped his head when he caught Jenny's eye and walked out. Jenny deduced he would catch up with her later.

Jenny sat down next to Jason, her eyes following her aunt across the room.

"I'm sorry," Jason whispered. "She started crying hours ago and just wouldn't stop. I didn't know what to do."

"I'm glad you came here," Jenny whispered back. "She'll be fine. Don't worry."

The baby finally fell asleep half an hour later.

"What if she starts crying again?" Star asked. "Spend the night here. We'll take good care of this little missy."

Jason stayed over at Seaview, too tired to argue with Jenny and Star.

Next morning, Jenny yawned all the way to the Boardwalk Café. She had woken up thrice to change the baby and feed her. A bank of heavy, storm filled clouds hovered over the shore, blotting out any light from the rising sun.

Jenny baked a few batches of muffins and diced vegetables and ham for western omelets. Two hours later, she finally pulled her apron off and sat down in the kitchen to take a break. Star had arrived an hour earlier.

Heather Morse walked in, looking for Jenny.

"Did you know they arrested Binkie?" she asked in a rush.

"I think they just questioned him." Jenny told her everything she had learned from Adam.

"This gets more confusing every day," Heather groaned. "Are we ever going to find out what happened to Kelly?"

Jenny didn't have an answer for that.

"At least Ada Newbury is not a suspect anymore," she said. "I want to go and give her the good news."

"Lead me on," Heather said cheerfully. "I've finished all my chores for the day."

Jenny neglected calling for an appointment. She assembled a big platter of chicken salad sandwiches for lunch and promised her aunt she would be back at the earliest.

"How can I ever thank you enough?" she asked Star.

"Stop worrying about me and get out of here," Star said.

The two girls set off in Jenny's car under an overcast sky. Heather regaled Jenny with an account of the tremendous response her shrimp curry was getting on Instagram.

"People who tried it can't stop talking about it," Heather said, smiling broadly. "They want to come back and bring their friends."

"It's a simple recipe, really," Jenny said modestly.

"I know what you should do," Heather said eagerly. "Have cooking sessions. Like those master classes they show on TV. You'll be sold out."

"I suppose it will be good advertising for the café," Jenny mused. "It's a great idea, Heather. I'm going to think about it."

They stopped at the gates when they reached the Newbury estate. The guards did their thing. Jenny handed over a bag of muffins, raising a smile out of a big, sullen guard.

Ada Newbury wasn't too pleased to see them.

"I have a golf lesson in half an hour," she said, frowning at her wrist watch. "You should really call before you come."

"This won't take long," Jenny said, refusing to be affected by Ada's grumpiness.

Ada led them into the parlor. Jenny and Heather sat down without an invitation, forcing Ada to take a seat.

"You're in the clear, Mrs. Newbury," Jenny informed Ada. "The police don't think you had anything to do with Kelly's death."

"I could have told them that," Ada quipped.

Jenny hadn't expected any compliments from Ada. But she couldn't help being a bit disappointed.

"So my work here is done?"

"Do you know who killed that girl?" Ada asked.

"That hasn't been determined yet," Jenny said.

"I want you to keep looking," Ada said. "I can pay you anything you want."

Jenny herself was curious to find out what had happened to Kelly. She had been thinking of continuing her search anyway.

"I thought you didn't like Kelly," she said. "Why do you care what happened to her?"

"I didn't like the girl for a reason," she said. "She was wrong for my Brandon. I'm sure she was just taking advantage of him."

Jenny knew that was true. She told Ada what they had found out about Kelly.

"So I'm not senile yet," Ada said triumphantly. "My instincts do mean something. My poor boy! He's well rid of this nuisance."

Although Jenny thought Ada was being harsh, she couldn't help but agree with her.

"How is Brandon doing?" Heather asked.

"Don't tell him about this other guy," Ada warned. "Who knows how he will react."

"I think Brandon knew Kelly was involved with someone," Jenny said.

"Then why didn't he boot the girl out of here?" Ada asked, shocked.

"I guess he loved her too much," Heather said.

"Love!" Ada spat. "Love means nothing without honor. Honor and respect. And whatever happened to trust? I couldn't love a person I don't trust."

Heather and Jenny listened to Ada's tirade with their heads down. They knew she was right this time. Neither of them could say anything to console her.

Zac Gordon walked into the parlor. Jenny hadn't known he was around.

"Zac's giving me a ride to the club," Ada said curtly.

Jenny and Heather thought about the fleet of luxury cars housed in the big garage outside. They couldn't help but exchange a look.

What was Zac doing there?

Zac's hair was wet and looked like it had been finger combed. He greeted the girls cheerfully.

"Nothing like a swim to recharge you," he said. "When are you coming to the club?" he asked Jenny. "I have a long waitlist but I can make an exception for you."

"Jenny doesn't belong to the country club," Ada said haughtily. "She

416

will need someone to sign her in as a guest."

"I told you I can sneak you in," Zac told Jenny with a wink. "Just say when."

Ada was getting impatient.

"Is it too late for our lesson?" Ada asked Zac apologetically. "These girls turned up without an appointment."

"The lesson begins whenever you are ready," Zac said smoothly, taking Ada's hand.

They walked out together, hand in hand. Zac bent down to whisper something in Ada's ear, making her giggle.

Jenny and Heather watched them go, feeling bewildered. Ada Newbury never giggled.

Chapter 15

The Magnolias sat on the windswept deck of the Boardwalk Café and exclaimed over Jenny's latest parfait. It was made with strawberry yogurt, macadamia nuts and toasted coconut flakes. There were generous layers of plump, juicy strawberries in between.

"I'm beginning to take a shine to these," Betty Sue said, licking her spoon.

A small storm was brewing and the waves lashed against the shore with more than usual force.

"We are getting a lot of rain this year," Star grumbled. "I have hardly ever been out painting."

"That's my fault," Jenny owned up. "You have been stuck here, helping me out."

"Tell us about your trip to Ada's," Molly said. "Did she at least thank you for your efforts?"

"She wants me to keep looking," Jenny sighed. "I'm not sure if I can help. Every time I think I'm on to something, it turns out to be a dead end."

Heather looked up from her phone.

"Remember what that maid told us about Enrique?"

"The pool boy?" Molly asked with a hint of mischief. "Are you looking for a chance to meet him again?"

"He's barely legal," Heather sighed. "Just a boy, really."

"What about Enrique?" Jenny asked, ignoring their banter.

"He lied to us about being asleep. The maid saw him walking around."

"She might have been mistaken," Jenny reasoned.

"Why don't we ask him outright?"

Jenny's face set in a frown.

"If he lied to us the first time, what makes you think he won't lie to us again?"

"Second time's the charm?" Heather asked hopefully. "Anyway, I fancy a swim. Are you coming?"

"Isn't it too cold?" Molly asked.

"Doesn't matter," Heather supplied. "It's a heated pool."

Jenny stole a glance at her aunt. She didn't want to lean on her aunt and take off again.

"A swim sounds perfect," Star said, reading Jenny's mind. "It will perk you up."

"But …" Jenny began.

"Go! Don't worry about me."

Jenny insisted on helping her aunt get ready for lunch. She stirred a big pot of vegetable barley soup as she made her mint and parsley pesto. She made pesto chicken and sweet pepper sandwiches for the lunch special. An hour later, Star literally pushed her out of the kitchen.

Heather had gone home to get her swimming things. She stood out on deck, waiting impatiently for Jenny to get going.

Jenny drove into the hills toward the Newbury estate. The girls took the path that skirted the main house and walked directly to the pool house.

"How do we get in?" Jenny asked as they stood before the access panel.

"Enrique will let us in," Heather shrugged, pushing the button that acted as a doorbell. "Or I will call Brandon and ask for the code."

"Maybe we should just go back if Enrique is not here," Jenny said uncertainly.

She wasn't keen on getting an earful from Ada Newbury.

"We are here for a swim," Heather said stoutly. "Just relax, Jenny. Don't worry about that old trout."

"Hush Heather," Jenny warned, looking over her shoulder.

She admitted to herself that she was jittery. She didn't know why.

Enrique ambled out of the pool house and grinned when he saw them. He punched in the code to unlock the gate. Heather rushed in, waving cheerfully at Enrique.

"Great day for a swim, huh?"

Five minutes later, Heather and Jenny were swimming laps in the pool. Enrique sat in a chair on the patio, looking bored.

"What's he doing, watching us like a creep?" Heather wondered.

"He doubles as a lifeguard," Jenny reminded her. "He's just doing his job."

She swam a few laps and decided she was sadly out of shape. The girls floated on a couple of rafts for some time and finally climbed out of the pool.

"We should do that more often," Heather said eagerly. "I feel so energized."

Enrique got to his feet and beckoned them inside. He pointed to an array of soda cans in the refrigerator. Jenny and Heather both chose one.

"Are you a habitual liar?" Jenny asked casually. "Or do you just have a bad memory?"

"What?" Enrique asked, looking cool as a cucumber.

Heather joined in.

"You told us you were drunk and asleep the night Kelly died. But you were seen walking on the beach that night."

"That's not all," Jenny added. "You talked to Kelly. I think you had a fight with her."

"I never met Kelly that night," Enrique stressed. "I don't know where you are getting your information. But someone's obviously leading you on."

"How do we know you are not the one doing that?"

Enrique shrugged.

"What can you do? You just have to trust me."

"We don't really know you," Heather said, crushing her soda can.

"Why should we believe you?"

Enrique muttered an oath.

"Believe me or don't believe me. I don't care. I have to go now."

He buttoned his shirt and strode out of the pool complex, acting as if he didn't have a care in the world.

"He's just putting on an act," Jenny said, her hands on her hips. "I'm sure he's lying to us."

"Have the police talked to him yet?" Heather asked. "What do they say?"

"I don't know," Jenny replied. "I can ask Adam."

Jenny didn't get a chance to talk to Adam until later that evening. She had invited him home for dinner.

"What's on your mind?" Adam asked as she served him a big steak of fish.

"Enrique," Jenny admitted. "What do you think about him?"

"Do we have to talk about this now?" Adam grumbled. "Can't we have a single meal without you trying to pump me for information?"

Jenny apologized. She knew Adam would clam up if he was angry. She didn't broach the subject again until they were sitting out on the patio. The big stone fountain gurgled merrily and Adam sat with an arm around her shoulder. The storm had moved past Pelican Cove and a bright moon shone in a clear sky.

"We questioned that pool boy," Adam volunteered. "He doesn't have a strong alibi. But he doesn't have a motive either. He has nothing to gain by harming Kelly."

"I think he's hiding something," Jenny insisted.

They talked about their kids after that. Adam wanted to know if the kids were coming to Pelican Cove for the spring festival. Jenny didn't know but hoped the kids would turn up for the special weekend. She was looking forward to spending more time with her son.

Jenny got to work at the café the next morning with a firm resolve to stay put. Heather had offered to come and help. Jenny convinced her aunt to take the day off.

It was a Friday and the weekend tourists were beginning to flock to town. A group of suburban moms about Jenny's age occupied a big table. They gushed over Jenny's parfaits and asked for the recipe. Jenny was making shrimp po'boys for lunch.

Adam Hopkins rushed into the café around noon, looking for Jenny. His face was brimming with impatience as he waited out on the deck.

"What is it?" Jenny asked, hurrying out to talk to him.

"You were right about the boy," Adam gushed. "I don't know how you do it, Jenny."

"Did he confess?" Jenny asked with bated breath.

"No such thing," Adam said, shaking his head. "I couldn't stop thinking about him so I ordered my men to search the pool house."

"I thought you already did that."

"Not very well, apparently," Adam cursed. "My men found a key in a gym bag."

"A key?" Jenny was puzzled.

"Let me finish," Adam said. "Luckily, I was familiar with the key. It opens a locker in the local bank. You will never guess what we found."

Jenny waited for Adam to go on.

"A bunch of jewelry," Adam said. "A really expensive string of pearls, a diamond necklace and some emerald earrings."

"Where did they come from?" Jenny asked.

"That's what I would like to know," Adam spat. "The boy maintains they belong to him."

"Can I see these jewels?" Jenny asked.

Adam pulled out his phone and showed her some pictures. Jenny had a good eye for jewelry.

"If these are real, they cost a pretty bundle."

"We got a jeweler to check them out," Adam told her. "These are the real deal."

"Do you think these jewels belong to Kelly?" Jenny asked Adam.

"We thought of that," Adam said. "It seems Kelly was wearing some fine jewels at the party. And she was still wearing them when she drowned."

"That means she wasn't killed for money," Jenny said.

Adam was looking frustrated. Jenny convinced him to stay back and have lunch.

"Don't go after that boy, Jenny," Adam warned her when he left. "Let the police do their job."

"See you later tonight," Jenny said, heading back to the kitchen.

Heather's mouth dropped open when Jenny told her about the jewels in Enrique's locker.

"Who do you think they belong to?"

"Kelly, Ada and Megan are the only women involved here," Jenny said thoughtfully. "Surely Ada wouldn't give away her jewels to the pool boy?"

"Kelly's our best bet," Heather said. "But how do we find out if these jewels belonged to her?"

"We can ask Brandon," Jenny suggested. "Or what about that roommate of hers? That girl we met in the city?"

"Excellent idea," Heather approved. "Did you get her phone number?"

"I don't think Adam will send me those jewelry photos," Jenny reasoned. "What am I going to say to this girl?"

"Just talk to her," Heather said. "She might recognize the jewels from their description."

As it turned out, the girl was very familiar with Kelly's jewels.

"I borrowed those emeralds once," she told Jenny. "Kelly was pretty cool about letting us girls borrow her stuff. She said it was meant to be shown off."

Jenny asked her about the pearls and the diamonds. The girl had borrowed them too.

"Any idea where Kelly keeps them?"

"She took all her bling with her," the friend confirmed. "Said she couldn't get married without her favorite pieces."

Jenny hung up the phone and looked at Heather.

"How did Enrique get his hands on Kelly's jewels?" she wondered.

"Let's go ask him," Heather said, jumping down from the kitchen table.

"Adam kind of warned me not to go and see Enrique," Jenny said meekly.

"What if Enrique comes to see you?" Heather asked, a broad smile lighting up her face.

"Wishful thinking?" Jenny asked.

Heather turned her around and pointed at a spot in the café's dining room. Enrique sat at a table near the window, wringing his hands.

"Are you here for lunch?" Jenny asked a few moments later.

Enrique looked resigned.

"Yes, please. I'll eat whatever you have on hand."

Jenny brought out a sandwich bursting with plump, deep fried shrimp. She placed it on the table and sat down before Enrique. She let him eat a few bites.

"Why did Kelly give you her jewelry?"

Enrique's eyes popped open. He swallowed a mouthful in haste and looked about to bolt.

"Don't even think about lying again," Jenny warned. "I know about the stuff they found in your locker. I am sure you got it from Kelly."

"Can you keep this between us?" Enrique urged.

"Depends on what you are going to tell me," Jenny said sternly. "Out with it."

Enrique leaned forward and spoke softly.

"I was blackmailing Kelly. I saw her kissing that cousin of hers, what's his name? Bunky or something like that."

"Binkie," Jenny corrected automatically.

"Yeah, him," Enrique nodded. "I threatened to tell Brandon."

"What else did you do?" Jenny asked. "Did you push her into the pool?"

Enrique looked alarmed.

"I had nothing to do with that. You have to believe me."

"You lied to us before," Jenny pointed out.

"Kelly had agreed to pay me a lot more," Enrique said. "The jewels were just a down payment. Why would I kill my golden goose?"

Chapter 16

The Magnolias gathered for their mid-morning coffee break. Betty Sue and Heather had called ahead saying they would be late because Betty Sue needed to go to the bank. Jenny was pouring the coffee when they came in, Betty Sue looking flustered and red in the face.

"I know what I saw," Betty Sue Morse said indignantly.

She was so distressed she had set her knitting aside. Betty Sue rarely did that.

"Calm down, Grandma," Heather said, stroking her back. "We need to watch your blood pressure."

"Leave me alone, girl!" Betty Sue cried, flinging off Heather's hand. "How could she!"

"Take a deep breath, Betty Sue," Star said, "and start at the beginning."

"Ada Newbury was kissing a man," Betty Sue said again.

"Go Julius!" Star chortled. "So their romance is still going strong."

Julius Newbury was Ada's husband.

"She wasn't kissing Julius," Betty Sue said, her chest heaving. "I never saw the man before."

Jenny laughed. Molly and Star joined her.

"Did you see her too?" Jenny asked Heather.

"I wasn't paying attention," Heather said.

"You must be mistaken, Betty Sue," Jenny said. "Ada's well into her seventies. I don't see her having an affair at this age."

Star added her opinion.

"Forget her age. I can't imagine Ada Newbury developing an affection for anyone."

"It was Ada alright," Betty Sue persisted. "She was driving that fancy car of hers. The man was sitting next to her. They were parked in that little alley behind the bank."

"Kissing a man in broad daylight, that too in the heart of the town?" Star frowned. "That doesn't sound like Ada."

"Can you describe the man, Grandma?" Heather asked.

Betty Sue thought for a few seconds and shook her head.

"I was too shocked to notice."

"The only strange man I have seen around Ada is that golf coach of hers," Heather said. "You don't think she's carrying on with him?"

"Zac Gordon?" Jenny asked incredulously. "He's half her age."

"It's not impossible," Heather said.

Heather had recently been in love with a much older man. She didn't believe age was a barrier for true love.

"It's her private business, I guess," Jenny said.

"But she's cheating on her husband," Betty Sue protested.

"Let them handle it, Betty Sue," Star said diplomatically. "Why should we interfere?"

None of the women really believed that Ada Newbury could be involved with a mere golf pro.

Jason Stone walked down the boardwalk carrying the baby in a carrier. The ladies hailed him and Jenny invited him for a cup of coffee. Heather, Jenny and Molly took turns holding the baby, smiling and blowing kisses at her as she gurgled and smiled.

"When is Emily spending the day with us?" Jenny asked Jason.

"You're always busy at the café," Jason pointed out. "When do you have the time to take care of my girl?"

"How about Sunday?" Jenny asked. "Spend the day with us. We can have a barbecue in the evening."

She invited the Magnolias for the barbecue. Jason told them how he had set up a crib in his office for Emily.

"I still need to go to the city sometimes though," he said gloomily. "I hate leaving Emily."

Jenny marveled at how easily Jason had stepped into the role of a father. She couldn't imagine Adam doing that. But she had to concede he had raised two daughters on his own after his wife passed away. Then she chided herself for comparing the two men. It wasn't fair to either of them.

The day passed in a blur. Jenny stayed busy making lunch and preparing for the next day. She walked to the seafood market on her way home.

Chris Williams greeted her with a big smile. He and Molly were seeing each other. Chris moonlighted as a part-time realtor and was a kind hearted young man.

"How are you doing, Jenny?" he asked, wrapping up her usual order of whitefish fillets and shrimp.

Jenny chatted with him for a while before heading back.

Jenny and her aunt had a quiet dinner at home. Jenny had pan grilled the fish and made a salad. She put on her sneakers after some time and went for a walk on the beach. A yellow Labrador ran up to her, his tail wagging and put his paws on her chest.

"Tank!" Jenny exclaimed happily, fondling the dog.

She pulled a ball out of her pocket and threw it in the distance.

Adam walked up to her, leaning on his cane. He didn't look very happy.

"You look tired," Jenny murmured. "Have you had dinner? I saved a plate for you."

"I'm not hungry," Adam snapped.

They walked away from the house, Adam unwilling to say a word. Jenny let him brood for a while.

"Do you ever listen to me?" he burst out suddenly. "What am I going to do with you, Jenny?"

"What have I done now?" Jenny asked, her hands on her hips.

"I told you to stay away from that pool boy."

"He came to the café. I didn't go looking for him."

"What did you talk about?" Adam demanded. "Tell me everything right now."

Jenny told Adam how Enrique had been blackmailing Kelly.

"And I bet he didn't stop there."

"I don't think he is involved in Kelly's murder," Jenny said. "He had a lot to gain by keeping her alive."

Adam held Jenny's arms and shook her.

"You need to be more careful, Jenny," he cried. "There's a killer on the loose."

"Why are you so upset, Adam?" Jenny asked. "Has something else happened?"

Adam looked grim when he gave Jenny the news.

"Paul Briggs is dead."

"Binkie's dead?" Jenny echoed.

"They found him in his room at the country club," Adam reported. "Don't know why he was still hanging around town."

"What happened to him?" Jenny asked.

"Don't know for sure. My guess is he was poisoned."

"Who would do that?"

"Isn't that the big question?" Adam growled. "Until we catch the culprit, everyone is under suspicion."

"What does anyone gain by killing Binkie?"

Adam shrugged. They turned around and walked back to Seaview. Jenny barely slept a wink before it was time to get up and go to the café.

Brandon Newbury turned up at the Boardwalk Café for breakfast. Jenny was surprised when she saw him standing in line.

"Chocolate chip muffin?" she asked. "My treat."

"Can I talk to you?" Brandon pleaded.

Jenny led him out to the deck. A brisk wind whipped her hair against her face. She shivered a bit as she waited for Brandon to speak up.

"A cold front's coming in," Brandon began.

"Are you here to talk about the weather?" Jenny asked impatiently.

She had a mountain of work waiting for her in the kitchen.

"Did you hear about Binkie?" he asked.

Jenny nodded affirmatively.

"The police think I did it."

Jenny sat down at a table and motioned Brandon to do the same.

"What did you have against him?"

"He wasn't Kelly's cousin," Brandon explained. "He was her lover. The police think I wanted revenge."

"Did you?" Jenny asked simply.

Brandon ran a hand through his hair. His blue eyes looked troubled as he stared beseechingly at Jenny.

"I never had a clue," he said. "At least not at first. Binkie was so friendly. He was a guy's guy, you know. He was the only family Kelly had, or so I thought. Then I saw them together. I got the shock of my life."

"You had no idea?"

"I knew Kelly was up to something," Brandon admitted. "I thought maybe she was just having a last fling. But I never guessed she was carrying on with Binkie."

"Do you know what their plan was?" Jenny asked.

"My grandma told me," Brandon said. "I still can't believe it."

"Anyone in your position would feel cheated. You might have decided to get revenge."

"I couldn't stand the sight of him," Brandon admitted. "But I didn't do anything to hurt him. You have to believe me."

"Can you tell me anything about him?" Jenny asked. "What did he do in the city?"

"Binkie was between jobs," Brandon told Jenny. "As far as I know he didn't seem concerned about it."

Jenny didn't want to make any tall promises.

"Nothing about this business makes any sense," she told Brandon. "I'm not sure if I'll be able to help you."

"You are close to the sheriff, aren't you?" Brandon said. "At least put in a good word for me."

Jenny felt her temper flare.

"I don't interfere in Adam's work."

Brandon knew when to shut up. He implored Jenny to help him in any way she could. Jenny was relieved when he left.

The Magnolias came in for their daily ritual. None of them said anything much. The news of Binkie's death had spread through town. People were beginning to look worried. They huddled together and talked in soft voices, blaming the police for inaction.

Jenny was too distracted to cook anything elaborate for lunch. She made her strawberry chicken salad and added in some freshly picked basil for flavor. She packed a lunch basket and headed to the police station, hoping to get the latest scoop.

Adam greeted her with a scowl.

"Thanks for getting lunch," he said. "I'm sorry I won't be able to join you."

"I can go back to the café and eat on my own," Jenny said meekly. "Actually, I might look in on the baby. I need something to cheer me up."

Adam gave in, just as Jenny had expected.

"You can eat here," he said, rolling his eyes. "Just make sure you don't talk shop."

"We don't have to talk at all," Jenny said.

Adam ate half his sandwich in a couple of bites. Jenny took one dainty bite and chewed slowly. The phone on Adam's desk trilled, shattering the silence.

Adam picked up the receiver and listened. His face turned darker with every passing second. He slammed the phone down after a while and muttered something under his breath.

"Bad news?" Jenny asked sympathetically.

Adam stuffed the remaining sandwich in his mouth, refusing to answer Jenny. She could sense he was bursting to tell her something. He guzzled the lemonade Jenny had brought along and looked at her.

"A witness has come forward. Brandon Newbury was seen at the country club two nights ago."

"So he spent time at his club," Jenny shrugged. "No big deal."

"He was seen skulking around Binkie's room," Adam thundered.

"How do you know this witness is telling the truth?" Jenny demanded.

"It's my job to determine that," Adam said. "Lunch is over."

Jenny took the hint and picked up her basket. She walked back to the café, trying to guess who might have called the police against Brandon. Did someone in town have a grudge against him?

Ada Newbury was waiting for Jenny at the Boardwalk Café.

"Where have you been?" she complained. "I have been waiting for an hour."

"How can I help you, Mrs. Newbury?" Jenny asked, ignoring the old woman's outburst.

"My Brandon's in trouble," Ada sobbed. "That poor boy! Please say you will help him. I will pay you anything you want."

"It's not that easy," Jenny said, trying to be honest. "Nothing about this affair has made any sense."

"You know my Brandon works for a senator?" Ada asked. "He has big aspirations. Who was this Binkie? A good-for-nothing loafer. Why would my Brandon risk his life's work over someone like that?"

A tear rolled down Ada's rheumy eyes. Jenny felt sorry for her. She decided not to mention the witness.

"Calm down, Mrs. Newbury," she consoled. "If Brandon's innocent, he has nothing to worry about."

Jenny wasn't sure he was. Brandon had motive and opportunity and it was going to be difficult to prove he was completely free of blame.

Chapter 17

Jenny smoothed her hands over her golf dress, gazing at herself in the mirror. She hoped it wasn't hopelessly out of fashion. She didn't want to look out of place.

Jenny needed an excuse to go scout around the country club. She had decided to take advantage of Zac Gordon's offer. She had called him the previous day and set up a lesson with him.

"Are you sure they will let me in?" she had joked.

Zac had boasted about the clout he wielded at the club.

"The golf course is my domain. Don't worry about a thing."

Two hours later, Jenny stood on the green, ready to tee off. Zac Gordon had painstakingly given her some directions, and attempted to correct her posture.

Jenny found out her game wasn't too rusty after all. She chatted with Zac as they traversed the famous course.

"This place is beautiful," Jenny breathed. "Do you like working here?"

"It's more than just a job," Zac told her. "I'm not complaining. I get to do what I love most. And the tips aren't bad either."

Jenny spotted a familiar figure in the distance. She waved at the tall black haired youngster and called him over.

"What are you doing here?"

Enrique looked surprised to see her.

"I'm here to pick up my girlfriend. Her shift ends in a few minutes."

"Do you come here often?" Jenny asked.

Enrique shrugged.

"Pretty much, I guess."

Jenny turned to smile at Zac.

"You know Enrique, don't you?"

A look of annoyance flashed across Zac's face.

"Sure," he said. "The pool boy."

"Yes," Enrique grinned. "I'm the pool boy."

He said goodbye to Jenny and started walking away.

"You don't like him much, do you?" Jenny asked Zac.

"Is it that obvious?" Zac asked. "I told Ada, I mean Mrs. Newbury, she should fire him. He's a crook if I ever saw one."

"He's just a kid," Jenny said mildly. "He's a bit cocky, I guess."

"He's hanging around here all the time," Zac spat. "I saw him 2-3 nights ago, prowling around."

Jenny's mind connected the dots. That was the night Binkie had been killed. What had Enrique been doing at the country club?"

"Are you sure it was Enrique you saw?" Jenny asked Zac.

"I'm pretty sure," Zac nodded. "I had just finished a lesson and was going to the café to grab a drink. He came over to say Hi. Wanted to know if I could give him a free lesson sometime."

Jenny thought about Zac's words on her way back home. What could Enrique possibly have against Binkie? Binkie, on the other hand, could have had a grudge against Enrique for blackmailing Kelly. None of it made sense.

Jenny took a long hot shower, trying to relax. She decided to have a quiet evening at home, reading a book or watching some cooking show on TV. She had barely put her feet up when her phone rang. Heather and Molly were at the local pub for drinks. They wanted Jenny to join them.

Jenny pulled on a dressy top over her jeans and drove to the Rusty Anchor, Pelican Cove's favorite watering hole. Molly and Heather sat at a table, facing Chris and Jason.

"Where's the baby?" Jenny asked Jason as she greeted everyone.

"Betty Sue's watching her."

"We insisted Jason join us for a pint," Molly explained. "He hasn't had an evening to himself since the baby got here."

"I can spare thirty minutes," Jason said, glancing at his watch. "Then I'm gone."

"What's Adam doing tonight?" Chris asked Jenny.

"Working," Jenny said with a shrug.

"No he's not," Heather said, looking up.

Adam Hopkins had just entered the pub. He spotted Jenny and limped toward her, leaning on his cane.

"When are you two setting a wedding date?" Heather asked Adam.

"What is this, an ambush?" Adam asked grumpily.

He looked at Jenny.

"Did you put her up to this?"

"No, she didn't," Heather butted in. "I'm asking because I am getting too old to be a bridesmaid."

"No Heather, you're getting too old to be a bride," Adam smirked. "Why don't you take pity on your poor grandmother and find someone who will tolerate you for the rest of your life?"

Heather looked like she had been punched in the face. Jenny gave Adam a quelling look and went around the table to console her.

"What's the matter with you, Adam?" she cried.

"Sorry, long day," Adam apologized. "Don't mind me, Heather."

He stood up to leave.

"I should go."

He looked at Jenny.

"I need to take Tank out. We'll come to Seaview in a bit."

Jenny stopped at Mama Rosa's on her way home. She picked up two large pizzas and salads for dinner. She drove home, telling herself to be patient with Adam.

Star was chatting with Adam when Jenny got home. Tank gave her his usual exuberant welcome. They devoured the food Jenny had brought and sat in the living room, eating bowls of chocolate ice cream.

Adam offered to call Heather and apologize again.

"It's your leg, isn't it?" Jenny asked. "Have you been doing those exercises the therapist recommended?"

"It's not just my leg," Adam sighed. "It's this case. It gets more complicated every day."

Jenny knew a direct question would not get her any answers. She stayed quiet.

"I did a background check on Paul Briggs," Adam said. "He just received a big sum of money in his bank account."

Jenny sat up, looking surprised.

"There have been multiple deposits into his account, all from different places in the area," Adam continued. "They add up to a pretty large amount."

"What does it mean?" Jenny asked.

"Looks like someone was paying him off," Adam said. "But I don't understand why."

"The only people Binkie knew in town were Kelly and Brandon," Jenny said.

"Brandon Newbury is implicated again," Adam said, rubbing his eyes.

"How so?" Jenny asked.

"Binkie must have seen something. Say he named a price for his silence. Brandon paid him once but Binkie got greedy and asked for more. Brandon decided to silence him forever."

"That's just a theory," Jenny protested.

"It's a strong motive," Adam said seriously.

"Can you prove Brandon deposited the money in Binkie's account?"

"Not yet," Adam said, clenching his jaw. "The money was deposited in cash. It will take us some time to locate the person who made those payments."

"I'm sure you will get to the bottom of this soon," Jenny soothed.

They went for a walk on the beach after that. Adam and Tank left around ten, Adam feeling considerably better after stretching his legs.

Jenny spent a restless night, tossing and turning in bed. She had to prove Brandon's innocence, but she needed to believe in him herself before she did that.

A bright and sunny day dawned in Pelican Cove, putting a smile on Jenny's face. She hoped they had seen the last of the dark clouds. The citizens of Pelican Cove turned out to enjoy the fair weather. The Boardwalk Café was packed for breakfast, with some people waiting in line outside to get a table. Jenny stayed busy baking batches of muffins and making her special puttanesca omelets.

Once the breakfast rush receded, Jenny started a pot of tomato soup and cooked teriyaki chicken for lunch. The Magnolias arrived as usual, eager to talk about Jenny's day on the golf course.

"Can you handle the lunch crowd again?" Jenny asked her aunt. "Please?"

"Don't worry about the café," Star assured her. "But promise me you will be careful."

"I will," Jenny promised. "There's nothing to worry about. Heather's going with me."

"Where are we going?" Heather asked as the car sped over the bridge connecting Pelican Cove to the mainland.

Jenny brought her up to speed. Heather's eyes widened as she heard about the money.

"What's the plan?" she asked Jenny.

"I have thought of something," Jenny said. "Not sure if it's going to work, though."

Jenny had shortlisted a few banks in neighboring towns. They entered the first one on her list and looked around. Jenny zeroed in on one young girl who seemed to be chatting freely with all the customers.

"Excuse me," Jenny said meekly, approaching her.

"How can I help you?" the girl asked.

Jenny hunched her shoulders and widened her eyes.

"I'm not sure you can. I'm getting married in a few weeks, see?"

The girl squealed and congratulated Jenny.

"We didn't register anywhere because we decided not to accept gifts. But you know how some people just have to send you something. Some of my friends and relatives put money in my account."

"How sweet!" the girl said sincerely.

"Yes," Jenny agreed. "But I have a problem. They deposited cash so I have no way of knowing who did it. I can't even write a thank you note."

The girl sympathized with Jenny.

"Can't you just guess?" she asked. "Must be someone who is close to you."

"I thought the same!" Jenny exclaimed. "I have some photos of my wedding shower. Can you take a look at them please?"

The girl hesitated for a second and then nodded. Jenny pulled out her phone and scrolled through photos of Brandon and Kelly's wedding shower. She had been clicking pictures of her food but she had managed to capture a lot of the guests in the process.

The girl looked at the pictures twice and shook her head.

"I'm sorry, but none of these people look familiar."

Jenny thanked her and stepped out of the bank with Heather.

"Now what?" Heather asked.

"Now we repeat the same thing at other banks in the area."

They hit pay dirt at the third bank they visited. One of the tellers, another young, bubbly woman pointed to a picture of Ada Newbury.

"She was here a few days ago. I remember because very few people make cash deposits."

Jenny thanked her and hurried out, her mind already churning with possibilities.

"What has Ada been up to?" Heather voiced as they got into the car. "Are you going to tell the police?"

"Not yet," Jenny answered. "I want to talk to Ada first."

"Won't Adam be mad at you for withholding information?"

"We don't know if a crime was committed."

"Why would Ada pay Binkie?" Heather asked. "I'm sure she barely tolerated him."

"You remember that argument Ada had with Kelly on the night of the party? She was offering to pay Kelly to leave Brandon."

"She didn't need to do that once Kelly was gone," Heather said patiently. "I think you are getting your timelines mixed up."

"You're right, Heather," Jenny said, slapping herself on the forehead. "What am I thinking?"

"Your brain needs food," Heather laughed. "I, for one, am starving. Let's look for some place to have lunch."

Jenny spotted an old, faded sign for a diner at the corner of a country lane. She yanked her wheel and turned on to the road, hoping the diner was open and still serving food. It turned out to be a gem of a find.

"What will you have?" an elderly woman with gray hair arranged in a neat bun asked them, pointing toward a chalkboard on the wall.

Jenny thought of Petunia, the previous owner of the Boardwalk Café. Jenny missed her every day.

Jenny chose the whitefish sandwich and Heather chose a grilled trout salad. Their meal came with crispy crinkle cut fries seasoned with Old Bay.

Jenny closed her eyes as she savored the fish, delicately flavored with dried herbs.

Heather dug her fork in her salad and took a big bite. Her eyes narrowed as she chewed the soft, flaky fish. She voiced the question that had been rolling around in Jenny's mind for the past hour.

"Do you think Ada's been playing you all along?"

Chapter 18

Jenny dropped Heather off at the Bayview Inn. She headed into the hills toward the Newbury estate. Heather's question had riled her up. Jenny felt sure Ada Newbury had been lying to her. The more she thought about it, the angrier she got. Her face was flushed when she pulled up outside the massive iron gates. The security guard did his thing and let her through. Ten minutes later, she was jabbing her finger against the doorbell, trying to calm down.

A maid led her to the parlor. Ada was sitting on a sofa next to Zac Gordon, sipping tea and laughing at something he said. Her face fell when she saw Jenny.

"How many times have I told you to call before coming?" she snarled.

"We need to talk, Mrs. Newbury," Jenny said firmly.

"I'm busy at the moment," Ada said. "Why don't you wait out on the patio?"

She rang a small silver bell to summon the maid.

"This is important," Jenny stressed.

"I'm sure it can wait," Ada insisted.

"Ladies, ladies ..." Zac Gordon interrupted. "Take it easy."

He urged Jenny to take a seat.

"How about some tea?" he asked.

Jenny couldn't wait to confront Ada but she didn't want to do it in Zac Gordon's presence.

"Actually, Zac, could you excuse us? I need a moment alone with Mrs. Newbury."

"No problem," Zac said, getting up.

The smile on his face was intact.

"I'll be outside. A stroll through the garden sounds perfect."

He patted Ada on the shoulder and left the room.

Jenny took a chair opposite Ada and settled down.

"What do you want?" Ada asked Jenny.

"Why did you put money in Binkie's account? Were you paying him off for something?"

"Who is this Binkie?" Ada wrinkled her nose in disgust.

"You know Binkie. Kelly's cousin. The guy they found dead at the country club."

"You mean her lover?" Ada snorted. "I was right. Kelly was cheating on my Brandon. And she had the gall to bring that man to my party."

"All that is water under the bridge," Jenny dismissed. "I want to know if you made any payments into Binkie's account."

"Of course I did no such thing," Ada replied.

"You were seen at some banks in nearby towns. You made certain cash deposits. Do you still deny that?"

Ada had turned white. She didn't say anything for a few minutes. Jenny let her stew.

"The police will be on to you soon, Mrs. Newbury."

"I did make a deposit," Ada said hoarsely. "But it had nothing to do with Kelly's lover."

"Why should I believe you?" Jenny asked. "You have been keeping secrets from me since the beginning. You didn't tell me about your argument with Kelly. And now this!"

"I'm not lying about this," Ada pleaded.

"Couldn't you just write a check?" Jenny asked. "Why sneak off to a town fifty miles away and pay cash? Are you in some kind of trouble?"

"I can't talk about it. You'll just have to trust me on this."

"That's a tall order, Mrs. Newbury," Jenny sighed. "Someone's been depositing money into Binkie's account. The police are trying to find this person. It won't be long before they identify you."

"Do you think they will arrest me?"

Jenny didn't have an answer for that.

"They will suspect you again at the very least."

"I can tell you when I made the deposits," Ada said hesitantly. "And the amount I paid. But I can't tell you who I gave the money to."

"That might help," Jenny said.

She had a strong suspicion about who the recipient of Ada's largesse was. She was ready to bet he was strolling in the garden outside.

Zac Gordon peeped in at a window just then.

"Are you two done?" he asked. "The wind's a bit harsh out here."

"Come on in," Ada said.

Zac ambled in and sat on the sofa again. Jenny noticed he wasn't dressed for golf. The jeans and shirt he wore indicated he was off duty.

"I enjoyed my golf lesson the other day," Jenny said to Zac. "You are a really good coach."

"You are a good player," Zac offered. "Spend an hour with me every day and you will be ready to go pro."

"I don't have time for that," Jenny smiled. "I have a café to run."

"And some sleuthing to do on the side, huh?" Zac asked.

His eyes hardened for a second and then he was his genial self again.

"Ada tells me you like to snoop around."

"I just talk to people," Jenny said modestly.

"It's time for our golf lesson," Ada said to Zac.

She gave Jenny a pointed look.

"Didn't you have a stiff neck?" Zac asked Ada.

"I'm leaving anyway," Jenny said, getting up.

Jenny stepped out into the hallway outside the parlor and looked around. She urgently needed to use a restroom. A couple of passages forked off in different directions making Jenny hesitate. She had used a powder room at the Newbury mansion before but Heather had guided her to it.

Jenny walked down a bunch of closed doors, trying to remember the right one. Every door looked the same. She paused in front of one tentatively and sucked in a breath. She knocked twice just in case and pushed the door in, walking in on a couple locked in a tight embrace.

"I'm sorry," Jenny began.

Then her eyes widened in shock.

"Brandon! I'm sorry, I didn't realize this was your room."

"It's not," Brandon said cheerfully. "It's a guest room. It's unoccupied at present. Were you looking to use the powder room?"

Jenny nodded mutely.

The girl next to Brandon had straightened up a bit.

"How are you?" she greeted Jenny.

"I'm good, Megan. How are you?" Jenny said mechanically.

She rushed to the door Brandon pointed at. Brandon was alone in the room when she came out five minutes later.

"Megan had to leave," he said.

"So …" Jenny said. "You and Megan, huh?"

"We never really stopped loving each other," Brandon clarified.

"But I thought she was the one who dumped you."

"It was all a big misunderstanding," Brandon said with a frown. "Megan thought I was interested in someone else. She didn't want to be a burden. So she took the initiative and let me go."

"But you were still in love with her," Jenny prompted.

"That's right," Brandon said proudly. "Megan and I have been friends for years. She is my first love."

"Are you two engaged?"

"We are going to wait for a few weeks before we announce our engagement," Brandon said soberly. "I might just tell my grandma. She adores Megan."

"Congratulations," Jenny said warmly. "I hope you will be happy together." She wavered a bit before asking her next question. "Tell me one thing. Were you really going to marry Kelly?"

"Frankly, I don't know. I feel like such a fool now. She had me wound around her finger. I never realized she was just using me."

Jenny wondered when Brandon had realized that. Had he confronted Kelly on the night of the party?

The sky had darkened by the time Jenny said goodbye to Brandon and stepped out. The orange ball of the sun had almost set, painting the sky around it in shades of pink and tangerine.

Jenny yawned deeply and started her car. Multiple theories were churning in her mind but she didn't have the energy to process any of them. All she wanted to do was go home and soak in a hot bath. Jenny's eyes glazed over as she thought of lighting a bunch of scented candles and using the lavender bath salts her aunt had got for her.

Suddenly, a pair of bright headlights appeared in her rearview mirror, almost blinding her. The portion of road Jenny was on was on the outskirts of town. There was hardly any traffic on the road. Jenny changed the lane and veered to the right, allowing the car behind her to pass. The headlights stayed behind her.

Jenny realized they were too close. Her car was almost on the shoulder now. She guessed the vehicle behind her was some kind of big truck. Jenny put on her turn signal and pulled her car completely on the shoulder. Surely the other car would pass her once she came to a stop?

Jenny felt her car skid as the car behind her rammed into her. Jenny spun her wheel round and round, trying to remember what she was supposed to do in this kind of situation. Her car tipped over and plunged into a ditch, with one wheel spinning in the air.

The car behind her flashed its lights and sped off.

Jenny wriggled in her seat, trying to reach her bag. Then she remembered her cell phone was in the cup holder right next to her. Finally, she dialed the emergency number with trembling fingers and waited for help.

Adam arrived on the scene within minutes, along with the ambulance. He stood by impatiently while Jenny was pulled out of the car. The paramedics treated her for a few bruises and recommended she go to the hospital to get checked out.

Three hours later, Jenny was tucked in her bed with a bowl of hot chicken soup. Her aunt sat next to her and Adam paced the room, his face as black as thunder.

"You could have been hurt, really hurt," he said hoarsely.

Jenny's hand shook as she spooned some soup into her mouth. She knew Adam was right. So she let him rave at her.

"There's a lot of maniacs out there," Star said. "Jenny was in the wrong place at the wrong time."

"I don't agree," Adam said heavily.

Jenny had been briefly questioned by the police. They had wanted to get a description of the car or driver. Jenny hadn't had a glimpse of either. All she could say was it was a big truck, much bigger than her small sedan.

Jenny had told them how the car had followed her for a long time and rammed into her a couple of times. She agreed it had seemed like a deliberate move and not an accident.

"How do you always get into these scrapes?" Adam asked hoarsely. "Why can't you stay out of trouble for once?"

"Take it easy, son." Star's voice had a warning note in it.

"Why would someone want to hurt me?" Jenny asked.

"You have made someone feel threatened," Adam said. "You must be getting close."

"If I am, I don't know it."

"What have you been doing in the past two days?" Adam wanted to know.

Jenny gave him a brief account of where she had been.

"So Brandon Newbury knew you were going to be on that road," Adam said. "I don't trust that guy one bit."

"Brandon, really?" Jenny asked. "Well, if you want to put it that way, everyone at the Newbury estate knew I was going to drive back to town. Ada knew, so did her entire staff."

"You need to take it easy for a while," Adam said. "Promise me you won't leave the house."

"That's impossible," Jenny exploded. "What about the café"?"

"We can take care of the café," Star said. "Don't worry about it."

"I'm not going to be cooped up in here just because some coward tried to run me off the road."

"My men are working on this now," Adam said, pausing next to Jenny's bed. "At least give them a couple of days."

"The doctor advised you to rest," Star reminded her. "Why don't you take this opportunity and relax a bit?"

"One day!" Jenny said, holding up a finger. "I will stay home for one day. Then I am going back to the café."

"And you will stop trying to solve this case?" Adam asked hopefully.

Jenny stirred her soup and smiled wanly at Adam. She didn't make promises she couldn't keep.

Chapter 19

Star knocked on Jenny's door the next morning and entered bearing a loaded tray.

Jenny reclined against a mound of pillows, reading a book.

"Good Morning," Star greeted her. "I hope you are hungry."

Jenny stared at the stack of blueberry pancakes, bacon, eggs and toast. A dewy pink rose from the garden rested on the tray.

"Breakfast in bed?" Jenny exclaimed, staring at the food in fascination. "What am I, an invalid?"

"I'm allowed to spoil my niece a bit," Star pouted.

She sat down at the edge of the bed and gave Jenny a worried look.

"I have loved having you here with me," she said.

"I'm not going anywhere," Jenny soothed. "Now let's eat this delicious breakfast you have cooked for me."

Jenny forced her aunt to eat along with her. There was plenty of food for the both of them.

"I need to get going," Star said. "Heather must be waiting for me."

Heather had volunteered to open the Boardwalk Café that morning and get breakfast started.

"Thank her for me, will you?" Jenny said. "Tell her I owe her one."

"You can tell her yourself," Star said with a smile. "We look out for each other in this town."

There was another knock on the door and Jason Stone entered. The baby was strapped to his body in a sling like carrier.

Jenny's face lit up when she saw Jason.

"This is a surprise!" she cried, holding out her arms toward Emily. "Give me that darling."

Jason gently pulled Emily out and handed her over to Jenny. Jenny kissed the baby's forehead and cuddled her. The baby gurgled and pulled a lock of Jenny's hair.

"We heard about your little mishap," Jason said. "What's the damage?"

"I'm perfectly alright," Jenny said. "My car, on the other hand, needs some care."

"Carry on, you two," Star said.

Jenny had completely forgotten her aunt.

"Will you keep an eye on her?" Star asked Jason. "I have to go to the café."

"Emily and I will stand guard," Jason said with a smile. "Don't worry about a thing, Star."

"Are you guys in collusion?" Jenny asked after Star had stepped out. "I would be very cross, except, you brought this little bundle of joy. Emily and I are going to have a fine visit."

Jenny chatted with Jason for a while. Jason brought in his bag after some time and pulled out some files.

"I hope you don't mind?" he apologized to Jenny. "I need to get this done by evening."

Emily took a nap after a while. Jenny went down to the kitchen and hunted around in her freezer for a casserole for lunch. She found a pan of Star's famous six layer lasagna and slid it into the oven.

"You must be getting close," Jason said as he prepared Emily's bottle. "You are beginning to threaten someone."

"I have no idea who," Jenny sighed. "It's all like a really intricate web. And there's something in the water, Jason. Every person I meet seems to be having an affair."

"You drank a bit of that water yourself," Jason teased.

"That's different," Jenny argued. "Adam and I are in love."

Jason's eyelids flickered a bit and he squared his shoulders but Jenny didn't notice any of that.

"I'm talking about a proper affair, the kind you have when you are cheating on someone."

"Oh?" Jason asked with interest.

Jenny started counting off her fingers.

"Kelly was having an affair with Binkie, she was sweet on the pool boy too. Ada is having a fling with the golf pro at her club …"

"Wait a minute," Jason interrupted. "What?"

"Have you met the golf pro at the country club?"

Jenny knew Jason was a member and enjoyed a good round of golf. It was all part of being a successful lawyer.

"I haven't been on the links in a while," Jason explained. "I was too busy earlier and now with Emily, it's out of the question."

"Zac Gordon is tall and attractive, and he says all the right things."

"Surely he's younger than Ada?" Jason sputtered.

"By decades," Jenny nodded. "They were seen smooching in a deserted alley."

"Now I've heard it all," Jason sniggered.

"Not really," Jenny said. "Brandon's back with Megan."

"They have been in love since they were kids," Jason told Jenny. "I was shocked to learn Brandon was marrying someone else."

"What if Brandon got back with Megan while Kelly was still alive?" Jenny asked. "He knew she was cheating on him. How do we know he didn't do the same?"

"He would have been justified," Jason said.

"I don't know about that," Jenny said. "But having an affair with Megan gives him a motive."

They went back and forth over it for a while.

"Are you sure about Ada? I can't imagine Ada Newbury being friendly with someone of the working class."

Emily woke up with a cry and Jason hastened to feed her. By the time Jenny set the table and served the lasagna, Emily's eyelids were drooping again.

Father and daughter left after lunch, Jason urging Jenny to take better care of herself.

Jenny had barely had time to flip through the latest issue of her favorite cooking magazine when she heard some familiar voices outside. She sprang up and flung the door open, just as Heather raised her hand to knock.

"What are you all doing here?" Jenny beamed. "This is a pleasant surprise."

Betty Sue, Heather and Molly bustled in, followed by Star. Star gave Jenny a withering look.

"You were supposed to take it easy, take a nap or something."

"I'm fine," Jenny assured her. "You worry too much."

She pointed to the container Molly held in her hands.

"Dessert?"

"You bet," Molly said. "My special espresso brownies."

Betty Sue settled in a comfortable armchair and pulled out her knitting. Her needles clacked in a familiar rhythm as she spoke to Jenny.

"We decided you needed our help. This whole sordid business has gone on too long."

"What did you have in mind?" Jenny asked, taking a big bite of Molly's gooey, rich brownie.

She hadn't waited for Molly to serve them on a plate. Molly handed the plate around and nodded at Betty Sue.

"We know you're the real sleuth, Jenny, but maybe if we brainstorm together, we might see something you have missed."

"Five heads are better than one," Jenny agreed.

"Where should we start?" Heather asked eagerly. "Enrique?"

"Heather told me that pool boy was blackmailing the poor girl who died," Betty Sue said. "Why would he kill her? He had lots to gain from her. And he seems to be the greedy type."

"That's right," Jenny said. "But he also has a criminal past. He was forcing Kelly to pay him for his silence. Let's not forget he was right there at the pool house. He could have let Kelly in."

"You think they had an argument?" Molly asked.

"They might have been fighting over money," Jenny agreed. "He could have pushed her in accidentally."

"What about the bruise on her head?" Heather asked. "I don't see Enrique hitting her on purpose."

"I agree," Jenny said. "But I'm not ready to rule him out completely."

"Okay," Molly said. "I think we are all in agreement on that one. Who else?"

"Brandon," Jenny said, looking at Heather. "I know you are related but we are trying to be objective here."

"It's okay," Heather said. "Let's get this out of the way."

"Brandon knew that girl was cheating on him, didn't he?" Betty Sue asked.

Jenny told the Magnolias about Megan and Brandon.

"I'm beginning to think he was cheating on Kelly too."

This was news to the other women. They exclaimed over this new theory, amazed at why the young couple had been going ahead with their wedding. Neither of them seemed interested in each other.

"Brandon may have wanted to break it off with Kelly," Jenny mused. "But Kelly wanted the wedding to happen. That was the whole point of the plan she hatched with Binkie. She wanted to trap Brandon in marriage and then maybe get a big divorce settlement."

"How does all this implicate Brandon?" Heather asked.

"Brandon decided to confront Kelly. He could have let her into the pool house. Maybe that was their rendezvous point."

"And then things got out of hand?" Molly asked. "That's possible. What about Binkie though? Why would Brandon kill him too?"

"Binkie was always hanging around Kelly," Jenny said. "Remember the night of the party? Those two were literally joined at the hip. Binkie could have followed Kelly to the pool house. He might have seen what Brandon did."

"And then he blackmailed Brandon?" Star spoke up. "There's a lot of that going around too."

"So what? Brandon got Binkie out of the way too?" Heather scoffed. "I can see Brandon losing his temper once but killing someone in cold blood, that's just not him."

"I understand your feelings, Heather," Jenny said. "But the evidence points toward him. He wasn't in bed when Kelly died, and he was at the country club around the time Binkie died. Like it or not, Brandon is the top suspect."

"What about that boy Binkie?" Betty Sue asked.

"That's right," Star spoke up. "He was a crook from what I can tell."

"There is one possible scenario," Jenny said. "Kelly might have changed her mind about ditching Brandon. She must have realized how rich the Newburys really were. What if she wanted to marry Brandon for real? That would leave Binkie in the lurch."

"And make him really angry with Kelly," Molly breathed, licking her chocolate stained fingers.

"Binkie could have argued with Kelly," Heather said, her eyes shining with hope. "Isn't it possible he hit her in a fit of anger?"

"There is only one problem with that theory," Jenny sighed. "Who killed Binkie?"

"That's it?" Star asked. "Are we out of suspects?"

"There's one other person who hated Kelly," Molly said.

"You are thinking of Ada," Betty Sue snorted. "Ada Newbury hates pretty much everyone other than her immediate family. If she started killing everyone she had an objection to, there would be a bloodbath in Pelican Cove."

"Funny how you always take her side," Star quipped.

The two older women squabbled for some time.

"Give it a rest, you two," Jenny said.

She stood up and began pacing the room. The shadows were beginning to lengthen outside. The sheer white curtains at the windows flapped around in the breeze coming off the ocean. The day had turned cooler, making Jenny shiver all of a sudden.

"Are we missing something?" she spoke out loud. "Or someone?"

"There is the staff at the Newbury mansion," Heather said. "I don't care how many times they change the access code for that pool house, some of them must have known what it was."

"Why would they have a grudge against Kelly though? I don't think any of the staff has a clear motive. It just doesn't make sense."

"What about the people at the party?" Molly asked. "Maybe Kelly pulled the same racket on someone else before. This person could have followed her to Pelican Cove."

"It was a very exclusive gathering," Heather said. "You know how snobbish Ada is. She went over the guest list with a fine toothcomb. Anyway, the party was for her friends, not Kelly's."

"We are back where we started," Jenny groaned. "Looks like whoever it was escaped long ago."

"That's not true," Star spoke up. "You must be getting close, Jenny. That's why someone tried to hurt you."

Heather and Molly bobbed their heads in agreement. Betty Sue summed up what they were all thinking.

"Whoever it is, he or she is watching every move you make, Jenny."

Chapter 20

"I still can't believe Ada invited me today," Jenny said, tapping her hands on the steering wheel.

Jenny had become familiar with the winding road that led into the hills and the Newbury estate.

"She's warming up to you, Jenny." Heather laughed shrilly and teased her friend. "Ada Newbury is giving you time of day. Count your blessings."

She sniggered again, shaking her head.

"That's enough," Betty Sue Morse said from the back seat. "Make sure you behave yourself when we get there."

"Yes, Grandma!" Heather said with a roll of her eyes.

"What's the occasion?" Jenny looked into the rearview mirror and caught Betty Sue's eye.

"Brandon said it's a surprise," Heather spoke up before Betty Sue had a chance to respond.

"We'll find out soon enough," Betty Sue nodded. "Why are you so impatient?"

"I just hope I am dressed appropriately," Jenny said self-consciously.

She was wearing a figure hugging silk dress in a light peach color. It was from an expensive label and she had worn it several times over the years. She hoped it was fancy enough for whatever event Ada had invited them to.

"You look fine," Heather reassured her friend.

"Is that fella of hers going to be there?" Betty Sue asked. "Maybe I can get a good look at him this time."

Ada had been spotted with Zac Gordon again. Star had come upon them when she was walking on the bluffs, trying to look for a good spot to set up her easel. Molly had seen them driving out of town once. The Magnolias had concluded that Ada Newbury was definitely involved in some way with the golf pro. Whether it was a light flirtation, an amorous affair or just an innocent friendship, they had no idea. The younger women were willing to bet that it was a hot affair. Especially since Ada's husband Julius had been away on business for the past few months.

"She wouldn't dare!" Heather exclaimed. "You think Brandon knows what Ada has been up to?"

"Brandon has been keeping himself busy," Jenny reminded her.

Brandon and Megan had been hanging out together for the past few weeks. There was nothing hidden about their relationship.

Heather's face assumed an 'I told you so' expression.

"Brandon and Megan are meant for each other," she parroted.

Jenny pulled up at the Newbury's entrance and the security guard waved her in through the big iron gates.

A maid took their wraps and ushered them out to the garden at the back. Fairy lights glittered in the dusk, covering the extensive veranda. Paper lanterns were interspersed between them and hung on trees, bathing the surroundings in a soft glow. Jenny had a déjà vu moment as she thought of the night of Kelly's party.

Brandon rushed forward to greet them. Jenny saw Ada holding court over a small group of people. Megan sat next to Ada on a sofa. Zac Gordon reclined in an armchair.

Brandon showed them to their seats, making sure they were comfortable.

Greetings were exchanged. Betty Sue sat with her back ramrod straight. She gave Zac Gordon a withering look.

"I don't believe we have met before," she said loudly.

Zac Gordon opened his mouth to speak. Ada beat him to it.

"Zac is a close friend, Betty Sue."

Betty Sue's cheeks turned pink.

"Friend, huh?" she murmured. "Nice to meet you, Zac."

Brandon offered the ladies a drink.

"We are all having champagne. Will that do? I can get you a soda or tea if you like."

They chose champagne and Brandon poured some bubbly into flutes. Jenny noticed he had another glass beside him filled with a dark, amber liquid.

"Are we all here?" Heather asked. "Or is anyone else coming?"

"It's a small group," Ada said. "Just people I care about."

"What's the occasion?" Heather asked again. "Are we celebrating something?"

Brandon took Megan's hand in his. They looked at each other and beamed at the assembled group.

"We wanted you to be the first to know," Brandon began. "Megan and I are engaged."

Heather squealed in delight. She stood up and gave Brandon a tight hug. Then she turned around and hugged Megan.

"I knew it!" she exclaimed. "You two are meant to be together."

Megan blushed like a new bride.

"Congratulations, you two," Jenny said, raising her champagne flute toward them. "Aren't you having a proper engagement?"

"We feel it's too soon," Brandon said. "You know, after Kelly ..."

Megan put a hand on his shoulder.

"We'll have a long engagement and then have a lavish wedding next year. Right, Mrs. Newbury?"

She turned toward Ada, seeking her approval.

"That's right, dear," Ada said. "And how many times have I told you? Call me Grandma, like Brandon does."

"Okay, Grandma Ada," Megan said shyly.

Jenny felt she was seeing a new version of Megan.

"Do you approve of this one then, Ada?" Betty Sue asked from her perch. "She may be local but she's not a Pioneer."

The five oldest families in Pelican Cove were called the Pioneers. They considered themselves superior to the rest and generally married among themselves.

"The Pattersons have lived in Pelican Cove for many generations," Ada said. "That's good enough for me."

"Are you sure about that, Grandma?" Brandon asked.

His voice was a bit slurred. Jenny decided he had imbibed a bit too much of hard liquor.

"Of course, dear," Ada said sharply. "Whatever do you mean?"

"Make sure she likes you, Megan," Brandon said, shaking Megan by the shoulder. "Or you'll be gone. Just like Kelly."

Megan looked weary. She picked up a tray of stuffed olives and offered them to Brandon.

"Why don't you eat something, sweetie?"

Brandon swept her hand aside.

"Grandma will make you go away. Look what happened to Kelly. She made her go away."

Megan's eyes darted between Ada and Brandon. She stood up and began to coax Brandon to his feet.

"Let's go get some solid food," she urged. "That whiskey's gone straight to your head."

"I'm not drunk, Megs," Brandon said, swaying on his feet.

He threw back his head and laughed. Then he pointed a shaky finger at Ada.

"You think I don't know what you did? You made Kelly go away. You, you witch…"

Ada's face turned white first, then red spots appeared on her cheeks.

"Take him inside, Megan," she said sternly. "Let him sleep it off."

"I'm not a child," Brandon cried suddenly. "And I'm not helpless like Kelly. You can't kill me off, you witch!"

Before Ada could respond to this latest insult, Zac Gordon shot out of his chair and lunged toward Brandon. His fist flew and caught Brandon on the jaw. Jenny heard a crack as the next punch broke Brandon's nose. He flailed his arms and crashed to the floor.

"Stop it!" Ada cried. "Stop fighting at once."

Megan had pulled out her phone and called the police.

Jenny and Heather huddled together and watched as Zac sat on Brandon's chest, continuing to pummel him. Betty Sue had obliged everyone by fainting on the spot.

Jenny finally spurred Heather and Megan into action. Together, they grabbed Zac by the arms and the collar of his shirt and tried to drag him away.

Ten minutes later, sirens sounded outside and the police rushed into the garden. Adam hobbled up to Jenny, his eyes full of concern.

"What just happened here?"

Brandon was sitting in a chair, holding a linen napkin against his nose. The girls had torn off Zac's sleeve and he sat opposite Brandon, shooting daggers at him. Ada was sobbing openly and Betty Sue fanned herself, muttering a prayer.

Jenny, Megan and Heather started talking at once. Adam held up his hand and asked Jenny to go on. Jenny gave him a precise account of how Zac had beaten Brandon to a pulp.

"We are taking you in," Adam told Zac.

He turned toward Brandon.

"I assume you want to press charges?"

"Of course I do," Brandon roared.

Ada opened her mouth to protest, but said nothing.

The police left the house with Zac in handcuffs.

Jenny caught Heather's eye and nodded at her. Heather helped Betty Sue to her feet and they started to leave.

"You really think I had something to do with that girl's death?" Ada asked Brandon. "How could you?"

Brandon looked uncomfortable.

"I'm sorry, Grandma!" he said. "I don't know what came over me."

Megan stood close to him, stroking his back.

"I really love Megan, Grandma," Brandon pleaded. "I always have. I couldn't take it if anything happened to her."

"I like her too," Ada said, bewildered. "She's been in an out of this house since she was a child. Your Grandpa and I always figured she would marry you one day."

Brandon sat down next to Ada. He looked like a lost child.

"I'm afraid, Grandma. Until we find out what happened to Kelly, I'll never feel safe. I know I didn't do it. And Binkie's dead. So who did it?"

Jenny, Heather and Betty Sue quietly said goodbye to Megan and walked out. Betty Sue sat wheezing in the back seat on the drive home. All the excitement had been too much for her. Heather couldn't stop talking.

Jenny was thoughtful, trying to process the scene she had witnessed. She felt she was on to something but she couldn't quite put her finger on it.

"What made Zac flip like that?" she asked Heather.

"Flip?" Heather laughed. "He went mental!"

Betty Sue spoke up from the back seat.

"Brandon called Ada a witch. That's what set off that young man."

"So Zac couldn't tolerate hearing anything bad against Ada," Jenny spoke out loud.

"He might have killed Brandon if we hadn't pulled him off," Heather crowed.

Jenny felt the pieces of the puzzle fall in place. Apparently, Zac Gordon could do anything for Ada. Had she hired him to get Kelly out of the way? She thought of Ada Newbury, an imposing old shrew. How could a snob like Ada have a romantic relationship with a common golf pro? Maybe she had paid him to do her dirty work and he was forcing her now. Hanging out with Zac Gordon might be something Ada was doing under duress.

Jenny pulled the car onto the shoulder and came to a stop. She turned around in her seat and looked at Heather and Betty Sue, her eyes gleaming.

"Remember how we talked about who could have killed Kelly? We thought it had to be Brandon or Enrique. But there's one person we haven't considered all this time. Someone who was right in front of us."

"Zac Gordon?" Heather cried.

Jenny nodded.

"You just saw what happened. Zac seems to be Ada's personal watchdog."

"So Ada paid him to get Kelly out of the way?" Heather echoed Jenny's thoughts.

"I don't believe it," Betty Sue protested. "Ada would never do that."

"Ada may not have been specific," Jenny reasoned. "Maybe Zac went a bit overboard."

"Things got out of hand," Heather agreed. "And Kelly lost her life. But what about Binkie?"

"I haven't figured that out yet," Jenny admitted. "Binkie might have seen something and Zac had to get rid of him."

"I think Ada is innocent," Betty Sue argued. "That boy must have acted on his own."

"But why?" Jenny and Heather chorused.

"To impress Ada?" Heather mused.

"Or try to please her?" Jenny added.

"Are we going to stay here all night talking about this?" Betty Sue demanded. "Take me home now."

Jenny started the car with a sigh. She needed to talk to Adam immediately. He would decide if he wanted to bring Ada Newbury in for further questioning.

Chapter 21

Jenny wiped down a table at the Boardwalk Café, deep in thought. The breakfast rush had just ended. Jenny had started making her parfaits in a smaller serving size. Most people ordered them as a side or dessert to go with their hearty breakfast. Jenny's customers, both locals and tourists, wanted sumptuous fare like omelets and frittatas for their first meal of the day. She had learnt it the hard way and accepted that she didn't cater to a yogurt and granola type of crowd.

"Why don't you come into the kitchen and grab a bite?" Star said to her.

Jenny took a last look around the room, made sure everyone's coffee was topped up and went into the kitchen with her aunt. She picked up a spoon and began eating the special parfait of the day, strawberries with toasted coconut and hazelnuts.

The phone mounted on the kitchen wall trilled. Jenny set her food down and sprang up.

"Heather! Is everything okay?"

She nodded her head and listened quietly for a while before hanging up.

"Aren't they coming over today?" Star asked.

"The police just took Ada in for questioning," Jenny told her. "Brandon called Heather. He's going to pick up Jason and go to the police station."

"Wonder who's watching Emily," Star said. "Why don't you call Jason? We can take her for some time."

Jenny's cell phone rang just then. It was Jason, in dire need of a baby sitter. Jenny told him to drop the baby off at the café.

"We knew this was coming," Star said, referring to Heather's phone call.

"You think Ada will break down and confess?"

"Betty Sue is sure she is innocent," Star reminded Jenny. "But you think Ada is hiding something, don't you?"

"You know how finicky she is about status and bloodlines and all that crap," Jenny said. "And she really hated Kelly."

"Let's see what Adam finds out."

The Magnolias came in at ten and took turns singing and talking to the baby. Heather offered to take her back to the Bayview Inn.

"Call that young man of yours," Betty Sue told Jenny. "Find out what's happening with Ada."

"You know he doesn't like to be disturbed, Betty Sue. I'll let you know as soon as I find out anything."

The Magnolias dispersed soon after. Heather was eager to go back to the inn with Emily. She had pulled her old crib out of the attic and set it up in a corner of their living room. She was eager to see how the baby liked it.

Adam came to the Boardwalk Café around noon, making Jenny's eyes widen in surprise.

"Got something to eat?" he asked Jenny. "I had to skip breakfast. I'm starving."

Jenny set a big bowl of mushroom soup before Adam and told him to get started. She brought out a couple of buffalo chicken sandwiches and sat down before him.

"Ada insists she is innocent and I am inclined to believe her," he said, between spoonfuls of soup.

Jenny was surprised Adam was willingly sharing information with her but she wasn't going to stare a gift horse in the mouth.

"So she didn't hire Zac Gordon to do her dirty work," Jenny asked, her mouth drooping in disappointment.

"She says she didn't and there is no evidence to prove otherwise."

"What about her relationship with Zac?" Jenny shot back. "Did she deny that too?"

Adam bit into his sandwich and chewed appreciatively.

"This is like chicken wings dipped in blue cheese with a side of celery," he said. "Yum!"

Jenny wasn't interested in Adam's compliments.

"Adam!"

"Ada was very forthcoming about it," Adam said with a smile. "She is having a fling with the golf pro."

"But why?" Jenny cried. "He has to be at least thirty years younger than her."

"Is that your only objection?" Adam quirked an eyebrow.

"She's married, of course," Jenny added. "How could she cheat on Julius?"

"Ada doesn't feel the need to explain herself," Adam said.

"Did she ask you to release Zac Gordon?" Jenny asked.

Adam shook his head.

"Blood is thicker than water. She was shocked by how he behaved. She said she wasn't aware he had a violent side. He's been all lovey-dovey with her, obviously. She is going to insist that Brandon press charges against Zac. She wants us to put him away forever."

"That's quite an about turn," Jenny laughed.

"She's nothing if not whimsical," Adam said.

"What do you think about this whole business?" Jenny asked. "Do you think Zac could have done it?"

"We never considered Zac as a suspect before," Adam said. "Now we are looking into his alibi for both the murders. And I'm doing a background check on him too."

Adam coaxed Jenny into sharing a sandwich with him. He left soon after.

A few more customers wandered in for a late lunch. The café emptied after that. Star and Jenny did a quick job of cleaning up and went into the kitchen to prep for the next day.

They were almost ready to leave when Jenny heard someone out on the deck.

A young man stood outside, biting his nails.

"Enrique!" Jenny exclaimed. "What are you doing here?"

"Can we talk?" he asked hesitantly.

"Sure," Jenny said, pointing to a chair. "What's on your mind?"

"Can you keep this between us?" Enrique asked. "I need to be sure you won't turn me in."

Jenny looked alarmed.

"What have you done? I can't promise anything."

Enrique's brow pinched as he wavered for a minute. Then he let out a deep sigh and started talking.

Jenny's eyes grew larger as she listened to Enrique's story. Her mouth dropped open after a while. She almost jogged to the police station to bring Adam up to speed on Enrique's story.

Things happened rapidly after that. Adam told Jenny about it when they were having dinner two days later.

Zac Gordon confessed to the murder of both Kelly and Binkie. The first murder had happened at the pool house and Enrique witnessed it when he woke up and went to the kitchen for a drink of water. He had watched Zac bash Kelly in the head with a golf club and push her into the pool. He had rushed to help Kelly as soon as Zac left the scene. It had been too late to save Kelly. Afraid of being harassed by the police, he went in and pretended he had been asleep in the pool house all night. Then he got greedy and tried to blackmail Zac.

Zac Gordon had threatened to report Enrique to immigration. It had been a shot in the dark but it had found its mark. It turned out Enrique was undocumented. Faced with the threat of being deported, he didn't say a word against Zac.

"What about Binkie?" Jenny asked Adam.

She was still trying to wrap her head around all the facts. It seemed Zac, Enrique and Binkie had all been crooks, using blackmail to extract money from someone.

"Binkie spotted Ada and Zac together," Adam smirked. "He threatened to expose their little affair. Zac thought that would be a big embarrassment for Ada, so he paid up at first. Then Binkie's demands increased. So Zac got him out of the way."

"I always thought Zac was a player, I mean, a womanizer," Jenny said, "but I never took him for a cold blooded killer."

"He had a violent past," Adam reported. "He beat up a few people when he was on the golf circuit, apparently for no reason at all. If he hadn't injured his shoulder and left himself, he would have been banned from the game."

"I don't understand one thing," Jenny said, taking a sip of her wine. "What was his motive? Why did he murder Kelly?"

"He did it for Ada," Adam said.

"What?" Jenny exclaimed.

"You know Ada can be outspoken. She made it very clear that she didn't like Kelly. She didn't want Brandon to marry her."

"There were other ways to break them up."

"He saw Ada trying to bribe Kelly into leaving Brandon. He asked her to meet him by the pool and threatened her. She scoffed at him. That's when he attacked her. He thought it would make Ada happy."

"I guess it did, in a way," Jenny mused. "What does Ada say about all this? Did she know what Zac was up to?"

"She's in shock. She had no idea what was going on in Zac's mind. She kept repeating it over and over again. I believe her."

"How did those two get together anyway?" Jenny asked, thinking she hadn't come across a more unlikely alliance in a long time.

"Zac flirts around with women his age," Adam said. "Mostly women at the country club. I guess he used to mooch off them. He never expected to fall for Ada."

"Was it mutual?" Jenny asked.

"Both of them say it was. Ada decided to learn golf while Julius was away on his extended trip. She wanted to surprise him when he got back. She met Zac at the club and they became friends. You know the rest."

"What happens to Enrique?" Jenny asked. "Will they send him back?"

"Enrique is working with an immigration lawyer. Brandon recommended one. I think he's going to be fine."

"Two young people lost their life, all for nothing," Jenny said sadly.

"Don't forget Kelly and Binkie were out to dupe Brandon. They might have met with trouble sooner or later."

"Brandon's back with his first love now," Jenny smiled. "He's happy with Megan."

Adam took Jenny's hand in hers and gazed deeply into her eyes.

"What about us, Jenny? Do you think it's time?"

Epilogue

The spring sun bathed Pelican Cove in a bright glow. Flowers bloomed everywhere and lawns were carpeted in newly sprouted grass in rich emerald hues. A barbecue was in progress on Jenny's patio, amidst a vibrant garden heavy with the scent of roses and gardenias.

Jason and Chris stood at a large grill, roasting hot dogs and flipping burgers. The Magnolias sat a short distance away, sipping tall glasses of cool lemonade, playing with the baby. Emily sat in her stroller, her big, round eyes taking everything in. She clapped her hands and cooed at the women, speaking in her own special baby language.

"Where is that young man of yours?" Betty Sue asked Jenny. "I hope you are still seeing him?"

Jenny smiled smugly, as if laughing at a secret joke.

"Adam's working. He should be here soon though."

Star leaned forward and whispered loudly.

"It's not too late, niece! I still think you should go for Jason."

Jason looked up from the grill just then and caught Jenny's eye. He gave her a wide smile that reached the corners of his ears. Jenny knew Adam never smiled like that.

"It's too late for a summer wedding," Heather complained, flipping through a wedding magazine. "Stop trying our patience, Jenny."

Jenny went up to the grill and started loading plates with the meat. A side table was loaded with side dishes everyone had brought. Molly had made her brownies and Betty Sue had made bread and butter pudding using a two hundred year old family recipe.

Jenny loaded her plate with coleslaw, potato salad and a bean salad and squirted mustard and relish on her hot dog. She urged everyone to start eating.

Jenny had just taken a bite of her food when Adam arrived, looking tall and handsome in his sheriff's uniform. He made a beeline for the food. The friends talked and laughed together as they enjoyed the food and the company.

Finally, after the second helping of dessert had been eaten and everyone was sitting back, groaning and holding their stomachs, Adam cleared his throat.

He took Jenny's hand and gave her a nod.

"We have an announcement," Jenny began.

"It's about time," Heather cried.

"Just say when," Star added enthusiastically.

"Fall," Jenny said shyly. "We are having an autumn wedding."

THE END

Acknowledgements

I hit a few unexpected hurdles while writing this book. What kept me going was the support and encouragement from my family and reviews, emails and messages from readers eagerly awaiting the next book.

I am so thankful for everyone who takes the time to read my books. Beta readers and advanced readers deserve a special mention. So do friends and family who keep me going no matter what curve balls life throws at me.

I am grateful for the tremendous response my books have garnered. I hope you keep it coming because it motivates me to write more.

Thank you from the bottom of my heart. I really appreciate your being here.

Truffles and Troubadours – Pelican Cove Cozy Mystery Series Book 8

By Leena Clover

Chapter 1

It was a scorching summer day in Pelican Cove. At the Boardwalk Café, Jenny King hummed a tune as she gently poured scalded cream into a bowl of chopped chocolate. She was trying her hand at making truffles. Jenny and her friends had a big sweet tooth and they all loved chocolate. She couldn't wait to see their reaction when she placed a platter of her fancy truffles before them.

Jenny added orange zest to the chocolate mixture and spooned in some orange liquer. The mixture was poured into fancy moulds. Jenny hurried to place the trays in the refrigerator as she heard a flurry of footsteps.

Two young women burst into the kitchen, vying for Jenny's attention.

"Something smells good," Heather Morse said, closing her eyes as she took a deep breath. "What's cooking, Jenny?"

Heather was a bold, attractive 35 year old woman who believed in making her own rules. She called herself Jenny's wing woman.

"Are you making your six layer chocolate cake?" Molly asked.

Tall and scrawny with thick Coke bottle glasses, she was the same age as Heather. The two couldn't have been more different.

"It's a surprise," Jenny admitted. "It's a new recipe. You will be my first tasters, promise."

"That's not fair!" Heather grumbled. "Can't you give us a hint?"

The friends parried back and forth, laughing and teasing each other.

Jenny felt a warm glow in her heart as she gazed lovingly at her friends. She couldn't imagine life without them.

Dumped and discarded by her cheating husband of twenty years, Jenny had sought shelter in the small town of Pelican Cove. Jenny had been at a crossroads when her aunt Star opened her home and her heart to her. She grabbed her aunt's invitation like a lifeline, arriving at the small barrier island off the coast of Virginia without any expectations. She had never imagined the path her life would take.

Jenny started working at the local café at her aunt's insistence. Her skills in the kitchen had earned instant approval with locals and tourists alike. The Boardwalk Café soared in popularity and Jenny flourished along with it. People flocked from far and wide to eat her tasty food.

Jenny had bought a seaside mansion with her divorce settlement and proudly called Pelican Cove home. She had found purpose in life. She made lifelong friends and then she had found love.

"Are you dreaming about Adam?" Heather trilled in her ear.

Adam Hopkins was the sheriff of Pelican Cove. He was also Jenny's betrothed. The two had finally set the date for their wedding after a long engagement. Jenny's friends were very excited about the impending nuptials and were urging her to start planning for the big day.

"We had lunch together," Jenny admitted with a blush.

"That doesn't answer my question," Heather said with a laugh. "The big day isn't far away, Jenny. It's high time we started planning for it."

"Save the wedding planning for another day," Molly interrupted, glancing at the clock on the kitchen wall. "We need to get going."

"She's right," Jenny said. "I don't want to miss a minute of the town meeting. All the funny stuff seems to happen at the beginning."

"Are you saying the town hall meeting is a joke?" Heather asked in mock horror.

The three friends laughed out loud.

"Where's Betty Sue?" Jenny asked, referring to Heather's grandmother.

Betty Sue was a formidable woman in her eighties, and wielded a lot of power in the small town. She was the direct descendant of James Morse, the founder of Pelican Cove. James Morse had travelled south from New England with his family in 1837. He had bought the island for $125 and named it Morse Isle. He built a house for his family on a large tract of land. Fishing provided him with a livelihood, so did floating wrecks. He sent for a friend or two from up north. They came and settled on the island with their families. They in turn invited their friends. Morse Isle soon became a thriving community.

Being a barrier island, it took a battering in the great storm of 1962.

Half the island was submerged forever. Most of that land had belonged to the Morse family. A new town emerged in the aftermath of the storm and it was named Pelican Cove.

Betty Sue had retained the Morse name even after marriage. Heather was the last Morse on the island, and the Morse bloodline was in danger of extinction unless she got married and produced a young one soon.

"Grandma's already there," Heather told Jenny. "There's going to be a big announcement."

"Must be something about the fall festival," Molly said. "It's going to be bigger and better than anything we ever put on."

"Didn't sound like it," Heather said with a frown.

"Why are we standing here playing the guessing game?" Jenny asked, pulling off her apron. "Let's head over there. We'll find out soon enough."

Pelican Cove was experiencing a bright and sunny summer day. Sun worshippers lined the beach, sprawled on colorful beach towels and chairs, working on their tan. Kids laughed as they frolicked in the water, the little ones squealing in delight as they jumped over the ocean waves. The sun had moved closer to the horizon but the days were long with sunset several hours away.

The girls walked along the boardwalk, arm in arm, chattering nineteen to a dozen. Soon they were inside the town hall building, greeting friends and acquaintances.

"Jenny," a tall, older woman bellowed from the front. "I saved your seats."

The girls walked up to Star, Jenny's aunt. Star was an artist who painted seascapes of the surrounding region. Her art was popular among the tourists. Jenny had recently helped her set up a web portal for selling her work. Star could barely keep up with the demand.

Like Jenny, Star was a chicken necker. It was a term the islanders used for someone who wasn't born in the region. Star had been hitchhiking around the country in the seventies. She had arrived in Pelican Cove, fallen in love with the town and a local and never left.

"Where's my grandma?" Heather asked Star.

Star pointed toward a small stage at the front of the room. A few chairs were arranged behind the podium. Betty Sue sat in one of them.

"There's something big going on," Star told them. "That's why she's up there."

Nothing important happened in Pelican Cove without Betty Sue's approval. A short, plump woman stood at the podium and called for silence. The crowd gradually settled down.

Jenny noticed a couple of new faces and wondered who they were.

"Welcome!" The woman at the podium beamed at everyone. "I see we have a good turnout today. You won't be disappointed. We have a big announcement."

A tall, black haired man sprang up from the row behind Jenny.

"Wait a minute. I got something to say."

"We can talk about it later." The woman stared the man down.

Her name was Barb Norton and she was generally found at the helm of some committee or the other.

"No!" the man said flatly. "This is urgent. It affects the whole town."

People began to murmur and guess what the man was going to say.

Betty Sue Morse leaned forward and tapped the woman at the podium on the shoulder. Barb let out a big sigh.

"Very well, Peter Wilson," she said to the man. "But make it quick."

Peter Wilson whirled around and pointed to a young man slouching on a bench in the last row.

"You there," he roared. "Come forward. I want everyone in this room to see you properly."

The man stood up and blinked. He was one of the strangers Jenny had spotted earlier. She guessed he was in his early twenties, maybe a couple of years older than her son Nick. His blond hair stood up in tufts and his green eyes lit up as he smiled at the crowd. He ambled to the front of the room and stood there, his hands in his pockets.

"Who is this?" Barb Norton asked.

"I'm Tyler Jones," the boy smiled.

"Forget about his name," Peter Wilson dismissed. "He's a bloody nuisance, that's what he is."

"Mind your language!" Barb said sharply.

She looked at the boy called Tyler and gave him a motherly smile.

"What have you done?"

The boy shrugged and said nothing. Jenny noticed he was what the kids called 'cool'. He didn't appear to be ruffled at all.

"This young buck has made my life hell," Peter Wilson yelled, jabbing a finger at Tyler. "He stands in front of my house, playing his guitar and raising a ruckus. We need to drive him out of town."

"You play your guitar on the street?" Barb Norton asked the young man.

Tyler nodded.

"I'm the troubadour. I filed my paperwork two months ago."

"Oh!" Barb's face relaxed and her shoulders settled. "Don't you play on the boardwalk?"

"Sometimes," Tyler said with a shrug. "I prefer the town square. I have a favorite spot near the gazebo."

"Right in front of my house, he means," Peter Wilson broke in. "Tell him to get out of town, Barb."

"No can do, Peter," Barb said. "He's the troubadour."

"What crap is that?"

"You're not from here, are you?" Barb said condescendingly. "The troubadours are a long standing tradition in Pelican Cove." She turned toward Betty Sue. "Isn't that right?"

Betty Sue bobbed her head. "My ancestor James Morse welcomed the first troubadour to the island back in 1892."

People began whispering among themselves and another murmur rose through the crowd. Jenny was as clueless as Peter Wilson. Heather brought her up to speed.

"Troubadours are traveling musicians. They write their own songs and compose their own music. It's been a while since one of them came along though. Not since I was in high school."

Peter Wilson heard her.

"Why does he sing on the street though?"

"It's my job," Tyler Jones said, rubbing a reddish mark on his cheek.

It looked like a birthmark of sorts.

"I sing and entertain people," Tyler continued.

"Who asked you to?" Peter Wilson fumed. "And why don't you sing in a pub or something?"

"Stop hounding the boy, Peter," Barb commanded from the podium. "There is a system in place here. As long as he filed his papers, he's good to go."

"So he's going to bang that guitar of his all hours of the day or night and there's nothing I can do?" Peter Wilson thundered. "What kind of joint are you running here?"

"The troubadours are known for their special brand of music," Betty Sue spoke up. "Their music uplifts the soul."

"He's doing us a favor," Barb nodded.

"Sounds fishy to me," Peter Wilson grimaced. "I bet he's charging an arm and a leg for all that noise he makes."

Tyler Jones smiled. His whole face lit up and his eyes crinkled.

"I don't sing for money."

Peter Wilson's mouth dropped open.

"You don't say. Why do you stand in the sun all day making that awful racket?"

"That's enough, Peter," Barb Norton called out. "We need to move on to the next item."

Tyler Jones flashed another smile at the crowd and walked to the back of the room. Jenny decided to catch up with him after the meeting. She wondered if she could request him to pick a spot outside the Boardwalk Café. Her guests would surely enjoy some live music along with their food.

Barb Norton banged a gavel, trying to get the crowd's attention again.

"And now for an important announcement …"

"Wait!" a voice drawled from the back.

Jenny whirled around to see Tyler Jones raising his hand.

"What is it now, young man?" Barb asked.

"May I have a minute, please?" Tyler asked, standing up. "I need to file a grievance."

Chapter 2

The room erupted in chaos as everyone started speaking at the top of their voices. Barb Norton looked a bit flustered.

"You are not a resident of this town," she said. "I am not sure if you can address the town meeting with a complaint."

She turned around and gave Betty Sue a questioning look. There was a hurried conference between the two.

"I bet Grandma's loving all the attention," Heather said to Jenny.

"I may not be born here but I have lived in town for forty some years," Star said. "No outsider has ever been allowed to air a complaint at the town meeting."

"Does he have a problem with the town?" Molly wondered out loud.

Barb Norton and Betty Sue had come to a decision. Barb pounded her gavel again and waited for the noise to die down.

"This is highly irregular," Barb said. "But we have decided to hear you out. Why don't you come forward and state your problem?"

Tyler Jones smiled and ambled toward the front.

"Thank you," he began. "I want to report a trespasser. I filed my papers with the town in July and became the official troubadour of this town. According to the troubadour code, there can be only one of us in a town this size."

"That sounds right," Barb nodded. "What's the problem?"

Tyler pointed toward the back of the room.

"Him!"

A tall, middle aged man with a heavy beard stood up and bowed before the crowd, folding his hands together in greeting.

"He turned up last week," Tyler said. "He shouldn't be here at all."

"Can you please come forward, Sir?" Barb asked. "Please introduce yourself."

The man shuffled to the front of the room and stared at his feet. He mumbled in a low voice.

"Can you speak up?" Barb spoke loudly. "I can barely hear you. I'm sure the people at the back want to know your name."

"Ocean," the man said, clearing his throat. "My name is Ocean. I'm the troubadour."

"You may be *a* troubadour," Tyler Jones protested, "but you can't play your music in this town."

Ocean gave him a beatific smile.

"There's plenty of space for the both of us."

"I didn't make the rules," Tyler said, beginning to turn red. "You need to go somewhere else."

Peter Wilson was staring at the troubadours with an expression of disbelief.

"Here's a thought," he said, taking an aggressive stance. "Why don't you both pack your stuff and get the hell outta this town?"

The crowd guffawed. Barb Norton pounded her gavel again.

"This is not funny. The town has never faced this situation before."

"My permit is valid for six months," Tyler reminded Barb. "This is my turf until the end of the year."

"Why don't we discuss this later?" Barb reasoned. "We are already running late."

"There is nothing to discuss," Ocean said. "We can both pick a spot in town."

"Don't you get it, man?" Tyler said, beginning to look provoked. "I got here first."

Jenny thought Tyler sounded childish.

"Let's have a sing-off," she suggested, springing up.

"What's that?" someone in the crowd asked.

"We'll have them play their music until one of them gives up," Jenny explained.

"Or they can each play five songs and we will vote on who's the best," Heather said, joining Jenny enthusiastically.

"You can't do that!" Tyler exclaimed. "What about my license? It gives me exclusive rights."

"Let's be reasonable, young man," Barb called out from her perch. "Don't forget the town gave you that permit. The town can revoke it anytime."

Tyler stomped a foot and pointed at the bearded man.

"Are you happy now, you gatecrasher?"

"All I want to do is entertain people with my music," Ocean said quietly.

His face had the same serene expression it had worn before. A smile tugged at the corner of his mouth.

"There's enough for the both of us," he added.

He held up his hand in a peace sign.

"I'm gonna wipe that irritating smile off your face," Tyler thundered.

He stalked out of the room without a backward glance. Ocean gave Barb a deep bow and turned to face the crowd. He bowed again and walked to the back of the room.

"I say we drive both these nut jobs out of town," Peter Wilson yelled.

Barb Norton banged the gavel again. A stream of sweat trickled down her forehead and beads of perspiration lined her upper lip. She dabbed at her face with a lace handkerchief. She cleared her throat and began. "We have an important item on the agenda today."

"Is it the fall festival?" someone cried from the crowd.

Barb held up a hand to ward off the fresh wave of hecklers.

"This is a historic moment for Pelican Cove," Barb said, puffing up. "Mayor Franklin is stepping down."

Jenny knew the mayor of Pelican Cove was just a figurehead. Younger than Betty Sue, he was still pushing eighty. His bow tie was crooked and his suit was wrinkled. He sat on the podium next to Betty Sue, dozing with his neck lolling on his chest. Other than special appearances at town meetings, people barely saw him these days. Most of the civic work was done by his staff and a bunch of volunteers like Barb Norton.

Mayor Franklin sat up with a start when Betty Sue gave him a sharp nudge. He flashed a toothless smile and waved at the crowd.

The crowd had exploded in frenzy again.

Barb pounded the gavel with all her might and kept talking.

"Pelican Cove will have a mayoral election for the first time in fifty years. Nominations will be accepted at the town hall for the next three days."

"We know who's going to be first in line," Star said with a snort.

"Maybe I should throw my hat in," Heather joked. "I'm a Morse, after all."

"You can't be serious," Jenny said.

Barb concluded the meeting. Heather walked over to give Betty Sue a hand as she joined Jenny and the girls.

"We are coming to your place," Molly reminded Jenny. "What's for dinner?"

"Let's just grab a pizza," Heather suggested and everyone agreed.

The women started walking toward Mama Rosa's, the only pizza place in town.

"Did you know about the election?" Star asked Betty Sue. "You sure kept it close to your bosom."

"I knew about it," Betty Sue admitted. "But I was sworn to secrecy. Barb wanted to make a big splash. You know how she loves attention."

"Are you going to be our new mayor, Betty Sue?" Molly asked.

Betty Sue looked pensive as she shook her head.

"Ten years ago, I might have considered it. But I'm getting on now. The town doesn't need another Mayor Franklin."

"She's right," Star said. "We need some young blood to steer us into the twenty first century."

"The twenty first century arrived two decades ago," Heather said with a smirk.

"Not in Pelican Cove," Star shot back.

"Give it a rest, you two," Jenny said, trying to diffuse the situation. "What toppings do you want on your pizza?"

Everyone wanted something different. They decided to go for one loaded veggie pizza and one loaded meat one.

A small crowd had gathered outside Mama Rosa's.

"Looks like everyone wants pizza for dinner," Heather joked.

"I don't think that's it," Molly said, pointing to a tall, bearded guy who stood shaking his head.

"Isn't that the troubadour?" Jenny asked.

"That's him," Star confirmed. "The second one — the trespasser."

"We don't know anything about that," Jenny argued. "Let them sort it out."

"Looks like that's exactly what they are doing," Star said.

Jenny and the girls stared as Tyler, the blond guy, put his hands on the bearded guy's chest and pushed. Offering no resistance, the bearded man toppled like a tree and crashed to the ground. Tyler turned around and stalked away without a backward glance. A couple of people in the crowd rushed to help the fallen man.

"That young one has a temper," Star said.

"What do you think they were fighting about?" Betty Sue asked.

"Weren't you paying attention?" Star asked her. "This tall guy is encroaching on that young one's turf. Neither of them is ready to back down."

"I'm beginning to agree with Peter Wilson," Molly said. "Neither of them deserves to be here. We don't need this kind of violence in our town."

Heather was talking to the man called Ocean.

"Are you hurt? Do you need to see a doctor?"

He shrugged off her concern.

"I'm fine. Thanks for asking."

"He shouldn't have hit you," Heather sympathized. "Like you say, the town's big enough for the two of you."

Ocean brushed the dirt off his clothes and shrugged. "He will get what's coming to him."

He thanked Heather again and walked away.

Jenny had gone ahead to order their food. She came out lugging big boxes of pizza and salad. Twenty minutes later, the ladies were at Seaview, Jenny's sea facing mansion, sipping wine and noshing on breadsticks.

"What a day!" Star exclaimed. "The town hall meeting never fails to entertain."

Heather cleared her throat.

"Let's talk about some more pressing things."

Everyone except Jenny nodded their heads.

"This looks like an ambush," Jenny said as she narrowed her eyes.

"Call it whatever you like, sweetie," Star said. "But it's high time we had this conversation."

"We need to start planning your wedding," Molly explained. "Unless you are hiring a wedding planner."

"She doesn't need one," Heather pouted. "She's got us."

"But we are not professionals," Star argued. "We may not be able to come up with a fully coordinated function like a seasoned planner would."

"But I've been looking forward to this since Jenny and Adam became a couple!" Heather cried.

"Relax, you two," Jenny interrupted them. "We are not hiring a wedding planner."

"But why?" Star and Molly chorused.

"I already told you. Adam and I want a small but tasteful wedding.

Nothing over the top, nothing too expensive. Hiring a wedding planner is out of question."

"Put me in charge, then," Heather said. "Let me coordinate everything."

"What about us?" Star asked. "We have some ideas too, you know."

Jenny held up her hand.

"You can all share your ideas," she said. "But the final decision is going to be mine."

"Of course, dear," Betty Sue spoke up. "You are the bride, after all."

"Let's start with the date," Heather said. "Fall is almost here. So you will have to be more precise than 'fall wedding'. Pick a date."

"She's right, Jenny," Molly said softly. "How about the first Sunday in November?"

"Weather should be mild enough," Star observed. "Although it could get chilly if there's a winter storm up north."

Jenny gave her approval for the date.

Heather wrote it down in a small notebook she pulled out of her bag.

"This is my official wedding planning notebook. The date's written here now, Jenny. You can't change it."

Jenny popped the lid off a bowl of salad and plunged her fork in. She nodded quietly as she speared an olive and a chunk of feta cheese.

"What about the venue?" Molly asked. "How about the gazebo in town? We can have a marquee in case it rains."

"I would go with the town hall," Betty Sue said. "You don't have to worry about the weather there. And it's got central heating."

"I want a beach wedding," Jenny said. "Do you think that's possible?"

"Have you forgotten you live in a beach house?" Star asked with a laugh. "You can get married right here, on the beach in front of Seaview."

"That's a wonderful idea," Jenny said approvingly. "Let's eat now."

Chapter 3

Jenny was up before the sun the next morning. Dressed in a light summer frock, she set off for the Boardwalk Café at 5 AM. She brewed her first pot of coffee and stood out on the deck, breathing in the cool air laced with a salty tang. The sun crept up the horizon, a large fiery orange ball. Jenny spotted a few early walkers on the beach and waved at them.

By the time Jenny opened the café doors at six, she had baked a few batches of blueberry muffins and brewed some more coffee. Her favorite customer stood on the step outside, ready to barge in.

"Good Morning, Captain Charlie," she greeted him cheerfully. "Ready for your blueberry muffin?"

Captain Charlie took the brown paper bag and large cup of coffee from Jenny.

"That was some meeting last night, huh?" he said. "I was in high school when they elected Mayor Franklin. Can't imagine anyone else in that position."

"I suppose he's getting on," Jenny offered. "Are you thinking of becoming our new mayor?"

Captain Charlie laughed heartily.

"Are you yankin' my chain, missy? I'm ready to hang up my hat. Two more years on the water, tops. You'll find me on the beach in a camp chair with a cooler by my side."

"That's the dream, isn't it?" Jenny sighed.

Jenny stayed busy making crab omelets for the breakfast crowd. The town hall meeting was the talk of the town. Jenny heard snatches of conversation as she went from table to table. The troubadours were a hot topic, so was the mayoral election.

Heather walked in with Betty Sue an hour later.

"Is it 11 already?" Jenny asked as she dabbed her forehead with a tissue.

The ladies went out on the deck and sat at their favorite table. The mid-morning coffee break was a ritual among the friends. They had christened themselves the Magnolias based on Heather's favorite movie. They met every morning come rain or shine, eager to share what was going on in their lives.

Betty Sue pulled out her knitting the moment she sat down. Her needles clacked in a rhythm as she worked on a bright orange scarf. Star pulled out a sketch pad and started doodling. Molly took a book from her bag. Heather was busy tapping keys on her phone.

Jenny placed a plate of warm muffins on the table and took a big bite from one.

"The town's buzzing," she said. "All anyone can talk about are those singers and the election."

"Pelican Cove has always welcomed artists," Betty Sue said, looking up. "There was a really handsome troubadour one year. I must have been sixteen at the time. Lily and I were both smitten."

Lily had been Betty Sue's childhood friend. She had gone missing one night twenty five years ago.

"I don't remember anyone singing songs on the street," Star said.

"We did have a couple of them troubadours when you were new in town," Betty Sue said. "You probably don't remember. But we haven't had any of them traveling singers since Heather here was a teenager."

"I think they are obsolete," Heather said. "Why not just upload a song online?"

"That's a question for Tyler," Jenny said. "Maybe you should ask him the next time you see him."

"Why would I see him again?" Heather scowled. "It's not like I have his number."

"Don't you remember?" Molly asked. "He's got a spot by the gazebo. You can go over any time you want."

"You can take his picture and put it on that Instagram," Star suggested. "It's one more attraction to draw tourists to town."

"That boy sure is pretty," Betty Sue said, nodding as she twirled a piece of wool over a needle. "I saw you staring at him yesterday, Heather."

"I did no such thing," Heather protested indignantly.

"Hello ladies!" A voice hailed them from the boardwalk.

The Magnolias smiled broadly as a tall, brown haired man walked up the café steps, holding a baby carrier. A bonny baby with large brown eyes clapped her hands as she spotted the women.

"Jason!" Jenny exclaimed. "And Emily. What brings you here this morning?"

Jason Stone was a lawyer, the only lawyer in town. He had recently become a single father. He was juggling work with his parenting duties with plenty of help from his friends. He was in love with Jenny but she had chosen Adam instead.

Jenny sprang up and lifted the baby out of the carrier. The baby grabbed Jenny's hair in her hands and pulled.

"Ouch!" Jenny cried. "You are becoming very naughty, Emily."

Emily cooed and pulled harder.

"She's been doing that a lot lately," Jason said with a grimace.

Everyone wanted to hold the baby. Jenny handed her over to Molly and hugged Jason.

"How about some coffee?" she asked. "It's almost time for lunch."

"Lunch can wait," Jason said seriously. "Haven't you heard yet?"

"Heard what?" the women chorused.

"Did you all go to the town hall meeting?" Jason asked. "I didn't get a baby sitter and Emily was being cranky. So I missed it."

"We were all there," Jenny confirmed. "We know about the election."

"What election?" Jason asked.

"The mayor's election, of course," Heather said. "What are you talking about?"

"I'm talking about the musician," Jason said. "Something called a troubadour."

"They are traveling musicians," Jenny nodded. "There were two of them."

"What about them?" Betty Sue asked imperiously. "Did they get into another fight?"

"I don't know about that," Jason said. "One of them was found dead a couple of hours ago."

"What?" the Magnolias cried in unison.

"How's that possible?" Star muttered. "They were both very young."

"He didn't die naturally," Jason said.

Emily let out a cry and Jenny rubbed her back, trying to make her stop.

"You don't mean ..." she stared at Jason, wide eyed.

Jason pursed his lips and shrugged.

"He was found near the gazebo, strangled to death with a guitar string."

"But who was it?" Heather asked urgently. "Was it Tyler? Or Ocean?"

"I don't know," Jason said. "But I guess you'll know soon enough. Nothing ever stays hidden in this town for long."

Jason stayed long enough to eat a muffin and have a cup of coffee. Emily ate a few crumbs of muffin that Jenny fed her.

"She already loves your cooking, Jenny," Jason laughed.

Father and daughter bid goodbye and walked down the beach.

"What's wrong with this town?" Betty Sue moaned. "The new mayor needs to focus on crime prevention."

"We don't even have good street lights," Heather pointed out. "And our police force is sadly understaffed."

"Adam's been trying to get the funds for a night patrol," Jenny said. "But the recent budget cuts pushed him to the back of the line."

"But why?" Star asked. "Shouldn't the security of the citizens be the town's top priority?"

Jenny jumped as a shrill voice interrupted them.

"Yooohoooo ..."

A short, plump woman huffed up the café steps, looking full of herself.

"Hello Barb," Betty Sue snapped. "You look like you are about to burst."

"I'm sure you must have guessed," Barb Norton panted.

"Enough with the guessing games," Star drawled. "Why are you here?"

The Magnolias, especially Betty Sue and Star, were always a bit short with Barb. Jenny could never understand why. Barb was at the helm of every project or committee, and she worked tirelessly for the good of the town. But she could be pompous at times. She also took credit for everything she did.

"I'm running for mayor." Barb beamed at them. "I just put my name in this morning."

"We kind of guessed you would do that," Star said dourly.

"That means I can count on your support, right?" Barb asked.

"Who's going to run against you, Barb?" Jenny asked. "I am sure you will be unopposed."

"That's what I think too," Barb said. "But you never know. This is a democracy, after all. It's a great opportunity to serve the people in this town. Anyone can contest. Even you, Jenny."

"I have my hands full with the café," Jenny smiled. "I don't think I'm qualified, anyway. I don't know the town like you do, Barb."

"What are you going to do to prevent crime in this town, Barb?" Betty Sue thundered.

"We already have a good police department," Barb Norton said. "I thought you would be more interested in promoting tourism, Betty Sue."

"Tourists are great for business," Jenny said. "But they can stretch the town's resources."

Heather spoke up.

"I have a whole list of things we can do to attract more tourists. We can have lifeguards on the beach, for starters."

"What about the library?" Molly asked. "You remember we had talked about allowing tourists to check out books?"

"Hold those thoughts," Barb said. "I'm going to formally announce my candidature soon. There will be a box there for suggestions. Don't forget to drop these in that box."

"What about that dead guy?" Star asked.

Barb Norton had not heard about the dead troubadour. The ladies told her the little they knew. She scurried off, promising to find out more.

Someone struck up a tune on the beach. Jenny shielded her eyes with her hands and peered into the distance. A small crowd had gathered around a tall, bearded fellow. He sang lustily, describing a beautiful woman he had met at a bar.

"That looks like that man called Ocean," Jenny said.

"That means Tyler ..." Heather said, her eyes bright with unshed tears.

Jenny patted Heather on the back. There was nothing they could do about it.

The Magnolias dispersed soon after. Star stayed back to help Jenny with lunch. Jenny was quiet as she spooned strawberry chicken salad over slices of bread.

"He was so young," she sighed. "What do you think happened?"

"I don't know, sweetie," Star said. "I hope you are not thinking of getting involved."

"Why would I do that?" Jenny asked with a shrug.

"Adam won't like it," Star warned. "Things are finally coming together for you, Jenny. Don't do something he will frown upon."

"Adam can't dictate what I do," Jenny said. "He knows that very well."

"That's not what I meant," Star said. "Just don't go borrowing trouble. Focus on planning your wedding. Have some fun with your friends."

"Don't worry about me," Jenny assured her aunt. "I didn't even know the guy. Although I do feel sorry for him."

Jenny went to Williams' Seafood Market after she closed up the cafe. Adam was coming over for dinner and she wanted to make something special for him. She got two pounds of shrimp and some fresh sea bass for dinner. Back home, she made her special orange and dill marinade for the fish. She decided to make Adam's favorite tequila lime shrimp along with fresh corn salsa and cilantro rice.

Jenny took a quick shower and dressed simply in a pair of linen shorts and a tank top. Star was already grilling the fish when she went down to the kitchen. Star's beau Jimmy Parsons was also joining them for dinner.

Jenny set the table and lit a few white tapers. She arranged a bunch of fresh roses in a vase. Adam arrived right on time and announced he was starving.

"Tough day?" Jenny asked.

Adam gave a brief nod.

"Any idea what happened to that poor kid?" Jimmy asked.

"We are looking into it," Adam said tersely.

Jenny knew he didn't like mixing his personal life with his professional one. He rarely welcomed any questions related to work, especially any status reports on one of his cases.

"Can you confirm it was Tyler?" Jenny asked meekly.

Adam looked up sharply.

"How do you know his name?" he asked, narrowing his eyes.

"He was at the town hall meeting yesterday," Star explained. "The whole town knew his name, son."

"The victim was one Tyler Jones," Adam said with a sigh. "That's all I can tell you at this time."

Chapter 4

Adam Hopkins sat at a table in the Boardwalk Café, eating a cheese omelet. Jenny topped up his coffee and gave him a secret smile. Adam wasn't fond of showing affection in public, so Jenny resisted planting a kiss on his cheek.

"You're in early," she remarked.

"My shift starts at seven," Adam said. "I thought I might begin the day with a hearty breakfast."

Adam's phone rang just then. He looked sharp as he listened to the voice at the other end.

"I'll be right there," he promised as he hung up.

"What's the matter?" Jenny asked, quirking an eyebrow.

"Nothing for you to worry about," Adam said. "See you later, Jenny."

Jenny watched him hurry out and wondered if it was something related to Tyler Jones. She got her answer soon enough.

The kitchen phone rang just then and Jenny rushed to answer it. Jason Stone's voice came through.

"They just took my client in for questioning," Jason told her. "He swears he is innocent."

"Who's your client? What are you talking about, Jason?"

"It's that troubadour fellow," Jason explained. "He hired me last night."

"Do you mean Ocean?"

"That's the name he goes by," Jason said with a sigh. "I need you, Jenny."

"I don't see how I can help."

Jenny had been involved in solving a few murders in the past couple of years. She wasn't a professional but she managed to get involved for some reason or the other.

"I need to check this guy out," Jason said. "You're the only one I trust."

"I've got a lot on my plate now, Jason," Jenny protested. "Have you forgotten I have a wedding to plan?"

"Just talk to him once," Jason said. "Feel him out. I trust your instincts."

"Adam will flip if I go to the police station now."

Jason paused for a minute.

"You don't have to go there. Let me go and see what's happening there. I'll bail him out if necessary. Why don't you come to my office after we get back? You can talk to him then."

Jenny agreed to talk to the troubadour once he was done with the police.

The Magnolias arrived at their usual time. Jenny placed a plate of truffles before them.

"What's this?" Betty Sue asked suspiciously. "Don't you have anything to eat?"

"Muffins are just coming out," Jenny assured her. "I'm trying my hand at these chocolates. Why don't you try one?"

"You don't have to tell me twice," Heather said as she popped a truffle into her mouth.

She closed her eyes and moaned with pleasure.

"These are so sinful," she crooned. "You have surpassed yourself, Jenny. These are better than your baked goodies."

Molly and Star were also sucking on the delectable chocolates.

"They just melt in your mouth," Star said. "Where did you learn how to make them?"

"I watched a few videos online," Jenny said modestly. "Then it was trial and error."

"Are you going to sell these in the café?" Betty Sue asked, picking up her third truffle.

"I might," Jenny said. "I'm thinking of making small gift boxes with these. The tourists can buy them as souvenirs."

"I know what!" Heather exclaimed suddenly. "They will make great party favors at your wedding."

"That's a great idea, Heather," Molly said. "We can wrap these up nicely and place them on each table. The guests are going to love them!"

"So you like them?" Jenny asked.

"We love them, sweetie," Star assured her.

"These are made with orange liquer," Jenny explained. "I'm making some with roasted almonds and raisins. And white chocolate."

Jenny was feeling excited. She had created recipes for a dozen different truffles. She couldn't wait to try them all out.

"Wait till you hear the scoop of the day," Heather said, taking the last truffle from the plate. She paused dramatically until she was sure everyone was looking at her.

"Tyler Jones was a trust fund baby."

"What does that mean?" Molly asked.

"I mean he was loaded. He was richer than any of us can imagine."

"How do you know that?" Jenny asked, her hands on her hips.

"The Pelican Cove grapevine, of course," Heather said. "The masses haven't been idle."

"Why did he sing on a street corner if he had money?" Star asked. "I don't believe it."

"Why shouldn't he?" Heather asked. "It's not like he had to earn a living. I guess he was living his dream, entertaining people with his music."

"Whatever the reason, it didn't end well for him," Molly said seriously.

"They arrested that bearded guy this morning," Heather continued.

"You know that too?" Jenny burst out. "How do you find out these things?"

"I have my ear to the ground," Heather said primly. "I'm surprised you didn't know that, Jenny."

"Ocean seemed like a mature guy," Molly said. "Why would he kill Tyler?"

"Turf wars," Heather said matter-of-factly. "Gangs do it all the time."

"Don't be ridiculous, Heather," Star said. "Those two young men didn't belong to a gang."

"But they were fighting for their turf," Heather said. "You were there at the town hall meeting. Didn't you hear what they were saying?"

"Tyler did want to drive Ocean out of town," Molly said slowly. "The opposite happened."

"I think Ocean took care of the problem," Heather said, widening her eyes meaningfully. "He's sly, that one."

"Think before you speak, Heather," Jenny said. "Don't malign someone before you know the whole truth."

"What do you care?" Heather asked, pouring herself a cup of coffee.

"Ocean hired Jason as his lawyer."

"And you are going to help Jason prove his innocence," Heather said. "You better not get too busy for wedding planning, Jenny."

"Relax, I'm just going to talk to him."

"That's what you always say," Star quipped. "And then you end up in a ditch by the side of the road."

"That happened one time," Jenny said. "Ocean seems like a harmless guy."

"A harmless guy who might have strangled someone with a guitar string," Molly reminded her. "I hope you will be careful, Jenny."

The Magnolias joined Molly in expressing their concern. Jenny assured them she would take care of herself.

"Stop!" Jenny held up her hands. "You worry too much. Let's talk about something else."

"Like the fall festival?" Molly said. "They didn't bring it up at yesterday's meeting. Wonder if we are still going ahead with it."

Betty Sue's needles stopped clacking.

"Of course we are," she said. "Pelican Cove takes pride in its festivals. The fall festival will go ahead as planned on the last Sunday in September."

"And we are still having the concert?" Star asked.

"Oh yeah," Heather said breathlessly. "Ace Boulevard is coming to town."

"Ace Boulevard?" Jenny asked. "Aren't they an 80s band?"

"Not just any band, Jenny. They have five gold records to their name. They topped the charts for three years running. Ace Boulevard ruled the eighties."

"But they must be old," Jenny said, scrunching up her face.

"You know the average age of people in this town?" Heather laughed. "They are perfect for us."

"I had cassette tapes of all their albums," Molly said, her eyes gleaming. "This is quite a coup."

"We did say we were going to make a big splash this year," Heather reminded her. "The Bayview Inn is booked solid for the month of October."

"You better start making plenty of these chocolates," Betty Sue told Jenny. "And what about your special menu for the fall festival?"

"I'm still working on it," Jenny said.

"Something with pumpkin?" Molly asked eagerly. "I love pumpkin."

"I do have something in mind," Jenny said evasively. "You'll find out soon enough."

Jenny's phone buzzed and she glanced at the screen quickly. She pressed the talk button and spoke for a couple of minutes.

"Jason wants to see me at his office," she told her friends.

"Go ahead," Star told her. "I'll take care of lunch."

"Thanks, Auntie," Jenny said. "I should be back before that. The sandwiches are ready and so is the soup. The cookies are ready to go in the oven."

"I know the drill, sweetie," Star assured her.

Jenny chose to walk along the beach, enjoying some fresh air as she hurried to Jason's office. It was barely two blocks away. The August sun was hot but the breeze flowing over the ocean made Jenny shiver.

Jason Stone had a visitor.

"You two know each other, right?" he asked, nodding at the tall, bearded man who sat before him.

"I saw him at the town hall meeting," Jenny explained, "but we haven't been formally introduced."

She extended a hand toward the man called Ocean. He shook it and gave her a small bow.

"The police asked him the usual questions," Jason reported. "They let him go now but Adam seems very keen on detaining him."

"I am their top suspect," Ocean said calmly.

"You don't seem worried," Jenny observed.

Ocean shrugged.

"I know I am innocent. The truth will prevail."

"I would try to be a bit more practical," Jason cautioned. "Why don't you tell us something about yourself?"

"That's against the troubadour code," Ocean said. "The troubadour is a man of mystery, an enigma. The only way he communicates with his people is through his poetry and music."

"Man of mystery, huh?" Jenny smiled. "What are you, James Bond?"

"Let's start with your real name," Jason said. "I'm sure the police asked you that."

"My name is Ocean," the man said. "That's exactly what I told the police."

"This kind of attitude will work against you, man," Jason warned. "Where are you from?"

"Planet Earth," Ocean replied. "Any place where the sun shines is my home."

"Where were you born?" Jenny asked. "Are you from around here?"

Ocean had to answer that one.

"I come from a faraway land, the land of the setting sun."

"You mean you are from some place out west," Jenny said. "And you traveled cross country to come to Pelican Cove. Why?"

"I go where the road takes me," Ocean told them. "I don't look at maps or make a plan. I take any turn that takes my fancy."

"So you came here by chance," Jenny summed up. "That doesn't explain why you are so keen on staying on."

"I like the place," Ocean said. "Is that hard to believe? It's a beautiful town."

"Where did you say you were staying?" Jason asked. "You're not at the Bayview Inn, are you?"

Ocean shook his head.

"Let me guess," Jenny said. "It's against your code to tell people where you live."

"Do you have a phone?" Jason asked. "How will I get in touch with you?"

"I don't believe in being addicted to those death traps," Ocean said. "The radiation from a cell phone can fry your brain."

Jason was looking helpless.

"You will have to be more forthcoming if you want Jason to help you," Jenny warned. "He's a great lawyer but he can't save you unless he has all the facts."

"All you need to know is I didn't kill my fellow troubadour. He was just a kid."

"Why were you fighting with him then?"

For the first time since Jenny had seen him, Ocean looked a bit irritated.

"He pushed me! I almost broke my hip. I walked away without saying a single word."

"Did anyone see him push you?" Jason asked.

"We did," Jenny confirmed. "So did a bunch of other people."

"That's good, I guess," Jason said.

"Good or bad," Jenny reasoned. "People will remember Tyler provoked him."

She turned around to look at Ocean.

"How do we know you didn't go back to get even?"

Chapter 5

"Are you sure you have the right address?" Heather asked Jenny.

The two girls were driving to Richmond to visit Tyler's family.

"It's the one Jason gave me," Jenny said. "I asked Adam to confirm it but he refused to speak about it."

"I bet he's mad you're butting in."

"I'm not," Jenny said. "We are just doing the neighborly thing. We are offering our condolences to a grieving family."

"Stick to that story," Heather snorted. "Why are we going there, exactly?"

"Ocean is the only suspect the police have so far," Jenny said. "I need to find out more about the victim. The logical approach is meeting his family."

"Let's hope they don't drive us out," Heather said grimly.

Jenny entered the city of Richmond and followed directions to Riverside Drive. She had looked it up on the Internet. It was supposed to be a posh area. Houses in the neighborhood cost upward of a million dollars. Nothing could have prepared her for the sight that greeted them though.

A wide drive took them to a plantation house that must have been built in the antebellum days. The stone façade and tall Grecian columns would have impressed anyone. Jenny and Heather stared with their mouths hanging open.

A butler answered their knock.

"We are here to offer our condolences," Jenny spoke up, trying not to be daunted by the inscrutable man towering over her.

"The family is not home for visitors," the butler said dourly.

"We are from Pelican Cove," Heather said. "We saw Tyler the day before he … err, passed."

The butler hesitated before giving in.

"This way please."

He walked down a wide foyer covered in a Turkish carpet and ushered them into a wood paneled room. Tall glass windows channeled in the warm sunlight. Jenny could see the James River gurgling in the distance.

The butler left without a word.

"That's one scary dude," Heather said, laughing nervously.

Jenny motioned her to be quiet.

Half an hour passed without anyone showing up. Jenny had almost decided to get up and leave when she heard someone dragging their feet in the foyer.

A shriveled old man with a shock of white hair shuffled into the room. He wore a three piece suit in a steel gray shade. He flashed a smile at the girls, his gleaming white teeth taking over his tiny face. Jenny guessed they were dentures.

The butler arrived and helped the old man into a wing chair near the fireplace. He made sure he was settled in before leaving the room.

"What brings you here, my dears?" the old man asked in a feeble voice.

A maid came in pushing a trolley loaded with a tea service. She poured tea for everyone and placed a delicate China cup in Jenny's hands. Jenny recognized it was a really expensive brand. Apparently, the Jones family was rich enough to use fine porcelain every day.

Jenny took a sip of her tea and hesitated. The old man gave her an opening.

"You knew my boy Tyler?"

"Not exactly," Jenny said honestly. "He spoke at our town hall meeting. The next day, he was gone."

The old man pulled a white linen handkerchief out of his pocket and dabbed at his eyes.

"He was the joy of my life. He was a good boy. Too young to be taken from us in this manner."

"Jenny's looking into what happened to him," Heather spoke up.

The old man sat up straighter.

"Are you some kind of detective?"

"No," Jenny admitted. "I just meet people and talk to them."

"She's being modest," Heather interrupted. "Jenny has helped solve quite a few murders in our town."

"Find out who killed my boy," the old man said suddenly. "I can pay you whatever you want. I will give you a blank check right now."

"I don't do it for the money," Jenny said, feeling uncomfortable. "A friend of mine is representing one of the suspects. He wanted me to look into the matter."

"So you just want to collect evidence that proves this man's innocence?" the man asked shrewdly.

Jenny shook her head.

"I want to find out the truth. That's what I do. If Ocean, that's this other man, if he is guilty, so be it."

The man's hand shook as he picked up his teacup and took a sip.

"How can I help?" he asked. "You must have come here for a purpose. What do you want from me?"

"I want to know more about Tyler," Jenny said immediately. "Everything you can tell me about him. Leave nothing out."

"I can do that," the old man said, bobbing his head up and down.

A faraway look appeared in his rheumy eyes. Jenny let him take his time.

"Tyler had a kind heart. He was always doing things for other people."

"Did he always like music?"

The old man's face broke into a smile.

"He started playing the violin when he was six. He began piano lessons a year later. There wasn't an instrument Tyler didn't play. His fingers could create magic."

"He sang too, didn't he?"

"He didn't sing until he was much older," Mr. Jones said. "He joined the choir. He sang like an angel."

"Why didn't he pursue a more traditional form of music career?"

"I don't understand," the old man said, his eyes clouding with confusion.

"You know Tyler was a troubadour?"

"That's a word I haven't heard in decades. You mean those gypsy like singers who go around singing for their supper?"

Jenny nodded.

"Why would my boy do that?" Mr. Jones asked, surprised.

He waved a hand around him.

"He had all this. He could feed a hundred people every day and not feel the pinch."

"Mr. Jones," Jenny said gently. "Tyler came to Pelican Cove as a troubadour. He even applied for a six month permit. He used to stand in the town square and sing all day."

It was obvious Mr. Jones didn't believe them. The tea cup in his hands rattled as his hands shook and his face set in a grimace.

"You wouldn't lie to me, would you? Are you trying to sully my boy's name?"

Heather spoke up in Jenny's defense.

"Mr. Jones, I live in Pelican Cove too. Believe me, we are telling you the truth. Tyler came to our town as a troubadour."

A large young man ambled into the room. His hair was cropped close to his head. His massive belly wobbled when he walked. He flopped down in a chair and spread his legs before him.

"Hey Gramps," he said. "Who are these people?"

"Did you know Tyler sang on the street?" the old man asked the new arrival.

"Must be his latest fad," the man said with a roll of his eyes.

Jenny introduced herself.

"We are here to learn more about Tyler."

"This is my other grandson, Billy," Mr. Jones told her. "He's older than Tyler."

"I'm your only grandson now," Billy said callously.

A golden retriever bounded into the room. A striking pearl and diamond collar glittered around its neck.

"I've seen that dog somewhere," Jenny exclaimed. "She looks very familiar."

"This is Toffee," Mr. Jones said. "She belonged to Tyler. The police brought her over."

"Oh yeah, she was with him that night," Jenny nodded.

She told Mr. Jones about the argument they had seen Tyler have with Ocean.

"Why was Tyler so adamant about not sharing street space?" Jenny asked. "Did he have any old feud with Ocean?"

"Never heard of him," Mr. Jones said. He turned to look at Billy. "Did you?"

Billy picked up a shortbread cookie from the tea cart and munched on it, spilling crumbs on his shirt.

"Tyler was a weirdo. He didn't have any friends."

"You mean he was smarter than you," the old man croaked. "You were always jealous of him, Billy."

Billy picked up another handful of cookies and stalked out of the room.

"Speaking of friends," Jenny said. "Did Tyler have any enemies, anyone who might have disliked him for whatever reason?"

"Billy was right in a way," Mr. Jones said. "Tyler was a quiet one. He spent most of his time making music. He wasn't the kind to hang out at bars and clubs. Most people were attracted to him because of his music."

"But someone must have hated him enough to kill him," Jenny reminded him. "What other motive could anyone have to harm your grandson?"

"What's going on here?" a voice snarled from the door. "Who are these fillies?"

"Mind your manners, Andrew," Mr. Jones bellowed. "These ladies are here to talk about Tyler."

"What do they want? Some kind of donation in his name?"

"This young lady here is going to find out who killed Tyler."

A tall, balding man wearing an expensive suit strode into the room. He didn't spare a glance toward the women. Jenny guessed the man to be in his fifties. She assumed he was Tyler's father.

"This is my son, Andrew," Mr. Jones said. "He thinks everyone is after the family's money."

"And why shouldn't I?" Andrew Jones demanded. "Someone's here for a handout almost every day."

"We have plenty," Mr. Jones said. "There's nothing wrong with sharing a bit with the less fortunate."

"You sound just like that ninny Tyler," Andrew Jones fumed. "He could have made millions with his music. But he had to go and give it away for free. Singing on some street corner like a beggar!"

"You knew he was a troubadour?" Mr. Jones asked, his eyes wide with surprise.

"What the dickens is a troubadour?" Andrew Jones asked. "All I know is he had pitched his tent in some dingy town on the coast. He stood there in the sun all day, playing his songs on that guitar."

"Why didn't you tell me about this?"

"What's the use?" Andrew asked in disgust. "You would probably have gone and joined him there."

"You didn't approve of your son being a musician?" Jenny asked.

"Tyler wasn't my son," Andrew Jones said in a clipped voice.

Jenny noticed the old man's eyes fill up.

"Tyler was an orphan. His parents died in a plane crash when he was seven."

Jenny didn't know what to say. She muttered something about being sorry.

"You need to leave," Andrew Jones ordered. "My father needs his rest."

"Come back anytime," the old man said hoarsely. "I'm counting on you."

Jenny and Heather walked out under the watchful eye of the butler.

"That was awkward," Heather breathed. "Can't imagine Tyler came from such an uptight family, huh?"

"He didn't have to worry about paying the bills," Jenny reasoned. "He could do anything he wanted with his life."

"Now we know why he was so stubborn," Heather observed. "He wasn't used to sharing."

The girls drove to Cary Street in downtown Richmond for lunch. Jenny ate her grilled steak sandwich with relish. Heather had chosen the roast duck.

"Have you thought about your wedding gown?" Heather asked Jenny. "I know Molly will have my hide if we go shopping without her, but there's a couple of good shops right around the corner."

"I guess there's no harm in looking?" Jenny asked uncertainly.

"Now you're talking, sista!" Heather gave her a high five.

"One thing's for sure," Jenny said. "I won't be wearing white."

"I guessed as much," Heather said, taking a sip of her sweet tea. "We should have plenty of choices in ivory."

"I don't know how to say this, Heather," Jenny said seriously, unable to hide the twinkle in her eye. "Will you be my maid of honor?"

"Only if you say pretty please," Heather shot back.

The girls clinked their glasses and whooped loudly, their eyes shining brightly.

Chapter 6

Jenny worked the breakfast rush at the Boardwalk Café the next morning. It was a hot and humid summer day in Pelican Cove. The town was flooded with families trying to squeeze in a vacation before school started.

Jenny had placed a box of her truffles at the counter for people to taste. The response was overwhelmingly positive.

"Are you selling these by the dozen?" One woman wearing a gauzy cover-up over her bathing suit asked. "I need to take back some presents for my family. I will take a few dozen of these."

Another man standing behind her was nodding his head.

"I say, that's a great idea. My wife takes care of the shopping but she couldn't come because of a last minute work thing. These will be a nice treat for her."

Jenny beamed at them.

"These are just a sample batch. I haven't decided if I am going to sell them at the café yet."

The woman looked disappointed.

"Why not? They are going to fly off the shelves."

Jenny felt pleased as she put a fresh batch of blueberry muffins in the oven. She was trying to calculate when she could squeeze in an extra hour to make the chocolates.

A tall raven haired man cleared his throat and rapped his knuckles on the counter impatiently.

"Hello Peter," Jenny greeted him.

Peter Wilson wasn't a regular at the café. Jenny was a bit surprised to see him there that morning.

"Wife and kids are away," he muttered. "I need some breakfast. How about a couple of those muffins with coffee?"

Jenny poured coffee in a cup and packed two muffins in a paper bag.

"I guess you heard about Tyler?" she asked.

"Who?"

"That young troubadour," Jenny elaborated. "Haven't you heard what happened to him?"

"Unbelievable, huh?" Peter said without emotion.

"Can I talk to you sometime?" Jenny asked quickly as she sensed his impatience.

"I need to get back to the garage. Is it important?"

"Sort of," Jenny nodded. "Why don't you grab a table outside? I'll join you in a few minutes."

Peter Wilson grudgingly agreed.

Jenny quickly worked through the rest of the line and went out to the deck with a fresh pot of coffee. A couple of people wanted a top up.

She finally sat down before Peter. He had worked through the muffins and was wiping the crumbs off his face.

"What's the matter?" Peter asked, leaning forward. "You in any trouble?"

"No, no ..." Jenny hastened to reassure him. "Everything is fine."

Peter Wilson had been a friend of the café's previous owner. He had kept an eye on her for twenty five years. Jenny guessed he still felt a bit possessive about the café.

"Then what?" Peter prompted.

"I saw you at the town hall," Jenny began. "You seemed pretty riled up."

"You have no idea," Peter grumbled, furrowing his brow. "That kid made my life hell."

"How long was he in town, do you know?"

"He's been banging that guitar for the past four weeks. I thought he would leave in a day or two but he just dug his heels in."

"You didn't like his type of music?"

"I never actually listened," Peter admitted. "I just didn't care for that type of thing. What is this? Las Vegas? We don't want any street performers out here."

"Troubadours have been welcome in Pelican Cove for centuries," Jenny parroted. "At least that's what Betty Sue said."

"He didn't stand outside her window, did he?" Peter shot back. "Now people are making me out to be the bad guy."

"No one thinks you are bad," Jenny assured him.

Peter Wilson hailed from the New Jersey mafia. He had left that life behind when he married a local woman and settled in Pelican Cove. Very few people knew about his past. But it was his Achilles' heel.

"We'll know soon enough," Peter said cryptically, giving one of his habitual shrugs.

"How's that?"

"I'm going to contest the elections," he smirked. "I could be your next mayor."

Jenny was speechless. She stared at the flannel clad figure before her and tried not to be too judgmental. She knew how snobbish the people in Pelican Cove could be. Peter Wilson was a blue collar worker and an outsider. Would the town people accept a virtual foreigner as their mayoral candidate?

"You don't think I can do it?" Peter asked, narrowing his eyes.

"You'll be up against Barb Norton," Jenny burst out. "Everyone knows her."

"But do they like her?" Peter asked. "She's a bossy old shrew from what I have seen."

"Barb may not have been the mayor all these years," Jenny said carefully, "but she as good as ran the town. She's on every committee, you know."

"The way I see it, it boils down to what this town needs," Peter said seriously. "I am willing to work hard to do that."

"That's admirable," Jenny soothed. "I am sure the people will appreciate it."

"So I can count on your support?" Peter asked eagerly.

"Sure," Jenny shrugged. "Why don't you work on your manifesto? We can discuss it when you are ready."

"That sounds like a plan," Peter said, slamming his fist on the table. "I knew I could count on you."

Jenny decided to change the subject before Peter got carried away.

"Did you ever see Tyler talking to anyone?"

"What?" Peter asked. "Are we talking about that kid again?" He sounded irritated. "Why are you so hung up on him, Jenny?"

"I am trying to find out what happened to him."

"Are you playing at being a detective again?" Peter asked with a frown. "Just forget that little twerp."

"I can't do that," Jenny said, feeling incensed. "That young man had his whole life ahead of him. He didn't deserve such a gruesome death."

Peter Wilson was looking uncomfortable.

"I guess you are right."

Jenny bottled her own emotions and said goodbye to Peter Wilson.

The day passed in a blur. Jenny had a dinner date with Adam but she was so tired she almost cancelled it. Adam arrived at her doorstep later that evening, holding a long stemmed rose in his hand.

"This is from your garden," he said sheepishly. "I didn't have time to get anything else."

The devil on Jenny's shoulder told her Adam was always busy.

"I have reservations at that bistro you like near Chincoteague," Adam told her. "We need to start right away."

Jenny brushed aside her exhaustion and tried to look upbeat. But her thoughts kept straying to Tyler Jones and his grieving grandfather.

Adam kept up the small talk through drinks and the main course, trying to draw Jenny out. He finally slammed his fork down in frustration during dessert.

Jenny was staring listlessly at her crème brulee.

"Didn't you like the food?" Adam asked. "Why are you so quiet,

Jenny?"

"I'm just tired," Jenny admitted. "Summer's always a busy time at the café."

"And we have double the usual tourists nowadays, thanks to you."

There was a note of pride in Adam's voice. Jenny's delicious food had put Pelican Cove on the map. It had always been a popular holiday destination. But the Eastern Shore of Virginia was lesser known compared to other places in the north. Jenny and her friend Heather had made clever use of social media to advertise the Boardwalk Café and the town itself.

"Do you think the twins will be my bridesmaids?" Jenny asked, referring to Adam's college going girls.

"They will love it," Adam assured her. "I think they are waiting for you to ask them."

Jenny hadn't really given it a thought. She decided to call the girls later.

"You're used to big crowds at the café," Adam mused. "Something else is bothering you."

"Star and the Magnolias are expecting a big wedding."

Jenny told him about having the wedding on the beach. Adam liked the idea a lot.

"So we have the venue," he said cheerfully. "That's a big item off the list."

Jenny stared at the floor, her eyebrows drawn close in a frown.

"You are not thinking of that dead guy, are you?" Adam asked suddenly. "You have no excuse this time, Jenny. Absolutely no reason to get involved."

"Jason needs my help," Jenny said stoutly. "And Tyler's grandpa wants me to find out what happened."

"Where did you meet that old man?" Adam burst out. "How do you even know that kid's family?"

"Heather and I went to Richmond," Jenny admitted.

Adam balled up his napkin and called for the check. Neither Jenny nor

Adam said much on the way back. Jenny stared out of her window and Adam concentrated on getting them home as soon as possible without breaking the speed limit.

"I thought you would be happy planning our wedding!" Adam stomped off after delivering his parting shot.

Jenny tossed and turned all night and was just falling asleep when her alarm went off at 5 AM. She dragged herself out of bed and got ready for the café.

Crab omelets were on the breakfast menu and Jenny was worked off her feet all morning. Her aunt arrived at 8 to help her out. Jenny felt she couldn't make enough of anything. They were already out of the parfaits she had assembled the previous day. The tourists had gone through four dozen muffins and endless pots of coffee since that morning.

Jenny was feeling harried when Betty Sue Morse barged in, her needles clacking as she twirled white wool around them. Heather was right behind.

"You'll never guess who wants to be mayor," she chortled.

"Peter talked to me yesterday," Jenny said with a smile. "We should support him."

Molly arrived a few minutes later and Jenny joined the Magnolias at their favorite table out on deck.

"I know Barb can be too much," Betty Sue said. "But she's worked hard for the town all these years."

"She's done the time, you mean," Molly said. "But what does she propose to do as mayor? Has she said anything?"

"She is in favor of promoting tourism," Heather told them. "She wants Pelican Cove to be the hottest beach town on the Eastern Shore."

"That's great," Star said. "Good for business."

"Wait a minute," Betty Sue interrupted. "Are you sure more tourists are the answer? The town's resources are stretched already. More crowds mean more litter on the beach, more noise and cars, more pollution…"

"But Grandma," Heather argued. "It's going to be good for our inn. We do well in the summer but our rooms are empty for most of the year."

"We are getting by, aren't we?" Betty Sue said with a shake of her head. "Greed is insatiable."

"You sound just like Peter Wilson," Molly spoke up. "He was at the library yesterday, printing out some flyers. He wants to drive the tourists away."

"That sounds extreme," Jenny offered. "Has he lost his mind? He knows this town runs on tourism."

"He is quoting the dangers of over-tourism," Molly explained. "He is citing the example of European cities like Venice."

"Is the island going to sink because of the tourists?" Jenny sniggered.

"That's not a laughing matter," Betty Sue said, wagging a finger at Jenny. "We can only take so much. It's just never been an issue so far."

"So what you're saying is, thousands of new tourists may not be good for the island?" Heather summed up.

"I think we need a balanced approach," Molly said. "Peter Wilson is incensed because of the troubadours. He is forgetting he himself doesn't belong here."

"That's a bit harsh," Star protested. "He's lived here for twenty five years. And I have lived here for forty five. Jenny here has been here for barely two years. I suppose we don't belong here either."

"That's not what I meant," Molly said, turning red. "I mean Peter Wilson is being unfair, just as he was to Tyler Jones."

Jenny wondered why Peter had taken such a dislike to the young singer.

Chapter 7

Jason Stone swept into the Boardwalk Café, holding a baby carrier in his hands.

"Emily!" Jenny cried as soon as she spotted them. "It's about time you brought her for a visit, Jason."

"This is not a social visit, Jenny," Jason said seriously as Jenny made faces at the baby.

Star heard him as she came out of the kitchen with a fresh pot of coffee.

"Why don't you two sit outside? I can handle everything here."

The breakfast crowd had thinned and Jenny had been ready for a break. She placed some warm muffins on a plate, added a crock of butter and ushered Jason out.

"I bet you missed breakfast."

Jenny nudged the plate toward Jason and put Emily's carrier on the seat next to her. The baby grabbed her finger and wailed heartily. Jenny blew kisses at her and ordered Jason to eat up.

Jason didn't need an invitation. He was already slathering butter on Jenny's banana nut muffin.

"What's got you all hot and bothered?" Jenny asked as she bit into a muffin herself.

"They took Ocean in again."

"What has he done now?" Jenny asked.

"The police searched his van. They found a guitar."

"He's a musician, isn't he? Of course he has a guitar."

"This one had one string missing," Jason said meaningfully.

Jenny's eyes widened as she connected the dots.

"Are you saying this guitar belonged to Tyler?"

"We don't know that for sure," Jason admitted. "But the police think the missing string is the murder weapon. That's why they took Ocean in for more questioning."

"What does he have to say about all this?" Jenny asked, lifting Emily up into her arms as she began to cry.

"Ocean says he found the guitar lying somewhere. He said it looked alright so he picked it up."

"Do you believe him?" Jenny asked, narrowing her eyes.

She stood up and began pacing the floor. Emily stopped crying and grabbed a fistful of Jenny's hair.

"Now you want to play, huh?" Jenny asked in a babyish voice as Emily pulled hard, making Jenny scream in protest.

"Watch out, Jenny," Jason cautioned.

"I'm fine," Jenny assured him. "So do you believe Ocean?"

"Clients always lie in some form or the other," Jason said, starting on a second muffin. "I don't think he's guilty of murder. He could have stolen the guitar, though."

"What do the police have to say about it?"

"You know they found a guitar string on Tyler? They sent it for some forensic testing. Now they will run tests on this guitar too."

"That's it?"

"Things don't look good for Ocean," Jason admitted. "He was already the top suspect. The police are leaning more toward him now."

"You have to defend him because he is your client," Jenny pointed out. "But I don't. I am looking for the truth here. If it turns out that Ocean did it, I will be the first to report him to the police."

Jason nodded as he sipped his coffee.

"I know that, Jenny. I respect your integrity. I won't ask you to do anything you are not comfortable with."

"Thanks, I appreciate that," Jenny told her friend.

Jason Stone had been one of the first people to befriend Jenny when she moved to Pelican Cove. Jenny adored him and didn't want anything to come between them.

"I came here to pick your brain," Jason admitted. "What do I do now?"

"Did you ask Ocean where he found the guitar?" Jenny asked.

"Somewhere on the beach," Jason explained. "He was pretty vague about it."

Jenny waved her hand at the ocean stretching before them.

"You think he can narrow it down?"

Emily had fallen asleep while they talked. Jenny gently put her down in the carrier. Jason had walked to one side of the deck and was waving at someone. Jenny looked up to see a bearded figure ambling along the beach.

"Let's ask the man himself," Jason said, pointing at Ocean. "Looks like the police are done with him."

Ocean climbed up the café steps, looking unruffled. He folded his hands and bowed before Jenny.

"We were just talking about you, Ocean. So they let you go?"

Ocean nodded and sprawled in a chair.

"I am innocent," he said. "Sooner or later, they will realize that. They are free to question me as much as they want until then."

"Why did you pick up that guitar?" Jenny asked him. "And where exactly did you find it?"

"I was planning to hock it," Ocean admitted. "Normally, I would have turned it in, or tried to find out who it belonged to. But there isn't a Lost and Found on the beach, is there?"

He laughed nervously.

"Actually," Jenny corrected. "The town maintains a Lost and Found for all the public beaches. People are leaving stuff behind all the time. Towels, sunglasses, chairs, you name it … sometimes even bathing suits."

"I didn't know that, I swear." Ocean looked contrite for the first time. "I was just looking to make a quick buck."

"It doesn't matter now," Jason said, placing a hand on Ocean's shoulder. "Just tell us where you found the guitar."

"It was on the beach," Ocean said with a shrug. "I already told you that, man."

"You will have to be more specific," Jenny said sternly. "There's miles of beach around us."

Ocean gave them some vague directions.

"What were you doing when you found that guitar?" Jenny asked in frustration.

"I was driving out of town," Ocean told them. "I had a meeting with a fellow in the next town."

Jenny hid her surprise. What was Ocean doing holding meetings with people? It didn't make sense given his zen attitude about everything. She decided to let it slide.

"Go on," she prompted.

"I had to make a pit stop," Ocean said, looking sheepish. "I stopped the car and walked into the beach grass. I saw something shine as I was doing my business."

Jenny tried not to flinch at the image that flashed before her eyes.

Ocean continued.

"What do I see but a perfectly good guitar buried in the sand. I saw dollar signs flashing before my eyes."

"Did you touch it?" Jason asked.

"How else do you think I picked it up?" Ocean quipped as Jason stifled a groan.

The guitar was going to have Ocean's fingerprints all over it.

"Didn't you notice the missing string?" Jenny asked impatiently.

"Not right away," Ocean admitted. "But I wasn't worried. I could easily get it fixed."

"You didn't wonder who the guitar belonged to?" Jenny pressed.

She couldn't believe Ocean was that naïve. Had he really not made the connection with Tyler?

"I didn't give it much thought," Ocean said breezily. "Finders, keepers."

Jason and Jenny shared a glance. This philosophy was going to cause Ocean a lot of trouble.

"Did you look around?" Jenny asked, wondering if Ocean could help them pinpoint the location.

"You bet I looked around," Ocean laughed. "There wasn't a soul in sight. It was a golden opportunity. I wasn't going to let it pass."

"A golden opportunity for what?" Jenny asked angrily. "Stealing something that didn't belong to you?"

"Calm down, sister," Ocean drawled. "Who said anything about stealing? That thing almost walked into my arms. Some rich dude with too much money must have chucked it without a thought."

"So you didn't see anyone," Jenny said with a sigh. "So no one can vouch for you and tell the police they saw you pick it up."

"Not unless someone from that garage saw me," Ocean said.

"What garage?" Jenny asked sharply. "Do you mean Peter Wilson's auto shop?"

"I don't know," Ocean said. "It's that garage before the bridge. Someone told me it's the only garage in town."

"You found the guitar on the beach off the bridge?" Jason asked. "Why didn't you say that before, Ocean?"

The bridge connected Pelican Cove to the mainland. It was the only way to enter or leave the town by road.

"Guess I didn't know it was important," Ocean said, scratching his head. "Can I go now? I need to go set up for the day. People expect me to entertain them, you know."

"Go ahead," Jason said.

"You think the bridge is important, don't you?" Jenny said after Ocean left.

Jason looked excited.

"Consider this, Jenny. Whoever ditched that guitar probably drove out of town."

"You are thinking it was someone from out of town?"

"Makes sense, doesn't it?" Jason continued. "Tyler Jones wasn't local. It follows that anyone he knew wasn't from here either."

"It's possible, I guess," Jenny agreed. "But how are you going to prove it? And how will you find this person?"

"I leave that to you, my super sleuth!" Jason teased. "I need to get going. Emily and I have a date at the library."

Jason picked up the baby carrier and set off. Jenny went into the kitchen and started prepping for lunch. She sliced strawberries for her chicken salad and tried to arrange everything she knew about Tyler in a logical order. The Magnolias arrived at their usual time, ready to share some gossip and nosh on something sweet.

"Have you made any more chocolates?" Betty Sue asked her. "I have been craving them all morning."

Jenny shook her head and placed a plate of warm muffins on the table.

"I can barely get through breakfast and lunch. I guess I need to put in some extra time."

"Ask Heather and Molly to help," Betty Sue ordained. "Heather needs to fill her time with something constructive."

"We need to go shopping for your wedding gown," Heather reminded Jenny. "It's a long process and time's running out."

"I know you two looked at some dresses," Molly said with a pout. "Have you already picked something, Jenny?"

"I wouldn't do that without you, Molls," Jenny said quickly. "We just did some window shopping, that too because the store was right next to the restaurant where we had lunch. We couldn't help but look at the display windows."

"Jenny has something to say to you, Molly," Heather said, staring hard at Jenny.

"I do?" Jenny muttered.

She looked bewildered for a minute but she caught on quickly. She grabbed Molly's hand and pulled her to her feet. Then she placed both her hands on Molly's shoulders and beamed at her.

"Molly Henderson, will you be my maid of honor?"

Molly squealed appropriately and hugged Jenny. Heather clapped her hands and Star and Betty Sue followed.

"I'm not done yet," Jenny said. "I want Star to give me away. Molly and Heather, you are both dear to my heart and I don't want to choose between you two. That is why I want you both to be my Maid of Honor. I hope you don't mind sharing."

"We don't," Heather assured her. "But you have to fall in line now, Jenny. Time is short and there's tons of things to do."

"What about Adam's best man?" Molly asked shyly. "Do you think he will ask Chris?"

Chris Williams was Molly's beau. He was a Pelican Cove native and knew Adam well.

"He's not asking Jason," Star said drily, referring to the unspoken rivalry between Adam and Jason.

"Adam's probably forgotten he has to choose a best man," Jenny said.

"Both of you need to start thinking about the wedding now," Heather stressed. "Molly and I are going to take Adam to task."

"Don't forget he's the sheriff, Heather," Jenny said morosely. "He won't rest until he solves this latest case."

"Or you can solve it for him," Betty Sue cackled, looking up from her knitting.

Chapter 8

Jenny walked to the town square after winding up at the Boardwalk Café. She was on a mission. She sat in the gazebo, placed a big frosty cup of sweet tea beside her on the bench and pulled out a book. She leaned back and held the book before her eyes.

Any casual passerby would have assumed Jenny was enjoying a leisurely summer afternoon in the shade. But Jenny had other things on her mind. Her eyes flickered as she took in the space around her. They rested on a bunch of dried bouquets someone had placed below a tree. A sign proclaimed it as Tyler's spot and wished him eternal peace.

A lush green lawn grew around Tyler's spot. There were a few stores bordering the street that ran next to it. The ocean sparkled in the distance. Some houses sat in an alley across an empty parking lot.

A two storied Cape Cod sat on the corner just across where Tyler Jones must have crooned his songs. Jenny assumed it belonged to Peter Wilson. She could see how Tyler's music might have bothered someone living in that house.

An old woman came out of one of the houses and began pottering in her garden. She looked up after some time, spotted Jenny and waved at her. Jenny recognized her as one of the café's regulars.

"Catching up on your reading?" The woman asked in a friendly tone.

"Molly says this is the best book of the year," Jenny replied. "I'm not much of a reader, I'm afraid. I barely have the time."

"That café keeps your nose to the grindstone," the woman nodded seriously. "But you need to take some time off and relax too."

"Music is my relaxation," Jenny offered. "I can't fall asleep without playing some of my favorite records."

The woman bobbed her head emphatically and leaned over the fence.

"Music feeds the soul, doesn't it? I can't imagine life without it ... unlike some philistines."

"You mean ..." Jenny prompted.

"I just made some fresh lemonade. Why don't you come and have some?"

Jenny finally remembered the woman's name.

"That's kind of you, Trish," Jenny beamed and walked over to the house.

She admired the roses and the wisteria. Trish looked happy as she ushered Jenny into a small parlor. White lace curtains billowed in the breeze. Chintz covered chairs in a quaint primrose shade faced a pale pink Chesterfield. A large seascape hung over the fireplace and a bunch of photo frames in wood and silver graced the mantel. Jenny recognized the painting as one of her aunt's.

"We bought that from Star a few years ago," Trish supplied. "That was before my Andy passed. He loved that painting. He used to sit right there in that chair and gaze at it for hours."

"I'm sorry," Jenny offered. "You must miss him."

"Only every day," Trish said frankly. "He was the love of my life, you know."

"How do you fill your time now?" Jenny asked with genuine interest.

"I try to keep busy," Trish sighed. "I take care of the garden. We have our share of festivals in Pelican Cove so there's a lot of opportunities for volunteer work."

"Do you have any family in town?" Jenny nodded at the pictures on the mantel.

"The kids all live in the city now. They rarely come to visit. You get used to it. They are busy with their lives, I guess."

Jenny guessed there was a lot Trish wasn't saying. She seemed like a lonely woman.

Trish excused herself and went inside. She came out a few minutes later with a tray loaded with tall glasses of lemonade. There was a plate with chocolate chip cookies.

"Not as good as yours," Trish said generously, offering Jenny the cookies.

Jenny took one and bit into it. She gave Trish a thumbs up.

"These are so good. I might ask you to bake some for the café."

"Really?" Trish perked up. "Do you mean that?"

"I do," Jenny promised. "I am stretched thin at the café. I have been thinking about getting some help. The townsfolk will appreciate something made by one of their own."

Trish regaled Jenny with the different types of cookies she could bake. Jenny's mind drifted as she sipped her lemonade. She didn't notice when Trish changed the subject and started talking about music.

"He was such a nice boy," Trish was saying.

"I'm sorry, who are you talking about?" Jenny asked.

"Tyler, of course," Trish said. "He sang like an angel."

"What type of songs did he sing?" Jenny asked. "Something by Elvis?"

"Tyler wrote his own songs," Trish said with devotion. "He produced his own music too. That guitar just came to life when he played it."

"Did people come and listen?"

Trish nodded vigorously.

"He always drew a crowd. People tipped handsomely too. He made almost twenty bucks in a day."

Jenny thought about the Ferrari sitting in Tyler's garage. Why had he chosen to sing on a street corner in an obscure place like Pelican Cove?

"So he was really popular," Jenny said. "It's hard to believe someone wanted to harm him."

"Not that hard," Trish said, leaning forward. "And you don't have to look too far."

"What are you saying, Trish?"

"You know Peter Wilson, don't you? That car mechanic? He lives right next door."

Jenny nodded.

"He had a big grudge against Tyler. You can say he hated him."

"But why? Tyler's hardly been here a month."

"Said Tyler was disturbing the peace. He used to yell at the poor boy every few hours."

"What did Tyler say?"

"That boy stuck to his guns, said he had a license from the town. He was the troubadour and he was just doing his job."

"But he could have sung his songs anywhere," Jenny argued. "Why did he stick to that spot, knowing he was being a bother?"

"Stubborn, I guess," Trish shrugged. "Or fearless? If someone had threatened me with dire consequences, I wouldn't risk my life."

"You don't think Peter really meant any harm?"

"I hope not," Trish said. "That's the man who wants to be our mayor."

Jenny tried to give Peter Wilson the benefit of doubt as she drove home. She knew he had a criminal past but he had left it all behind him. Could Tyler's music have driven him to insanity?

Heather and Molly were waiting for her at home. The looks on their faces made Jenny wince.

"You were supposed to be here an hour ago," Heather pounced. "When are you going to start taking this seriously, Jenny?"

"We missed our appointment at the bridal store," Molly clucked.

They had planned to go to a boutique in Virginia Beach. It was owned by a new designer who displayed her latest designs on her website. Heather had sent her the links to some of the dresses and Jenny had really liked them. But they needed an appointment to go try on the dresses.

"I'm so sorry," Jenny apologized. "I ran into someone and lost track of time."

"Were you playing hooky with Adam?" Star asked with a laugh.

She was sitting next to Jimmy Parsons, her special friend. Jimmy had admired Star from a distance for several years. They had recently reconnected and were taking it slow. Neither of them was in a hurry to take the next step in their relationship.

"I wish," Jenny groaned. "Adam had to attend a seminar in the city. He's going to be late getting back."

"That's good," Heather said. "We need to make up for lost time."

Molly backed her up.

"That's right. Let's start with the guest list. How many out of town guests will you have, Jenny? We will need to make arrangements for their stay."

Jenny's mother hadn't approved of her divorce, even though she had been the victim. She felt everything would be as it was if Jenny just groveled before her ex-husband and asked him to take her back. Relations between mother and daughter had cooled considerably in the past two years. Jenny's mother had declared she was never setting foot in Pelican Cove. Star, who had always been the odd one out in the family, was supposed to be a bad influence on Jenny.

"No one from out of town," Jenny said, knowing her mother would never give her blessing for a second wedding.

Star gave her a sympathetic look.

"Remember, we want it to be small and intimate," Jenny reminded the girls. "Fifty people at the most."

"Fifty people from your side, right?" Heather said. "What about Adam's family?"

Jenny and the girls argued over the list while Star started prepping for dinner. Heather had the first draft of the guest list ready by the time the linguini in clam sauce was ready. Jenny had already poured her favorite Chardonnay for them. Star set the table and dished up the hot, flavorful pasta.

The talk turned to the fall festival.

"Who's going to head the festival committee, now that Barb is running for mayor?" Molly asked.

Barb Norton was an active organizer when it came to town festivals.

"Who says she can't do both?" Heather giggled. "She has enough energy for all of us."

"Why don't you do it?" Jenny asked Star. "It's one of your favorites, isn't it?"

"I'm going to be busy with wedding prep," Star said hesitantly.

"Don't worry about that," Heather said, fanning her mouth. "We got that covered."

"Talk to Barb," Jenny urged her aunt. "I am sure you can convince her to let you take the lead this time."

"I have attended all the meetings," Star said, "so I know what's going on. You are going to love it, Jenny. We took your suggestion from last year. There's going to be a big concert on the beach. We don't really have any space constraints since it will be out in the open."

"That sounds great," Jenny praised. "The Boardwalk Café will provide dessert," Jenny told them. "What about the rest of the food?"

"We are having a big barbecue," Star told them. "Chris and Jason have already volunteered."

"That's what I want for my wedding," Jenny said, feeling inspired. "A barbecue right here on the beach. And a potluck."

"But I already shortlisted a few caterers from up and down the coast," Molly protested. "I was thinking oyster bar, champagne and filet mignon."

Jenny poured some more wine for herself.

"Keep the champagne but ditch the steak. Too fancy schmancy."

"Nothing wrong with having a fancy dinner at your wedding," Heather retorted.

"You forget," Jenny sighed. "I have already done all that."

"Twenty something years ago …" Heather began.

"Whatever," Jenny insisted. "We want something down home and friendly. What could be more coveted than a dish lovingly cooked by our friends?"

"So what? You want corn casserole and potato salad?" Molly wrinkled her nose.

"Adam and I talked about this," Jenny nodded. "We just want your blessings and best wishes. Money can't buy that."

"You don't really need our help, do you?" Heather asked glumly. "You've already got everything figured out."

"On the contrary," Jenny said. "I need you to put it all together for me."

"What about flowers then?" Molly asked, sounding defeated. "I suppose you want roses from your garden?"

Chapter 9

Jenny settled into the plush seat of Jason Stone's fancy car. Even though it was the peak of summer and the air conditioning was on full blast, she was tempted to press the button for the heated seats. There was just something decadent about them.

Jason and Jenny were driving to Richmond. Jenny had received a call from old man Jones. He had suggested Jenny pay a visit to the family lawyer. Jenny didn't know what to expect from the visit so she had asked Jason to go along.

"I really don't see why this lawyer wants to meet us," she said out loud. "I hope it's worth the trip."

"Relax," Jason soothed. "You work too hard, Jenny. Just enjoy your time away from the café."

Jenny tried to follow Jason's advice. She cranked up the radio and enjoyed the view outside the window. They were crossing the Chesapeake Bay Bridge-Tunnel and the Bay sparkled around the long curving road.

They stopped at a rest area on the way. It was too hot for coffee but they both craved a snack.

"How is the wedding prep coming along?" Jason asked as he handed her a large glass of soda and a cinnamon roll.

"Heather and Molly are immersed in it," Jenny told him. "I couldn't do it without them."

"It's your special day," Jason said gently. "Make sure you don't let them steamroll you."

"They mean well," Jenny said. "Sometimes I think they are more excited about the big day than I am."

Jason pulled up before the offices of Gold, Mason and Arlington a few minutes before 11. The reception area was carpeted in burgundy. It had a look of understated opulence. Jenny guessed most of the firm's clients were as affluent as the Joneses.

A pretty young girl escorted them to a large corner office. A small, wizened man perched in an overstuffed leather armchair, dwarfed by a massive cherry wood desk. He nodded at Jenny and offered his hand to Jason.

"Phineas Gold, at your service."

He offered them coffee and nodded at the girl. She came back a few minutes later, carrying a tray with a silver coffee urn and delicate mugs. Jenny accepted a cup and thanked the girl.

"Thanks for driving all the way to town," Phineas Gold began. "I suppose you are wondering why I called you here."

Jenny nodded as she took a sip.

"The Jones family has a long association with the firm. Josiah's father hired my great grandfather sometime in the 19th century. We have taken care of their legal affairs since then."

Jenny had a lot of questions but she let the man continue.

"Josiah told me you are looking into Tyler's death for him. I have some information that might be relevant to you."

Jenny sat up in her chair, feeling hopeful.

"You know Tyler's parents died when he was young. He was their sole heir. All the money was tied up in a trust until he reached twenty five."

"When was he coming into this trust?" Jason asked.

"This week," Phineas said meaningfully.

Jenny was two steps ahead.

"Who gets the money now?" she asked.

"Tyler could have left it to anyone, but he didn't have a will. He ignored our professional advice and never made one. Said it made him feel morbid."

"He was barely twenty five," Jenny whispered. "Of course he didn't think he needed one."

Phineas Herb looked impatient.

"Tyler's parents did think of this scenario though. They left everything to Tyler's uncle."

Jenny remembered the tall, rude man she had encountered at the Jones residence.

"Doesn't he have a son too?"

Phineas nodded.

"It will all go to him, eventually. But Tyler's uncle gets it for now."

"Did Tyler get along with his uncle?" Jenny asked. "I had the impression he didn't approve of Tyler's music."

"Tyler wasn't interested in the family business," Phineas told them. "It was a source of friction between him and his uncle."

"What about old Mr. Jones?" Jenny asked.

"The Jones family is loaded. Tyler could live in the lap of luxury without having to lift a finger. The old man just wanted him to be happy."

"Isn't this all kind of personal?" Jason asked. "I'm surprised you are telling us all this."

"I am acting on my client's instructions," Phineas Gold grumbled. "I don't see how this is going to help you find Tyler's killer."

"It opens up a line of investigation," Jenny told him. "Tell me, what is your opinion of Tyler's uncle?"

Phineas Gold looked scandalized.

"I don't gossip about my clients, Madam."

"Was he short of funds?" Jenny asked doggedly.

Jason caught Jenny's eye and gave a slight shake of his head. The old man must have pressed some kind of button. The pretty young girl came in and started to show them out.

"Tyler may not have been practical but he was kind," Phineas said as they were leaving. "I hope you find out who murdered him."

Jason knew Jenny liked Chinese food. He drove to a local restaurant tucked away in a strip mall.

"Save room for dessert," he told Jenny. "Their fried banana fritters are not to be missed."

They ordered a generous lunch and began eating with gusto. Jenny deftly picked up a steamed dumpling with her chopsticks and looked at Jason speculatively.

"What was the whole point of that visit?" she asked. "Does the old man want us to suspect his son?"

"I've been wondering that myself," Jason said, scrunching his face.

"Money is always a strong motive," Jenny said. "And the uncle didn't seem too fond of Tyler."

"Shouldn't the uncle be rich in his own right, though?" Jason asked.

"He might have needed the money for a secret project," Jenny pointed out.

"So what?" Jason scoffed. "He bumped his nephew off? It sounds farfetched."

"You know who else is beginning to look like a suspect?" Jenny asked. "Peter Wilson."

"Come on, Jenny, Peter can be hot headed. But you don't seriously think he's guilty?"

"He hated Tyler and had several confrontations with him," Jenny reminded Jason. "And he even threatened the poor kid."

"That still doesn't mean he did it."

"We don't have any other suspects," Jenny muttered. "Unless you want to consider Ocean."

"What does Ocean gain by getting Tyler out of the way?" Jason asked.

"He's the sole troubadour in town now. That seemed important to him."

"You're getting mixed up," Jason said, shaking his head. "Tyler is the one who wanted to drive Ocean out."

"Whatever," Jenny shrugged. "Ocean is the only entertainer in town now. He gets to rake in the moolah."

Jason laughed at that.

"So he earns twenty bucks more than he would otherwise. Not a strong enough motive to kill someone."

Jenny stared moodily at her Sichuan chicken.

"I'm completely out of ideas," she admitted.

"What does Adam say about all this? The police must be doing something other than harassing Ocean?"

Jenny rolled her eyes.

"You know Adam doesn't like talking about his work. He's already warned me to leave this alone."

"He's not completely wrong," Jason considered. "You are about to be a bride. Enjoy all the pre-wedding fun, Jenny. Forget all this running around."

"But you're the one who wanted help with Ocean," Jenny reminded him.

Jason slapped his forehead.

"Guilty as charged. But you've been a big help so far. I don't think there is any hard evidence against Ocean."

"So you want me to drop all this?" Jenny asked, scraping the last bit of fried rice off her plate. "It's not that easy. And I promised old Mr. Jones I would look into it."

"I think you've done your bit," Jason said with a sigh. "Forget all this for now. Let's order dessert."

Jason mentioned the wedding again on their way back to Pelican Cove.

"Where are you going to live after the wedding?"

Jason knew Jenny was very fond of Seaview, the beach facing mansion she had bought with her divorce settlement. She had clearly expressed she didn't want to live anywhere else. Adam was equally adamant about his own house. Jenny's friends had secretly started a pool about where the couple would live after they got married.

"We are still talking about it," Jenny divulged. "But Adam will come around."

"Now this wouldn't have been a problem if you were marrying me," Jason joked.

Jenny knew the remark was only half in jest. Jason had made it clear he would follow Jenny to the end of the world if needed. Everyone wondered why Jenny had chosen Adam instead of Jason. But as they said, love didn't always follow logic.

"Emily's growing up real fast, isn't she?" Jenny asked glibly.

Betty Sue and Heather were watching Jason's baby for the day. Jason's hands tightened on the steering wheel.

"Am I doing right by her, Jenny?" he wondered out loud. "A baby girl needs her mother. Do you think I should get married?"

"What are you planning to do? Order a wife online?" Jenny scoffed. "Don't be silly, Jason."

"That's not what I meant," Jason murmured.

"If you are thinking about dating again, I think you should go ahead. You don't lack baby sitters. We will gladly take care of Emily while you go out."

"You think anyone will want to date a single father like me?" Jason asked, his doubt splashed clearly across his face.

Jenny gave him an encouraging smile and began to check off his attributes on her fingers.

"You are a successful lawyer, you own the house you live in, you are not bad on the eyes, and you have a heart of gold ... wait a minute, you have a lovely baby girl. You, my dear, are a great catch!"

"If you say so, Jenny," Jason mumbled.

Jenny tried to cheer Jason up. She fiddled with the radio and tuned into Jason's favorite station.

"You like Springsteen, don't you?"

They both sang their hearts out to 'Born in the U.S.A'. Jenny broke off as Jason turned onto the bridge leading to Pelican Cove.

"What in the world!" she exclaimed, pointing to a large billboard.

Barb Norton's face stared back at them, flashing a 1000 mega watt smile. 'Barb Norton for Mayor', proclaimed the large letters splashed across the poster.

"Barb does everything in style," Jason laughed. "She's going to win in a landslide."

"I wouldn't be so sure," Jenny said as Jason drove off the bridge.

She pointed toward the side of the road.

Peter Wilson's auto shop was festooned with hundreds of balloons. Music played in the background and a small crowd had gathered. Jenny spied people holding small paper cups of lemonade. A line of cars snaked along the road leading to the garage. A car wash event was in progress. High school kids were busy cleaning the cars while the guests mingled. Peter Wilson could be seen moving around, shaking hands.

"Looks like Peter has upped his game too," Jason remarked.

"Election canvassing is on alright," Jenny said as they drove further into town.

Lawn signs had gone up before most of the houses. Jenny counted the election placards and tried to calculate who was leading the race.

"Barb may be a busybody but she has done a lot for this town," Jason said. "She definitely has my vote."

They came upon another crowd as they drove up to the town square. Barb stood in the gazebo, getting ready to give a speech. People waved tiny American flags and cheered her on.

"What is Peter offering to do anyway?" Jason asked.

"He's going to put a stop to over-tourism," Jenny said, putting double quotes around the word. "He doesn't want the town to change too much."

"You mean he's against growth?" Jason frowned.

"I'm sure he doesn't see it that way," Jenny replied.

Jenny's phone rang then. She stared at the unknown number, then made up her mind and pressed the green button. She spoke briefly before hanging up and stared at Jason meaningfully. He had just pulled up before Jenny's home.

"That was old Mr. Jones," she said in a hushed voice. "He wants to see me again."

Chapter 10

Jenny bustled about in the Boardwalk Café, chatting with customers and topping up coffee. The sun shone brightly outside, and the beach behind the café was packed with sun worshippers and families enjoying summer vacation. Most of the townsfolk were out too, canvassing for their favorite mayoral candidate.

The café crowd thinned after a while and Jenny finally went back inside to prep for lunch. Her strawberry chicken salad was so popular she was making gallons of it every day. Soft shell crab season was on and it was another item Jenny couldn't make enough of.

"You look tired," Star observed as she drained the poached chicken.

"I'm fine," Jenny muttered without looking up.

She had sliced a mound of strawberries and was ready to start mixing the salad.

"You need to take better care of yourself," Star droned. "Can't have you looking like a hag on your wedding day."

"Why does everything come around to that nowadays?" Jenny complained.

Star just shook her head quietly, opting not to say anything.

"Tell you what," she said after a few minutes. "Why don't you go out for lunch? Take a picnic basket and meet your young man."

"Adam's going to be busy," Jenny said with a grimace. "I don't think he can spare the time."

"Nothing wrong with asking," Star said. "Better yet, go surprise him and ask him sweetly. I am sure he won't be able to say no."

The Magnolias arrived at their usual time.

"You need to ask Adam about his guest list," Heather reminded Jenny.

Jenny promised she would do that when she met Adam later.

"Mandy is in town," Molly informed them. "I saw her going door to door with Barb as I was coming here."

Mandy was a publicist the town hired from time to time. She had been instrumental in modernizing a lot of things in town. She could be pushy but Jenny admitted Mandy had helped spread the word about the Boardwalk Café. Tourism had boomed in town since Mandy's arrival.

"Barb must have hired her for the election," Betty Sue observed, her hands busy knitting an orange scarf.

"Does that mean she won't be helping with the fall festival?" Star grumbled. "I was counting on her assistance."

"Why don't you ask her?" Jenny asked, pointing in the distance. "I bet those two ladies are on their way here."

The Magnolias looked up from their coffees and muffins and stared at the beach. Two familiar figures were hurrying along the sand, weaving their way around people lying on towels or lounging in camp chairs under colorful umbrellas.

"Yoohoo …" Barb Norton called out her signature greeting and waved at them.

She huffed up the steps a few minutes later, trying to catch her breath. Mandy was at her heels, holding a pen and notepad in her hands.

"Looks like you are painting the town red, Barb," Betty Sue cracked.

"I believe in a job well done," Barb said pompously. "You know that about me, Betty Sue. I have always taken care of this town. I will continue to do so when I become mayor."

"You are that confident of winning, huh?" Star quipped.

"Of course I am going to win. People like you fully support me and can't wait for me to be mayor."

She gave them a speculative look.

"I can count on your vote, right?"

"What do you propose to do for the town?" Betty Sue asked. "I need to know you won't turn this place into a circus. Jenny here said you are angling to bring more tourists down here?"

"Of course!" Barb beamed. "Boosting tourism is one of the top items on my agenda. We need the money these people bring in. Most of the businesses in town depend on tourists, Betty Sue. Your own inn needs them."

"That doesn't mean you should flood the town with these folks."

Barb Norton looked flustered.

"Why don't you just come out and say it, Betty Sue?" Barb thundered. "You want to vote for that chicken necker Peter Wilson."

"He is talking about preserving our heritage," Betty Sue said stoutly. "This is the land of my ancestors, Barb Norton! I don't want to see it sink because you brought in a boat load of outsiders."

The two women continued to bicker over the issue. Jenny, Heather and Molly looked at each other and tried to suppress their smiles.

Star took Mandy to task.

"Can I still count on your help for the fall festival?"

"Don't worry," Mandy said smoothly. "I am working on a presentation for our next meeting. Everything is running on schedule. Barb told me you are heading the festival committee now?"

"That's right," Star said proudly. "And I want everything to go off without a hitch."

"The concert is going to be big," Mandy told her. "That itself should help us reach our fundraising goal."

"What about games and rides?" Star asked. "Hay wagon rides are absolutely must. And people expect the usual contests like pumpkin carving, best yard decorations and so on. Are you keeping track of that?"

Mandy reassured Star she had everything under control.

"For shame, Betty Sue!" Barb roared suddenly, springing up. "I didn't expect this from you."

"What's wrong with having a debate?" Betty Sue asked with a frown. "It's what happens in every election."

Barb was breathing fire as she clattered down the steps without a word.

"Now you've done it, Betty Sue!" Star drawled. "Did you have to rile her up?"

"Did you see her?" Betty Sue cackled. "She got as red as a tomato."

The Magnolias chattered for a while longer. Heather reminded Jenny of plenty of wedding related chores before they left.

Jenny went into the kitchen and started assembling a picnic basket. She added chicken sandwiches, chips and Adam's favorite chocolate chip cookies. Two bottles of lemonade went in along with some truffles Jenny had made that morning.

"Don't forget a blanket," Star called out.

The noon sun felt scorching as Jenny walked to the police station. She was glad she had remembered to wear her straw hat. The breeze coming off the ocean offered some relief from the heat.

Adam's face lit up when Jenny peeped into his office.

"Jenny! What a nice surprise!"

"Can you get away for lunch?" Jenny asked, holding up the picnic basket before him.

"Why not?" Adam said with a shrug. "I need a break from these files. And I'm starving."

Adam picked up his cane but Jenny noticed he didn't lean on it much. Adam was a war veteran who had been injured in the line of duty. She knew he was trying hard to get rid of the cane for their wedding. It was supposed to be a surprise for her so she didn't make any comment.

They walked out and strolled to the beach. Jenny pointed to a spot and Adam spread the blanket in the sand.

Adam guzzled the cool lemonade before picking up his sandwich.

"What's new at work?" Jenny asked.

"The usual," Adam said between bites. "Nothing worth talking about."

"Is it always going to be like this?" Jenny bristled. "When are you going to learn to trust me?"

"What do you want to know, Jenny?" Adam asked with a sigh. "Is this your way of digging for information?"

"I'm not always doing that," Jenny snapped, putting a half eaten sandwich down.

"Are you still helping Jason?" Adam asked sternly. "Tell me you don't care what happened to that kid."

"I can't," Jenny said. "An innocent young man was struck down in the prime of his life. I can't just forget about that, Adam, especially when the police don't seem to be doing anything about it."

"There you go again," Adam muttered.

"Do you have any new leads?" Jenny asked. "The only two suspects we have are Peter Wilson and the uncle."

"Uncle?" Adam asked.

Jenny told him about the trust fund.

"You never cease to amaze me, Jenny."

"Is Ocean still at the top of your list?" Jenny asked. "Or do you have any other evidence."

"The guitar came back from forensics," Adam told her. "There were three sets of fingerprints on it. We identified two of them as belonging to Tyler and Ocean."

"What about the third set?" Jenny asked eagerly.

"Unknown."

Jenny's eyes widened as she processed this latest piece of information.

"Could it be Peter Wilson?" Jenny mused. "Ocean told us where he found the guitar. It was just off the bridge near Peter's garage. He could easily have thrown it there."

"What would Peter be doing with that guitar?"

"He was known to have shouting matches with Tyler. He found Tyler's music offensive. Maybe he grabbed the guitar sometime in a fit of anger."

"Believe it or not, we thought of that," Adam said drily. "Peter's prints are already on file."

"So it's someone other than Peter?"

Jenny didn't hide her relief. Peter Wilson had always been good to her. She thought he hadn't behaved well with Tyler. But she didn't want to believe he had actually harmed the boy.

"As of now, we have no idea who those prints belong to."

"Try matching those prints with Tyler's uncle."

"Tyler and his uncle lived in the same house, right? So any of his family could have touched that guitar. I am surprised we found only three sets of prints."

"I bet it was someone Tyler knew from out of town."

"Enough of all this, Jenny," Adam said. "Stop pumping me for information. I don't have anything else to tell you."

Jenny smiled coyly as she offered Adam some cookies.

"Have you worked on your guest list?"

Adam looked sheepish.

"I haven't had the time. But I think you already covered anyone I want to invite."

"How is that possible?" Jenny asked. "What about your family or friends from the military?"

"Most of my family are gone," Adam explained. "The rest are relatives of my first wife. I don't think it's appropriate to have them here for our wedding."

"And your friends?" Jenny asked.

"Some are still deployed. Some aren't around anymore."

"I'm sorry," Jenny mumbled as she worked out what Adam meant. "So it's just you and the girls and your brother?"

"We don't need too many people, Jenny," Adam said, holding her hand. "Just a few close friends and their blessings."

"What about your suit? You are not getting out of wearing a tux, mister!" Jenny said sternly. "No shorts or floral shirts."

"Why not?" Adam teased. "Aren't we getting married on the beach?"

"Don't let Heather hear you say that," Jenny warned. "And you need to ask Ethan to be your best man, unless you have someone else in mind."

Adam assured her he would get all that done. Adam wanted to get back to work. Jenny offered him the chocolates she had made earlier.

"Something for your 4 PM sugar rush," she smiled.

Jenny swung her basket from side to side as she took the scenic route back to the café. She wondered if Adam was being sufficiently enthusiastic about their wedding. How could he not have any guests of his own? Then she dismissed her thoughts as being obsessive.

Had Heather's constant nagging finally turned her into a bridezilla?

Chapter 11

A low hum of conversation rippled across the dimly lit pub. The Rusty Anchor had provided sustenance to the locals since 1879. The Cotton family and its descendants had been running it proudly since days of yore, when Pelican Cove had been Morse Isle.

Jenny and her friends had decided to gather for drinks that evening. Jason had squeezed an hour out to be with them, reluctantly letting Betty Sue and Star watch Emily.

"This is nice," Heather said, sipping a glass of wine. "I don't remember the last time we all got together like this."

Jenny stared moodily into her own glass of wine. Adam was working late again and wasn't going to join them. She tried not to be jealous of Molly and Chris, standing close together with their arms around each other. Her relationship was different and she would have to get used to it.

Eddie Cotton came over to their table with two large mugs of beer. He set them on the table and stopped to chat with them.

"You are not going to some fancy city pub for your drinks, are you? It's been a while since I set eyes on you."

"Of course not," Heather said cheerfully. "Everyone is just too busy."

She pointed toward Molly and Chris.

"These two love birds can barely spare a glance at anyone else. Jason's busy with the baby, as he should be. Jenny's swamped at the café. And I am the official wedding planner for the wedding of the year."

"What's that music you are playing, Eddie?" Jenny asked. "Sounds captivating."

"That's the poor kid who got bumped off," Eddie said.

Jenny sat up straighter.

"How do you have his music?"

"He gave it to me ... he had to cut something, he said."

"He cut a disc for you?" Heather prodded. "That was nice of him."

"Came here every night after he wound up for the day," Eddie told them. "Had a beer."

"So you knew Tyler well?" Jenny asked eagerly.

Eddie shrugged.

"We talked a bit. He was loaded, you know. He tried to hide it but I knew he came from money the moment I laid eyes on him. Drove here all the way from Richmond every day."

Jenny was surprised Eddie knew so much about Tyler's background. She wondered what else he had shared with Eddie.

"He was a shy one," Eddie said, anticipating her questions. "Sat in a corner over there and barely spoke to anyone."

"Surely the locals must have recognized him?" Jenny asked.

Eddie scratched a spot on his face and pursed his lips.

"He sat facing the wall. He made it clear he wanted to be left alone."

"How did you know who he was?" Jenny asked.

"I saw him singing in the town square, didn't I?" Eddie puffed up. "My missus heard him first. She was a big fan. She took me there to listen to this guy. Didn't believe me when I told her he had a beer at our pub every night."

The group plunged into an animated discussion about the upcoming elections.

"Peter Wilson may turn out to be a dark horse," Jason said seriously. "Nothing wrong with having someone new at the helm, of course. He will keep everyone on their toes."

"I think Barb will pack her bags and move to Florida if she doesn't win the election," Heather chortled. "She wouldn't be able to handle the shame."

As everyone in town knew, Barb Norton's daughter lived in Florida. Barb was a snowbird, spending every winter with her daughter down in the sunshine state.

"She won't give up that easily," Molly said thoughtfully. "And why should she? She has toiled hard for this town."

"So you are in Barb Norton's camp?" Jenny asked her.

Molly looked uncertain.

"I don't know, Jenny. Part of me feels I should be loyal to Barb."

"It's not a question of loyalty," Chris Williams spoke up. "It's just an election, for heaven's sake."

"You poor sod," Heather laughed. "It's never 'just' anything. I guess we were better off with that old fogey for mayor."

"Now that I don't agree with," Jason said strongly. "Anything is better than that. Both Barb and Peter seem fired up to do some work. Whoever gets elected, they will finally be taking action. We might even get parking meters on Main Street."

Heather punched Jason in the shoulder.

"No parking meters! We are not that evolved yet. Don't go spouting these crazy ideas, Jason."

"What's wrong with having parking meters?" Jason asked, rubbing his shoulder dramatically. "Ouch, Heather, you do pack a mean punch."

"Parking meters are a blot on our rustic charm," Heather stated, draining her wine.

"Stop squabbling, you two!" Molly reproached them.

She nudged Heather and tipped her head toward Jenny. Jenny was absently twirling her wine, staring in the distance.

"What's eating you, Jenny?" Molly asked solicitously. "You know you will meet Adam in a few hours, right?"

"You love birds!" Heather sighed, rolling her eyes.

"She's going to get worse," Molly said. "I bet she's dreaming about the wedding."

Heather grew alarmed when Jenny didn't call them out.

"Are you okay, Jenny?" she asked, coming around to hug her friend. "What's the matter with you?"

Jenny's eyes were bright with emotion.

"I was thinking about Tyler," she admitted. "All my efforts have been futile. I have never felt so helpless."

"You just haven't talked to the right people," Jason soothed.

"Tyler was popular, right?" Jenny said with exasperation. "He must have talked to someone other than Peter Wilson?"

Chris let out an exclamation.

"I just remembered … that kid was talking to someone in a fancy car."

"You mean like a limousine?" Jenny asked eagerly.

"Way more expensive," Chris said. "Like a Porsche or a Ferrari. Something that costs six figures."

"Which one was it exactly?" Jenny prompted.

"I couldn't say," Chris apologized. "I wasn't really paying attention. I noticed it because it was red and shiny and low slung. No one in Pelican Cove owns such a car, at least as far as I know."

"Tell me more," Jenny said urgently. "Did Tyler get into the car? Did anyone get down from it? What were they talking about?"

"How would I know, Jenny?" Chris asked. "I spotted them from a distance."

"Think harder, Chris."

Chris was shaking his head and shrugging his shoulders when he exclaimed again.

"Looked like a heated discussion. Tyler didn't look too happy."

"Are you sure you are not making this up?" Molly asked.

"To be honest, I don't remember much," Chris admitted. He looked at Jenny and winced. "Sorry, I guess?"

Jenny waved off his concern.

"Don't worry about it. How about another drink? This round's on me."

Molly and Chris stayed for a while and then said goodbye. Molly had cooked a pot roast and they were both looking forward to a cozy dinner at home.

Heather took her leave next.

"Don't worry about Emily," she told Jason. "Her Auntie Heather will look after her until you get back."

Jason had switched to water after one beer.

"I just want to talk to Jenny for a bit," he said. "I'm right behind you."

"Why don't we walk to the Bayview Inn?" Jenny suggested some time later. "We can talk on the way and I can say hello to Emily."

"What's really bothering you, Jenny?" Jason's voice was full of concern as he peered at Jenny in the dark.

The waning moon was a thin sliver and the inky sky was studded with stars. Jenny still couldn't help marveling at them. She had barely noticed them when she lived in the city. Now she reveled in the beauty that surrounded her, right from the thundering ocean right outside her house to her lush garden.

"When will you stop worrying about me, Jason?" she asked softly.

"Never," Jason declared vehemently.

He made no attempt to hide his fervor. For the first time, Jenny wondered if she had chosen the wrong man.

"Adam's a cad," Jason exclaimed, as if reading her mind. "Is he really so busy?"

"He's taking a week off after the wedding," Jenny said meekly. "We are going to drive north to Maine, to Acadia National Park. I have never been there."

"At least he's planning a honeymoon," Jason conceded.

"He can't shirk his responsibilities," Jenny said staunchly. "Being sheriff comes with its own burden."

"Speaking of which ... does he know about this man in the car?"

"Adam doesn't exactly swap notes with me, Jason. You should know that by now."

"Maybe you should tell him."

"You think this man is important? He could just have been a tourist, asking for directions."

"Don't forget the third set of prints," Jason reminded her.

"That's a long shot," Jenny said, turning around to face Jason. "And how are we ever going to locate this guy? We don't even know his name."

"I suppose you can't ask your customers if they saw a fancy red car?" Jason joked.

"If you ask me, that car is long gone. So are any tourists who might have been in town around that time."

"You're right, Jenny," Jason nodded. "I'm just grasping at straws. Ocean is still the prime suspect. Funnily enough, he doesn't seem to be too bothered about it."

They reached the Bayview Inn and Jason rushed in to gather his daughter in his arms. Jenny wanted to hold her next. She cuddled the baby and breathed in her special baby smell. Emily grabbed her hair and pulled hard.

"Stop that, Emily," Jason said in a stern voice, trying to pry her fingers apart.

"She's a feisty one," Betty Sue laughed, looking up from her knitting. "She's going to lead everyone a merry dance."

Jason put Emily in her carrier and said goodbye to the ladies.

"I didn't expect you to be here," Jenny said to her aunt.

"Betty Sue was craving my lasagna," Star explained. "So I made a pan and brought it over. We are eating here tonight. Is that okay with you, honey?"

"No complaints from me," Jenny laughed, "as long as I have a couple of slices of your special lasagna."

"You better eat up," Heather said purposefully. "We have our work cut out after that."

"More wedding chores?" Jenny groaned. "Can't we have a night off, Heather?"

"Not tonight," Heather said firmly. "We need to finalize the invitations. You need to send 'save the date' cards at the very least."

"You sound like a sadist," Jenny said viciously. "You get some perverse pleasure from all this, don't you?"

Heather's eyes filled up.

"Am I being too hard on you?"

Jenny rushed to console her friend.

"You are the best wedding planner a girl could possibly have, Heather."

"Come on, you two," Star called out. "Dinner's getting cold."

"Let's look at the designs you shortlisted after we eat," Jenny promised Heather.

Jenny pushed all thoughts of Tyler from her head and went in to have dinner with her friends.

Chapter 12

The stifling heat of the summer had finally receded. The lower humidity put a smile on everyone's face. The Magnolias sat on the deck of the Boardwalk Café, sipping iced coffee and trying out Jenny's latest batch of truffles.

"White chocolate and orange liquer," Heather moaned in pleasure. "This is my favorite so far."

Molly shook her head.

"I think orange works better with dark chocolate."

"I am making both," Jenny told them. "People either love white chocolate or don't. It's mostly butter, though. Not as healthy."

Betty Sue looked up from her knitting and peered at the beach.

"I thought I heard that woman," she muttered.

Betty Sue seemed to have a sixth sense when it came to Barb Norton. Barb and Mandy came up the beach, looking flustered.

"What's up, Barb?" Star asked. "You look like a child who's lost his favorite toy."

"Ladies," Barb said heavily, collapsing in a chair. "We have a crisis on our hands."

"Someone else is contesting the elections?" Heather asked.

"This is about the fall fest," Mandy corrected her. "You remember that 80s band that was going to headline our concert?"

The Magnolias nodded with varying degrees of interest.

"They pulled out," Mandy said grimly.

"Wait a minute," Star said. "Does Barb know about this?"

"Of course I know," Barb said. "Why do you think I'm here?"

"Why does Barb know and I don't, Mandy?" Star roared. "I am the head of the fall festival committee. Anything goes wrong with the festival, you come to me first."

Mandy stared at Star, her mouth hanging open.

"Stop acting like a child, Star," Barb snapped. "How does it matter who she goes to? She did the right thing coming to me."

"No she didn't," Star said stoutly. "You handed me the reigns of the festival committee. Or have you forgotten already?"

"Yes, yes," Barb said impatiently. "We all know who's running the show. But aren't you missing the point, Star?"

"Stop this nonsense, you two," Betty Sue spoke up. "You can figure out who comes first later. We have a problem on our hands."

"Didn't you have a contract with that group?" Heather asked Mandy. "I thought you take care of things like that."

Mandy shook her head.

"We were in the process of doing that. It appears that this band is going on tour with someone. It's a much more lucrative deal for them than a small town festival."

"So what?" Star grumbled. "They just abandoned us?"

"They have apologized," Mandy offered. "The lead singer says he is really sorry he has to pull out at short notice."

"A fat lot of good that's going to do us," Betty Sue said with a frown.

"You should have come to me first," Star said to Mandy. "Why don't I try talking to him once?"

"You think I haven't done that?" Barb asked. "It's no use. They know where the real money is. They are not coming here."

"Who asked you to butt in, Barb?" Star argued again. "Why don't you stick to the election?"

Betty Sue rapped the table with her hand.

"Stop beating a dead horse, Star, and shut up! Mandy, tell us what happens now."

"The concert is already sold out," Mandy said, reading something off her smart phone. "People from the surrounding states bought tickets because everyone wanted to hear this guy sing."

"So what now?" Molly echoed.

"We either cancel the concert and refund the tickets ..."

"Can we really do that?" Jenny asked.

"The tickets were sold online so yeah, it's possible," Mandy nodded. "But it's not desirable. It gives the festival a bad name. And it will mean we won't reach any of our fund raising goals."

"Do we have any other option?" Star asked, finally looking beyond her perceived insult.

"We need to get someone else," Mandy said with a shrug. "Someone as famous as Ace Boulevard."

"Good luck with that," Heather muttered.

"What are the chances?" Jenny asked.

"Slim," Mandy said frankly. "It's short notice and most of these singers have full calendars."

"Looks like you have your work cut out then, young lady," Betty Sue said imperiously. "Start looking for a new artist for our concert."

Everyone pitched in with suggestions about what Mandy could do next. Barb settled down a bit after sampling some of Jenny's chocolates. The two women finally left, Barb spouting a steady set of instructions and Mandy bobbing her head up and down as she noted them all down.

"The nerve of that woman," Star fumed as soon as Barb was out of earshot. "She wants it all."

"Enough already, Star," Betty Sue said. "Think about how to salvage the festival."

"What about some local band?" Jenny suggested. "I am sure they will be happy to get the exposure."

"They will," Heather said sarcastically, "but the people who bought the tickets won't. They are coming here to listen to a star, don't forget that."

Jason Stone hailed them from the boardwalk. He was hurrying along, pushing Emily's stroller.

"What's the matter, Jason?" Jenny cried when she noted his anxious expression.

"The police have arrested Ocean."

The women bombarded him with questions. Jason held up his hand.

"It's not entirely unexpected. I need to go bail him out. Can one of you look after Emily?"

"We need to prep for lunch," Star reminded Jenny.

"I can stay back and help watch the baby," Heather assured Jason.

Jason looked relieved. He promised to keep them posted and hurried off toward the police station.

"Ocean is that bearded fellow, right?" Betty Sue asked. "He sure looks like a thug."

"Looks can be deceiving, Grandma," Heather said, dangling a set of keys before Emily. "Ocean is harmless."

"I say he's a thug," Betty Sue maintained.

"We don't have a lot of suspects," Jenny mused. "Ocean is the most obvious because he had a fight with Tyler."

"But Tyler was the one who pushed Ocean, remember?" Heather said. "We saw it with our own eyes."

They went back and forth over it for a while. Molly left to go back to her desk at the library and Betty Sue went back to the inn, pleading exhaustion. Heather took the baby back into the kitchen with Jenny and Star.

Jenny added fresh pesto to rotini pasta and tossed it with some finely diced olives and peppers. Jason arrived as the lunch rush was winding down.

"They let him go for now," he said, wringing a hand through his hair. "He is going to be their top suspect until he can prove he found that guitar on the beach."

"How is he taking it?" Jenny asked.

"Ask him yourself," Jason said. "I invited him here for lunch."

Ocean arrived and sat at a table on the deck. He ate the crab sandwich Jenny placed before him with relish.

"I suppose you are sorry you ever set foot in this town," Jenny said.

"We can't predict what's around the corner," Ocean said with a shrug. "It could have happened anywhere."

"What made you come to Pelican Cove?" Heather asked. "We are so off the beaten track."

"I was driving north from Georgia," Ocean told them. "Someone mentioned this scenic route via the Chesapeake. I thought I would check it out."

"There are plenty other towns along the Eastern Shore," Jenny prompted. "Why this one?"

"Why do we do anything?" Ocean drawled. "It just happened."

"Are troubadours always confrontational?" Heather asked. "Why didn't you leave when you found Tyler was already here?"

Ocean flashed a toothy smile.

"I fell in love with this town. It's become my muse. I have written some really good songs since coming here."

"Isn't there a troubadour code?" Jason asked, drawn into the conversation. "I remember reading about it when I did some research for the case."

"It's more of a guideline," Ocean dismissed.

"That doesn't sound right," Jason said with a frown. "In fact, I distinctly remember that troubadours are like a close knit family. They look out for each other."

Heather was tapping some keys on her phone. She looked up and waited impatiently for Jason to stop talking.

"I just did some quick research," she burst out. "There's a nationwide group where you can register yourself. And there is an active database that lists who is playing in which town. A troubadour is supposed to check the status before he enters a town."

"We don't know if Tyler used that database," Jenny pointed out.

"But he did," Heather cried. "He is listed here as the official troubadour of Pelican Cove. That means no one else is allowed to play their music here."

Jenny put her hands on her hips and stared at Ocean with raised eyebrows.

"I don't follow all that crap," he muttered. "Isn't there enough external influence in our life? The government dictates how we should live and how much tax we should pay. Now some unseen, unknown group is telling me where I can play my tunes?"

"So you knew you were barging in on Tyler's territory," Jenny summed up. "You just didn't care."

Ocean gave one of his habitual shrugs.

"Tyler didn't need the money. He had a big trust fund to fall back on. Unlike the rest of us."

"How do you know about Tyler's trust fund?" Jenny asked suddenly.

She thought hard, trying to remember. Had they discussed Tyler's background with Ocean?

Ocean struggled to his feet.

"I need to make a move. Already lost a few good hours of work today."

"You are hiding something," Heather said suddenly. "How did you know how rich Tyler was?"

"Can't say," he said, scratching his beard. "Must have heard it somewhere."

"I advise you to come clean, man," Jason said, speaking softly for Emily's sake.

She had fallen asleep after he fed and burped her.

"I am beginning to think you knew Tyler before coming here," Jenny said, taking a shot in the dark. "Admit it."

"No, I didn't," Ocean said.

"You are not telling us the whole truth," Jenny insisted. "How did you know Tyler came from a rich family?"

"Jenny will find out sooner or later," Heather warned. "She is good at ferreting out secrets."

"What happens when the police find out?" Jason asked Ocean. "You will be in more trouble than you are now. I need to know the truth if I am to defend you."

"Okay, okay," Ocean said, holding up his hands. "Give me a minute."

Ocean scratched his head and stared out at the waves for some time. He gave a deep sigh and started talking.

"I was paid to come here," he began.

"What?" Jenny and Heather echoed.

"I was playing my music in the Shenandoah valley when this rich dude came up to me. He placed a big bundle of cash in my hand."

"What did he want?" Jenny asked.

"Who was he?" Heather asked at the same time.

"This man said he was Tyler's uncle. Apparently, Tyler was supposed to run a fancy business. This dude didn't want him playing his guitar on the street."

"Did he ask you to harm Tyler?" Jenny narrowed her eyes.

"Not exactly," Ocean said with a shake of his head. "I was supposed to come here and make life hell for him."

"Did he say why?" Jason asked.

"Guess he wanted Tyler to give up this gig and go home."

"And you thought you could make him leave?"

"I thought it was a piece of cake," Ocean said. "I reckoned all I had to do was dog his steps. It was easy too. Turned out he had a really short temper. I thought he would pack up his guitar and hit the road."

"But he didn't leave, did he?" Jenny asked.

"No," Ocean nodded. "The kid had spunk."

"How far were you willing to go, Ocean?" Heather asked. "Did you sell your soul for a bit of money?"

Ocean looked disturbed.

"I just wanted the kid to go home. I didn't harm a hair on his head, honest."

Chapter 13

It was another busy day at the Boardwalk Café. Jenny had flipped dozens of blueberry pancakes, the special of the day. The parfaits were almost gone and she had run through four trays of banana nut muffins. Jenny was glad breakfast was almost over.

Heather came bouncing in, her face red with excitement. Jenny could tell she was bursting to share some news.

"Good Morning," Jenny greeted her with a smile. "What's got you all hot and bothered, my friend?"

"You'll never guess who just checked into the Bayview Inn," Heather beamed.

She grabbed Jenny by the arms and spun her around in a circle.

"Who?" Jenny asked, playing along.

"Bobby Joe Tucker!" Heather exclaimed.

Her eyes widened as she waited for Jenny to respond suitably.

"Should that name mean something to me?" Jenny asked drily.

"You have never heard of Bobby Joe Tucker?" Heather sucked in a breath as she stared at Jenny in disbelief. "Have you been living under a rock?"

"Apparently," Jenny laughed. "So who is this guy? Some old flame?"

"I wish," Heather sighed. "Bobby Joe is a top country singer. His latest single 'You are my everything' is top of the charts."

"I didn't know you were a country music fan."

"I'm not. I mean, not really. But I do know the latest hits."

"Is he from around here?" Jenny asked Heather.

"He's not," Heather confirmed. "What's he doing out here in the boonies?"

"Why don't you ask him?" Jenny suggested.

Heather couldn't get over her shock. She sat in a kitchen chair and went over different scenarios. She couldn't believe a big music star had checked into her inn.

"Shouldn't you be at the inn, making sure he's taken care of?" Jenny asked.

"He went out," Heather told her. "He's got this big RV. It's like a tour bus. He's in there working."

The Magnolias arrived for their daily coffee break. Heather repeated everything she had told Jenny.

"I don't like the look of him," Betty Sue said suspiciously. "He better not steal our towels."

"Come on Grandma!" Heather said, scandalized. "He sold a million records just last month. He doesn't care for our towels."

"You never know," Betty Sue said staunchly. "He's not an islander after all."

Heather looked irritated.

"Most of the people who come to our inn aren't," she told Betty Sue.

"And they steal stuff," Betty Sue said triumphantly. "Don't they? Didn't we just replace a dozen towels and five bath robes?"

Heather opened her mouth to object. Jenny stepped in to calm them down.

"Let it go, you two. How long is this illustrious guest staying in town?"

Heather's face lit up again.

"He's paid a big advance. He should be here for a couple of weeks at least. Why?"

"Just a thought," Jenny said. "Do you think he will sing at our fall festival?"

Jenny's question created an uproar. Everyone started talking at once. Star wanted to go and talk to him at once.

"Isn't the Pelican Cove fall fest too low key for this guy?" Molly provided a practical opinion.

"Fall festival is a month away," Betty Sue said. "Surely he won't stay with us that long."

"How much will he charge?" Jenny asked. "Can we afford to hire him?"

"All of these are good questions," Heather said. "We need to come up with a solid plan before we approach him. I think we need Mandy's help."

"What does she know that we don't?" Star asked.

She was still holding a grudge against Mandy.

"Mandy's good at her job," Jenny reasoned. "She is used to dealing with celebrities. She will know how to approach this Bobby Joe."

"What's this country music star doing in Pelican Cove?" Molly asked.

"I think he needs a break. This is the best place for someone who wants to fly below the radar."

"I'm tired of talking about this boy," Betty Sue said, pulling out her knitting from a tote bag. "And I'm hungry."

Jenny took the hint and went in to get some fresh muffins.

"When are we going to the city, Jenny?" Heather asked. "I thought you wanted to leave early."

Jenny had received another call from Mr. Jones in Richmond. He wanted to meet her.

"You can leave now," Star told them. "Lunch is caprese sandwiches. I can easily make them."

Jenny made sure her aunt had everything she needed. She packed some lunch for herself and Heather and they set off for Richmond. It was a good two hour drive.

The butler ushered them into the parlor. Mr. Jones was waiting for them this time. He looked pale and had a racking cough.

"Are you sick, Mr. Jones?" Jenny asked with concern.

"Don't worry, gel," he croaked. "I'm not dying anytime soon."

Jenny couldn't figure out if he was irritated or being humorous. Mr. Jones asked about the progress Jenny had made.

"I seem to have hit a wall," Jenny admitted.

She told the old man about the two suspects.

"But you don't think much about them, eh?" the old man asked shrewdly.

"I do believe they are both innocent," Jenny admitted. "But that leaves us with no suspects."

The old man cleared his throat.

"What do you think of my son?" he asked bluntly.

Jenny hesitated.

"I haven't really met him, Mr. Jones. What possible motive could he have to harm Tyler?"

The old man was quiet. Jenny gave him some time and then spoke up tentatively.

"How is he situated financially?"

"My son is a very wealthy man," Mr. Jones said. "So is my grandson."

"And he gets even more money now that Tyler is gone?"

"He does," the old man nodded. "My son believed he was entitled to that money."

Jenny sensed there was more to the story. She sat back in her chair and waited for Mr. Jones to continue.

"Tyler …" the old man began. "Tyler was the apple of my eye."

His rheumy eyes filled up as he spoke about his grandson.

"He was a good person, a better person than my son."

Heather nudged Jenny and pulled a face. Was the old man just rambling or did his talk have a purpose? Jenny gave Heather a stare, silently warning her to be quiet.

"I loved Tyler very much," the old man continued. "That didn't sit too well with my son."

He looked up at Jenny and she sensed he was about to say something important.

"You see, Ms. King. Tyler was adopted."

Jenny let out a gasp. She hadn't seen that coming.

"I still remember the day his parents brought him home," the old man reminisced. "He was barely a month old. He was a Jones from that moment on."

"Was he related to you?" Jenny asked.

She wondered if Tyler had been adopted from a poor relative.

"No idea where he came from," Mr. Jones said. "It was a closed adoption. My son, Tyler's uncle, was against it at the time."

"How did he treat Tyler?"

"He rallied around," the old man told them. "Tyler was such a sweet kid. He looked up to his uncle, especially after his parents died."

"What changed?" Jenny asked.

"It was the music," Mr. Jones said with a sigh. "Tyler was supposed to start learning the business. But he seemed more interested in writing songs. My son thought it was a waste of time."

"Tyler could have written his music in his spare time," Jenny mused. "Surely he was brought up with certain expectations?"

"He was," the old man agreed. "Tyler was groomed to be at the helm of a bunch of companies."

The old man's gaze hardened.

"Tyler was doing fine until he found out he was adopted."

"You had never told him?"

"His parents might have at some point. But he was just a child when they died. I guess it was my job to tell him when he grew up. But I decided not to. Still don't know how he found out."

Jenny thought it was kind of obvious but she didn't say anything.

"He took it hard?" Jenny guessed.

The old man's voice shook as he replied to Jenny.

"He started behaving erratically. He stopped going in to work. I think he must have latched on to this troubadour business around that time."

"Your son didn't like that, I guess?"

"They had a big fight," the old man said. "My son warned Tyler to clean up his act."

Jenny leaned forward and patted the old man's knee.

"What are you afraid of, Mr. Jones?"

"He wouldn't … he wouldn't do something drastic, would he? He can't be that heartless."

"I don't think so," Jenny soothed.

She told him what she had learned from Ocean. It seemed like Tyler's uncle just wanted him to come back home.

"That does seem more plausible," Mr. Jones said, sounding relieved. "Sounds like something he would do. Throw money at a problem and expect it to go away."

Jenny wasn't taking any chances. She asked Mr. Jones if she could look around a bit. She pointed her phone toward some photos on the mantel and started clicking pictures. She did the same thing with a couple of cars parked outside.

"What are you doing, Jenny?" Heather whispered. "I thought you agreed the uncle was innocent."

"I'm just making sure," Jenny said softly. "I will explain later."

Mr. Jones was talking to his son when they went back in. He gave Jenny and Heather a withering look.

"Are you here to poison the old man against me?"

Jenny decided to beard the lion in his den.

"You have made it clear you didn't like Tyler."

"I didn't like how he was throwing away his life. He was going to be twenty five soon. He needed to get his act together and start acting responsibly."

"That's all?"

"Believe it or not, yes," the man thundered. "If you think otherwise, prove it."

"I am working on that," Jenny said boldly.

"You are on the wrong track," he said, his voice full of scorn. "Obviously, you have nothing better to do. Tell me, how much is my father paying you? I will pay you triple to stop nosing around."

"You fool!" Old Mr. Jones roared. "Everything can't be measured in money. Ms. King has very kindly agreed to help us. She isn't taking a cent from me."

"Don't be naïve, Dad. Someone else must be paying her. Some trashy tabloid, probably."

Jenny tried to curb the anger she felt. She decided to exit gracefully. She said goodbye to Mr. Jones and promised to stay in touch. She walked out with Heather following close behind.

"That was intense," Heather gushed as Jenny drove her car out of the massive iron gates. "Were you provoking him on purpose?"

Jenny cracked a smile and shrugged.

"Where to?" she asked Heather.

"You still haven't chosen your wedding dress," Heather reminded her dourly. "Why don't we check out a few bridal stores while we are here? I have a list with me."

"Molly's not with us again," Jenny reminded her.

"I know," Heather grimaced. "But do you want to waste this opportunity?"

"I still think we should look closer to home," Jenny said. "Coming to Richmond for fittings sounds like a chore."

"Why don't you choose something first?" Heather sighed. "We can figure out the rest later."

"What about your dress?" Jenny asked. "You can choose any style you want. No hideous bridesmaid dresses at my wedding."

"We already thought about it," Heather smirked. "We are going with fall colors. We are all wearing shades of yellow, orange or russet."

"That sounds beautiful," Jenny said, her eyes filling up.

"Don't you get maudlin now, Jenny King!" Heather warned. "We are just getting started on our wedding chores."

Chapter 14

The town square was jammed with people. Tourists mingled with locals, looking on with interest as volunteers set up a makeshift stage. It was the day of the debate. Peter Wilson had challenged Barb Norton for the first public debate before the election and she had no choice but to accept.

Supporters on both sides had plastered the town with flyers advertising the event. Everyone was invited. No one would have dreamed of missing it.

People sat on camp chairs with coolers by their side, ready to enjoy a good show. Some people had brought picnic hampers and reclined on blankets. Kids scurried about, chasing each other and screaming their heads off.

Jenny had her own agenda for the debate.

The Magnolias had set up their chairs in two semi-circles. Betty Sue and Star sat at either end. Heather and Jenny sat in between. Molly sat in the second row with Chris. The other two spots were reserved for Jason and Adam. Adam was on duty, keeping the crowd in check. Heather had made gallons of popcorn. Jenny had brought her latest batch of truffles and Molly had brought brownies. They were all set to listen to arguments from both sides. Star was confident Barb would win. Betty Sue was the only one who supported Peter Wilson.

A lot of locals stopped by them to greet the ladies. Jenny had her phone out. She flipped through the screen and showed them the photos she had taken at the Jones residence.

"Do any of these people look familiar?" she asked. "What about these cars?"

Most people barely glanced at the screen before shaking their heads. Others peered at the screen ghoulishly and reluctantly gave it back.

"You really think you can catch a murderer that way?" Star asked skeptically.

"I just want to find out if one of them came to town."

"What if they did?" Molly asked. "That doesn't prove anything."

Jenny didn't have an answer for that. She admitted to herself that she was just grasping at straws.

Captain Charlie came and sat with the women. Betty Sue started talking to the old salt.

"Do you agree we don't need more tourists in town?"

Captain Charlie ran fishing tours. His business depended on the tourists.

"I wouldn't say that exactly," he said, stroking his beard. "This town as good as runs on tourists, you know."

"But what about all the mess they create?" Betty Sue cried. "Look around you. The town's never been this dirty."

"We need more people on cleaning duty then," Captain Charlie said with a shrug.

He looked at Jenny for support. Jenny thrust her phone in his face.

"Can you take a look at this?" she asked. "Anyone look familiar?"

Captain Charlie scrolled through all the photos patiently before shaking his head.

"You better eat some of this popcorn, Jenny," Heather said, her fingers smeared with butter. "It's almost gone."

"She's right," Chris said, licking his fingers.

Jenny could barely think of food.

She started working the crowd, showing the photos to random people, urging people to look carefully as her frustration rose.

Someone grabbed her arm and pulled her aside. She whirled around to complain and found herself staring into a familiar pair of blue eyes.

"Adam!" she breathed. "It's you."

She put her arms around his neck and leaned in for a kiss. Adam jerked back and flung her hands away.

"Not here, Jenny. I am working."

Jenny's face fell as she tried to hide her disappointment.

"We saved a seat for you," she told him. "You can't miss us. Almost everyone's there except Jason and Emily. But they will be along soon."

"What do you think you are doing, Jenny?" Adam asked angrily. "People are beginning to complain."

"I have some pictures of Tyler's family," she began to explain. "I just want to know if anyone saw them in town."

"I don't care," Adam snapped. "I am warning you, Jenny. Stop this nonsense right now."

"Nonsense?" Jenny asked, placing her hands on her hips.

"I don't have time to argue with you," Adam said, starting to walk away. "Stop harassing people or I will have to take you in."

"You can't do that," Jenny challenged.

"I can and I will," Adam said, sounding exasperated. "Don't test my patience, Jenny. I won't be able to do you any favors. You are being a nuisance."

Adam turned his back on her and walked away. Jenny's eyes filled up as she stared at him. Why couldn't he cut her some slack? Then she remembered how Adam preferred to keep his professional life separate from his private one. She forced herself to admire his integrity.

"You look like someone slapped you," Star commented as soon as she spotted Jenny.

"Adam must have said something," Heather piped up. "He can be so nasty."

Jason had arrived with Emily. She sat in her stroller, dressed in a cheery yellow frock and stared around her with interest. Jason's nose twitched in annoyance as he looked at Jenny.

"What is it? What grave crime are you supposed to have committed this time?"

"Forget it," Jenny said feebly. "It's nothing."

"Why don't you eat something?" Molly coaxed. "Jason brought pizza."

Jenny forced herself to eat a slice and immediately felt better.

Eddie Cotton from the pub joined them. He sat with Betty Sue and

Star, arguing about whether Pelican Cove needed tourists or not.

"I thought you would be at the pub," Star said.

"Most of the people are here," he said. "I thought I would stretch my legs. I wanted to put up a beer stand but Barb said no."

Jenny flipped through her phone again, moodily staring at her pictures.

"What's that you have there, Jenny?" Eddie asked.

Jenny handed over her phone to him.

Eddie scrolled through the photos half heartedly, continuing an impassioned dialog with Betty Sue and Star. A few moments later, he let out a sudden exclamation.

"I know him," he said, jabbing his finger at the screen. "I bet he has been to the Rusty Anchor a couple of times."

Jenny realized he was pointing at a picture of Billy Jones, Tyler's cousin.

"Tell me more," she pressed. "Was he alone? Was he talking to someone?"

"I don't remember that much," Eddie said, handing the phone back to her. "At least not now. Maybe it will come to me."

"Please try to remember," Jenny urged him. "This may be important."

"Okay, missy," Eddie nodded. "Give me some time."

The loudspeaker crackled as Mandy came on stage and began testing the microphone. Both the candidates climbed up on stage and greeted the crowd. A wild cry went up. Both Peter Wilson and Barb Norton had worked hard for the debate. Jenny forgot everything else as she listened to them in rapt attention. Questions flew from the crowd and both candidates handled them deftly. The debate ended in a tie.

"That went better than I expected," Star said as Jenny drove them home. "I never expected Peter would speak so well. Not with his background."

"He did seem prepared," Jenny admitted grudgingly. "And sounds like he is passionate about the cause too."

"He can't really be against tourism though, can he?" Star quizzed. "He is a business owner too."

"Most of his customers are locals," Jenny explained. "How many tourists are going to get an oil change at his garage?"

Back home, Star set up her easel in the garden. Jenny decided to take a nap.

Two hours later, Jenny woke up refreshed. She fired off a text to Adam and confirmed that he was coming for dinner. She decided to make her special paella.

"You can win any man's heart with your cooking, Jenny," Star offered as she chopped vegetables. "But not Adam's. He's a tough one."

"I already have his heart," Jenny said smugly.

"Doesn't look like it," Star muttered.

She had never hidden the fact that she wasn't a big fan of Adam. Jenny worried about their living situation after she got married. She had invited her aunt to make her home with her at Seaview. But would Adam and Star get along?

Adam arrived with a bottle of Jenny's favorite wine and a bunch of daisies. Jenny melted as soon as she saw the look on his face.

Star pleaded exhaustion and decided to eat in her room.

Jenny and Adam sat out on the patio, sipping wine and watching the sun creep closer to the horizon. The sky was aflame in shades of orange interspersed with pink and purple. The water glistened in the rays of the setting sun.

"Did your hunting expedition yield anything?" Adam asked.

Jenny felt Adam was taunting her. She decided to say nothing about Eddie.

"You were right, Adam. I shouldn't have bothered those people."

"You have been an invaluable help to the police many times, Jenny. I will be the first one to admit that. But I think you are stumbling in the dark this time."

"There does seem to be a dearth of suspects," Jenny said glumly.

"I say we have the right suspect," Adam argued. "My money is still on that Ocean chap."

"You don't have any concrete evidence," Jenny reminded him.

"I still believe he is guilty," Adam insisted. "I won't rest until I put him away."

"What about motive?" Jenny questioned. "Ocean is an easygoing chap. What could he possibly have against Tyler?"

"He was jealous," Adam said. "He just wanted to eliminate the competition. Men have been killed for less."

"Peter Wilson should be top on your list in that case," Jenny pointed out. "He was spitting mad at Tyler. He even threatened him."

"I don't think Peter did it."

"You are willing to ignore his past record?" Jenny wondered. "Why, Adam?"

"Peter Wilson has been an exemplary citizen of this town for the past twenty five years. This Ocean chap is an outsider."

"Is that all?"

"Give me some credit," Adam sighed. "We ran a background check on Ocean. His movements are highly suspicious. He has been in regions where there were break-ins and robberies. One of the towns he was in had a fire just the night before he left town."

"You are saying he committed all those crimes?" Jenny asked with contempt. "You are just determined to pin something on him."

"I have my reasons, Jenny."

Ocean's serene face swam before Jenny's eyes. She couldn't believe Adam wanted to pin a litany of crimes on him.

"I think you are on a witch hunt."

"I'm just doing my job, Jenny," Adam said grimly.

Jenny forced herself to change the subject. She didn't want to end the evening on a sour note.

"How are the girls? Nicky said they should all be here in a couple of weeks."

Adam's girls were doing a summer internship in the city. So was Jenny's son Nick. Much to their relief, Jenny and Adam's kids were good friends. They were looking forward to spending a few days in Pelican Cove before going back to college in the fall.

Adam relaxed at the mention of his girls.

"Have you asked them yet?"

"I want to talk to them in person," Jenny told him. "I hope they will say yes."

"Of course they will say yes. It's all they have been talking about all summer."

Adam's phone trilled just then, making him frown. He answered gruffly and his mouth hung open as he listened to the voice at the other end.

Jenny leaned forward, waiting for Adam to speak. Adam looked very upset as he stared at Jenny.

"You were right about Ocean."

Chapter 15

The Magnolias chatted at the top of their voices, guzzling coffee and commenting on the tourists that lined the beach. Jenny felt she was the only one affected by Ocean's death. Murder, she corrected herself.

They had found Ocean's body on a deserted beach. Based on initial examination, the police were thinking he had walked into the sea and drowned. He had luckily been washed ashore. Jenny wasn't sure she believed that.

She felt Heather staring at her and snapped to attention.

"Did you say anything, Heather?"

Heather rolled her eyes.

"I have been asking you the same question three times. Have you heard 'You are my everything'?"

"Is that supposed to mean something to me?"

"It's only the name of Bobby Joe's hit single," Heather gushed. "It hit the top spot last night."

"Oh," Jenny muttered. "I don't listen to country music."

"You have to give it a chance," Heather insisted. "Especially since Bobby Joe is staying right here with us."

"That does it," Star said. "He's not going to sing for us now. He's too famous."

"You haven't even asked him yet!" Heather cried. "He has a big fan base here. Why would he refuse?"

"Let's go ask him now," Betty Sue said, struggling to her feet.

"Yes, let's," Star said, scrambling up. "I want to get this done before that maniac Barb Norton thinks about it."

"Too late," Molly said, nodding at the boardwalk.

Barb Norton and Mandy were walking toward the café.

"Yoohooo!" Barb called out her usual greeting. "Going somewhere?"

"No time to waste, Barb," Star quipped. "We are on an important mission."

"Never mind, then. I thought you would want to go with us. Mandy and I are going to invite Bobby Joe Tucker to play at the fall festival."

"That's where we are going," Betty Sue objected. "No need to waste your time, Barb. Go talk to your voters."

"The voters can wait," Barb said lightly. "This is more important."

Then she giggled like a school girl.

"Mandy says this boy is quite the looker. I can't wait to see him."

"Have you ever heard him sing?" Heather asked skeptically. "Do you even know what kind of music he plays?"

"Of course I do," Barb said in a huff. "It's country with a pop influence. Mandy played his hit single for me. I have been humming it all morning."

"That's more than I can say for my grandma," Heather said grudgingly.

"Who cares if we know his music or not?" Betty Sue spat. "We want to go and talk to him. He is living in my house so there is no doubt I am going."

"Let's all go," Mandy said, trying to placate the older women. "We will look like a delegation and he will feel more welcome."

Betty Sue and Star joined Barb and Mandy, talking eagerly about how to approach him.

"This is going to be the best fall festival yet," Heather sighed dramatically. "Just imagine! Bobby Joe Tucker playing in tiny old Pelican Cove!"

"He hasn't said yes yet," Jenny pointed out. "I imagine he will charge a pretty penny."

"I didn't think of that," Heather admitted. "I thought he would just sing for the sake of his fans."

"That's not how these stars function," Molly said practically. "They have to make a living too, I guess. What's he doing in Pelican Cove though?"

"Living off the grid," Heather parroted. "That's what he calls it."

"I'm going to the Rusty Anchor this evening," Jenny told them. "I need to talk to Eddie Cotton. You girls coming?"

Heather and Molly promised to meet Jenny later at the pub.

Jenny got busy prepping for lunch. She made a pot full of watermelon gazpacho. The cold Spanish style soup was a summer favorite. Jenny had chucked in some leftover watermelon in it once and it had been a huge hit.

Star came back just in time to help her serve some lunch. She wasn't looking too happy.

"What's the matter? Didn't you get to meet that singer guy?"

"I met him alright," Star grumbled. "But he's beyond our reach. There's no way we can afford to hire him."

"Didn't you ask him to give us a discount?" Jenny asked later when they sat down for their own lunch.

Star bit into her crab salad sandwich and shook her head.

"He's taking a big chunk off his usual rate, apparently. He said he wants to do something for the people of Pelican Cove. But it's still more than our budget."

"Guess we will have to hire some other band," Jenny said. Her eyes flickered with emotion. "Ocean would have done it for free."

Star helped Jenny clear up and prep for the next day. Jenny drove home with her. She had a couple of hours before she had to be at the pub. She decided to relax in her garden until then. Jenny changed into a pair of shorts and a bikini top and settled into a cabana she had installed in her garden. Putting her arms below her head, she stared out at the ocean. She started to get hot after some time and walked into the water for a quick dip. She almost forgot she needed to go out again.

The Rusty Anchor was packed when she got there. Every table was taken and there was barely a space open to stand at the bar. Eddie Cotton pointed at a battered door. She had never noticed it before.

"It's a little hidey hole for my special people," he told her. "The pub gets too crowded in the season."

Jenny entered a small, darkened room, barely lit by an ancient bronze chandelier. Heather and Molly were seated at a table under it. They both had a glass of wine before them.

"I'll come back and check on you soon," Eddie promised.

Jenny chatted with the girls half-heartedly, waiting for Eddie to come back. He arrived with a platter of chicken wings Heather had ordered earlier.

"Do you remember the photos I was showing you?" Jenny asked him. "You said one of them looked familiar. What can you tell me about him?"

"You mean that chubby kid with a paunch? He came here a lot a few weeks ago."

"Do you remember who he talked to?"

"Was a bit of a weirdo, if you ask me. Picked a few fights over nothin'. Had to warn him to lighten up."

"Is that all?" Jenny pressed.

Eddie's face cleared as he remembered something.

"Now that you mention it – I saw him talking to that troubadour a couple of times."

"Did you hear what they were talking about?"

Eddie hesitated.

"I wasn't paying attention. I can't be too sure but I think they were arguing about something."

Jenny wondered why Tyler's cousin had come all the way to Pelican Cove to pick a fight with him.

"Do you know what Tyler did after he left the pub every night?"

"Drove home to Richmond," Eddie said.

"Are you sure?" Jenny asked.

"100%. Talked about what a pain it was driving a couple of hours each way."

Jenny was stumped. If Tyler had gone home every day, Billy could have easily met him at home. What had he been up to? Had Tyler been in on it?

"Gotta go," Eddie said before rushing to take care of someone else.

"What's this, Jenny?" Heather pouted. "I thought we were having a girls' night."

Jenny devoted herself to her girlfriends after that. Heather was lamenting the lack of eligible men in Pelican Cove.

"Adam and Chris were the only handsome hunks and you both grabbed them," Heather said, her tongue loose after her second glass of wine.

"What about Jason?" Jenny asked. "He is as eligible as they come."

"Ewww …" Heather cried. "Jason is like a brother to me."

"What about Ethan?" Molly asked, referring to Adam's brother. "Didn't he just break up with his girl?"

Ethan Hopkins was a divorcee with no kids. He had been dating someone for the past few years. They had recently had a very public breakup when the girl left him for someone living in the city.

"Ethan's still licking his wounds," Heather clucked. "And I have a feeling those two aren't done yet. City life is not for everyone."

"He can still be your date for the wedding," Jenny offered. "He is the best man and you are my maid of honor."

"I don't know, Jenny," Heather slurred. "Those Hopkins boys are trouble."

"Do you have any other date for Jenny's wedding?" Molly asked.

"Why can't I go alone?" Heather challenged. "I am a modern independent woman. I don't need a man to hold my hand."

"Bravo!" Jenny clapped her hands. "That's the kind of spirit I like."

"Speaking of the wedding," Molly said. "We still need to talk about flowers. Do you have a city florist in mind?"

"We don't need a florist, Molly," Jenny deadpanned. "I want flowers from my garden. My very own roses and gardenias. I can't imagine any other bouquet for the wedding."

"If you insist," Molly said. "I guess that's one more item we can check off the list."

"Please tell me you are not baking your own cake," Heather said drily.

"I want to," Jenny confessed. "But I am not sure if I will have the time."

"I know a very good bakery in Virginia Beach," Molly told them. "Please order your cake from them, Jenny. They are really good."

"You are skimping on almost everything," Heather pointed out. "Barbecue instead of caterers, flowers from your own garden … splurge on the cake. Order a lavish four tiered thing. You deserve it."

"I will set up an appointment for us," Molly said before Jenny could object. "We need to go cake tasting."

Jenny and the girls lingered at the pub for a couple of hours. Jenny was ready to call it a night by the time she got home. A bank of clouds had crept up the horizon, shadowing the moon. She spotted a familiar figure on the beach as she parked her car. A large furry body came bounding up as soon as she stepped down. Jenny hugged the yellow Labrador and scratched him below the ears.

"Tank! I missed you!"

Tank had been with Adam through thick and thin. Jenny was besotted with him. He had been staying with Adam's brother for the past few weeks, keeping him company while he mooned over his lost love. Jenny had missed spending time with him.

Adam walked up to Jenny. He was using his cane again. Jenny wanted to ask if his leg was hurting badly but she forced herself to stay quiet.

"Looks like you had a wild time."

His tone was clipped and Jenny decided he was definitely in pain. She wondered if he would give in and take a pain pill.

"It was just Heather and Molly," she said with a shrug. "You coming in?"

Adam shook his head.

"Tank and I need to get back. I have to get up early. I am going to the city."

"Is everything alright?" Jenny asked, picking up on the tension.

Was Adam jealous of the time she had spent with the girls? They would need to have a talk about it again. She wasn't ready to be shackled down in any way just because she was getting married to him.

Adam swallowed and sighed deeply.

"It's official. Ocean was murdered. The news has already leaked out. I thought I would tell you myself."

"I knew it!" Jenny crowed. "So he didn't just drown?"

Adam shook his head.

"According to the autopsy report, Ocean was strangled."

Chapter 16

Jenny wasn't having a good day. She had barely slept, thoughts of Ocean's last moments keeping her awake. When she did manage to fall asleep toward dawn, she had nightmares. She woke up drenched in sweat, shaking in fear at some unknown assailant who had been about to choke her.

She had overslept after that and hadn't reached the café until 6 AM. That meant breakfast had been late. She had to send Captain Charlie away without his muffin.

Star had been on the phone for twenty minutes. Jenny felt her irritation rise. She tried to tune out the one sided conversation and focused on making her stuffed French Toast. Loaded with fresh strawberries, it was a summer favorite at the Boardwalk Café.

Star gave a whoop and finally hung up.

"Guess what?" she crowed, clapping her hands.

"Why don't you just tell me?" Jenny asked crankily.

"Someone woke up on the wrong side of bed today," Star said with a smile.

"Star ..." Jenny groaned.

"Okay, okay. You will never believe what just happened. The town has agreed to pay that Bobby Joe person. We have one hot concert coming up, Jenny Right here too, in Pelican Cove."

"I thought we couldn't afford him?" Jenny quizzed.

"You know how Barb is when she wants something. She called a meeting of the town council. They just voted to cough up the money."

"Where is this money coming from?" Jenny asked, sprinkling powdered sugar over a plate of toast.

"From the reserves," Star explained. "This is historic, Jenny. The town has never dipped in the reserves. The reserves are sacred."

"What's so special about this guy then?" Jenny asked with a grimace.

"His song is number one in the country, Jenny. And he is willing to perform it live for the first time. Right here on our beach."

"He better be worth it," Jenny muttered.

"Aren't you going to Richmond today?" Star asked.

Jenny nodded.

"I was planning to go after lunch. We are going to be super busy, judging by the breakfast crowd."

Jenny's prediction proved to be right. She made dozens of sandwiches and salads while Star ladled endless bowls of seafood chowder. Both women were exhausted.

Jenny put her feet up on a chair as she wolfed down her own sandwich.

"Look at those cracked heels," Star clucked as she stared at Jenny's feet. "How many times should I tell you, Jenny. You are going to be a bride. You need to take better care of yourself."

"Maybe we should have a spa night," Jenny said grudgingly.

"I have a better idea," Star said. "Let's all go to that day spa in Cape Charles. We need to do a test run before your wedding anyway. We can book all your bridal treatments there if you like the place."

"Sounds pricey." Jenny made a face.

"It's your wedding," Star said. "You can afford to spend a bit."

"Whatever you say, Aunt," Jenny sighed. "I wonder what's keeping Heather."

"I'm right here," Heather said, sweeping in.

She was grinning from ear to ear.

"Bobby Joe came out of his room to get coffee. I said hello to him and he said hello back."

"Shouldn't he?" Jenny asked.

"Oh Jenny! You don't get it. Bobby Joe Tucker spoke to me! It was my big fan girl moment."

"You sound as mad as the rest of the town," Jenny said. "They are going to shell out the big bucks needed for his gig."

"I know!" Heather beamed. "We are going to be famous. People are already asking each other where this island is where Bobby Joe Tucker is hiding out at."

"Shouldn't you get going?" Star reminded them.

Jenny took off her apron and freshened up a bit. She asked Heather to drive, pleading exhaustion.

Heather kept up a monologue all the way to Richmond. Jenny napped fitfully, barely hearing anything Heather said. Two hours later, Heather wove her way through downtown traffic to the more upscale River Road area.

The Jones residence loomed over them, reminding Jenny once again of Tyler's exclusive background. The butler greeted them with a smile.

"Mr. Jones will be happy to see you."

"Actually, we were hoping to talk to Tyler's cousin."

"Master Billy is a bit indisposed," the butler said, clearing his throat.

"This could be important," Jenny told him.

"I will see what I can do," the butler promised.

Jenny had remembered to bring a big box of her truffles for Mr. Jones. She hoped he liked chocolates.

Billy Jones waddled in fifteen minutes later, looking like he had just got out of bed. He looked freshly showered but his eyes were bloodshot and his mouth was set in a frown.

"What do you want from me?" he grumbled.

"We need your help," Jenny began. "I hope you don't mind answering a few questions."

Billy spotted the box of chocolates and tore it open. He popped a couple of truffles in his mouth and chewed noisily.

"This is good stuff," Billy spoke, his teeth smeared with chocolate. "I don't suppose you get these in that hick town of yours?"

"Jenny made them herself," Heather said curtly.

"You don't like Pelican Cove?" Jenny asked Billy.

"Never been there," he drawled. "Tyler was crazy about that place though."

"We know you visited the Rusty Anchor a few times," Jenny said to him. "The bartender recognized you."

"Why would you lie about going to Pelican Cove?" Heather asked.

"I don't want my Dad to find out," Billy said, looking over his shoulder.

"We won't tell him anything," Jenny promised. "Will you talk to us?"

Billy pulled his shirt down over his ample belly and frowned. He gave them a brief nod as his mouth settled into a pout.

"Okay."

"What were you doing in Pelican Cove?" Jenny asked a straightforward question.

"Tyler and I grew up together, in this house," Billy told them. "I am a lot older than him but we were buddies while growing up. Very few kids in class were as rich as us. We got kind of isolated."

Jenny and Heather got caught up in Billy's story.

"What I'm saying is, I was used to looking out for Tyler. He told me everything he did. He wanted to write music for the rest of his life. My dad didn't want that, of course. When Tyler found this little island in the middle of nowhere, he was excited. He said they would let him play his songs all day long. He was happy."

"Based on what we learned, your father found out about it," Jenny told him.

"That was my fault," Billy admitted. "I let it slip. I went there to warn Tyler about it."

"What were you afraid of?"

"My father has a lot of influence," Billy said. "He would have made sure Tyler packed up his guitar and came home. I just wanted to give Tyler a heads up. We did that for each other all the time."

"Was Tyler going to come home with you?"

Billy shook his head.

"He was really fired up this time. He said people loved his music. He asked me to book a recording studio here in town. He was going to go all out with his song."

"Eddie at the pub told us that Tyler drove home every night?" Jenny asked.

"That's right," Billy laughed. "He tried roughing it out for a couple of nights. Get the authentic experience. But he wasn't cut out for it. Said he could bear standing in the sun all day but he needed his feather bed at night and fresh squeezed orange juice in the morning."

"So why did you go to the Rusty Anchor to talk to him?" Jenny asked. "You could have talked to him right here?"

"I wanted to see what the fuss was about."

"Surely you had heard him sing before?" Heather asked.

Billy's manner changed abruptly.

"I don't have to explain myself to you."

"Did you need a change of scene?" Jenny asked diplomatically.

"Hey, it's summer. And there's not much to do here. So I wanted to get some beach action. So what?"

"So you took a road trip with Tyler and worked on your tan," Jenny said with a smile.

"Nothing of that sort," Billy said, shaking his head. "I drove there in my own car and came back on my own. Tyler didn't want to let on he knew me."

"Do you drive that Ferrari in the garage?" Jenny asked impishly.

"Sometimes," Billy said noncommittally. "Sometimes I take the Porsche."

"What did Tyler drive?" Jenny asked.

"He wanted to look poor," Billy said, fighting off a yawn. "He borrowed our housekeeper's ancient Toyota. Took him hours to get there in that trap."

"You and Tyler were brothers, right?" Jenny asked. "Did you fight like brothers too?"

"Who said we had a fight?" Billy asked sullenly.

"You were seen arguing with Tyler at the pub," Jenny said softly. "What was that about?"

"It was between us," Billy said. "Family stuff."

"Tyler's gone," Jenny reminded him. "And I am trying to find out who had it in for him. This is not the time to withhold information."

Billy looked around before leaning forward. His voice had dropped to a whisper.

"It was that girl."

"What girl?"

No one had mentioned a girl in connection with Tyler until now.

"Must be some local chick," Billy said with a frown. "Tyler was crazy about her."

"What was the problem?"

"She was a gold digger," Billy said flatly. "They all are. She just wanted Tyler's money."

"How can you be so sure?" Heather asked. "And wait a minute, how did she know Tyler had money?"

"Tyler let it slip that he was coming into money very soon. That's when she started acting smitten."

"Was she hoping to marry Tyler?" Jenny asked.

"I don't know," Billy said. "My guess is she was going to blackmail Tyler. His whole street singer cred was based on him being poor."

"What were you arguing about exactly?"

"He wanted to bring her here to meet the old man. Not a good idea!"

Jenny couldn't determine whether Billy was right about the girl.

"Do you know her name?" Jenny asked. "Did you meet her yourself?"

Billy shook his head.

"Tyler was very protective about her."

Jenny looked up at the sound of shuffling feet. A voice could be heard grumbling outside. Mr. Jones came in a few moments later, followed by the butler.

"Jenny King!" he exclaimed. "Were we supposed to meet today?"

He glared at the old retainer.

"Why didn't anyone tell me she was here?"

Jenny picked up the open box of truffles.

"Do you like chocolates? I brought these for you."

The old man stared suspiciously at the box she held out. His hand shook as it hovered over the box. He finally made a choice and picked one up. He popped it in his mouth tentatively and a smile lit up his face.

"Who makes these?" he asked. "I want to invest in this company."

"Jenny made these herself," Heather supplied. "You can say they are home made."

"You can make a fortune with these," Mr. Jones told Jenny. "They are that good. Why don't you make an appointment with my office? I will ask my assistant to make a project plan. We can produce this on a large scale and sell them all over the country."

"Thank you Mr. Jones," Jenny blushed. "But I am not here to sell the truffles."

The old man's face fell as he snapped back to reality.

"Have you made any progress, Jenny?" he asked with a quaver. "Do you know who killed my boy?"

Chapter 17

Back home, Jenny got ready for dinner but her heart wasn't in it. It had been a while since she had spent any quality time with Adam. So she should have been excited about their date. But her mind kept drifting back to the troubadours and the fate that had befallen them.

Her search for Tyler's killer hadn't led to any new suspects. Now Ocean had met a similar fate. Jenny wondered if their profession had anything to do with the tragedy. Was there some kind of music hater out there who had a silent vendetta against singers? The idea seemed ridiculous even as she half heartedly considered it.

Adam would be no help in discovering anything about Ocean. Jenny was sure he would fly off the handle if she mentioned either crime during dinner. She reminded herself to stay away from the topic.

Adam had reservations at their favorite restaurant a couple of towns away. His eyes darkened as he gazed at Jenny over a plate of Beef Bourguignon.

"Just a few more days to go, Jenny," he said softly. "I can't wait."

"Me neither," Jenny said honestly.

Apart from the unsolved issue about their living arrangements, Jenny was looking forward to wedded bliss with Adam.

"How is the wedding planning coming along?" Adam asked. "Have you thrown any tantrums yet?"

"Not much scope for that," Jenny said, spearing a piece of thyme and lemon scented roast chicken. "We have kept everything pretty simple. I just need to order my dress."

"Isn't that supposed to be the most difficult?" Adam raised his eyebrows.

"I have been busy," Jenny said apologetically. "There's so much going on."

"Are you still playing Nancy Drew?" Adam asked irritably.

His visage had changed from romantic to grouch in a fraction of a second.

"There's very little to find," Jenny said honestly. "There are hardly any suspects and no motive. You should know. Your top suspect turned up dead."

"I was wrong about Ocean," Adam said readily. "Not entirely though. He wasn't completely blameless."

"What do you mean?"

"I told you we ran a background check, remember? His real name was Daniel Garcia. He is from California."

"I think he mentioned that once," Jenny nodded. "Not his name. Where he is from. I did think that Ocean was an assumed name."

"Daniel Garcia has a record as long as my arm," Adam said grimly. "He was involved in a lot of petty crimes. Confidence schemes, petty theft, blackmail. The police found it hard to track him because he was always on the move. Wonder how he landed in Pelican Cove."

"He may have been a crook," Jenny said. "But I believe Ocean was good at heart. He was just trying to survive."

"What are you saying, Jenny?" Adam asked angrily. "It is okay to steal if you are doing it for survival?"

"I didn't mean that," Jenny said quickly. "I mean Ocean didn't deserve to die like this."

"Don't tell me you are going to look for his killer too?" Adam said with a groan.

Jenny said nothing. She had already decided that she would try to find out what happened to Ocean.

Adam and Jenny were both quiet on the drive back. Jenny figured Adam wasn't too happy with her when he didn't stop for a walk at their favorite beach.

Jenny slept well that night and woke before her alarm went off. She reached the café on time and hummed a tune as she baked muffins for breakfast. She flung the doors open at 6 AM and greeted her first customer of the day.

"Good Morning, Captain Charlie. Here is your coffee and your chocolate chip muffin. All packed and ready to go."

"You seem chipper this morning," the old sailor said with a smile. "Counting down to the big day?"

Jenny blushed.

"I am so busy here I barely have time to think about the wedding," she confessed.

"I know what's keeping you busy," Captain Charlie said with a glint in his eye. "No luck this time, eh?"

"Are you talking about Tyler?" Jenny asked. "You are right. I am stumped. No suspects and no motive."

"What about that other fella?" Captain Charlie asked. "Heard he was done in too."

"You heard right," Jenny nodded. "Did you know Ocean?"

"Talked to him a few times," Captain Charlie said with a nod. "He was camping out in the woods by my cabin. He had me over for a pint."

"I thought he was living out of his van," Jenny said.

"It's more like a bus," Captain Charlie explained. "What they call a camper van. He had a bed inside and everything. But this weather, he just put out a sleeping bag and slept under the stars. Said it was the best sleep a person could have."

"Did anyone else visit him while you were there?"

"I don't think so. He didn't know anyone locally. Said his friends were drifters like him, driving around the country. They met once every year, at a different location. They were meeting at Corpus Christi in November."

Jenny said goodbye to Captain Charlie and went inside. Star arrived as she began mixing batter for her blueberry pancakes. Breakfast was a blur and Jenny barely had time to gulp some coffee down.

The Magnolias arrived at 11, ready for their mid-morning break. Heather was smiling again. Betty Sue was muttering as she clacked her knitting needles.

"Her head's in the clouds," she said to Jenny. "What am I going to do with this girl?"

"Bobby Joe said Hi to me again," Heather crowed. "I think we are going to be friends."

"Why haven't we seen him around town?" Jenny asked.

"He's busy working in that bus of his all day," Betty Sue said. "Goes straight to his room when he comes into the inn."

"What about his meals?" Jenny asked. "Surely he must eat somewhere?"

"His meals are brought in by special delivery," Heather told them. "He has hired a chef in Virginia Beach. He prepares everything according to Bobby Joe's eating plan. He follows a strict diet."

Molly had come in behind the Morse women.

"He has to, I guess," she cooed. "Have you seen his abs?"

"Not really," Heather giggled.

Molly joined her.

"Do you think he will take his shirt off at the concert?"

"He won't," Star interrupted them. "That's another ten thousand bucks we can't afford."

"Are you saying he …" Jenny was speechless.

The girls dissolved into a fit of giggles again until Betty Sue rapped her hand on the table. Jenny went in to get coffee.

"When are you going to choose a wedding dress, Jenny?" Heather asked as she licked chocolate off her fingers. "Time's running out."

"How was your date with Adam last night?" Star asked, playfully poking an elbow in Jenny's side. "Is he getting impatient?"

"You know Adam," Jenny sighed. "He wants me to stop sniffing around."

"Did he tell you anything about Ocean?" Heather asked eagerly.

"Ocean was wanted in several states," Jenny told them. "He duped a lot of people, it seems."

"That bearded oaf?" Betty Sue asked. "Why am I not surprised?"

"He was like a cuddly bear," Heather said. "And he played bad music. I listened to him a couple of times, right there on the beach."

"The music must have been a disguise," Jenny said brightly. "He entered towns as a troubadour and got to know the people."

"You think he had some devious scheme in mind for our town?" Molly asked. "We are well rid of him, in that case."

"He didn't deserve to die, Molly," Jenny said. "No one does."

"You are turning into a big old softie," Heather said. "I think being a bride is doing that to you."

Someone hailed them from the beach and the ladies looked up to see Jason waving at them. He bounded up the steps and handed over the baby carrier to Jenny.

"Hello Emily," Jenny chuckled, pinching the baby's cheeks.

"We were just talking about your client," Jenny told Jason. "Do the police have any suspects?"

"I don't think they are trying hard," Jason said frankly. "They found out he had a record."

"What are your thoughts on the subject?" Jenny asked him. "What motive could anyone have for killing him?"

"Ocean's past opens up a few possibilities," Jason explained. "He must have made some enemies."

"So you think he cheated someone and this person or persons got their revenge?"

"It's an option," Jason said.

"What was he doing on the beach that night?" Jenny asked. "I thought he camped out in the woods."

"He must have gone there to meet someone," Jason replied. "That's the most obvious explanation."

"Where was this at?" Jenny asked.

"On the edge of town," Jason informed her. "On that beach next to the bridge."

Jenny uttered an exclamation.

"Near the bridge?" she asked. "Don't you remember? That's where Ocean said he found that guitar."

"You are right, Jenny," Jason said, widening his eyes. "That can't be a coincidence."

"Maybe Ocean just liked that beach," Heather said.

"I think we are missing something," Jenny said, shaking her head. "There was something about that beach. We talked about it last time."

"It's near Peter Wilson's garage," Jason reminded her.

"That's right!" Jenny exclaimed. "We keep coming back to him, don't we?"

"You really think he is involved?"

"I don't know," Jenny admitted. "You think Ocean knew he was a crook too?"

"Ex-crook, Jenny," Jason said. "Be careful of what you say about him. He's becoming a big man now. He might be our mayor soon."

"Over my dead body," Betty Sue said dramatically. "Peter Wilson is not winning this election."

"Have you seen all the yard signs, Grandma?" Heather asked. "More and more people are supporting Peter Wilson each day. I think he's going to win in a landslide. And I thought you supported him too."

"No one's actually going to vote for an outsider," Betty Sue clucked. "This is Pelican Cove, Heather. Tradition means something here."

Molly cleared her throat.

"You people haven't heard about the green tax yet, have you?"

Every pair of eyes stared back at her.

"Peter Wilson has proposed a tax for local businesses. He says they are damaging the environment with their excessive use of plastic. So he is going to make them pay a surcharge of sorts."

"That's insane," Jenny groaned. "And we don't use plastic at the Boardwalk Café."

"You use plastic somewhere," Molly reasoned. "And all your customers don't recycle."

"I don't control where a customer throws his trash," Jenny cried.

"Exactly," Molly said. "Peter says the business should take responsibility for that."

"There's no way any business will agree to this."

"The people love it," Molly told them. "They are calling it Trash Tax and they are in favor of it. Don't forget there are only a handful of businesses compared to the number of people in town."

"This is what I am talking about," Jason told Jenny. "Peter Wilson is all set to be mayor."

"That doesn't make him innocent, Jason. And being mayor won't absolve him of murder."

"It shouldn't, Jenny," Jason agreed. "But you know what a snob Adam is. You think he will investigate such a powerful person?"

"Adam is a highly scrupulous police officer," Jenny rushed to defend him. "How dare you question his character, Jason?"

"Look, I'm sorry, okay?" Jason backtracked. "That came out wrong. I just want you to be careful."

"I'm going to find out if Peter and Ocean knew each other. We can go talk to him after that."

"I will go with you," Jason offered. "You don't need to do everything alone."

Jenny smiled.

"I don't have to. Not when I have friends like you."

"Start by telling him you support him," Heather advised. "That will make things go smoother."

"Great idea, Heather," Jenny agreed. "I don't mind stroking his ego if it helps me get to the truth."

Chapter 18

Jenny worked nonstop all day. She served her customers with a smile but she couldn't wait to get away. She finally made her way to Williams Seafood Market to get something for dinner.

Chris Williams greeted her warmly.

"Have you heard about this Trash Tax, Jenny?" he asked. "I hope you will join us in protesting it."

Jenny assured him the local business owners could count on her support.

Chris packed her usual order of sea bass and shrimp.

"You seem preoccupied," he said as he rang up her purchase.

"I was thinking about Ocean," she admitted to Chris. "Did you ever see him talking to Peter Wilson?"

"They seemed to hit it off," Chris told her. "Saw them sharing a pint a couple of times."

"Maybe I should talk to Eddie," Jenny muttered.

She went to the Rusty Anchor, trying not to feel too hopeful. Eddie Cotton greeted her enthusiastically and offered her a drink on the house. Jenny opted for a glass of wine.

"What brings you here, little lady?" Eddie asked. "And where is your posse tonight?"

"I was hoping to pick your brain," Jenny admitted.

Eddie offered to help any way he could. Jenny asked him about Ocean and Peter Wilson.

"What did those two talk about. Any idea?"

Eddie wasn't sure.

"It was some kind of business deal, I think. Something which would benefit the both of them."

Jenny felt she had established that Ocean knew Peter. She called Jason and asked him if he had time to go visit Peter Wilson. He agreed to meet her at Wilson's Auto Shop.

Peter Wilson was working on a car when they reached the garage. Dressed in grease stained overalls with sweat lining his brow, he looked like an honest, hardworking man. He smiled when he saw the baby carrier Jason was holding. He had two daughters, one of them in college.

"They grow up really fast," he said to Jason. "She'll fly the nest before you know it."

He turned toward Jenny and smiled.

"Am I in trouble? You look fierce."

"That depends," Jenny said primly. "We are here to talk about Ocean."

Peter's expression was inscrutable.

"I was sorry to hear about him. He was a good guy."

"Did you know him well?" Jenny asked.

"Not really," Peter Wilson said with a shrug.

"He was found near here," Jason said. "Near your shop, I mean."

Peter Wilson's face hardened.

"Are you accusing me of something? This here is a public beach. I don't keep track of everyone who comes or goes here."

"So you never saw Ocean walking around here?" Jenny asked.

"I didn't, believe me. I close shop at 5 PM and go home. He might have come here after that. And I'm busy during the day. I don't sit and stare at the beach all the time."

"Eddie said you were hatching some kind of scheme with him."

"He was proposing a festival for troubadours," Peter Wilson told them. "The town would take money from them. He said he could supply at least a dozen of them singers."

"I guess he wanted money for that?" Jason asked.

Peter nodded. "Like a finder's fee."

"Why would he come to you with such a scheme?" Jason wondered.

"It's all this buzz about the election," Peter smiled. "He thought I was going to be mayor."

"Judging by all accounts, you might be," Jenny conceded.

Peter looked thoughtful as he wiped a wrench.

"I don't think so. When push comes to shove, people will vote for Barb."

"That's not a very positive attitude," Jenny remarked.

"I'm just being realistic," Peter shrugged. "And it's fine. I never thought so many people would support me. They have made me a happy man."

Jenny and Jason said goodbye to Peter. Jenny invited Jason for dinner and he accepted.

"Why don't I get us some dessert?" he offered. "You go on, Jenny. We are right behind you."

Star was happy to learn they were having company. She started helping Jenny prep for dinner. Jenny made carrot and avocado puree for the baby.

Then she made a rice pilaf and a green salad to go with the fish.

"Are you ready to cross Peter off your list now?" Jason asked as they sat down for dinner.

"I'm really not sure," Jenny grumbled. "Say we cross Peter off. What does that leave us with?"

"That's no reason to suspect him," Jason reasoned.

Jenny had to agree with him.

They gorged on the ice cream Jason had brought from the local creamery. Jason and Emily left and Jenny dragged herself upstairs, ready to turn in after a long day.

The alarm woke Jenny up the next day. She showered and dressed in her favorite pair of shorts and a chambray shirt. Labor Day had come and gone but the weather was still quite hot in Pelican Cove.

Jenny was surprised to see a line outside the café at 5 AM. Groups of people loitered on the beach. Jenny went in and started the coffee. The phone rang, startling her. It was Heather.

"Are you ready for the big day?" Heather screamed in her ear.

"What's going on, Heather?" Jenny asked. "Why are there people on the beach at this hour?"

"You don't know?" Heather asked. "Don't you check your Instagram?"

"What has happened?" Jenny asked with a sigh. "Just tell me, Heather."

"Bobby Joe is making an appearance today," Heather told her. "He has decided to have breakfast at the Boardwalk Café."

"He told you that?" Jenny asked.

"He told the whole world, Jenny," Heather giggled. "He posted it on his Insta last night. People are driving overnight to catch a glimpse of him here."

"That's why there are people on the sidewalk!" Jenny said, connecting the dots.

"Forget the people," Heather said. "What are you making for breakfast?"

"Whatever's on the calendar," Jenny said. "Wait a minute … it's crab omelets today."

"Bobby Joe likes chocolate chip pancakes," Heather informed her. "With extra chocolate chips."

"Didn't you say he was on some kind of diet?" Jenny asked sarcastically.

"Today is his cheat day," Heather quipped. "And he is willing to spend it at the Boardwalk Café. Just think of all the free publicity, Jenny."

"I'm worried about all those people outside," Jenny said. "What am I going to feed them, Heather? You better come here and help."

"On my way," Heather said. "I'm not missing this for all the gold in Pelican Cove."

Rumor had it there was a lot of gold in town. It came from sunken treasure.

Jenny managed to bake a few trays of muffins before 6 AM. People rushed in as soon as she threw the doors open. She could see Captain

Charlie on the sidewalk, struggling to make his way in through the crowd. She waved at him and pointed toward the deck. He got the message and went around the café to the back.

"What's all this ruckus?" Captain Charlie asked, pulling out a chair on the deck.

"Heather says that big country singer is coming here for breakfast," Jenny told him. "These are his fans, I think."

Jenny handed over a paper bag with two muffins and a cup of coffee. Captain Charlie thanked her before heading out. He turned around just as he reached the bottom step.

"Weren't you asking about that Ocean chap? I remembered something about him."

"Go on," Jenny urged.

"Saw him in a fancy car one evening," Captain Charlie said. "At least I thought that was him at the time. But what was he doing in a car like that?"

Jenny thanked him for the information and waved goodbye.

Pandemonium reigned inside the café. They had already run out of coffee and muffins. Almost everyone wanted the crab omelets. Jenny and Heather got busy beating eggs and flipping omelets. Jenny called Star and begged her to come in and help them.

Jenny had lost count of the number of omelets she made when Heather gave a cry.

"What's wrong now?" Star asked.

She had come in and taken charge of the cash register.

Heather waved her phone at them.

"It's Bobby Joe! He just started from the inn. He should be here in five minutes."

A roar went up through the café. Most of the customers had lingered over their food, refusing to give up their vantage point. People stood along the walls, sipping coffee or lemonade and waiting for their icon to come in.

Jenny peeped outside and sucked in a breath at the scene outside. She pulled Heather to her side.

"Can you believe that?"

The street was packed with people. Many of them wore T-shirts with Bobby Joe's face or name printed on them. Some people were waving flags with his picture on them. Someone began chanting Bobby Joe's name and the crowd took it up.

Heather began snapping pictures with her phone.

"This is priceless, Jenny. You can't buy this kind of publicity!"

The crowd parted and a tall, broad shouldered young man walked through, blowing kisses to the crowd. The sun glinted off his copper colored mop. A couple of burly security guys straddled him, keeping the crowd at bay.

"We love you, Bobby Joe!" a girl cried from the crowd and began pulling off her top.

Heather pulled Jenny inside.

"Better start making those pancakes."

A table had been miraculously cleared for Bobby Joe. Jenny went out to greet him and take his order.

"How are you, sugar?" he drawled. "Nice place you got here."

Jenny fought a blush. Bobby Joe was at least 10 years younger than her but she had eyes. Jenny had to admit he was one handsome hunk.

Jenny's hands shook as she arranged the crab omelet on a plate and added toast and bacon. Another plate held a stack of chocolate chip pancakes with her special chocolate and espresso sauce, topped with whipped cream.

Fans were clicking pictures with Bobby Joe when Jenny took the food outside. Heather made her pose with him and clicked several photos of Jenny and her food with Bobby Joe. Jenny knew she would post them online on the café's page.

"Delicious!" Bobby Joe exclaimed when he took a bite of the pancakes. "Best I have tasted in my life."

Some fans wanted Bobby Joe to say something.

"I am singing at the Pelican Cove Fall Festival. It's going to be lit. See you there!"

Bobby Joe surprised Jenny by cleaning his plate. He walked out with his guards, waving at the crowd.

People who had been hogging the café all morning tagged along after Bobby Joe. A fresh wave came in, thirsty and hungry after standing out in the sun.

Jenny and her friends spent the day churning out massive quantities of food. The Magnolias didn't meet that day. There was no time to relax and no place to sit. Every single chair on the deck was taken. People sat on the steps and on the beach, eating Jenny's food and giving high praise.

"We have done more business today than we did all month," Jenny told her aunt later, wiping her brow with the back of her hand.

The café stayed open longer than usual. The crowd finally thinned as people realized their star Bobby Joe wasn't making any impromptu appearances. People began driving out of town.

Jenny stood on the deck, enjoying the cool breeze rolling off the Atlantic. She was ready to drop with exhaustion. The sun was a big ball of fire, hanging low on the horizon. The sky was streaked with pink. Jenny stifled a yawn and smiled to herself. She had survived a tough day and she was proud of herself.

Something dark flew through the air and struck her ear. Jenny yelped in pain at the impact. She looked around sharply and spotted someone running away from the café.

"Hey, you!" she called out, holding a hand to her head.

She didn't have the energy to run after her assailant. He was already a speck in the distance. Jenny collapsed into a chair, wondering who was taking potshots at her.

Chapter 19

The Magnolias were looking at Jenny with concern. It was the day after Bobby Joe Tucker had graced the Boardwalk Café with his presence. Jenny was dragging her feet, still worn out from the previous day. The Magnolias were just learning about the attack on Jenny.

"Does it hurt?" Molly asked, peering at the spot above Jenny's left ear.

"It's a bit sore, that's all."

"Have you been to the doctor?" Betty Sue demanded. "Don't take this lightly, young lady."

"Relax," Jenny told them. "It was just a mud pie."

"But what if it had been something more deadly?" Heather asked.

"I think it was just a wayward tourist," Jenny told them.

She had told herself to believe that over and over.

Star wasn't taking any of it.

"I don't think so, Jenny. What if someone is trying to warn you off?"

"Someone who?"

"Someone who's not happy with your snooping, of course," Heather said. "Looks like you have ruffled some feathers."

"I don't think so," Jenny said, shaking her head in denial. "I don't have a single suspect."

"Then who's attacking you in broad daylight?" Molly asked worriedly. "Have you told Adam about this?"

Jenny hadn't but her aunt had. Adam had given her a lecture as usual and begged her to be more careful.

"He knows," Jenny said, giving Star a withering look.

"Normally I am pretty supportive of your sleuthing," Star said. "But I think you should call it quits this time. We are almost into October. It's time you started preparing for the wedding."

"Haven't we been doing that all this time?" Jenny asked, rolling her eyes.

She held up her hand as Heather and Molly both opened their mouths to object.

"I shortlisted three wedding dresses. Let's go and try them on one last time. I will make my final choice after that."

"Shall we go today?" Heather asked eagerly. "The fall festival is two days away and I am going to be busy volunteering tomorrow onwards."

"I am not missing this," Molly said. "I am going to call in sick."

"Molly, you already went in to work this morning," Heather reminded her.

"But I feel a migraine coming on," Molly said, widening her eyes. "Don't even think of going without me, Heather."

The girls squabbled over what to do. Star convinced Jenny to take half the day off.

"Don't worry about the café," Star told her. "I can handle it."

Jenny insisted on helping her aunt prep for lunch.

"Let's start in a couple of hours," she told Heather and Molly. "I will pack some sandwiches for us. We can eat in the car."

Jenny's excitement about the trip amped up as she thought about the three dresses she had narrowed down. She covered two platters of sandwiches with plastic wrap and placed them in the refrigerator. She packed some chicken salad sandwiches for their trip, along with potato chips and cookies. She added two bottles of sweet tea to the small basket.

"All set?" Star beamed at her. "Take some pictures."

"Don't worry, I am not going to order the dress without consulting you."

Star's eyes filled up. Jenny hugged her aunt tightly, swallowing the lump in her throat. Her aunt had offered her refuge when she had been alone and miserable. She would never forget what Star had done for her. She was determined to take care of her aging aunt for the rest of her life. It was the least she could do. Estranged from her own mother, Star was the only family Jenny had other than her son.

"Have fun, sweetie!" Star said, patting her on the back.

Jenny picked up the food hamper and breezed out of the kitchen, ready to hit the road with her friends. A young girl sprang up from a table when she saw Jenny. Jenny gasped at how beautiful she was with her wispy red hair and sculpted face. Jenny guessed she was barely twenty one.

"Are you Jenny King?" the girl asked. "I have been waiting for you."

Jenny looked into her deep cornflower blue eyes and smiled tentatively.

"Have we met before?"

The girl shook her head.

"My name is Rebecca Brown. I live here in Pelican Cove. I heard you were looking for information about Tyler Jones."

"I guess you can say that," Jenny said. "I was just about to leave for an appointment though. Can we talk some other time?"

The girl hesitated.

"I am not sure I will have the courage to come back," she said honestly.

Jenny made a snap decision.

"Why don't you come with me? We can talk in the car."

The girl seemed overawed when she saw Heather and Molly waiting by the car.

"I wanted to talk in private," she said.

"Don't worry," Jenny told her. "I share everything with Molly and Heather. You don't have to worry about them."

Introductions were made and the girls welcomed Rebecca.

"The more, the merrier," Heather said in her usual friendly manner.

"So? How did you know Tyler?" Jenny asked the girl.

"Tyler and I were engaged."

The girls stared at each other with wide eyes and raised eyebrows. They hadn't expected this.

"We know Tyler was seeing someone," Jenny told her. "But we had no idea he was engaged."

Tears streamed down the girl's face.

"Tyler was such a gentleman. He proposed when we found out I was pregnant."

Jenny dropped any pretense of being cool.

"You're expecting Tyler's child?" she asked incredulously. "How does anyone not know this?"

"Who am I going to tell?" the girl asked.

"The family, of course," Jenny cried. "Old Mr. Jones will be very happy."

"Tyler's grandpa?" Rebecca asked. "We were going to meet him soon. Tyler adored him."

"I can give you his number," Jenny offered.

"Billy said I should wait."

"You know Billy?" Jenny asked.

"I have met him a few times," Rebecca told them.

She looked like she had a bad taste in her mouth. Jenny guessed their dislike for each other was mutual.

"What do you do, Rebecca?"

"I am a college student. I was home for my summer break when I met Tyler."

"What was he like?" Jenny asked.

"Very shy," Rebecca told them. "You would never have guessed he performed in front of a crowd. He was so passionate about his music."

"So you like music too?" Jenny asked.

"We had that in common," Rebecca nodded. "I am going to minor in music. Tyler and I both loved the blues. His own music was a peculiar blend of country and pop."

"You started dating, then?"

"We hit it off right away. Tyler and I used to meet on one of the beaches after sunset."

"When did you find out about his background?"

"There were little signs," Rebecca told them. "His clothes, the really expensive watch he wore, the way he gave away most of the money he earned during the day … he would buy ice cream for the kids or give someone a ridiculous tip."

"So you realized he was rich," Jenny said frankly.

"He told me himself," Rebecca explained. "Right on our second date. He told me about some big trust money that was coming to him in a few weeks."

Was that the only reason Rebecca had fallen in love with him, Jenny asked herself cynically.

"Why did he tell you that? I guess he didn't want to come across as a poor musician."

"He wanted to make it on his own," Rebecca explained. "He told me it was really hard to do in the music industry. But he had a safety net. He didn't want me to worry about the future."

"Was Billy helping him with his music?"

"Billy?" Rebecca asked with disdain. "Billy only helps himself. He came into a big trust when he was twenty five, about five years ago. Tyler said he had squandered it all. Now he was after Tyler's money."

"So they didn't get along?" Jenny asked.

"Not really," Rebecca told her. "Tyler wanted Billy to take an interest in the family business. He felt that would allow him to focus on his music. But Billy doesn't want to work at all."

"How did Tyler get on with his uncle?" Jenny asked.

"Tyler's parents died when he was a child. His uncle was his big role model. The uncle wanted Tyler to start learning the business."

"And Tyler didn't want to?"

"He just wanted to do something on his own first. He had given himself six months. He was hoping to have a hit single in that time. He said he would happily take up the family business after that."

Jenny remembered how Tyler had been hung up on being the only troubadour in town.

"Do you know why he came to Pelican Cove?"

"Tyler discovered this town by accident when he took a wrong turn. He loved the vibe here. Said this town had become his muse."

"Was he making a lot of new music?" Jenny asked curiously.

"He recorded a song," Rebecca smiled sadly. "He was very excited about it. He was looking for a contract with some record label."

Heather had been driving the car while Jenny and Rebecca chatted in the back seat. She had reached a designer's studio two towns over. It was going to be their first stop that day.

Jenny took Rebecca by the arm and coaxed her to go in with them. The dress was tried on and pronounced beautiful. Heather took several pictures for Star.

"Are you ready to lock this one down?" Molly asked.

Jenny shook her head.

"I am going to try on all three dresses."

"Let's get going then," Heather quipped. "No time to waste."

Heather offered to drop Rebecca back in Pelican Cove before heading out to the city. Rebecca agreed gratefully.

"Where have you been hiding all this time?" Jenny asked her. "Why didn't you come forward before this?"

"Billy warned me to stay under the radar," she explained. "He said the tabloids would start harassing me."

Jenny's opinion of Billy Jones was changing rapidly.

"What made you seek me out now?" Jenny asked.

"You know how active the local grapevine is," Rebecca said. "Talk was that you were trying hard to find Tyler's killer. Everyone said you were really good at it. So I was just watching from a distance. Then someone said you have given up."

"There are no suspects," Jenny explained. "My wedding is just a few weeks away and the café keeps me busy."

"You are the only hope I have," Rebecca pleaded. "Please don't give up yet. I want to see Tyler's killer brought to justice."

"I can't promise anything, but I will see what I can do."

Jenny urged Rebecca to go meet the Jones family at the earliest. They entered Pelican Cove and dropped her off in the town square.

"What did you think of that girl?" Heather asked as they sped toward the Chesapeake Bay Bridge -Tunnel that would take them into Virginia Beach.

"She's so young," Jenny exclaimed. "She looks innocent."

"Are you going soft, Jenny?" Molly laughed. "Looks don't mean anything."

"What motive could she possibly have to harm Tyler?" Jenny asked. "She was marrying into millions. Now she is alone with a baby on the way."

"You just have her word for it," Heather argued. "What if Tyler broke up with her, huh?"

"Maybe that child isn't Tyler's at all," Molly offered. "She could have killed Tyler to get him out of the way. Now she can act the role of the poor widow and extract money from the Joneses."

"You are both crazy," Jenny dismissed.

"You taught us well, Jenny," Heather told her smugly. "Never take anyone at face value. Confirm it from different sources."

"Billy tried to paint Rebecca in a bad light. She is doing the same thing with him. Looks like they are trying to throw each other under the bus."

Heather turned toward Jenny as she pulled up in front of a toll booth.

"What if they are both lying?"

Chapter 20

The day of the fall festival arrived.

The town of Pelican Cove was packed to the gills. A sea of people thronged the town square. There wasn't a single empty spot left to stand on. The Boardwalk Café was bursting at the seams. Every table on the outdoor deck had been taken. People had set up camp chairs on the beach surrounding the deck. They bought food from the front counter and feasted on it at the beach.

Jenny was working like an automaton, helped by her aunt Star and her friends Heather and Molly. Betty Sue presided over the cash counter. Jenny had finally made several batches of truffles in honor of the occasion. Five dozen boxes had been sold out within the hour.

"We are running out of bread," Heather declared as she tore open a fresh loaf. "Only two loafs remaining."

"Those are our last ones," Jenny said. "Let's finish making these sandwiches and call it quits."

"People are still coming in," Star said, taking a peep outside.

"I can't help it," Jenny said. "We are out of everything. Time to let our hair down and enjoy the festival ourselves."

"Have you seen that stage they erected on the beach?" Molly asked. "We have never had anything like it before."

Jenny shook her head. She hadn't even gone out on deck all day.

"Bobby Joe's people had precise instructions on how to build that stage," Heather told them. "Mandy managed all that."

"What would we do without Mandy!" Jenny exclaimed.

Star made a face. She had reluctantly delegated any work related to the concert to Mandy.

"This is going to be the best fall festival ever!" Heather crowed.

They were all beginning to get excited about the concert. Finally, the last morsel was served and the Magnolias breathed a sigh of relief. They had all brought dresses to change into for the festival. The girls primped and got ready in half an hour and set off.

The mercury had finally dipped a bit in Pelican Cove, bringing some much awaited cool weather. It was a sunny evening and the crowd was getting excited as the musicians tuned their instruments.

A roar went up in the crowd as Bobby Joe appeared on stage. He started playing his guitar and the crowd erupted in a roar.

Molly stood arm in arm with Chris. Jason wasn't coming because he hadn't found a sitter for Emily. Adam was on crowd control duty. Star and Betty Sue were going to relax on the café's deck and listen to the music from a distance.

Someone tapped Jenny on the shoulder. She turned around, hoping it was Adam. It was Barb Norton.

"Isn't this great, Jenny?" she tittered. "Don't forget who brought this famous country music star to Pelican Cove. It was all my idea."

Jenny knew that wasn't true but she went along with it.

"This concert is going to be a big boost for tourism," Barb continued. "How's the take at the café been these past two days? Better than the whole summer, huh?"

Jenny had to agree with Barb.

"When I am mayor, I will be doing plenty more activities to boost tourism in the area."

"Thanks, Barb," Jenny said. "You can count on my vote."

Barb moved on to tackle her next prospect.

Things were heating up on stage. Jenny wasn't a country music fan so Bobby Joe's music wasn't very familiar to her. But she found herself tapping her foot and enjoying the atmosphere. She realized that was the beauty of a live music show.

There was another tap on Jenny's shoulder. It turned out to be Peter Wilson.

"You see all this, Jenny?" he demanded angrily. "They are destroying our environment, trashing the beach and the natural beauty of our surroundings."

Jenny nodded meekly.

"These are the dangers of excessive tourism. This is exactly what I want to curb when I am mayor. No crazy music concerts, that's for sure."

"You are right, Peter. We don't need these crowds."

"So I can count on your vote, right?" Peter asked directly.

"Sure," Jenny said.

Peter stood with his arms folded, glaring at the people around him. A couple stopped swaying to the music and moved away.

Up on the stage, Bobby Joe tapped the microphone and cleared his throat.

"Thank you all for coming. This is the one you have all been waiting for. My latest hit single."

The cheer that went up through the crowd was deafening. Peter Wilson turned red as a tomato. Jenny watched in amazement as he curled his hands into fists and pointed them at the stage.

The music started and the crowd grew quiet as Bobby Joe began crooning. He was barely two lines into the song when Peter let out a loud groan.

"Not this again. I'm fed up of listening to this crap."

Heather turned around and glowered at Peter.

"This is 'You are my everything'. It's top of the charts. Bobby Joe might even win a Grammy for it."

"So that kid was in cahoots with this goon all along?" Peter demanded

"What are you saying, Peter?" Jenny asked.

She had lost track of what Peter was fussing about.

"This is the same song that kid who died played all summer. It's burned into my brain. You know why? Because he stood outside my house and sang that same thing from sunrise to sunset. The same thing over and over."

"That's impossible!" Heather argued. "Bobby Joe released this song just a few days ago. Tyler couldn't have played it before that."

"What did I say?" Peter frowned. "It's burned into my brain. You want proof? Let me show you."

People around them were beginning to turn around asking them to shush. A couple of security guards surrounded them suddenly and asked them to stop causing a disturbance.

Peter looked like he was ready to burst.

"Let's go back to the café," Jenny said, grabbing his arm. "You stay here and enjoy the show," she told Heather.

Peter Wilson was already pulling a phone out of his pocket. He went into the café with Jenny and started playing a video. He thrust the phone into her face.

Tyler appeared on the screen. He was standing by the gazebo in the town square, playing his guitar. Jenny watched for a while, her eyes widening in surprise.

"This does sound like the song that country star is playing right now," she admitted grudgingly.

"What did I tell ya?" Peter crowed triumphantly.

"Do you know where Tyler heard this song?"

"He wrote it himself," Peter told her. "All his music was original. He used to boast about it."

"It's actually a great song," Jenny said. "What is it you don't like about it?"

Peter looked abashed.

"It's a good song," he said reluctantly. "Even I can see that. But you listen to anything twelve hours a day, day after day after day, it begins grating on your nerves. Know what I mean?"

"I think so," Jenny said.

She was trying to figure out how Bobby Joe had got hold of Tyler's song. Peter made it easy for her.

"So what? You think that hotshot country star stole this kid's song?"

"Sure looks like it, huh?" Jenny said. "I'm going to find Adam."

She didn't have to go too far. Adam burst into the café just then, looking for her.

"What's going on, Jenny?" he bellowed. "Heather said it had something to do with Tyler Jones?"

Jenny quickly brought him up to speed.

"Let's wait for the show to be over," Adam told them. "I will bring him in after that."

Captain Charlie barged into the café next.

"Remember that fancy car I told you about, Jenny?" he asked urgently. "The one I saw Ocean riding in?"

Jenny nodded.

"It's parked in the town square, near that big stage."

"Let's check it out," Adam said purposefully.

He strode out and Jenny, Peter and Captain Charlie followed him. It was a red Ferrari and it had been parked close to the stage. A few questions to the crowd revealed that the car belonged to Bobby Joe Tucker.

"Are you sure this is the same car?" Adam asked Captain Charlie.

He shrugged.

"Sure looks like it. We don't have another car like this in town."

"I think you should head home now, Jenny," Adam told her. "Things might get ugly here."

The Magnolias had already planned a spa night at Seaview, Jenny's home. They ordered pizza from Mama Rosa's and made strawberry daiquiris. Molly mixed her special face packs for all of them.

Three hours later, the ladies lay sprawled around the room, stuffed with pizza and Star's caramel pumpkin pie. Star and Betty Sue had each commandeered a couch while the younger girls lay on the plush carpet.

The doorbell rang and Adam came in, looking tired and hungry.

"Tell us what happened," Betty Sue ordered. "Did that stuffed peacock kill that poor boy?"

Adam collapsed in a chair and nodded. Jenny heated some pizza for him while he began telling his story.

"Bobby Joe came to Pelican Cove sometime in the summer."

"How do we not know that?" Heather cried.

"His tour bus broke down somewhere on the highway. He came into town one evening and heard Tyler sing in the square. He thought the song had potential."

"So what? He just stole it from Tyler?" Jenny asked, incensed.

"Not at first," Adam said. "Bobby Joe offered to buy the song from Tyler. Apparently, it's a thing. These street singers often sell their music to big stars. They don't have the money to record them or market them. And they need to survive."

"So Bobby Joe thought Tyler would sell him his music," Jenny said, catching on.

"That's right," Adam nodded. "But he didn't know Tyler's background. Tyler had more than enough money to buy his own record label. And I guess that was his long term plan."

"So Tyler refused to sell," Heather summed up. "What did Bobby Joe do?"

"He came here a few times, trying to convince Tyler," Adam explained. "They had a fight where Tyler called him names. Bobby Joe strangled him in a fit of anger. He said he just lost control."

"What about Ocean?" Jenny asked. "Did he kill him too?"

"Ocean's murder was more cold blooded," Adam told them. "He was familiar with Tyler's music. He caught on to Bobby Joe as soon as he heard his hit single. He wanted to blackmail him."

"Bobby Joe wasn't willing to pay him?" Jenny asked. "He did steal the song."

"Bobby Joe paid him once," Adam sighed. "But Ocean got greedy. Bobby Joe agreed to pay him a big sum to make him go away. They were supposed to meet at that beach near the bridge. Bobby Joe saw an opportunity and finished him off."

"Why did Bobby Joe come back to Pelican Cove after killing Tyler?" Heather asked. "Shouldn't he have gone miles away from here?"

"We asked him that," Adam told them. "He was hoping to get inspired and write some good music here, just like Tyler did. Personally, I think he got cocky. He thought he was invincible."

"Poor Tyler," Jenny said sadly. "He didn't deserve to die."

"Thanks to you, his killer won't roam free," Adam said, his eyes full of admiration. "You did it again, Jenny."

"We need to go to Richmond tomorrow," Jenny told the girls.

Jenny wanted to meet Tyler's grandpa and explain everything. Tyler's last wish had come true in a roundabout way. His song was Number 1 on the charts. Mr. Jones would use his resources to make sure Tyler got credit for it.

Jenny was looking forward to a pit stop on the way. She had chosen her wedding dress. She couldn't wait to order it.

Jenny gave Adam a secret smile. Their big day was just around the corner.

Epilogue

It was a mild fall day in Pelican Cove. The weatherman predicted a pleasant day with highs in the 60s. Cool winds blew in from the north, making the air a bit chilly.

A small group of people had assembled in the garden by the beach. They wore broad smiles as they waited for the ceremony. A beautiful arch decorated with roses and gardenias was erected at one end. The pale peach voile draped around the arch matched the giant bows tied to the chairs.

Jenny's son stood on one side, ready to give her away. Betty Sue had been chosen to officiate the wedding. She looked imposing as usual in a red silk dress and matching hat.

Jenny's closest friends waited inside the house with her. Adam's daughters looked beautiful in matching yellow dresses. Heather and Molly wore shades of russet and Star was dressed in a vibrant orange gown.

The bride was trying to quell the butterflies in her stomach. She was a vision in ivory, wearing the dress of her dreams. Long sleeved with a sweetheart neckline, it had a three foot long train and a bodice embroidered in tiny pearls. She wore a tiara on her head and a rose from the garden was tucked into her hair.

Everyone was eagerly waiting for the groom. His brother Ethan was going to drive him over.

An hour later, they were still waiting for Adam. Ethan Hopkins arrived with a screech of brakes. He looked at Star and shook his head.

Heather's phone rang just then. Her face turned ashen as she listened to the voice at the other end. She stared at Jenny, unable to utter a word.

"That was Adam," she finally whispered.

A single tear rolled down Jenny's face as she took in her friend's dismay.

"He's not coming, is he?"

THE END

Thank you for reading this book.

Jenny's story continues in Sundaes and Sinners, the next book in the series. https://www.amazon.com/gp/product/B07PXYPNG5

Acknowledgements

I would like to thank my indefatigable sibling for the constant support and encouragement which went a long way toward the release of this book. Thanks to my readers for waiting patiently for this one. These are the people who motivate me day after day and inspire me to write.

Thank You

Thank you for reading this collection. If you enjoyed these books, please consider leaving a brief review. Even a few words or a line or two will do.

As an indie author, I rely on reviews to spread the word about my books. Your assistance will be very helpful and greatly appreciated.

I would also really appreciate it if you tell your friends and family about the book. Word of mouth is an author's best friend, and it will be of immense help to me.

Many Thanks!

Author Leena Clover

http://leenaclover.com

Books by Leena Clover

Pelican Cove Cozy Mystery Series

Strawberries and Strangers – Pelican Cove Cozy Mystery Book 1

https://www.amazon.com/dp/B07CSW34GB/

Cupcakes and Celebrities – Pelican Cove Cozy Mystery Book 2

https://www.amazon.com/dp/B07CYX5TNR

Berries and Birthdays – Pelican Cove Cozy Mystery Book 3

https://www.amazon.com/gp/product/B07D7GG8KV

Sprinkles and Skeletons - Pelican Cove Cozy Mystery Book 4

https://www.amazon.com/dp/B07DW91NKG

Waffles and Weekends - Pelican Cove Cozy Mystery Book 5

https://www.amazon.com/dp/B07FRJ1FC1/

Muffins and Mobsters - Pelican Cove Cozy Mystery Book 6

https://www.amazon.com/dp/B07GRBCZG8

Parfaits and Paramours - Pelican Cove Cozy Mystery Book 7

https://www.amazon.com/dp/B07K5G2DDJ

Truffles and Troubadours - Pelican Cove Cozy Mystery Book 8

https://www.amazon.com/dp/B07N6FQTK2/

Sundaes and Sinners – Pelican Cove Cozy Mystery Book 9

https://www.amazon.com/dp/B07N6FQTK2/

Croissants and Cruises – Pelican Cove Cozy Mystery Book 10

https://www.amazon.com/dp/B082L2W6V2/

Pancakes and Parrots – Pelican Cove Cozy Mystery Book 11

https://www.amazon.com/dp/B082H1DJ42/

Hazelnuts and Halloween – Pelican Cove Short Story Book 1

https://www.amazon.com/gp/product/B07HG9R1QT

Candy Canes and Christmas – Pelican Cove Short Story Book 2

https://www.amazon.com/gp/product/B07L9T7R5D/

Meera Patel Cozy Mystery Series

Gone with the Wings – Meera Patel Cozy Mystery Book 1

https://www.amazon.com/dp/B071WHNM6K

A Pocket Full of Pie - Meera Patel Cozy Mystery Book 2

https://www.amazon.com/dp/B072Q7B47P/

For a Few Dumplings More - Meera Patel Cozy Mystery Book 3

https://www.amazon.com/dp/B072V3T2BV

Back to the Fajitas - Meera Patel Cozy Mystery Book 4

https://www.amazon.com/dp/B0748KPTLM

Christmas with the Franks – Meera Patel Cozy Mystery Book 5

https://www.amazon.com/gp/product/B077GXR4WS/

Dolphin Bay Cozy Mystery Series

Raspberry Chocolate Murder – Dolphin Bay Cozy Mystery Book 1

https://www.amazon.com/dp/B07VVQDGPN/

Orange Thyme Death – Dolphin Bay Cozy Mystery Book 2

https://www.amazon.com/dp/B07W226H71/

Apple Caramel Mayhem – Dolphin Bay Cozy Mystery Book 3

https://www.amazon.com/dp/B07YN35K2Y/

Cranberry Sage Miracle – Dolphin Bay Cozy Mystery Book 4

https://www.amazon.com/dp/B08538MP3Z/

Made in the USA
Columbia, SC
26 June 2020